Also by Tom Miller

The Philosopher's Flight

The Philosopher's War

A NOVEL

Tom Miller

Simon & Schuster

NEW YORK LONDON TORONTO SYDNEY NEW DELHI

Simon & Schuster
1230 Avenue of the Americas
New York, NY 10020

This book is a work of fiction. Any references to historical events, real people, or real places are used fictitiously. Other names, characters, places, and events are products of the author's imagination, and any resemblance to actual events or places or persons, living or dead, is entirely coincidental.

First Simon & Schuster hardcover edition July 2019

Interior design by Ruth Lee-Mui
Illustrations created by Michael Gellatly

Manufactured in the United States of America

1 3 5 7 9 10 8 6 4 2

Library of Congress Cataloging-in-Publication Data is available.

ISBN 978-1-4767-7818-1
ISBN 978-1-4767-7820-4 (ebook)

For my dad, who knows the best joke in every episode of M*A*S*H *and where the commas go.*

And for Abby, who keeps me flying.

PROLOGUE

EVERY NIGHT WHEN I WAS A CHILD, I WAS PUT TO BED WITH A STORY. Usually my big sister Vivian tucked me in. She favored anything with a moral—Grimm's fairy tales, Aesop's fables, the *Prudence Fairchild: Girl Philosopher* books. Regardless of what we read, Vivian always spelled out the lesson: be brave, be kind to strangers, follow directions, don't eat all your chocolates in one go.

On the other hand, when my mother put me to bed (on the rare occasion that she wasn't out on an emergency call, fighting in one of her domestic campaigns or deployed overseas), she liked to tell war stories. Sometimes she described historical battles, other times events she'd seen firsthand. But as thrilling as her stories were, I could rarely puzzle out a moral. In half of them, I wasn't even certain whether Mother had been one of the good guys. You can't hear the story of the Pacification of Manila or the counterinsurgency campaign in Hawaii and believe the women of the US Sigilry Corps were blameless, no matter how good their intentions might have been at the outset.

There was one exception among Mother's war stories: the Franco-Prussian Intervention. That was the Corps' good war, their brightest, most humane moment, when the perfect combination of cutting-edge sigilry, guile, and physical courage produced a stunning victory against impossible odds. You could learn any number of good lessons from that episode. It profoundly shaped the way that I—and most philosophers of my generation—viewed the world. You can't understand why the final days of the Great War played out the way they did unless you understand how badly we wanted to re-create the heroics that had taken place nearly five decades before.

The story goes like this:

In 1870, France and what's now Germany were spoiling for a fight. Both sides wanted land and glory, they had a grudge going back a hundred years—it doesn't much matter who fired the first shot. The Prussians had the better army and drove steadily through France, winning one battle after another, before the French dug in a few miles outside Paris and fought them to a standstill. The Prussians kept Paris under siege for months but couldn't crack the French defenses. As winter fell and public opinion back home began to turn against the war, the Prussian general staff decided it was time for drastic measures.

The Prussians had watched the American Civil War a few years earlier with interest, especially the final battle, in which the Union philosophers under Mrs. Cadwallader had unleashed a cloud of poison smoke that asphyxiated the defenses of an entire city. Impressed by this new form of warfare, the Prussians had founded their own group of military sigilrists, the Korps des Philosophs, borrowing their name from their American counterparts. (France, by contrast, had little in the way of practical empirical philosophy, having clung to the Napoleonic ideal that a woman's proper role was as mother and nurturer, hardly consistent with a philosophical career, much less one in the armed services.)

In January 1871, the ten-thousand-woman-strong Korps began shipping loads of smoke west, using trains made up entirely of tank cars. Over the course of weeks, the German smokecarvers—rauchbauers, they called themselves, or "smoke builders"—began constructing a giant cloud, a mile wide and a mile deep, thick enough to suffocate anyone it rolled over. The French government and two million civilians who had remained behind in Paris considered it a mere psychological weapon and refused to negotiate a surrender. After interminable delays, the rauchbauers pushed their cloud forward, smothering the French defenses and driving into the city, blanketing one neighborhood at a time, killing thousands and sparking a panic.

Back in America, Gen. Comfort Tyndale, who had assumed command of the US Sigilry Corps after Mrs. Cadwallader retired, watched with mounting alarm as reports came in by message board from the French capital. Though Tyndale herself had once been an instrument of destruction using similar weapons, the Germans were slaughtering civilians. It was a step too far—this sort of attack could only cause empirical philosophy to be hated and stamped out the world over. At an emergency joint session of Congress, Gen. Tyndale requested to deploy her women to France posthaste to counter the German attack. Not a war with Germany, she insisted, not a military adventure, but a humanitarian action by the Sigilry Corps to prevent the destruction of Paris. A woman—much less a Negro—had never before addressed Congress, but they could hardly ignore the Corps' undefeated record in the Civil War. They authorized Tyndale to relieve Paris.

Mrs. Cadwallader rushed east from her laboratory in Detroit and, together with Gen. Tyndale, crossed the Atlantic in ten minutes by serial transport—the first time such a journey had been attempted. They took with them two hundred handpicked women, the largest number that could fit into the balky transport bubbles of the age.

Putting her faith in a squadron of fliers wearing primitive respirators (and I should remind my readers that the modern hover glyph had been in use for less than a year at that time), Gen. Tyndale ordered them to land in the middle of the German cloud itself and draw a destination sigil. The fliers managed it and were swapped free to safety as Cadwallader, Tyndale, and their smokecarvers transported in, their defensive smoke already arrayed around them.

The corpswomen struck desperately at the German cloud from the inside out and then at the panicked rauchbauers themselves, who couldn't understand who was attacking them or where they'd come from. They surrendered in twenty-eight minutes. The Americans emerged victorious without the loss of a single woman.

Paris was saved. The French hailed Mrs. Cadwallader as "the American Leonidas," called Gen. Tyndale "the black Hannibal." There were not streets enough in France for all the parades they were given, not honors and knighthoods enough in all of Europe for the two women. Back home, the newspapers called it "The One-Hour War" or "Mrs. Cadwallader's Thursday Afternoon Picnic."

To guard against further attacks, the rest of the Corps was moved to France by steamship, including a scrawny, unlettered thirteen-year-old girl from the Ozarks who'd run away from home to join up—my mother, Emmaline. Ma's unit guarded the Riviera, while the German army dismantled the Parisian cloud and packed up to go home. Ma called the year she spent as part of the relief force "paradise on earth," as she fattened up on French cuisine and absorbed the tutelage of expert sigilrists. (It's still her favorite out of her five wars.)

The peace that followed lasted forty-three years.

Now, the lessons I took away from that battle as a child were not terribly different from the ones that the generals I served under during the Great War seem to have learned: the Sigilry Corps was invulnerable, even outnumbered fifty to one; it could impose its will and end any war it chose in a twinkling; and an overwhelming display of advanced philosophy was the surest way to accomplish that. The French learned that empirical philosophy was a terrible evil and led the international crusade to remove sigilry from warfare. Germany learned it would have been victorious had its Korps been equipped with better chemicals and techniques; it plowed millions of marks into philosophical research, as the peace treaty neglected to place limits on laboratory philosophy. In short: if ever there were another war in France, everyone involved planned to do exactly as they'd done in '71.

When the Great War broke out in 1914, that strategy cost four years of fighting, sixteen million lives in Europe, and many of the finest philosophers of my age, dead on the fields outside Reims and in the streets of Paris.

Whenever I've doubted the usefulness of writing an account of the World War while we seem determined to embroil ourselves in a second, I've continued on in hopes that my recollections might be of use to the new generation of philosophers and soldiers. After all, they were raised on bedtime stories, too, stories in which a shadowy group of conspirators, intent on overthrowing the American army, destabilized international politics for decades to come. Stories in which I'm one of the villains.

But I suspect that a few of those younger philosophers have encountered a slim little volume called *The Philosopher's Flight*, a book, I might add, that's banned in my home country for sigilristic content (though the odd copy sometimes slips across the Mexican border). Perhaps they'll give my story a more sympathetic ear. I don't know what moral I hope they'll draw, except that when you're convinced of the righteousness of your mission, no price is too high to pay. And when all the choices are bad ones, you choose the least worst and call it virtue.

In writing, I'm indebted to several friends or their estates, who have provided reminiscences and diaries. My thanks to: Professor Karl Friedrich Unger, lately of the Universidad de Tamaulipas; Brian F. Mayweather, Esq.; Maj. Gen. Sarah E. Stewart, US Army Philosophical Service; Dr. Edith Rubinski, Department of Neurology, Matamoros General Hospital; Gen. Tomasina Blandings, Caballería Aérea Mexicana; and former US Secretary of Philosophy Danielle Hardin. Any errors are my own.

BRIG. GEN. ROBERT A. CANDERELLI WEEKES
Commander, First North American Volunteer Air Cavalry
Chungking, China
November 11, 1941

Part 1

Rescue and Evacuation

Blood Upon the Harness

(To the tune of "Battle Hymn of the Republic")

She was just a rookie flier and she surely shook with fright.
She checked all her equipment and she cinched her helmet tight.
She had to sit and listen to those awful cannons roar,
"You ain't gonna fly no more!"

(CHORUS)
Gory, gory, what a hell of a way to die.
Gory, gory, what a hell of a way to die.
Gory, gory, what a hell of a way to die.
She ain't gonna fly no more.

"Is everybody happy?" cried the Sig-1 with a shout.
Our hero feebly answered, "Yes," and then they sent her out.
She flew into the inky black, her drop tab not secure,
And she ain't gonna fly no more.

(CHORUS)

She turned to land, she reached her hand, her sleeve caught on the tab.
Her powder bag it fell away, with nothing left to grab.
She felt the wind, she felt the drop, it shook her to her core,
And she ain't gonna fly no more.

(CHORUS)

She hit the ground, the sound was SPLAT, her blood went spurting high.
Her comrades, they were heard to say, "A hell of a way to die!"
She lay there rolling round in the welter of her gore,
And she ain't gonna fly no more.

(CHORUS)

(HALF SPEED)
There was blood upon the harness, there were brains upon the jute,
Intestines were a-dangling from her sigilwoman's suit.
She was a mess, they picked her up, and poured her from her boots,
But she ain't gotta fly no more.

Traditional Song of the United States Sigilry Corps, Department of R&E, 1898–1918.

Organizational Table for the Fifth Division

Franklin K. Lane
Secretary of the Interior
Supervisor for the US Sigilry Corps

Lt. Gen. Gillian Fallmarch
Commandant
US Sigilry Corps

Maj. Gen. Loes Niejenhuis
Commander
Rescue and Evacuation Department

Brig. Gen. Tomasina Blandings
Commander
Fifth Division of R&E

Lt. Adelgundis Drale
Executive Officer
Fifth Division

# of Rescue and Evacuation for July 1918

Squadron 1	Squadron 2	Squadron 3
SIG-1 Bernice MacMurdo SIG-2 Helen Dawes SIG-3 Pearl Hanover SIG-3 Minnie Zimmerman	SIG-1 Hortense Millen SIG-2 Sabine Vos SIG-3 Anna Wojciechowski SIG-3 Cora Devereaux	SIG-1 Fern Cunningham SIG-2 Sally Brodsky SIG-3 Ethel Gelbstein SIG-3 Gladys Moore
SIG-2 Odessa Roman SIG-3 Almira Maddox SIG-3 Irene Fitzpatrick SIG-3 Marjorie Krist	SIG-2 Hehewuti Nampeyo SIG-3 Carmen Delgado SIG-3 Maria Mondragon SIG-3 Eira Eirasdottir	BVT-2 Ruth Aielli SIG-3 Beulah Dunphrey
BVT-2 Mamie Wheelwright SIG-3 Agnes Murphy	SIG-2 Alta Andrada SIG-3 Kiyo Takahashi SIG-3 Louise Punnett SIG-3 Robert A. Canderelli	

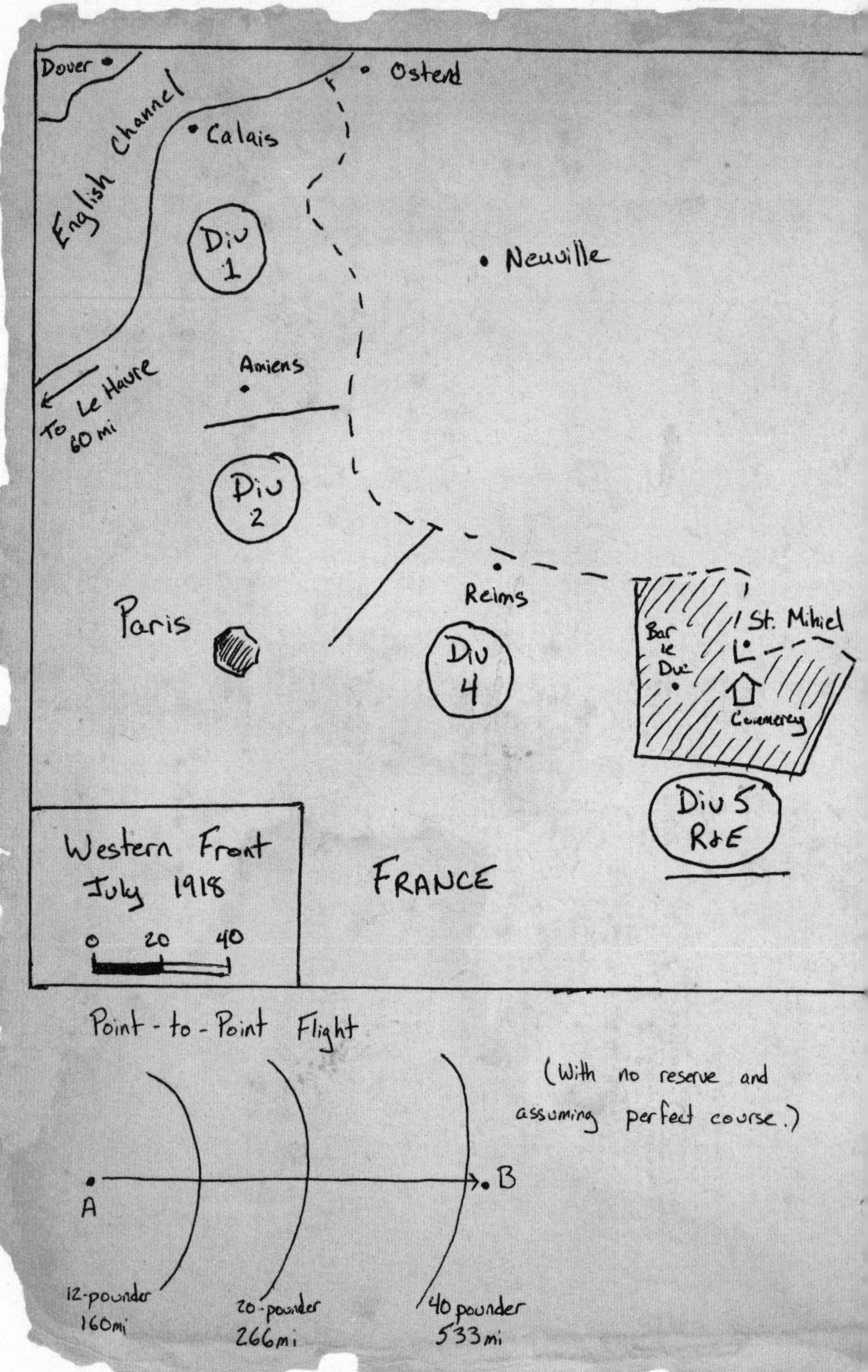

Dover
English Channel
Calais
Ostend
Div 1
Neuville
Amiens
To Le Havre 60 mi
Div 2
Reims
Paris
Div 4
St. Mihiel
Bar le Duc
Commercy
Div 5 R&E
Western Front
July 1918
0 20 40
FRANCE
Point-to-Point Flight
(With no reserve and assuming perfect course.)
A
B
12-pounder 160mi
20-pounder 266mi
40 pounder 533mi

Evac Max Range

12-pounder - 8 minutes outbound (26.6 mi)

20-pounder - 14 minutes outbound (46.6mi)

40-pounder - 29 minutes outbound (96 mi)

Standard flight speed 3.33 miles/min (200 mph)

Range & Powder Load

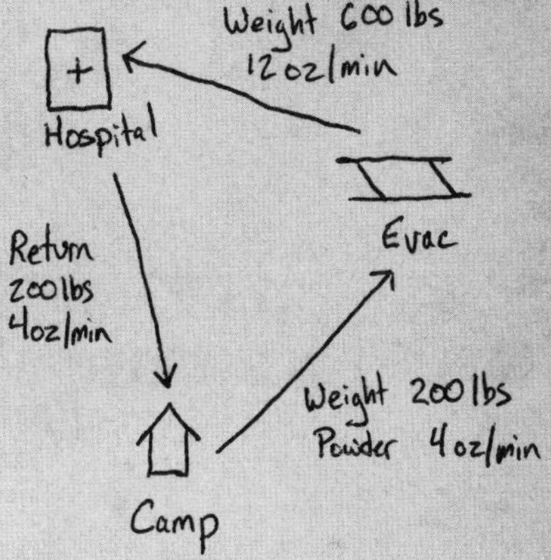

Millen's Rules

① It's never where they say it is.

② You'll <u>Always</u> get lost

③ Our scale was last calibrated in 1915, so God help you if you trust it.

Drake's Rules

① Always assume 2 casualties

② Assume they're 200lbs each

③ Hold 25% powder in reserve for emergencies

1

JULY 1918

I am a philosopher.	*Je suis une philosophe.*
I am an American.	*Je suis une américaine.*
I am a friend.	*Je suis une amie.*

United States Sigilry Corps, *Phrasebook #4 for Overseas Use*, 1915

THREE HUNDRED OF US SAT SHOULDER TO SHOULDER ON THE rickety wooden bleachers of the stadium in which we would make the transatlantic crossing, sweating under the afternoon sun without a lick of shade. One hour passed, then two. As we waited, the mood went from nervous anticipation to annoyance to dull, stupid endurance.

We were a mixed group of new officers in the United States Sigilry Corps—Logistics hoverers, messagists, smokecarvers, medical philosophers, and sixty-eight freshly minted Rescue and Evacuation fliers, who had just that morning finished our six weeks of advanced flight training. On the infield in front of us sacks and cargo crates were stacked twenty feet high, with a small clearing in the middle in which ten women stood—the Corps transporters who would be jumping us to France in rapid sequence. They at least had parasols. One of them was fanning herself with the cargo manifest.

I shifted on the hard bench.

"They've got us arranged backwards," whispered Essie Stewart, who was sitting next to me. "They should have *us* in the center and the supplies around the edges. In case the transport bubble comes up short."

"Well, if we lose something, they'd probably rather keep the cargo than a lot of green recruits," I joked.

Essie swallowed. We'd heard a lot of talk like that in training from our flight instructors about replacements such as ourselves: *disposable; worse than useless; won't survive ten weeks.* We'd tried to chuckle over it, except when our dread that they were right stuck deep in our throats and we weren't able to force a laugh past it.

And then, without so much as an announcement, the first heavyweight transporter took a knee on the infield, drew a sigil, and jumped the entire stadium from an empty field outside Presque Isle, Maine, to an isolated hilltop in New Brunswick. A few of the passengers cried out in alarm. I tightened my grip on the bench.

The earth beneath us settled into the new locale and the dilapidated stadium creaked and shifted with it—the building must have dated from the Franco-Prussian Intervention. Before I had time to take a breath, the next transporter drew and jumped us to a tiny island off the coast of Newfoundland called Killiniq.

Someone behind us was crying.

"Gosh," Essie whispered.

She and I had joined up together after a year at Radcliffe College and had gone through flight training in the same group. She'd been a godsend. I tried to imagine what it would have been like as the first man to join Rescue & Evac without Essie's constant reassurance to the other recruits that yes, I could do the work if they would only let me, and no, I wasn't some sort of pervert or sex maniac or transvestite or any of the hundred other delightful theories they came up with. Yes, he really was the first man to medal in the long course at the General's Cup. Yes, he really shot Maxwell Gannet, the crazed anti-philosopher who'd wanted to exterminate American sigilry in the name of God. Yes, he was really lover to Danielle Hardin, who'd rescued the entire Commonwealth army at Gallipoli, a hero without parallel to the young empirical philosophers we'd trained alongside.

Essie's word had carried a lot of weight. Her performance in the General's Cup had made her famous, too. She'd edged out the two fastest fliers in the world in what the *Detroit Defender* had called "the greatest upset of all time." Then the other girls had met her and, of course, Essie had been Essie: shy but determined, a prim, rail-thin rich girl who never put on airs. All through our grueling training in the dead of the Texas summer, she'd never flinched at floor scrubbing or powder bag filling or any other hard duty. She'd always volunteered for overnight watch and guard shifts. Always a spare minute to help patch a uniform or take dictation from her less literate squadmates so they could send letters home. They'd loved her. (That she could outfly the entire company in a race of any distance—one hundred yards or one hundred miles—didn't hurt either.)

I looked at her beside me now. Her lower lip was trembling.

We jumped again, making the long swap from Killiniq across the Labrador Sea to an ice-covered valley in western Greenland. Danielle had once told me that the Corps transporters intentionally mispronounced it as the "killing jump," because of the strain that the distance put on the sigilrist. Every few years, one of them dropped dead from the effort.

"That's the hard one," I said to Essie. "We're going to be okay."

She tried to put on a stoic face, but her eyes were full.

Six hours earlier, in morning assembly, the whole company had been in a celebratory mood: our last day of training. Graduation ceremonies would be held in the afternoon and then we would have three days' leave before our overseas deployment. My mother, a retired corpswoman, had planned to attend the formal commissioning ceremony; Danielle had arranged to come too and then stay on in San Antonio so she and I could spend my last stateside days together.

I'd stood in line with the other trainees, laughing and jibing, as our flight instructors handed out the single plain brown bar of rank that we would sew on the collar of our uniform in preparation for the afternoon's exercises. No longer Provisional Sigilwomen, but rather proper Sigilwomen Third Class, or Sig-3 as we called the rank.

Our chief flight instructor had skipped over Essie, much to the poor young lady's distress, only to return to her at the end: for her outstanding performance, she'd been promoted to Sigilwoman Second Class. We'd applauded and Essie had done her damnedest not to bawl. Not, I suspected, out of joy. The promotion meant she would outrank many of the more seasoned women in France, and R&E fliers were notorious for balking at orders if their socks had been in the service longer than their Sig-2.

Then came the bad news for the rest of us: pre-overseas leave, canceled. Graduation ceremonies, canceled. Immediate deployment. Ten minutes to pack. Dress in field skysuits with harness and tackle stowed at the ready.

Once the shock had worn off, we'd rushed to pack our things, the women in their barracks and me in my tent removed from the main building by fifty yards. It had taken me little enough time. I'd stuffed my duffel with two spare olive-green skysuits—the padded, high-necked coveralls we wore while flying—which I'd had to procure from a civilian vendor, as the Corps quartermasters were not in the practice of issuing suits to six-foot-tall men. One army dress uniform in place of the Corps' traditional jacket, blouse, and full skirts. And to complete the time-honored full-dress outfit, a parasol and saber, which had been presented by my mentors at Radcliffe—not that I seemed likely to be deployed to any formal balls.

We'd ridden the civilian transporter line to Maine, then hiked a half mile up the road to the Corps stadium to cross the Atlantic with our own women.

Now, we jumped to the eastern shore of Greenland, then a rocky field in Iceland and a beach in the Faroe Islands.

Essie put her head so close to mine that our foreheads were almost touching.

"What?" I asked.

"We're going to be there in two minutes," she whispered. "They could put me out there in command. In the field. Today."

"Not on the first day."

"If we catch a mass casualty—"

"Then you'll run it by the book and it'll be great."

"Robert, I can't." Essie had her chin to her chest and her eyes closed so she wouldn't cry. "I can't do this. I can't, I can't, *I can't!*"

We jumped to Inverness, Scotland, where a light rain was falling.

"You're not allowed to say that, ma'am," I whispered.

. . . to Manchester under gray skies . . .

"I'm allowed to say it today! I'm allowed to say it to you."

. . . to London . . .

"One time," I said.

"I can't do it," she said in a voice like a mouse's squeak.

My own chest echoed the sentiment every time I tried to take a full breath—*I can't, I'm not ready, they'll hate me, they'll send me home.* So, make a joke. Bear up under it. Don't let anyone see it, never admit it out loud.

Then the temperature rose fifteen degrees, the sky was clear, and it was early evening. We'd arrived in Le Havre.

A Corps colonel wearing a smokecarver's gray work apron over her uniform entered the stadium. She lifted a speaking trumpet to her lips, shouted, "Welcome to France!" and exhorted us to exit in an orderly fashion and find the representatives from our units, who were waiting outside.

I hefted my duffel and we made our way down the stairs and across the infield to one of the exits. Outside, the officers picking up their replacements seemed not to have been briefed on the "orderly" part of the operation. Dozens of them milled about, shouting out the numbers of their units or the names of the greenhorns they were trying to find. It would be a wonder if this sorted itself out by doomsday.

As we plowed through the confusion, Essie reached out and took my hand. Her fingers were thin and cool.

"Robert . . ." Her voice caught.

Essie didn't like strangers, hated crowds, and couldn't abide racket. She also didn't approve of hand holding. She gave me a desperate look, but no words came out.

I knew. Even for a callow young man, it was impossible to miss a crush as big as the one Essie had developed on me back at Radcliffe. But fraternization with a fellow officer would get me thrown out of the Corps so fast that I wouldn't even have time to hear the threads snap when they ripped the insignia off my jacket. And I was saving my heart for Danielle, with whom things were . . . tricky. Especially now that she and I wouldn't be spending three days' leave together.

Essie tightened her grip on my hand. She was headed to First Division along with most of the rest of our company. I was the sole flier assigned to Fifth Division. Outside of a major evacuation, we were unlikely to see each other. Maybe it was kinder that way.

"You yell 'First Division' loud as you can and let them find you," I said to her. "Give 'em hell, ma'am."

I swept a loose strand of hair out of Essie's eyes and tucked it behind her ear. She let go of me and clapped her hand to her face, as if I'd burned her skin where I'd touched her.

I turned to find my own wing. Behind me, I heard Essie bellow, "R&E! First Division reinforcements, on me!"

I did very little in the way of shouting, relying on Fifth Division to recognize the single male present. As I circled the crush, I spotted a lanky beanpole of a woman at the edge of the crowd. She'd made a sign out of a piece of cardboard tied to a stick: DIV 5 R&E. I made my way toward her.

She had a portable message board strapped to her forearm and was doubled over it, bobbing her head up and down like a crane. She looked about twenty-five years old. On her collar, she wore three brown bars edged with gold; on the left sleeve of her skysuit, a thin white stripe ran from shoulder to wrist. That made her a squadron commander with at least a thousand souls evacuated, plus the Corps' highest decoration for valor. A formidable woman.

I cleared my throat and came to attention in front of her. "Sigilwoman Third Class Robert A. Canderelli, reporting," I announced.

The name still sounded awkward in my mouth. After my brush with infamy a few weeks earlier, the Corps had requested that I enlist under an alias, to protect me against unwelcome attention. (Not idly, as it turned out. A gang of Trenchers had been caught trying to sneak on base at Fort McConnell during my second week of training, with me as their target.) I'd taken my father's surname.

The tall, skinny woman finished writing her message and looked up at me like I was the lowest worm in existence. My insides turned to slush.

"Hell," she drawled.

She pulled a harness out of her pack and began putting it on. It was only when she gave me an irritated look that I understood I was to ready myself for flight, too.

"A lot of girls going to be disappointed," the Sig-1 said.

"I'm sorry, ma'am?" I said.

"They took odds on whether it was Roberta or Robert A. Wagered their spots in the flight rotation. They said Gen. Blandings isn't crazy enough to take a man. I told them don't bet on it."

My Sig-1 had probably made that up, but had I been a woman in one of the R&E wings, a Roberta with a typo might have seemed likelier than a male philosopher.

"Are you a gambling man, Robert A?" the Sig-1 asked me.

It struck me as a question with a correct answer, though I couldn't decide which.

"Not often," I said.

"A Christian?" she asked, sounding suspicious.

"Not really."

She heaved a twenty-pound powder bag to me and attached a second to her own rigging.

"Gonna have to pick one," she said. "Serve long enough with Fifth Division and you're bound to believe in either Jesus Christ or the laws of probability."

I nodded, hoping I hadn't just given myself a reputation for indecisiveness.

"You belong to second squadron," she said. "So, I own you until such time as the Lieutenant decides you fit better with the layabouts in first squad or the incompetents in third. My name's Millen and there's no 'ma'am' or 'sir' or curtsying, unless we have a visiting dignitary."

"Understood," I said.

Sig-1 Millen put on her leather crash helmet and adjusted her goggles over her long, angular face.

"You're no fun at all!" she complained. "Were you born without a sense of humor or did they beat it out of you in training?"

"More the latter."

"Well, locate it. In the field, it's laugh or go mad."

"I'm not even supposed to be here today!" I blurted out. "We were supposed to have three days' leave and then come over on the *Olympia*."

The rumor, from the very first day in Texas, had been that our unit was one of the lucky ones that would ship to France aboard a luxury liner pressed into service as a troop transport. She was a beautiful Eupheus ship that put up four banks of kite sails and set a perpetually westward course at forty knots, blown by the hurricane-force winds summoned up by her philosophical officer. Our training instructors had spent the final weeks providing ever more lavish descriptions of the *Olympia*'s opulence: a swimming pool, wood-paneled staterooms, a seventeen-piece orchestra, a gourmet chef.

Millen slapped her thigh. "Now *that's* funny. The *Olympia*! Does she still have a shuffleboard court and Persian carpets in the bathrooms?"

"Umm . . . something like that."

"Robert A, the *Olympia* sank ten years before you joined up. Shit, they're making Sig-3s just as stupid as they used to. The *Olympia*. Oh, you'll do fine."

Possibly our training company hadn't been the first one to believe the story. Millen helped me secure my overseas bag to the back of my harness.

"I *am* sorry about your leave," she added. "First Division set a couple wings down in a minefield last week. Chewed up enough women that they cried for their reinforcements early and got near your whole training company. You ready?"

I clipped my powder bag to my right hip. I pushed the thumb lever on the mechanical regulator to open it and set the flow rate. The mixture of sand and fine-ground cornmeal, which provided the catalyst for philosophical flight, began to trickle out. I gripped the tip of the reg between my thumb and forefinger like a pencil.

On Millen's signal, I drew a glyph to launch and popped into the air. I redrew to adjust course, adding speed and altitude, then drew again every eight seconds to prevent my sigil from fading, following Millen southeast.

Being airborne was a relief. Even thousands of miles from home, the regulator had the same solid feel in my hand; the powder produced the same subtle hiss as it flowed out of the waxed canvas bag. The sigil's thrust lifted through the center of my body and the sense of buoyancy was as intoxicating as ever.

We flew for an hour. Beneath us, fields slipped by, a chaotic patchwork of yellow and gold instead of the orderly rows of farms I'd known in Montana. Even the grass looked foreign: it was the wrong shade of green, bending and swaying to a different rhythm than it had back home. Gradually, the ground became more scarred, the roads muddier, the earth marred with shell craters, the farmhouses and villages in ruins. This had been disputed territory as recently as a few months before. We didn't see any soldiers or artillery, though. They were farther east.

I glanced over at Millen, ten feet off my shoulder with her speed matched to mine. She had her eyes closed. She wasn't sleeping—not the way she was holding her course and redrawing sigils—but something akin to sleep. Even my mother, who was the most experienced flier I knew, didn't dare do that.

The sun was nearly touching the horizon by the time we reached Fifth Division's encampment outside the village of Commercy, twenty miles behind the front lines. Millen waved with her off hand to catch my attention.

She pointed to the ground, where a large landing field had been drawn with white paint on a flat stretch of grass. I put two fingers to my temple to indicate that I understood.

As we came over the landing field, Millen pirouetted to kill her forward momentum, then pulled her knees to her chest and reverse-drew to descend smartly. She halted a few inches above the ground and straightened her legs to set down. A classic tuck-and-groove approach, though too conservative for my taste.

I flared into a forward half somersault, so that I was flying upside down and backward, braked hard, and pushed toward the ground. At an altitude of fifty feet, I flipped back upright and drew for maximum upward thrust to stop my dive. I came to a halt just above the ground and settled my feet.

"Oh, holy Jesus in a wheelbarrow!" Millen howled. "He's a hotshot! Did you grow up in the circus?"

"No, ma'am," I said. "That's a standard flare and—"

"That's a circus landing for when the Germans take a shot at you! There's no one to impress out here and I can't replace you if you break a leg."

I'd spent months at Radcliffe working on that maneuver—the fastest and most precise landing approach possible—and then six weeks doing it at Fort McConnell, where no one had ever considered it showy or dangerous.

Millen led me down a row of eighteen canvas tents to the last one in line.

"This one's yours, so drop your gear," she said. "It's supposed to be two sigilwomen in each, but it'll rain lemon drops in hell before Fifth Division gets a full complement. You'll share with the foul-weather gear."

Half the tent was crammed with piles of rubberized capes and boxes of wool sweaters. The other half had a cot and a hat rack. It stank of mothballs and looked like the spiders had been busy in the corners.

"We'll find your squadmates," Sig-1 Millen said. "Unless you want one right now."

"One what?" I asked.

"*One*. An evacuation, a quick one. I'll take you forward and you can grab one."

I had flown passengers on hundreds of occasions, but the thought of taking one now made my heart stutter. I'd waited my whole life to fly a real evacuation. If the war ended tomorrow, I could at least say I'd had my one.

"Yeah," I said, not wanting to sound overeager.

"Of course he does!" Millen hooted. "The squadron hotshot's going to get his first evac before he even goes on duty. I love it!"

2

As the Sigilry Corps styles all its members "officers," we shall treat them as such. Enlisted men are to call corpswomen "ma'am" and offer a hand salute when appropriate.

Gen. John J. Pershing, US Army,
General Order #324, April 8, 1917

I FOLLOWED MILLEN TO THE FARMHOUSE THAT FIFTH DIVISION had commandeered for its headquarters. The ground floor was a single large room with a trestle table covered by a dozen message boards, plus numerous binders and handmade cardboard charts.

A black woman with graying hair pulled back into a bun sat at the table making notes in a logbook. She had three bars of rank on her collar, which made her a Sig-1 too.

"Evening, Bernice," said Millen.

"Evening, Teeny," the woman replied to Millen, who was at least six inches taller than the older woman.

"Please tell me the adjutant officer isn't covering board duty on her day off," Millen said. "It's not your turn, is it?"

Bernice cleared her throat in a way that made it sound as if she were rolling her eyes, though she kept her face motionless. "It was supposed to be Marjorie's turn, but she had another one of her . . . episodes. She knew a girl in First Division who bought a piece of it this afternoon. Margie was crying and shaking and carrying on."

"And she stuck you with the board over that? If you haven't taken that child out back and beaten her yet, I'll do it for you."

"The Lieutenant decided Marjorie's done. Sent her to Le Havre to see the doctor. She won't be coming back."

Millen bit the second knuckle on her index finger like she wanted to draw blood.

"That makes you *three* fliers short," Millen growled. "Fern's down six. And that's with two brevets for Sig-2s. They're trying to kill Fifth Division."

"Same as last month," Bernice said. "Or ever. You knew what you were getting into."

Millen smiled evilly at me. "But now I have young Robert A, who still has considerable enthusiasm for the trade. So, we've broken even for the day, at least."

Bernice and I shook hands.

"I'm the divisional adjutant officer," Bernice explained. "In the event of a court martial, I'm supposed to defend you. I also handle personnel transfers. Teeny, what's the record for the fastest a girl has ever tried to get out of your squadron—was it eight minutes?"

"Seven," Millen replied.

I furrowed my brow. "I thought it was a lieutenant colonel who served as adjutant."

"Ha!" Millen said. "Aren't they just darling on their first day?"

Bernice gave a half smile at that. "And how many working women did they tell you an R&E division was supposed to have when you were training at Fort McConnell?"

"One hundred and eight, ma'am," I replied, reciting the figure I'd learned.

"We have twenty-nine," Bernice said. "Back at headquarters in Le Havre, Gen. Niejenhuis has the American lines divided into equal sections for evacuations—one for each R&E division. Looks very pretty on the map. Doesn't matter that First Division has ten times as many women as we do. We cover the same amount of territory. I hope you came ready to work."

That may have been the moment when I realized the Great War wasn't going to be the grand adventure I'd imagined. We didn't even have women enough for a full wing, much less a division.

Millen was getting bored. "Find him a quick one. I'm taking his virginity."

Bernice massaged her temples. "Teeny, we've discussed not using that phrase. And we're off duty until midnight."

"So poach a call," Millen insisted. "Somebody must have something at this hour. Low priority—he doesn't care."

Bernice sighed and swept her hand over the sand on one of the message boards, smoothing the surface flat. With her fingertip she wrote a message, then traced a glyph in the corner to transmit it to the forward casualty clearing stations. We waited for a reply.

"Your best chance will be Point A for Adele," Bernice offered. "They were calling for ground ambulances a while back." She sorted through a pile of maps that had been rolled and stacked beside the table. "Mr. Canderelli, let's have you plot a course to evacuation point A while we wait. Do you have a compass?"

I reached into my pocket, but Millen waved me off.

"Don't bother. All you have to do is follow me."

Bernice glared over her steel-rimmed glasses at Millen. "Teeny—"

"Run your own damn squadron. By the time he plots a course to the evac point and then to the hospital and back here, we could already have run it. Are you capable of following me, Robert A?"

"Yes," I said, though not without trepidation. If we were to become separated or if, God forbid, something should happen to Millen, I would be lost over unknown ground in a country where I could speak all of two hundred words. Good sense dictated that I should plot my own course and commit it to memory.

But Millen was already walking out the door.

"You at least going to wait for them to respond before you fly out there?" Bernice called after her. "Teeny!"

Millen didn't dignify that with an answer.

Bernice scribbled her personal message glyph on a piece of paper and passed it to me. "If somebody shoots her, message me for directions."

I hurried out after Millen. She took me to the supply shed and we kitted out with forty-pound powder bags, as well as a satchel with passenger harnesses and extra straps.

"What's top speed for you with one passenger, rigged back-to-back?" Millen asked.

"Two twenty," I said.

Millen frowned at me. "Two hundred twenty *miles* per hour?"

"Yes, ma'am," I confirmed.

"A boy who makes two hundred twenty carrying another boy. Now I've seen it all."

We made final adjustments to our rigging.

"Stay close on me," Millen instructed. "Straight course, six minutes, then down without preliminaries. It's only two thousand yards back from the front lines, but it's a quiet area. The Huns haven't been shooting at fliers, so make a low-risk approach. No circus landings."

We launched and kept low at an altitude of a hundred feet. In a few minutes, we came upon the reserve trenches, which were deep and well improved with dugouts and wooden causeways. The aid station was a trench partially roofed with corrugated tin sheeting.

Beside it, the stretcher-bearers had cleared an open area twenty feet to a side, free of the tangle of barbed wire and telegraph wires that crisscrossed the rest of the trenches. As an indication of how quiet the section was, they'd also—in flagrant violation of army regulations—drawn out the borders of a square with whitewash and labeled it with a letter *A*. A good target for artillery, but also extremely convenient for us.

We put down in the center of the square. A senior stretcher-bearer climbed out to meet us and assisted us down a ladder eight feet into the trench.

"Didn't expect to see you this evening, Mrs. Millen," he said. "Bernice says you're freelancing?"

"For him," said Millen, pointing to me. "This is Sigilwoman Canderelli. He's new to the division today."

"Did you say—" The stretcher-bearer cocked his head. "Well, it takes all sorts, I suppose. Welcome to the war, ma'am!"

(American soldiers would call a rock "ma'am" if they thought there were the slightest risk of it being a corpswoman.)

The stretcher-bearer led us to a young man sitting on a stool, smoking a cigarette with his left hand. He had a blood-soaked bandage wrapped around his right.

"James," the stretcher-bearer called. "The fliers will take you to the field hospital so you can have that sewn up."

I looked to Millen, who nodded at me.

"Good evening," I said as I approached the wounded man, working from the script we'd memorized in training. "I'm Sigilwoman Canderelli with the Sigilry Corps. I'm going to evacuate you to the field hospital by air. You'll be in stasis, which is like being in a deep sleep. You won't feel any physical sensations or remember anything until you wake. Do you understand?"

"You said it was just a bad cut—why they gonna fly me?" the boy asked. He rose from his stool and backed away. "Why's *he* taking me?"

"It's his first day in the war," said the stretcher-bearer in a soothing tone. "They're getting him practice."

"It's his *first day*?" the boy asked. He turned to Millen, mistaking her for a reasonable person. "Why's there a man flying?"

"Where are you from, son?" Millen asked.

"Laurel, Mississippi," he said.

"Mr. Canderelli is from Montana. All the men can hover out there. He was the best male flier in the state, so we put him in the Corps."

"Really?" the wounded young man asked. He had to be the most unphilosophical soul in the world to buy that line.

"Put the harness on," said Millen.

The young man stepped through the leg loops and buckled the straps. Millen stepped behind him and took hold of one of the carabiners on his back. The stretcher-bearer held on to the other. I opened the collar of the boy's shirt.

"Indicator paper?" I asked.

"We do it the fast way," Millen said. "Twelve over four."

"Sure thing," I said, inwardly mortified to be discussing the logistics of performing a stasis sigil in front of the man we were evacuating.

Millen took a glass ampoule of silver chloride from her workbag and slapped it into my hand. I wrapped a turn of my skysuit's sleeve around it and snapped the neck off, discarding the glass tip.

"What are you doing?" the boy asked. He tried to take a step backward, but Millen and the stretcher-bearer, having correctly identified him as a runner, held him fast.

"Stand up straight and close your eyes," Millen said to him.

I poured a thin stream of silver chloride powder from the tube onto the boy's chest, tracing out a series of interlocking arcs. When I finished the glyph, his whole body went rigid. We laid him down on the ground.

The stasis sigil I'd drawn on the soldier placed his body in a state of suspended animation. While the sigil was in effect, he would lose no blood from his wounds; he would suffer no discomfort at being manhandled when we attached his harness to mine; if I encountered difficulties while in the air and had to dump him, he would hit the ground without further injury. Most importantly, it paralyzed him so that he didn't panic in the air and kick or buck, knocking us both right out of the sky.

The doctors at the field hospital liked to know how long our stasis sigils would last so they could jump into action at the appropriate moment. I'd grown up calculating it with chemical indicator paper, but that needed several minutes to provide results. Most R&E fliers preferred to take shortcuts. The stretcher-bearer loaned me a nickel and a ruler. I measured four inches above the boy's chest and dropped the nickel. The coin made a popping noise at it struck his chest and rebounded high into the air, accelerated by an electromagnetic peculiarity that even the best theorists couldn't explain. But the higher a nickel bounced, the longer the sigil lasted. Greater than twelve inches meant at least two hours of stasis.

Millen gave me a grease pencil and I wrote on the boy's forehead the sigil strength and on-time: *12+/4 20:16.* Millen and the stretcher-bearer pulled the paralyzed young man back to his feet and assisted in hooking the carabiners on the back of his harness into the clips on the back of mine.

"Couldn't ask for smoother," the stretcher-bearer said, supporting the body so that it didn't shift and pull me over. "He'll be one of the regulars?"

"With Louise Punnett," said Millen.

"Ah, Miss Punnett! A sturdy pair they'll be."

"A working pair, I hope," said Millen.

The stretcher-bearer took her meaning better than I did. "I'm sorry to see Marjorie go. But once a malingerer gets their claws into a unit, there's no saving it."

"Don't I know it," said Millen. She looked at the sun, which had nearly dipped below the horizon. "We need to move. Robert A, stay on me. At the hospital, circle the landing zone once and then go straight in. Corporal, come safe home."

The stretcher-bearer sketched out a salute to us. "Same to you, sigil-women."

We launched and made for the field hospital. Thanks to the hover sigil, the wounded man felt almost weightless as soon as we were in the air, but having him strapped to me still changed my center of mass. That meant a series of a thousand adjustments in head and body angle, powder flow, the length of time necessary to set up a turn. I could tell that Millen, even as she was trying to set a moderate pace, was annoyed at having to slow down for me.

After a few minutes' flight, I could make out a village in the distance. A squat little church stood in the center and I followed Millen as she adjusted course and made for it. Attached to the main building was a low-slung structure that (I was to learn) had served over the centuries as a hostelry for pilgrims, a plague hospital, a barn, and now as an operating theater where the wounded were stabilized before being shipped back to the States to convalesce. Outside the building, the medical staff had erected a large open tent with neat rows of cots to triage incoming casualties. They'd also chalked off a landing zone on a level patch of grass.

Millen set down and I followed her in. I had no more than the usual trouble landing with a stasied man strapped to me, trying to lever myself down to the ground and take his weight without throwing out my back. Two orderlies—old hands—were smoking cigarettes and watching our landings from a few feet away.

"Corpswoman on the ground!" one of them called out, making the traditional announcement.

"*L'aviateur a atterri*," the second tried, his French thickly American.

"Better, but not quite," the first said. He was a plump, balding man of about fifty with a professorial air. "You ought to use *aviatrice* as the feminine form of . . ." Then the cigarette sagged from his lips as he got a good look at me.

"Good evening, gentlemen," I said.

"Jesus, but Gen. Blandings is running out of fresh bodies," the second orderly said. "They're making the men evacuate themselves!"

"Well, get the poor fellow a stretcher before he strains a muscle," answered the first. His companion trotted off for a litter.

"What's wrong with this one?" the orderly asked me.

"Hand's cut up," I said.

"Left or right?"

"Right."

"Safer for him that way. If it's the left, the military police suspect self-inflicted to get out of the fighting. That's a capital offense. A righty usually holds the knife in his right hand and cuts the left."

The orderlies got the man detached from my harness, put him on a stretcher, and carried him into the tent.

"They're a good pair," Millen said to me. "It's a godsend when they're on. They don't leave you standing for hours with the wounded strapped to your back."

Having secured my patient, the two men ambled back out, their cigarettes still in place.

"Care for a smoke, Sigilwoman?" the second orderly asked Millen. "I won't charge but my usual price."

"Very well," said Millen. "Robert A, if you can teach this gentleman a new phrase in French, you earn a cigarette. Ah, let's see. *La lune se couche à minuit.* Do you know that one?"

The orderly smiled and rubbed his chin. "Perhaps . . . the moon dances a minuet?"

"It sets at midnight," Millen corrected.

"Ah! Though God willing we'll be in bed at that hour," the orderly said. He pulled a cigarette from his pocket, put it between Millen's lips, and lit it with a match. Then he looked at me. "And this one—does he call himself Sigilman or Sigilwoman?"

"Sigilwoman," Millen and I both answered.

That had been drummed into me from the first minute of flight training: the rank was Sigilwoman, the honorific was ma'am, and if I didn't like it, the army had a very nice draft on.

"Well, Sigilwoman," said the orderly, "have you any French?"

"Only what they taught me in training," I said.

"I already know all eight of those phrases," he replied.

"German?" I suggested. I'd taken two semesters at Radcliffe.

"Ah! So either we overrun them and yell '*Hande hoch!*,' or they overrun us and we yell '*Nicht schiessen!*' You can add something to that?"

"*Der Mond setzt am zwölf Uhr*," I said, trying to sound more confident than I felt in assembling the words. "The moon sets at midnight."

The orderly looked pleased by the phrase, but the older man shook his head.

"Not bad," he said. "But *um* rather than *am*. And *Mitternacht*, if you like a more literal translation. I'm afraid we have to uphold standards, even on your first day. Cigarettes for correct grammar only."

Millen took a long drag. She considered the sun, now only a sliver on the horizon.

"You're going to lose the light," the older orderly said.

Millen rubbed the tip of her cigarette against the leather shoulder strap of her harness to knock off the ash and then pinched it out. She handed it back to the younger one.

"I'll finish it next time."

"I look forward to it, Mrs. Millen," he said.

We launched and Millen got us back to our encampment as the western sky was going from orange to purple.

"So you got your one," Millen said to me. "First day in the war—first hour—and you got one. So, you're not allowed to have stage fright, or get lost, or say 'I don't wanna,' because you already did. Do you understand?"

What I mostly understood was that I had evacuated a single minor casualty with someone else navigating, in fair weather, with decent light, while adequately rested, with ample help on the ground. Under those circumstances, I could have flown the mission at the age of fifteen. I had less a feeling of accomplishment than a burning sense of embarrassment that Millen should think I needed so obvious a confidence booster.

"Yeah," I said. But something she'd said earlier was bothering me, too. "How'd you know I'm from Montana?"

"Oh, we know all about you, little brother. Gen. Blandings picked you out special. You're her secret weapon. You're going to win the war for her, right?"

I looked at her askance. "Are you joking?"

"You have no idea how deep you're in, do you?"

Millen spat over her shoulder.

"Go find your Sig-2," she said. "She's one of the well-behaved ones. Her name's Andrada. She's in the mess tent. You think you can find that on your own or you need me to hold your hand?"

3

> The senior Sig-3 is your big sister. Your Sig-2 is a young, stylish aunt. The Sig-1 is mother on her worst day (which is every day). The lieutenant is the minister's wife, for whom you must be on your best behavior. And captains and generals—well, they are creatures so strange and removed from the concerns of the everyday as to be of another species entirely.
>
> Constance Lattimore, *Flying with the First*, 1919

THE MESS TENT WAS LARGE ENOUGH TO SEAT THE ENTIRE DIVISION at a mismatched collection of benches and chairs. In one corner, a recirculating perpetual heat stove whirred, keeping a vat of soup simmering above a canister of specially made smoke. Barrels of flour and sacks of onions were stacked next to it. The smell of scorched beans permeated the entire place, and there was a fine film of grease over every surface.

At a battered folding table in the back, three corpswomen in skysuits with the necks unbuttoned were playing cards. When they caught sight of me, they stopped their game and stared.

"And he's nine feet tall," one of them laughed. She was an Asian woman of about thirty. On her collar, she had one bar of rank, edged in gold—a Sig-3, like me, but quite experienced. "Perfect. Why do the special projects always have to end up in my flight group?"

"In second squadron, that's for sure," said the second woman, a short, plump girl with beady eyes who looked like she ought to be a sophomore in high school. She had a single bar, too, but ordinary brown, which would make her one of the division's more junior fliers. More worried than sarcastic.

"Do you play?" she asked.

"Umm, I'm looking for Sig-2 Andrada?" I said.

"Come and sit!" said the first woman. "Do you play?"

I found a chair and sat with them. "I'm Robert Canderelli," I said. "I'm supposed—"

"Yes, yes, you could hardly be anyone else," said the first woman.

"Are you— I'm supposed to find Andrada?"

"Jesus," muttered the second. "Was I as dim as him my first day?"

"Louise, sweetheart, you were greener than the fresh-mown grass on an April morning," the first woman said. She laid down her cards to make introductions. "I'm Kiyo—I'm just a simple Sig-3. That's Louise Punnett, who'll be your babysitter. And that's the boss lady."

The last was directed toward the scowling, brown-skinned woman with two bars on her collar, who hadn't yet acknowledged my presence.

"Ma'am," I said, rising and saluting. "You're Sigilwoman Andrada? Millen told me I'm supposed to—"

"Sit," said Sig-2 Andrada. "We're off duty. *You're* off duty. We go on at midnight and we'll talk business then. In the meantime, play cards or shut up."

I did both.

"The game's high-low cutthroat," Kiyo told me as she dealt. "Queens are blush, jokers go left-handed, and we boot on twos."

It was not much different from no-look jiggery, which I'd grown up playing, except that we played each against the other, instead of in teams. After playing a couple hands, I decided that Andrada was an unusually smart player, Punnett was not much good at arithmetic, and Kiyo was determined to play the most exuberantly obstructionist strategy I'd ever seen.

"Oh, don't lead a two!" Punnett protested, as Kiyo moved to make the game even more excruciating. "Everybody scores negative for the round!"

I tried to parry it with an ace, but Kiyo capped me with a three to force a mudge.

"Here ten minutes and he's already trying to advance the common good," Kiyo said, chuckling.

We played a few more hands, but other than a comment or two about the cards, no one talked, much less explained what I was supposed to be doing.

"Should I just play until we go on duty?" I asked. "Or should I—"

"Christ," Sig-2 Andrada said. "Little brother here thinks he's working. Punnett, he's your partner. If you can't keep him quiet, explain how the schedule works."

"Sure," Punnett said. "Fifth Division covers evacuations from the southernmost sector of the lines. We're on duty for two days at a time and then have one day to rest—sleep, resupply, play cards, whatever. For our on-days, we divide the division in half. You're designated first-in for six hours, then backup for six hours, up again for six, and backup for six. Second day, you do it all over again. Understand?"

That was not how we'd trained down in Texas. It was supposed to be three wings, with each wing covering eight hours of the day.

"Does that mean we could theoretically be flying for forty-eight hours straight if there's a big attack?" I asked.

"See, he's not as dumb as he looks!" Kiyo said.

"Yeah, theoretically," said Punnett. "But the forward aid stations almost never call for us overnight—they get shelled if they light up a landing field. So, sunset to sunrise is quiet and the days are getting shorter. Our flight group's got it easy tomorrow. We'll take the overnight shift and the afternoon."

"That's first-up from midnight to six," I said, making sure I had it right, "then fly again noon to six in the evening?"

"Right," Kiyo said. "Except Bernice and Fern will find a way to screw up the morning shift and we'll end up running most of their calls, too."

"They do okay," Punnett countered. "Usually. Anyway, the schedule isn't as bad as it sounds."

"No, it's *exactly* as bad as it sounds," said Kiyo. "I was on a hundred and three hours last week and it wasn't even busy."

"It's better if you don't count," suggested Punnett. "We like to say we work harder because we're picked women."

"Picked by a batty old witch of a general," Kiyo said. "With an executive officer who doesn't believe in hot water. And a burnout for a Sig-1."

Sig-2 Andrada leveled a look at Kiyo that said, *Not in front of the children.*

Punnett played a jack to force a mudge and score four points and promptly lost them as Kiyo froze the deck with a queen.

"Evacuations are busiest right around dawn," Punnett continued. "All the overnight wounded plus morning sick call to evacuate. They're only supposed to call us for the really bad cases—too critical to waste time going overland by motor ambulance or too badly hurt to survive the trip. Everybody's supposed to go in stasis."

"That's a good joke," said Kiyo.

"We've been taking a lot of them awake," explained Punnett. "We're dead short on silver chloride. Everyone is."

"Yeah," said Kiyo, "but the divisions with generals who play politics feel it less. Our local brigadier doesn't bother with little-p politics. No, only capital-P Politics for her—treaties and conspiracies and international relations. She's going to politick us into our graves."

"Gen. Blandings likes to speak her mind," Punnett offered. "It means she doesn't have a lot of friends."

"Oh, she has plenty of friends," Kiyo said. "Too many friends. When's the last time you saw her? Two days ago? Three? Off playing ambassador somewhere."

"We are *not* starting this again," said Sig-2 Andrada. She turned to me. "Did you eat?"

With all the time changes, I had no idea how long it had been since breakfast. "Yes," I said. "Five thousand miles ago. I'm fine, though."

"That's wrong," said Punnett. "Go eat. You never know when we're going to get an all-hands call. Always eat, always pee, always sleep."

I retrieved a hunk of stale brown bread and dished myself a bowl of lentil soup that had the consistency of dried paste.

"So, how'd you get stuck in the last corner of France?" Punnett asked as I retook my seat.

"Nobody but Blandings is dumb enough to take a man," Kiyo answered for me.

"More or less," I said around a mouthful of dinner. "I joined as a Contingency student out of Radcliffe College. I wanted to be where the action was."

"I thought Contingencies were supposed to be the smart ones," Kiyo said with a *tsk*. "All that expensive education but no sense at all."

I shuffled and dealt the next hand.

Kiyo looked at Punnett. "So, go ahead and ask him," she said.

"God," Punnett said. "Could we not?"

"They warned us you were coming weeks ago," Kiyo said. "Louise won't shut up about your medal in the General's Cup. She's your biggest fan."

Punnett glared at me like I'd been the one to say it. "I just wanted to know how you beat Aileen Macadoo, is all."

It was a question I'd heard nine thousand times in training: How does a male philosopher beat the fastest flier in the world in a hundred-mile-long race?

"She got lost," I said. "She was a fancy city flier. Couldn't navigate."

Kiyo snorted in approval, but my answer no more satisfied Punnett than it had any of the girls at Fort McConnell.

"Yeah, I read that part," Punnett said. "I wondered about the end."

"Ah," I said. "I cut under Macadoo on my flare and settle."

"On his flare and settle!" Kiyo laughed. "Oh, Millen's going to have a conniption."

"Our last flare and settler cratered," Punnett explained. "Right in front of our dear Sig-1."

"Both legs, snap-snap," said Kiyo. "And off to the hospital for some pins and rods and a pension. On her third day. It was months before we got a replacement."

We played one more hand before Sig-2 Andrada collected the cards.

"Little brother and I need to take a walk," Andrada said. "I'll see you two at midnight."

Andrada found an oil lantern, lit it with a sigil, and led me into the night.

Overall, I was finding my wingmates' attitude reassuring. I'd expected skepticism, of course, but it didn't look like they were going to stick me in the mess tent and make me scrub pots for the duration. That was the important part.

Andrada took me down the line of tents, then another fifty yards, to a pair of tree stumps surrounded by tall, uncut grass. She sat, staring at the starry sky and motioned for me to sit too. The air was warm and humid, though less stultifying than coastal Texas.

"You know we joke around a lot," Sig-2 Andrada said. "But when it comes time to work, we're serious. You understand that, right?"

"Yes," I said.

"Then let me tell you something serious."

She spoke slowly, choosing her words with care.

"Millen and I didn't want you in second squadron. Gen. Blandings was very high on you. I told her he sounds smart and he sounds pretty good, but put him in first squadron or third. Because second squad carries the division. We have to, we're the only full squadron."

"I'll work as hard as—"

"I'm not finished," she said. "The divison has a third the number of women we should have. On top of that, we have three women who nobody trusts in the air and two more who are scared to fly but more scared to resign. And now we've got you."

That stung. What more could I do? Hadn't Millen taken me for my first evac before I'd even gone on duty?

"I came here to work," I said, my voice thick. "I grew up in Montana. My mother was the county philosopher and there weren't any other professional fliers within a hundred miles of us. We were it. I know how to work. I'll work harder than anybody."

"That's the part that worries me. You have everything to prove. I know that feeling."

"It's a little different for me," I said.

"Yeah, a little. But not a lot. Do you know where I'm from?"

"No," I said.

"I bet you could guess."

I'd seen pictures of people who looked like her in books on the Philippine Insurrection, which had taken place two decades before. There had been little love lost between the native Filipinos and the corpswomen sent to pacify them. Throats slit in the night and whole villages eradicated with poison or incendiary smoke. My mother still spoke bitterly about the conflict.

"From the Philippines?" I asked.

"Yes. I heard about that on my first day in the Corps and every day since. I had something to prove. Nothing good ever happened when I tried to prove it."

A couple blades of grass had taken fire from her lantern. Andrada ground them out with her foot.

"You listen, you pay attention, you don't volunteer for things, and you don't try to win medals. You don't ever fly alone. Because then you get killed and I have to take three women to wrap up your remains in a sheet. I don't have time for that."

I nodded in agreement, but every fiber of my being raged against the idea of holding back. I hadn't earned a scholarship to Radcliffe by being quiet and well behaved; I hadn't won the respect of my fellow collegiate fliers by meekly following directions; I hadn't seized a spot in R&E against the advice of every single one of my friends by staying out of trouble. Now that I was in France, I intended to be the finest officer R&E had ever seen.

Sig-2 Andrada was sneering like she knew just what I was thinking.

"You know, there's one other thing we should discuss," she interjected.

She pulled her belt knife out of its sheath and laid it in her lap. It was an extraordinarily large specimen, the size of a machete, with a heavy, leaf-shaped blade. The lantern light danced across the swirls in the thick laminated steel. The edge was honed razor sharp.

"That's a big knife," I said.

"It's called a barong," Andrada said. "This one was my uncle's. He fought in the uprising. He cut American soldiers in half with it. You've heard the stories, right? You know that's not just an expression."

"Yes," I said. "My ma served there."

"Wonderful. Maybe your mother killed my mother."

I closed my mouth. What answer could you possibly give to that?

Andrada picked up the blade and pointed it at me. I stopped breathing.

"You love your mother?" Andrada asked.

"Yeah," I managed.

"You have sisters?"

"Three."

"Every woman in this division is my sister. You treat them like you treat your mother or your sisters. I'm going to tell you one time: If you lay a finger on another corpswoman, if you so much as eye her up, I will cut out your heart and dump your body over the German lines. No one will ever find it."

I believed every word.

"Okay," I said.

"Good. We're on duty in an hour. Go get ready. And behave. Because I'll be watching."

4

In the full dark of the night watch, when the chilly wisps settle snug against the earth and the clouds brick off the moonlight, as the distant explosions flicker aurora-like, one cannot feel lonelier nor more exposed. Yet one senses the massive presence of the long guns, the thousand tons of steel at one's back, and feels invulnerable too.

Brian F. Mayweather, *The Last Barrage*, 1927

I WENT TO MY TENT AND SEWED THE SINGLE BROWN BAR OF RANK onto the collar of my skysuit, trying to keep my hands from trembling.

Andrada had rattled me. As a Sig-2, she would lead our flight group of four hoverers—her, me, Punnett, and Kiyo—in the field during larger evacuations. We would help one another load casualties, navigate, launch, and land. But how was I supposed to do all that while worrying she might knife me in the back? Of course, complaining about her would mean going to Sig-1 Millen, who seemed three seconds away from going completely barking mad.

I oiled the leather on my harness and buffed it. It still had some of the shine on the buckles and straps, even after six weeks of training. It marked me out as wetter behind the ears than a duckling in a thunderstorm. Several of the girls back at Fort McConnell had used emery boards to scuff their shoulder pads or had applied rubbing alcohol to their chest protectors to make them look more worn. I hadn't been able to conscience doing that to new equipment.

I could feel tightness creeping into my cheeks and forehead, the unsteadiness in my hands, the heat in my calves as they threatened to go weak. All the familiar physical signs of terror.

First-day jitters. And the overnight watch, no less. Like all fliers, I was afraid of the dark. On a moonless night, you couldn't judge distances. You couldn't see the ground. Were you at ten feet of altitude or ten thousand? Unless someone had been kind enough to light your landing field for you, you didn't know. The dark could kill you.

Jesus Christ or the laws of probability, Millen had said.

It wasn't funny. Run enough missions and you would end up dead, period. Fatigue, accidents, ground fire from your own troops or the enemy's. Each year, on average, two R&E fliers out of every five were wounded badly enough to be medically retired. One out of ten was killed. We'd spent nights at Fort McConnell doing and redoing the arithmetic: If the war lasted another twelve months, of my training company, twenty-seven of us would be seriously injured. Seven of us would be dead.

I re-laced my boots and put them on.

I couldn't afford to think that way. I had to make a good showing on my first shift. If I was lucky, they might let me have a couple runs. I'd show them what I was capable of.

"From ghoulies and ghosties and long-leggedy beasties and things that go bump in the night, oh Mother, deliver us," I whispered.

A child's prayer, but hell if I'd be the thing that went bump for forgetting to say it.

At a quarter to midnight, I made the short walk to the farmhouse. A bleary-faced Sig-3 from one of the other squadrons was slouched in a chair beside the trestle table, where ten message boards were set to receive under different glyphs.

"Hi," I said, my voice pitching up. "I'm Robert Canderelli, coming on for the midnight shift?"

The woman stood. "You know how to send messages, right?"

That couldn't be a real question. In fact, that was the favorite complaint about self-described male philosophers: can't do anything more complicated than send a message.

"Of course," I said.

"Then watch the boards."

"Um, I've never—"

She was already escaping into the night. "If something comes across marked *immediate*, ring the bell and the Lieutenant will come down. She and Gen. Blandings have their rooms upstairs. Ignore everything else."

"Okay," I said, eyeing a large dinner bell and a small triangle hanging beside the door.

I looked over the tabletop. Sheets of paper were strewn about with titles like "Meteorology Command" and "Sigil of the Week." They had dozens of glyphs crossed out and new ones haphazardly drawn in. Piled next to them were a bunch of formal leather-bound logs.

I poked through the mess.

A board in the center of the table was labeled with a piece of masking tape marked EVAC COMM. That would be the evacuation command center back in Le Havre, which relayed requests from the aid stations. A message came across it:

To Div 5:

relaying Charlotte:

"R&E x4 for wndd . . . ctu standby."

So, wound-dressing Point C (as in Charlotte) was requesting four fliers for wounded, but didn't want us to send them yet, just keep them ready to go. It was hard to judge the urgency on a request like that. I checked the logbook, where similar messages had been recorded every fifteen minutes for the past two hours. So perhaps not critical if this was the eighth time they were telling us.

The other boards, too, contained messages of unclear import: *Estimated overnight humidity 85%*, read one. Another said, *Test message—respond on the top to acknowledge glyph fidelity.* And, *For distribution: the movement of troops and supplies by philosophical means including but not limited to transport, hover, and Eupheus sigilry is strictly prohibited (Second Rouen Conventions; Ch 8, Sec 4, Item 11.3)*. Probably all of it was trivial, but I wasn't certain.

A moment later, Millen dragged herself in, a large mug of coffee in hand. For someone about to command a six-hour shift, she looked ready to drop.

"Who's on communications duty?" she asked me, setting her mug down on the board containing the meteorological information, obscuring the glyph.

"I believe I am," I said.

"You *believe* so. Who shirked and left ten minutes early?"

"I don't know her name," I said.

"What did she look like?"

Even if I had recalled, I wouldn't have answered too precisely. "She looked tired."

"Fine," spat Millen. "If you *believe* you're on board duty, then give me a status report."

"Uh, there's going to be significant humidity overnight. We're supposed to reply at the top of the hour to acknowledge glyph fidelity to—well, someone. And Point C for Charlotte wants four fliers for wounded on standby."

"Use your fancy college education," Millen said. "Only one of those is important."

"The four fliers."

"So, that goes first when you report. Let me have a look."

Millen compared the message from Evac Comm to the log. "They're jockeying the order," she decided. "They have wounded right now, but they'll get shelled if they light up a landing zone. So instead, they're going to message us every fifteen minutes to keep a spot at the top of the list for morning evacuations. It's bad manners, but they do it all the time."

As she cleared the board and reset it with a fresh glyph, Millen's eyes took on a predatory gleam.

"Did Andrada train you for communications duty already?" she asked.

"Not exactly," I said.

"Oh, Mother Mary in her Sunday boots!" Millen moaned. "We've got one with a case of volunteerism." She strode to the door and bellowed out into the night, "Andrada! It's an emergency. Andrada! Pass the word for Sig-2 Andrada!"

A minute later Andrada came sprinting up to the farmhouse on her short little legs. "What do we have?" she puffed.

"We have a brandy-new sigilwoman who volunteered for board duty. He's so green he can't tell the difference between shit and cherry soda. Mr. Canderelli, a status report, please."

"Yes," I said, "umm, Point C for Charlotte is requesting four fliers on standby for wounded for the past two hours. Sigilwoman Millen suspects they may be trying to jockey the order. There are a number of less crucial messages as well."

Andrada looked at me and ran her thumb over the polished wood handle of her enormous knife. "Didn't we just talk about not volunteering?"

"I wasn't trying to," I said.

Andrada clucked and sat beside me. She explained the other boards on the table: Humanitarian Command, which assigned missions to assist the local civilian population, though their office closed at five in the evening; Divisional Command, which was moot for us since Gen. Blandings was both wing and division commander; Medical Command, which we used to notify the field hospital about incoming casualties; the Meteorology Service, which sent updates every fifteen minutes and occasionally even succeeded in predicting the weather before it happened; Philosophical Compliance, which acted as an official channel for reporting illegal sigilry in violation of the Rouen Conventions (which banned all forms of military philosophy, except for aid to the wounded); and the Pan-Corps Emergency Sigil, which had never been used to issue commands, but sent a test message every hour.

"Overnight, just worry about Evac Command and glance at the rest every few minutes to make sure the world isn't coming to an end," Andrada said.

By then, the rest of second squadron had trickled into the old farmhouse. Twelve fliers in all, perched on the table or leaned against the walls. No one felt compelled to come over and introduce herself. All of them looked exhausted. It seemed impossible that in the event of an evacuation they wouldn't fall asleep in midair.

At ten seconds to midnight, a woman descended the stairs from the second story. It could only be Lt. Drale, our executive officer. She was in her late forties, skeletally thin and clench-jawed, with an expression that made Millen look like a cupful of sunshine. She carried a stack of folders in one hand and a cased typewriter in the other. Despite the warm evening, she wore a heavy winter-weight skysuit, immaculate and so crisply pressed I wondered if it had ever been worn into the field.

Drale set the typewriter on a side table. "What's the report from the board?" she asked.

Andrada laid a hand on my shoulder.

"Point C has been requesting four fliers on standby for evacuation of wounded," I said, "starting at 21:45 this evening with repeat messages every fifteen minutes."

"Fine," said Drale. "How many?"

"They're requesting four—" I began.

"They haven't said how many wounded or what acuity," Andrada supplied.

"That's unacceptable. If we get hold of their board technician tomorrow, tear his fingernails out," said Lt. Drale. "So, four on standby in case they decide they need us immediately. I'll take volunteers—Canderelli, Andrada, Punnett, and Takahashi."

An actual volunteer wouldn't even have had time to clear her throat.

"We have fifteen twelve-pound bags filled from earlier today," Lt. Drale continued. "If you need additional reloads, pull the top half of first squad to fill for you. Astronomically, moonset was at 22:17. Moonrise tomorrow morning is at 11:51, twenty-three percent illuminated. Meteorologically, the sky is seven-eighths clear with scattered cumulus crud at forty-five hundred feet. No precipitation expected. For landing field amendments, evac site E for Elaine is putting their observation tower back up two hundred feet north of the trench, so do not make a north-south approach. Any cautions or concerns to add?"

"We should have significant humidity overnight," I offered.

Drale looked directly at me for the first time. Not so much offended as baffled that this trifling creature should have mewled out an answer.

"Are you the one who flew a recreational evac without filing a Form 41?" she asked.

"I don't—"

"Don't *ever* do that again. Fill one out immediately. No flights until it's submitted."

"Where—"

Drale turned back to the assembled women and fanned out a bunch of index cards. "Nightly safety quiz. It's Devereaux's turn. Pick a card."

A beautiful brown-skinned woman with a pink cardigan over her skysuit and a sleeping mask on an elastic string around her neck stepped forward and plucked out a card.

"Inadvertent landing in enemy territory," she read, and recited from memory: "Immediate message for assistance. Launch if able. If unable, use tree branches or rocks to spell out *H* for Helen to mark a "Help" landing zone. If nighttime, do not light a signal fire or flares until the ready rescue flier requests that you do so."

"Fine," said Drale. "Additionally, in the event of imminent capture, you are to smash, destroy, or bury your regulator and burn any courier materials. Ladies, I really did fly pickup for one of these in '16 and the German patrol that found our downed flier splinted her arm, cooked her dinner, and cleared a landing field. So, if it happens to you, be cautious but don't panic."

That went against everything we'd been told in training: the Germans were murderous, slavering barbarians who would rape and mutilate any woman they captured. There had been whispering, some of it serious, as to what the fastest way would be to end one's life rather than be captured.

"All right, then," Drale concluded. "Four on standby. Morning assembly and shift change is at six. Defer noncritical casualties until afterward if possible—I'd like full attendance. Come safe home."

The Lieutenant went back upstairs. Millen took her place.

"Hold the standby fliers," she said. "The rest of the overnight watch is dismissed."

The assembled women slunk out of the farmhouse except for Millen and the four of us, who would await further word from the evacuation point.

"Since Robert A is suffering from acute volunteerism, he'll retain board duty," Millen said. "Punnett, you make sure your partner's adequately supervised."

"Yeah," said Punnett. She sat beside me while Andrada and Kiyo pulled cots and blankets out of the closet and prepared to lie down.

"So, now you have to stay up all night," explained Punnett. "You *cannot* fall asleep. That's the only rule. How long have you been up?"

I tried to count back the hours to reveille at Fort McConnell and couldn't figure it out.

"I'll be fine," I said. "I did this every night growing up."

Punnett bit her tongue and rocked her head from side to side, as if to say she'd heard that one before.

"Keep logging the requests from Point C," she told me. "At the top of every hour, send a one-word 'OK' message to Pan-Corps Emergency. If Meteorology is predicting storms, tell me. Otherwise your only job is to stay awake. That's not a joke. Women have been court-martialed for falling asleep."

"Understood," I said.

"I'll tell you the one other rule. Officially, the Corps prohibits personal messages while in the field. Unofficially, Gen. Blandings thinks we can't afford to fire every woman in the service. If you wanted to send a message to your girlfriend—well, everyone does."

Personal message boards were banned among frontline corpswomen such as ourselves because they would make it all too easy for a spy to send information to the enemy about the positions of American troops. Boards hadn't been allowed in training either. During our trip earlier in the day, I'd gotten two minutes at one of the public message systems in the transporter arena in Atlanta to dash off notes to Mother and Danielle, but hadn't had enough time to wait for their answers. There was nothing I wanted more than a few minutes alone with a board.

Millen was standing beside the farmhouse door, working at a chalkboard ruled with lines. On them were written the names of each flier in the wing and a string of numbers. Millen rubbed out Marjorie Krist's name and began to write in mine.

"Robert A, how do you spell your last name?" asked Millen.

"Canderelli, with two Es, one R, and two Ls," I said.

Millen grunted. "That's something, at least."

"You know why she says that?" asked Kiyo from her cot.

"No."

"If you can't spell a girl's name, then she must be good," Kiyo said. "R&E hates foreign fliers, they hate immigrants, they hate brown people. If they let one in, she's got talent. Blandings poached all of those for our wing."

"And she put them all in second squadron," Millen added. "I can't hardly spell anyone's name."

"Well, my name," said Punnett.

"Sometimes I only put one T," Millen said.

She wrote: *Canderelli, Robert A, 5,1,2,12*, and then in a separate column *1*. Fifth division, first wing, second squadron, twelfth flier. One soul evacuated.

The last number was the only one that mattered. It was the realest measure of an R&E flier's quality—or at least her longevity. Millen had the highest number in the division: 11,368. Enough lives saved to populate a decent-sized town. But, two passengers at a time, a few flights a day, two days out of three, for four years. Andrada had over eight thousand. Punnett, who was the next most junior Sig-3 after me, had 735.

Andrada noticed the intensity with which I was looking at the numbers.

"Don't do that," she warned. "It's not a contest. We're not keeping score."

Only they *were* keeping score. After one thousand evacuations, you wore gold-edged bars on your collar instead of brown.

"If it ends tomorrow you still got your one," said Andrada. She pulled her blanket over her head.

• • •

The first hours passed quickly enough, as I logged requests from Point C and tried to familiarize myself with all the different message glyphs. But by three in the morning, I could feel my eyes getting heavy. Reluctant as I was to break Corps regulations on my first night on duty, I decided it would be better to chat with someone back home than risk falling asleep watching a bunch of empty boards.

I glanced at Millen, who was sitting in her chair lost in thought, hands hanging loosely at her sides, mouth agape, eyes wide open. She'd been arranged in the same posture all night.

"Ma'am?" I said to her quietly, not wanting to wake the others. Millen didn't move. "Ma'am?" I tried again. "Is it okay if I . . ."

Punnett rolled over on her cot and opened one eye. "Robert," she croaked. "She's asleep. Let her be."

Even a deep sleeper fidgets or twitches, but Millen sat dead like lead. Not a snore, not a blink, not a twitch.

So, no one to catch me.

I swept my hand over the board for Humanitarian Command, smoothing the sand flat. Then I wrote Mother's personal glyph in the corner and drew sigils to pull up the messages from her. In reply to the note I'd sent that afternoon urgently telling her to cancel her ticket on the transporter chain and not come down to Texas, since there wasn't going to be a graduation ceremony, she'd replied: *That's the Crps for y.*

Give em hell, she'd added. *Don't let yr Sig-1 push y around. Always do mor than y have to. Writ whn y can.*

I smiled wanly and tried to imagine having Ma as a wing commander—hell on earth, probably, as strict as she was. (Unless you were the one who needed to be rescued, in which case there was no one you'd rather see.) I wondered what she would have done to a girl who sent private messages on a Corps board.

Y awak Ma? I wrote.

No answer. Away from her board, maybe.

I sent her an account of the day, a simple *made it overseas and already ran one, and didn't discredit myself and all my ancestors, and my Sig-1 is a standard-issue bastard, and my Sig-2 wanted a girl, and my partner needs two tries to add up six plus seven.* Ma could read it in the morning.

Then for the more delicate task. Danielle. I drew the private glyph we used for our missives. Her reply from several hours before was waiting for me: *Robert, I don't understand what happened. They can't just cancel your leave, can they? Write when you can. I miss you.*

Six hours earlier in Washington. She might be up. She might be at her board.

Thinking of her was shattering, delicious agony.

Ours had been a winter romance, bodies seeking each other out in the cold. My loneliness at being in a strange city two thousand miles from home paired with hers at coming back from the war to find her country and her place in it unrecognizable. Our courtship had ended with me promising her I wouldn't join the Corps and then joining anyway. She'd dumped me. Then we'd fought off an attack by a group of Trenchers and she'd decided she might not mind seeing me again after all. We'd written paper letters back and forth all through flight training. She'd found the very notion of training comical. *You already know how to fly. What do they need six weeks to teach you? We had a half-day orientation and a uniform fitting.*

Danielle was a Corps veteran, too, though a transporter rather than a flier. The Corps treated their transporters like a bunch of overfed princesses: every transporter detachment traveled with its own physician and on-call chef. If they wanted a steak and peppermint ice cream at three in the morning, they got it. (By contrast, the Corps fed its fliers like they were trying to keep our weight down.) The special treatment wasn't without reason; the Corps had to have transporters enough to run the transatlantic chain a couple times a day and several of the jumps were punishing. She'd made the long jump between Newfoundland and Greenland three times in her career and each time had had to be carried off the transporter field, after losing sixteen pounds in an instant. Then a month off to recover and regain the weight.

But a month of liberty at a time! We *hated* them for that. Some of the more senior R&E fliers hadn't had a month off since 1914. Their service was so different from ours that when Danielle wrote that she didn't understand the idea of flight training, she wasn't being facetious.

I'd filled my letters with anecdotes about our days: group physical training; calisthenics; conditioning flights; basic stasis sigilry; map and compass use; triage of the wounded; tactics for harnessing a man quickly on the ground; rigging approaches for casualties with one leg blown off, two legs blown off, all four limbs blown off.

That sounds excessive, Danielle had complained.

I disagreed. At the start of the war, training for R&E had lasted six *months*—they'd had lessons in French, astral navigation, edible plants, and hand-to-hand combat. But our early fliers had been killed or wounded in such great numbers that replacements like me got the brief version instead.

Danielle's letters had become cooler after I mentioned that.

I'd written about our endless practice of landings: solo landings; front-passenger landings; back-passenger landings; dual-passenger landings; conscious passenger versus stasied passenger; nighttime landings; water landings; and blindfolded landings, during which a woman on the ground coached us down the last few feet. We worried over landings the way transporters worried over the Killiniq jump. Landings were what killed and maimed fliers.

Danielle's letters had become more distant still.

I'd written about the indignities of being the only man in training. Of having to dig my own latrine. The ten minutes twice a week when the bathhouse was cleared and a guard posted so that I could shower. Instructors who called me "Miss."

In turn, Danielle had filled her letters with stories about her work as an aide to Josephine Cadwallader-Fulton, the only avowed sigilrist and only woman serving in the US Senate. Which senators and congressmen and judges she'd met. When I was in a good mood and read Danielle's letters, they'd made me feel proud to be involved with someone so important. On bad days (which had vastly outnumbered the good), I'd read them and wondered what she could ever see in a simple male philosopher headed for

France. That Danielle seldom wrote about her feelings for me only made it worse.

Then her last letter had taken quite a different tone. I could say the final lines by heart: *Robert, I have been so lonely these last weeks. Every night while I lie awake in bed, I remember being with you. How I could be my own self—petty or vain or pouting—and you still loved me. I remember the sheer pleasure of being with you. It was simple and holy and right. Would it cause a scandal for you if I came to San Antonio for your leave? Three days is not enough time for everything I would say to you. Three nights is not enough time to hold you to me. But could I see you?*

I'd received it in mail call minutes before my training company embarked on a weeklong backcountry bivouac on which we were to run simulated casualties round the clock and have no contact with the outside world. Essie had faked a sprained ankle to delay our departure long enough for me to find an envelope and scrawl out: *Please come. I'm yours for three minutes or three days. I have to go.*

That had been my last communication with Danielle before my message in the transporter arena.

I smoothed the sand on the board and drew my glyph in the sender's corner, then stopped. A letter might be safer. Look it over in the light of day. A few days for it to reach her, a few days for her reply to come back. Go slow, leave the embers banked and buried—they'd stay hot longer. If you dug through the ashes looking for something still glowing red, all you did was burn your fingers.

I'm still alive, I wrote on the board. I clenched my teeth, roughly drew Dar's glyph to send the message, and swept my forearm over the board to clear it before one of my wingmates could see.

Idiot!

But, the words were away and nothing I could do would call them back. Sand on a board somewhere back in America had already taken the shape of my three-word message, or it would when Dar said to herself "I wonder whatever happened to old Robert?" and doodled her glyph opposite mine.

I pushed back my chair and walked to the door. The night outside had grown thick and foggy. I wanted to swing my fist against the old stones in the farmhouse wall. I would be checking my personal glyph every five minutes for a reply for the rest of the war. I didn't need that distraction on top of everything else. I should have told her to let me go—find a nice young congressman instead. No more of this intolerable, halfway longing. Let me hurt and mourn and heal.

I stalked back to my post.

Where are you? the board read. *What happened to leave? I canceled my ticket on the transporter chain—should I get a new one?*

God, but I wanted her.

I exhorted myself to go slow, to think everything through. Don't get too excited. By the time I had finished forming those thoughts I had already dashed off:

Frnce. Theyr short flyrs. And our boat sank 10yr ago. So transpo here.

I subscribed to the flier's theory that you ought to write messages on the ground the same way you did while in the air—every second you reached across your body to write on a wrist board, you were out of proper flight posture. As a ground-hugger and a lady, Dar wrote longhand.

I'm so angry at them for ruining our long weekend! she wrote. *I had the hotel picked out and everything. I wanted to lie in bed with you for 3 days and just get room service.*

I blew out my breath—I'd wanted to hear that more than anything.

It's not the end of the world, she continued. *The senator has a lot of business in France. Select Committee for the Sigilry Corps. I can tag along if you have a day or two off at the right moment.*

Y, pls, I replied.

Do you know when? What days? Do you have a schedule?

Which was a preposterous notion of how things worked, even for a transporter. I would fly two days out of every three for the duration of the war. Even if my division gave me extended leave—which they were supposed to do every couple months—I could be recalled in case of heavy casualties from a major attack.

Dunno days off.

Too bad, she replied.

I described my day. My evac. My worries that Millen was sarcastic at best and insane at worst and that Sig-2 Andrada might be plotting to kill me.

When they made me a Sig-2, Danielle answered, *they told me my only jobs were to scare the new girls and keep my Sig-1 from going any crazier. It must be the same in every department.*

I found that reassuring.

So you're on overnight board duty all by yourself? Dar asked.

Squadmates asleep.

I could torture you for a few minutes. If you're all alone.

I didn't know what that meant, but I liked the sound of it.

Y.

I went out shopping when I thought we were going to have our weekend. I thought I might buy something to wear that was . . . provocative. But I don't know what you like.

Nt sure I undrstnd.

Anything was provocative. She could wear an old-model coverall skysuit with a parka and my skin would flush the moment I saw her.

What do you want me to wear in the boudoir?

We'd never put anything like this into writing before.

Nothng. I wnt y naked. I wnt our bodies wrpped arnd each othr.

A stupid answer. Maybe too much.

Oh, yes. But before we do all that? I'm offering to get tarted up for you. So what do you like?

I tried to close my mouth.

Dunno nothng re: ladies undergarments.

A frilly little negligee? she suggested. *A corset laced up with ribbons and have you unwrap me like a Christmas present? A garter belt and black stockings like the can-can dancers wear?*

Any of them. All of them. All of them at once (though I suspected that wasn't possible).

Silk, I wrote back, my nineteen-year-old's inexhaustible lust fully upon me, the itching, ravening desire. I switched to longhand to prevent any possibility of being misunderstood: *Thin layer of sheer silk between your breasts and my skin. Feel your nipples go hard under my fingers.*

There was a long pause. Too coarse?

Continue, please.

My breath caught.

Silk bloomers, I wrote. *Short ones. Thin enough to feel the heat of you when you straddle my thigh.*

More.

Kiss you through them. My lips and my breath on your thigh. And your bottom. And the jut of your hip. Your belly. And then . . . when you're cursing me up and down for teasing you . . . hook my thumbs in the waistband . . .

"All's well?" a voice at my side whispered.

I clapped a hand over my heart and nearly fell out of my chair.

It was a dowdy middle-aged lady wearing a hand-knit cardigan and a kerchief. Her gray hair was in a thick plait and she was carrying a picnic basket in the crook of her arm. She looked like someone's grandmother come to visit—the same harmless aspect, the slightly confused air.

I expelled my heart from my larynx, where it had become lodged, and scrubbed one arm over the message board to obscure my conversation with Dar. "May I help you?" I stammered.

"Status report, please," she said.

It had to be some sort of joke. Hazing the new boy on his first night by sending a civilian to visit.

"All quiet," I managed. "Significant humidity. No moon. And C for Charlotte has been asking for four on standby since a quarter to ten."

"They're trying to jockey the order," the woman said. She set her basket down on top of the message board for Evac Comm, smearing the glyphs and rendering it momentarily useless. She opened her basket's lid and rummaged among knitting needles, yarn, and scraps of fabric. "But you must never, never utter the Q-word overnight."

"I beg your pardon?"

"The Q-U-I-E-T word. The gods punish presumption."

We heard creaking above us and Lt. Drale descended the stairs.

"Addie," the visitor said to Drale. "A few friends from my quilting club came to visit. They're outside."

Drale scowled. "You're sure you want to say that in front of him?"

"Oh, young Robert is one of us!" the lady laughed. "He'll know all our secrets soon enough."

She gave the basket to Lt. Drale, who pulled out a dozen ornately knotted doilies and replaced them with an armload of folders. Drale took the basket, grabbed the typewriter, and went outside.

"Lt. Drale doesn't appreciate the decorative arts," the lady said, arranging one of the doilies under the board for Meteorology Command. "But I think they add a certain *je ne sais quoi.*"

I knew I'd seen her before, but I couldn't place her.

"You have me at a disadvantage, ma'am," I said.

"Well, we've only met once," she said. "I was having a terrible day and you told me every flier is going zero miles an hour when she hits the ground. And you didn't punch anyone, though you probably felt you had cause."

I thought back to the interview when I had tested for the Corps and the grumpy woman in pince-nez glasses who had knitted quietly while the other officers had interrogated me in the most insulting fashion.

"Gen. Blandings," I spluttered, and rose to salute.

She cackled and nodded in appreciation. "Welcome to Fifth Division. The report from my friends at Radcliffe was that you were the most unique hell-raiser they'd ever met. I plan on using you to cause a lot of trouble."

"What kind of trouble, ma'am?"

"The only kind worth causing in a war zone, sweetie. The kind that ensures we win."

5

One bell for commanders, two for a flight
Three bells and the wing will be working all night

Miss Goodbody's Book for Girls, 1899

BLANDINGS RETIRED TO HER QUARTERS.

When I was certain I wouldn't be interrupted again, I tried to reach Dar, but she'd gone to bed, too. She'd parted with *I hope to God you got called away to save someone's life. Because if you left me right on the edge on purpose . . .*

I was in the middle of a lengthy and salacious reply when Lt. Drale came back inside. I hurried to send my message and wipe the board.

"Mr. Canderelli," Drale said, "the privilege of covert personal messages hinges upon my not seeing you do it."

"Yes, ma'am," I said.

Drale sat down beside me and blew into her hands to warm them.

"Is C for Charlotte still calling?" she asked.

"Every fifteen minutes."

"They'll make their formal request for evac just before sunrise. Do you want to fly it?"

"Yes," I said. No question.

"When it comes, tell Millen you were up all night and you'll damn well take it. Before you go, fill this out. You should have another hour at least."

She handed me a sheet marked FORM 41.

"Some of the women cry doing it," she said, looking apologetic. "You're alone enough, right?"

Drale went back to bed as well. I looked over the page.

In the event of your death or capture, your wing executive officer, in consultation with the Corps casualty notification service, will contact your family. In-person notification will be attempted whenever possible.

Well, that was a cheerful thought.

1. NAME OF NEXT OF KIN, WITH RELATIONSHIP, ADDRESS, CITY, STATE, COUNTRY.
   I wrote in: *Emmaline Weekes. Mother. 14 Bryant St, Apt 2, Billings, Montana, USA*

2. RELIABLE MESSAGE GLYPH FOR PERSON ABOVE.

I drew Mother's glyph.

3. IS THERE A FAMILY FRIEND OR CLERGY MEMBER YOU WISH TO ASSIST WITH IN-PERSON NOTIFICATION?

A couple of Mother's acquaintances might serve—Dr. Synge, the smoke-carver in Helena with whom Mother had served in the Philippines, maybe—but I couldn't imagine Mother would want Synge knowing before she did. Instead, I wrote: *None.*

4. WHOM DO YOU WISH TO NOTIFY YOUR CHILDREN?
   Not applicable.

(Though I couldn't help but wonder whom Mother had designated back in the day.)

5. DO YOU HAVE FINANCIAL OR CONFIDENTIAL MATERIALS ABOUT WHICH YOU WISH TO INFORM YOUR FAMILY? (E.G., BOND COUPONS, SAFETY DEPOSIT BOXES, STOCK CERTIFICATES, KEYS.)
Also not applicable.

6. ARE YOU CURRENTLY PREGNANT OR DO YOU PLAN TO BECOME SO IN THE NEXT SEVERAL MONTHS? (IN THE EVENT OF CAPTURE, THIS ALLOWS US TO PURSUE ACCELERATED PAROLE PURSUANT TO THE SECOND ROUEN CONVENTIONS.)
Very not applicable.

7. DO YOU HAVE A PARAMOUR, PARTNER, OR SPECIAL FRIEND WHOM YOU WISH TO BE CONFIDENTIALLY INFORMED SEPARATE FROM THE PERSON INDICATED ABOVE? (INCLUDE GLYPH AND ADDRESS.)

The last one broke me. Somehow I'd never—well, I'd thought about dying, but never about the way in which someone might tell Dar. She'd gone near catatonic when a shipload of newly enlisted acquaintances had been killed a couple years before. What would she do if a corpswoman in a black dress showed up at her office carrying a Bible? Or even worse, if they did it by message? *The Corps regrets to inform you of the loss of your paramour.*

I wondered if she'd ever considered it in the other direction. She'd received death threats by the bagful. Had she left instructions on how I ought to be told?

I fought against the surge of emotions. Danielle's death, mine, being alone in the small hours of the morning, four wounded men awaiting evacuation for hours. The dark. My first day in the war. Every part of me was panicking at the same moment. I remembered Essie sitting next to me on the transporter chain, with the same expression I must be wearing: *I can't, I can't, I can't.*

"Fuck," I muttered. I wiped my eyes.

Punnett startled awake on her cot. "What? What happened?"

"Nothing," I said. "It's five in the morning. Paperwork."

"Oh," Punnett said. "Form 41? I hear even Millen cried."

Punnett resumed her unholy snoring.

At 5:40, Lt. Drale reemerged, her skysuit even more sharply pressed.

"Nothing?" she asked.

"Standby," I answered. "Again, a few minutes ago."

Drale cursed and kicked Millen's chair.

"Up!" Drale roared. "Everyone up!"

"It's a go?" asked Millen, who startled awake still sitting in her chair, her wide-open eyes going wider.

"No, they're screwing around," said Drale. "They should have called for us by now. We would have light enough to land by the time we got there. Get your women ready and we'll go as soon as they give the word."

"Ma'am," I said to Sig-1 Millen, choosing the wrong tone. "I had the board all night. I'd like to request—"

"Yes, Robert A, we couldn't possibly run the first evacuation of the morning without the squadron hotshot. Gear up, all four of you useless louts!"

I sprinted to my tent to grab my harness and then to the storage shed for a powder bag. Between a twelve-pounder, the humid morning air, and my general state of excitement, I was winded by the time I reached the farmhouse, a few seconds ahead of Andrada, Kiyo, and Punnett.

"Are you planning to win the war all by yourself?" Millen asked.

"No, ma'am," I puffed.

"Then stop making a scene."

We sat and sweated in full harness and buttoned skysuits for several more minutes. Under Drale's direction, I calculated and recalculated compass headings from our camp to the casualty evacuation point, then to the hospital, then back to camp. I committed them to memory. I did my best not to vomit.

My fingertips had gone cold, my shoulders pinched backward of their own accord, my calves twitched. *Mine.* I wanted it like a wildfire wants the next field of dry grass.

We just needed the word to go. Give us the word.

At 5:58, Ruth Aielli, the brevet Sig-2 from third squadron, relieved us. We took our bags and went outside to form up with the rest of the division for morning assembly. If the call came in the next two minutes, it would still be ours.

The rest of the women had already arranged themselves in rows by squadron. They'd kitted out with a variety of sweaters and dressing gowns over their skysuits. Here there was a felt cap, there a campaign hat—there were even women with their hair down and loose in a fashion explicitly forbidden by the Corps. My training instructors would have been appalled.

Gen. Blandings strode out at six, looking remarkably bright-eyed for someone who'd been up most of the night. The rank and file had a sour but attentive mood, a sense that today was just a bit different from the usual routine.

"Good morning," Blandings announced. "Today is July 20. This is the first day of our current two-day stint."

Her face turned serious and she pulled it off well—a career officer, a professional.

"By now, I expect everyone knows that Marjorie Krist became ill with a bout of nervous delirium yesterday and went to Le Havre to see the doctor. We hope that with rest and quiet she will recover. However, Lt. Drale and I believe the risk of a relapse is too great for her to return to duty with R&E. I need not tell you that the hazards in our line of work are more than merely physical. We must strive to support and care for one another, as I know you all did for Margie. I'm sure she would appreciate letters if you have the time."

A couple of women nodded in agreement. Everyone else was silent. Marjorie seemed not to have been the best-liked woman in the division.

Blandings continued. "On a happier note, I'm pleased to report that we've had word from Alice, who's arrived home safely in San Diego. She sounds perfectly content to allow Jim to dote on her for the next few months. For those of you working on booties or baby hats, Mrs. Macmurdo is taking charge of the care package, which we will send during the first week of September."

There were a few indulgent murmurs and an enormous eye roll from Millen.

"As a final matter, Alice's replacement arrived yesterday evening. Mr. Robert Canderelli, lately of Radcliffe College, comes with sterling qualifications, including two improvised mass-casualty evacuations in Boston and a memorable performance in the General's Cup. I should add that his mother, Emmaline Weekes, was a major in R&E who won the White Ribbon by plebiscite in '97."

Those who had not yet gawked at me took the opportunity to do so.

"We have seen women from every background come to the Corps and succeed brilliantly," Blandings continued. "There is no reason that a man shouldn't be an asset as well. All of you remember your first days in the field, with their attendant difficulties and anxieties, so I expect you to help him in any way possible. As ever, ladies, protect each other and come safe home. The Lieutenant also has a few matters to discuss."

Blandings gave us a polite nod and returned to the farmhouse. Lt. Drale marched out from the formation to take her place.

"First item!" Drale barked. "Roll call."

Bernice Macmurdo replied in a well-practiced cadence: "First squadron with nine, all aground."

"Second squadron," sang out Millen, "with twelve, all aground, coming off duty."

"Third squadron with six," reported a young, nervous-looking Sig-1. "One on the board, four on standby, all aground."

"Situational awareness report," said Drale. She gave a brief account of the recent British advances in Belgium and northern France. The American Expeditionary Force, however, had been content to remain dug in on the southern end of the lines for the past year, waiting for more reinforcements to pour in from home before they began an offensive.

"Make no mistake, though," Drale said. "The American army will attack the German salient at Saint-Mihiel by the end of the summer. It'll be big, it'll be ugly, and it'll be us. If you've not been up yet to observe where the bandaging stations are likely to set up shop, then do so soon."

That was a frightening prospect. The well-defended German lines near Saint-Mihiel stuck like a dagger twenty miles deep into Allied territory. When the Americans made their assault, we would see thousands of wounded in the space of a few hours. All of Rescue & Evac would be responsible for moving casualties, but we were the closest unit by fifty miles. A million and a half soldiers with the twenty-nine of us designated as first-in to support them. Not a textbook ratio.

"Third item," said Drale, "supply readiness. The division now has fewer than four hundred ampoules of silver chloride. Conservation, ladies. If you fly two wounded, use one tube and half-powered glyphs. If we get a mass casualty, Kiyo and Millen will draw for the whole wing using one gram per wounded."

"Lieutenant," broke in Sig-1 Macmurdo, "any word when we'll see more amps?"

"No," replied Drale. "First and Second Division are short, too, so I do *not* want to hear complaining that this is some sort of scheme singling us out." Drale fixed Millen with a glare. Millen shrugged.

"Fourth: The mess tent is a disgrace. It will be cleaned immediately by all available—"

The big bell in the farmhouse rang out twice, followed by four higher-pitched dings from the triangle—*evacuation request, four women.* I clenched and released my hands. It should have been *my* call, my grab. Turn my number on the chalkboard from a 1 to a 2. Or a 3.

The nervous Sig-1 from third squadron was already trotting toward the supply shed. "Brodsky, Gelbstein, Moore, and Dunphrey, on me," she shouted.

That made five fliers responding to a call for four women. A squadron's Sig-1 might go forward to help keep things organized on a big evac—or to break in the new girl, as Millen had done with me—but her leading this flight was excessive.

"That one's a new call!" Sig-2 Aielli yelled from the farmhouse door. "I still need four standing by for Charlotte!"

Macmurdo rolled her eyes heavenward—third squadron's fliers were now fully committed, which meant first squadron would cover it. "Helen, Pearl, Minnie, and Agnes, on standby in the farmhouse, please."

Before they'd even had the chance to fall out of formation, Aielli rang out an additional two low bells plus four high bells. Yet another call on top of the standby.

"Previous four to run this one," Bernice amended. "Odessa, Almira, Irene, and Marjorie to cover the standby."

"Ma'am?" the Sig-2 of that group said apologetically. "We don't have Marj—"

"Excuse me, and Mamie," Bernice finished. She looked meaningfully at Millen, who looked ready to drown a bag full of kittens. Both first and third squadron had assigned all their available fliers, which meant second squadron would be up for the next one, no matter that we'd just covered the night watch.

"There's work to be done," Lt. Drale said calmly. "See to it. Second squadron: fill sufficient bags for the morning and clean the mess tent. Dismissed."

My squadron went to the storage shed, where we had a large hand-powered paddle mixer for blending corn powder with sand. Flying during summertime, when the air was warmer and thinner, called for a fifty-fifty mix of corn and sand. I cut open a fifty-pound sack of corn dust and dumped it into the hopper, followed by a fifty-pound sack of high-grade sand. Then I heaved on the crank to get the paddles moving and mix the powder. My squadmates lined up with waxed canvas bags and one by one opened the spigot at the bottom of the machine to fill them while I kept the mixer turning.

We filled thirty-six twelve-pound bags—432 pounds of powder, all of which I lifted and poured and mixed.

"You know, I think I'm going to like having a man around," Punnett said to me. "That used to be my job."

When we'd finished, we went to the mess tent.

Because Fifth Division was so small, we didn't rate a permanent cook. Instead, we made do with a rotating cast of peasant women from the surrounding countryside, paying them with money from our officers' mess fund and in trade by drawing koru glyphs on their gardens to enlarge their vegetables.

"France is a goddamned backward country," Kiyo complained as we scrubbed the stove together—it ran on a high-powered form of compressed vapor that our smokecarvers back in Le Havre made. "Most of the farmers refuse to learn korus. Paris gets smothered by German smokecarvers in '71 and a whole generation says, 'Thanks, but I'd rather starve than learn philosophy.' "

"They're good cooks at least?" I asked.

"Terrible," Kiyo sniffed. "It's bean soup one day after another."

Our cooks also seemed to believe that their duties did not include washing pots or cleaning the stove, which meant basic kitchen maintenance was put off until it reached crisis proportions. Then I heard another two low bells and two highs. *New call, two women.*

Second squadron congregated in front of the farmhouse.

"Where the *hell* is Fern?" Millen complained. "She is *not* going to stick us with this."

With diminishing hope, she scanned the sky for returning fliers and saw none.

Aielli popped her head out the door. "What's the problem here? I need a pair to go to Point E for Eleanor."

"The problem is your fucking incompetent of a Sig-1 took five women on a four-woman call," Millen snapped. "Is she clear of the hospital yet?"

"I don't know!" Aielli answered. "She didn't message 'back in service'—she forgets sometimes. But you have to give me two women to fly."

"No," Millen insisted. "Get your Sig-1 on the board and tell her to run her own calls or I will take a rolling pin and beat her until she can't sit down on a six-foot-tall pile of silk cushions! What's the priority on this one?"

"Zero," said Aielli.

Priority Zero because it came before even a Priority One—*most critical.*

Millen had reached the end of her patience. "Canderelli and Punnett," she said. "Go."

Punnett and I kitted out in the farmhouse, with Andrada and Kiyo helping us with straps and bags, then dashed onto the field and launched.

We covered the fifteen miles to Point E in minutes. I was glad to have Punnett with me, because I was so jittery and tired and overwhelmed that I could never have found my way to the aid station by myself. As we approached Point E, nestled in a morass of barbed wire and mud, we saw one of the stretcher-bearers climb up and out of the trenches, waving a green flag to direct us to a clear spot.

"If they've got a flagger up, it's going to be terrible," Punnett said once we'd set down. "Let me do the talking and we'll make sure you get the carry, okay?"

There was no ladder, so Punnett and I scrambled over the edge of the trench. The stretcher-bearers grabbed hold of our straps and helped lower us to the ground.

"Medical evacuation," Punnett announced. "What do you have?"

"Jesus Christ, we've been calling for an hour!" shouted one of them. "Where were you?"

"We got the message seven minutes ago," Punnett replied. "One of the board girls in Le Havre must have misdirected it. Let's worry about the wounded first."

The stretcher-bearer led us past a handful of minor cases that would be taken to the rear by motor ambulance. Set aside from these were two men who would never survive such a trip.

"Oh, no," whispered Punnett.

The first lay on his back, his jaw clenched, eyes screwed shut. He was sweating profusely, panting for breath. Gut shot—six or eight rounds in the belly. The other was motionless and covered up to his chest with a sheet. His face was a mass of black and red blisters, his eyes swollen shut, his eyelids charred. He smelled of burned meat.

"Poor bastard was unloading cans of kerosene and the whole thing just blew up," one of the stretcher-bearers said. "We gave him all the morphine we could."

Punnett and I knelt next to the burned man.

"Stasis?" I breathed to Punnett.

"No shit," she said.

I reached for the top button of his jacket and it crumbled into ash between my fingers. The fabric stuck to his flesh. I didn't dare pull it away for fear of taking the rest of his skin with it.

This was going to be tricky. The stasis sigil required healthy tissue to work—it wouldn't work if I drew it on the dead, burned flesh. The only possibility I could see was a crescent of intact skin along the top of his forehead that his helmet had protected.

Punnett was holding a square of acetate film with the lines for a stasis glyph cut into it. She looked at her stencil, which was an inch wide.

"That's the only way you know how to draw it?" I asked her.

She nodded.

"I'll do it," I said. "Overlapped tricorn form. It'll fit."

"Are you asking or telling me?" Punnett said.

She cracked an ampoule of silver chloride and handed it to me. I exhaled and drew the glyph, aiming the stream of silver chloride at the strip of pink skin on his head.

The man brushed at me with one of his hands, bandaged so thickly it looked like a club.

"Sorry," I whispered. "Sorry!"

I reached back for a second attempt, but Punnett took the half-full tube from my hand and replaced it with a fresh one. "It could be bad powder," she suggested.

I swallowed and drew again. For a split second I thought the sigil had taken, but I could still see pink foam bubbling up between his lips.

"Damn it," I said. There was no way we could take him without stasis—strapping him in a passenger harness would probably kill him.

"Sometimes it doesn't work when they're almost gone," Punnett said.

"He just moved," I said. "He's not almost dead."

"I've only got one tube left," Punnett warned. "We could try to shave him with a knife, maybe, put it on his scalp or—"

"I can do it," I said. "Hold his hair back."

Punnett pulled back his hair and I drew with the last tube: tiny, deliberate, slow.

"Got it," Punnett said, as the man went rigid. She took a nickel from her workbag and dropped it from four inches over the man's chest. It stuck to his charred shirt instead of bouncing.

"Seriously?" she said.

"It's dead tissue," I said.

I plucked the nickel off him and dropped it on the top of his forehead. It popped high into the air. Punnett wrestled him into a harness while I turned to the other man.

Somehow I'd never considered the possibility that an evacuee might be all of eighteen, have a patchy three days' growth of beard, and look like any number of the boys I'd grown up with.

"Hello, sir," I said. "I'm Sigilwoman Canderelli with the Philosophical Corps. I'm going to evacuate you by air to the—"

"I know!" he screamed. "Do it."

"I'll be taking you in stasis," I continued. "Which is like a deep sleep—"

"Stop talking and do it!" he screamed. "I'm dying."

With the other half of the tube, I put a glyph on his chest and rendered him insensate, too.

Then I closed my eyes and took a step backward. The empty tube fell out of my hand. This wasn't how it was supposed to be. They were supposed to be stoic and grateful, not disfigured and beyond any hope of saving.

I felt Punnett's hand on my shoulder.

"Don't do that," she said. "Don't stop to think. Keep moving."

The stretcher-bearers had pulled the first stasied man to his feet and were clipping him into the back of my harness.

"One each?" the senior stretcher-bearer asked Punnett.

"You want them both, little brother?" Punnett said to me.

"Yeah," I answered.

"His second day in the war," Punnett explained to the stretcher-bearers. "Get him comfortable now and it'll save you time on the busy days."

That answer satisfied the men, who went through the more complicated process of attaching the second wounded to my chest while holding the one clipped to my back steady, so as not to upset my balance.

I messaged the hospital on my wrist board with our status, then launched with Punnett.

We hurried, more out of a desire to be rid of these awful cases than out of any hope of changing their fates. Both men were dead—their bodies just didn't understand it yet.

We saw a flight group of four women lifting from the hospital as we lined up our approach; they swung wide to give us an unobstructed path. We touched down and an orderly came out to assist us. He was much younger than the gentlemen the previous night.

"From Fifth Division, in with two," I reported.

"Well *of course* you've got two," he said. "Just drop them and we'll put them with the rest."

That was simple enough to accomplish. I pulled my release straps and allowed my passengers to fall to the ground.

"What did you do that for?" the orderly demanded. "Drop them *on the stretcher.*"

"But you just said—"

"It's his second day," Punnett said.

"I don't care what day it is. He should be better trained than to drop them on the ground!" The orderly turned and stalked into the building for a stretcher.

"Whatever you're thinking, don't say it," Punnett advised. "You won't win an argument with this guy. No one ever has."

The man returned with a stretcher and I helped lift the burn victim onto it.

The orderly looked offended. "This is a dead man!" he objected. "He can't survive that. We barely have room for the ones we *can* save. Did you bring him here just to die?"

"Yes," said Punnett. "With clean sheets and someone to say a prayer over him."

"What a beautiful sentiment," the orderly retorted. "Let's fly his mother in to visit him while we're at it. We'll find them a nice seaside villa. You corps-women are too stupid for words."

I took my end of the stretcher and we carried it into the triage tent, which was packed with three dozen men—a few of them writhing in pain on cots, but most of them in stasis, carefully laid out in rows by how long it would take their sigils to wear off.

"He's got no sigil on-time!" the orderly complained.

"It was ten minutes ago," I said.

"A lot of good that does! You think I can remember times on everybody who comes in?"

"Where's he supposed to write it?" Punnett asked. "That guy doesn't have any skin left to write on."

"On a tag tied to a hand or foot!" the orderly said.

As if we'd had time to go looking for cardboard in the middle of a war.

I felt as if my heart was going to burrow its way out of my chest, through my throat, and explode out of my face. Fortunately, the stasis glyph on one of the other immobilized soldiers chose that moment to wear off and the orderly broke away to tend to him.

"Keep breathing," Punnett said to me. "Take a breath before you pass out."

We found a stretcher and brought the second one in ourselves.

When we'd finished, Punnett led me to the supply room. I wrote the sigil time on a slip of paper and Punnett went to attach it to the burn victim. I stowed the passenger harnesses in my bag and then just stood there, frozen, until Punnett found me.

"How you doing, little brother?" she asked me. "Robert?"

My legs went out from under me and I sat down hard.

"I— he— they're going to die, Louise. That's not how it's supposed to work."

Punnett took a knee beside me. "Yeah. Yup."

"I'm sorry. I don't know what happened."

"What happened was that was a bad one. You've been here one day—you don't know what normal is. That was terrible. I've never seen anyone worse off than those two, just more of them at once. You did really good. I couldn't have gotten a stasis on the one."

"I couldn't even do that right. Three tries."

"It was either that or shoot him to put him out of his misery. And they don't let us carry guns."

Punnett caught me by the shoulder strap and hauled me to my feet.

"You're gonna be fine," she said. "Come on."

We flew back to camp. I prayed that Punnett wouldn't tell anyone how I'd reacted. The last thing I needed was a reputation for being oversensitive.

Lt. Drale was updating numbers on the chalkboard. "How many evacuated?" she asked.

"Two more for Sigilwoman Canderelli," Punnett announced.

Drale erased the appropriate spot with a damp rag and chalked in a *3*. "How many tubes?" she asked.

"Three," Punnett said.

Drale glared at her.

"I missed twice," I said, not wanting my partner to take the blame.

Drale glared at me instead. "The next time you're going to miss, have her do it."

"He had to put it on a half-inch of skin on the forehead," Punnett said. "The whole rest of the body was burned to char."

Drale looked as if she'd heard that excuse before.

Punnett and I went to stow our gear in the supply shed.

"Thank you," I said to Punnett.

"I'm big sister to you," she said. "I keep you safe. That's my job."

I gave a wan smile at that. "I think I'm a couple years older than you."

"Yeah, but I've been here six months longer. So, I'm big sister."

"Okay."

"We're off duty. Sleep. Millen will scream if she needs you."

She didn't have to tell me twice.

My alarm clock rang what felt like ten minutes later. Bland bean soup and brown bread for lunch, noontime briefing, six hours on with Punnett, during which we ran three evacuations, none as critical as that morning's, punctuated by one worthwhile nap. Then rain, continuous and moderately heavy, without lightning—enough to make flying cold and inconvenient, but not enough to ground us. Lentil soup (bland) for dinner, more brown bread, one apple each, bed until 23:30, then prepare for the overnight watch.

I went to the mess tent for coffee and oatmeal. I was so disoriented that I tried to eat with the wrong end of my spoon.

Punnett sat down next to me.

"How do people do this?" I asked. "This is insanity."

"You get used to it."

We hiked up to the farmhouse for the overnight briefing.

Carmen Delgado, a corpswoman from our squadron, was preparing to take over the board.

"Unless you're volunteering," she said to me with a smile. "I thought maybe you'd be trying for a record? Two in a row? I don't think anyone ever—"

"I did four nights in a row in the spring of '15," Millen said as she entered. Not bragging, but with conviction enough to make us glad we weren't serving during the first year of the war.

"We have nothing pending," Millen reported, after the rest of second squadron had assembled, "so this will serve as briefing: if there is a repeat of last night's standby nonsense, Lt. Drale is to be notified immediately so she can fly to evacuation point C and shoot the man operating their message board. Carmen's taking communication duty for the front half of the night with Eira to relieve her at three o'clock. You're dismissed."

The rest of second squadron, every bit as tired as I was, trickled out the door and back to their tents for what would be—hopefully, blessedly—six hours of rest. I should have gone with them, but I couldn't help but linger a moment, looking at the chalkboard: *Canderelli, Robert A, 7.*

"I love it," Millen said. "He's ready to drop and he still wants one."

"In the morning is soon enough," I said.

"More than soon enough," Punnett agreed. "You don't win any friends if you fall out of the sky. We have to train your replacement and that's a lot of extra bother."

Touching that she had such concern for my welfare.

Carmen saw something on the message board and let out a delighted squeal. "Oh my God, Teeny!" she called. "Teeny! Look at this."

Millen looked at it and snorted.

"Somebody's winding you up," Millen said. "You got a friend in First Division passing the night by playing pranks?"

"The glyph's real. That's Evac Comm's number three desk in Le Havre."

"Sure enough," said Millen. "They must be stuck in the sixth circle of Hell to call us."

"Who are you talking about?" I asked.

Millen turned toward me and Punnett, a slow, unpleasant smile creeping across her face. "And we have a couple of rustic types here. You were a farmer, weren't you Robert A?"

"Approximately," I said.

"How did you get your wagon out of the mud when it sank up to the axels?"

That was the sort of situation that had generally called for a couple neighbors with crowbars rather than the county philosopher.

"How large a wagon?" I asked.

"Three motor ambulances," said Carmen. "*American* ambulances."

"Oh, no!" I said, grinning.

The rivalry between R&E and the motor-ambulance companies had escalated over four years until it was just short of a shooting war within a war. Even though R&E moved more wounded, the ambulances had captured the fancy of the American newspapers and people. A newfangled form of adventure, sleek, modern, and full of ingenuity—and infinitely more male. By contrast, R&E had been running casualties by air for forty years and the novelty had worn off. For the ambulance boys to strand a couple of their beloved vehicles, much less come begging to the delicate little ladies for help—well, it was a treat.

"How in God's name did they end up *there*?" asked Carmen as we looked at Evac Comm's estimate of their location. "That's almost ninety miles to the south-southwest of us. They must have driven in the wrong direction for three hours. Are they even in our sector?"

"It's nobody's sector—there are no troops there," Millen decided. "But we're closest. And I'd *hate* for First Division to have to cover all that distance from Amiens. But fuck if I know how a flier gets a truck unstuck."

"A winch or windlass," I suggested. "Anchor it to a tree and start cranking."

"Look through the shed and see what you can find," Millen said. "I'll send instructions for them to light a signal fire. If you find them, you get to brag about it for the rest of the war."

6

"Why do they call it dead reckoning?" I ask.

"Ah!" my Sig-1 says. "It's the navy's corruption of 'deduced' reckoning. They use compass, clock, and speed to set their course, same as us!"

"It's called that," my Sig-2 whispers, "because if you reckon wrong, you're dead."

Constance Lattimore, *Flying with the First*, 1919

IT WAS A DOG OF A MISSION. WE WERE LOOKING FOR A BUNCH OF men so directionally impaired that they'd driven ninety miles in the wrong direction. They'd tried to describe their location to some well-fed board monkey back in Le Havre and then our sister at Evac Comm, who'd never flown in her life, had settled back into her easy chair and probably picked a grid square off the map at random. Maybe a one-in-ten chance of finding them. Or that we were even looking in the right country.

We flew for half an hour, climbing above the cloud cover to get out of the rain. I was heavily laden with spare powder bags and harnesses, a block and tackle, three hundred feet of rope, tent poles, stakes, several packs of cold chemical flares, and a pair of tarps. Nevertheless, I kept up easily with Punnett, who was not a strong flier. When we finally reached the designated coordinates, we dropped back under the clouds, circling in the rain. We saw nothing.

"They couldn't get a fire started?" I shouted.

"I dunno!" Punnett called back. "Are we even in the right place?"

We messaged Evac Comm, who was unable to raise the ambulance drivers by message.

"Are they playing a joke on us?" I yelled to Punnett. "Because this isn't funny."

"Let's set down," Punnett said. "Light us a target."

We were several hundred feet above the ground, but it was too dark for us to be any more certain of our altitude than that. I took a smoke-carved safety flare from my cargo bag, cracked it, and shook it up. Inside the tube, the vapors from two different compartments intermixed and produced a bright blue glow. I let go of the flare and counted. It shrank to a pinpoint of light as it fell, then winked out. Hidden by high grass, perhaps. Or trees, which could kill us if we hit them unexpectedly.

"Nine seconds until it disappeared?" I called to Punnett. "What did you count?"

"Six seconds?" she answered. "I don't know!"

So, maybe we were four hundred feet above ground or maybe eight hundred. And that was why nice young people went *splat* trying to land over unfamiliar terrain on rainy nights.

"Down real slow," I suggested. "We'll go one minute and I'll drop more flares."

"How many you got?"

"Ten," I answered. "Or nine now."

"Drale's gonna kill you for taking that many."

"She'll kill me if we die, too."

We flew downward at a crawl. After a minute, I tossed another flare and saw nothing, then repeated and repeated until we saw one hit and jerked to a stop only ten feet above the ground. Beneath us, tall blowing grass had obscured our lights.

"Me first," Punnett said.

God knew what else was in the grass—rocks or rabbit holes. Punnett lined up and made it down with a simple point and touch. I followed and settled to the muddy ground without injuring myself. I shucked my bags.

"We're never going to find them!" I said. "If they're even here to begin with."

"Let's look at least," Punnett replied. "You go a thousand steps that way. I'll go a thousand steps the other. Look for a road, a stream, a house. Anything to give us a clue where we are. We'll meet back here."

I stumbled through the night, the blue light of my safety flare doing very little to penetrate the darkness. I scanned the ground, looking for tire tracks or footprints. Two stumbles and one out-and-out trip and fall later, I realized that not only was I not going to find so much as fleas, but I also wasn't holding a straight line.

I shouted for Punnett. No answer. I spent half an hour stumbling in circles before I heard her calling for me. Somehow she'd found our bags.

"We should go back to camp," I said.

"Millen said stay until we find the ambulances."

"That's stupid," I said. "We can come back at dawn. We won't even lose any search time—we'll never find them in the dark."

"No, we have to bivouac. Millen says."

"Why?" I asked. Other than ensuring we came down with the grippe, there was no use in camping in the field in a rainstorm.

Punnett scrubbed her hands over her cheeks, looking embarrassed. "Because I said something smart. I'm being punished. And you're along for the ride."

I set about putting up a shelter. I pounded one of the tent poles into the ground, tied a rope to the top and staked it out, then hung one of the tarps over it, making a simple open fly. Punnett and I crawled inside and lay down beside each other. Remembering Andrada's threats, I tried to not even brush up against Punnett.

"Am I allowed to know what you said?" I asked.

"Oh, you'll hear about it," Punnett sighed. "It was a little clever. I think that's why Millen was so offended—Louise Punnett is supposed to be a lot of things, but clever ain't one. It had to do with Alice."

"The woman I replaced?"

"Right. So, Alice was career Corps. She joined up in peacetime in '06, back when everyone said you could put in twenty-five quiet years and then collect your pension. The Great War came as a shock for her. From what I hear, Alice was a pretty good egg at first. She spent two years with First Division when they were evacuating French and British casualties. She was in one of the wings that got overrun at the Somme and had to flee on foot. She got her gold bars. Then by the end of '16, she had ten years of service and her a married woman, too. You know what that means."

"She's allowed to have a baby," I said.

"No! It means a lot more than that. It means, 'During such times as the Corps is not committed to the defense of the American realm, reasonable accommodations must be made for the conception, carriage, delivery, and nursing of a child.' Ask me why I know that by heart."

"Why do you know—"

"Because I heard it nine million times. It's one thing in peacetime, right? You live off base with your husband and fly in to work every morning. If you're on time for assembly, who cares where you spend the night? Even over here, a few women in specialties with regular hours have managed it—the messagists and Logistics hoverers."

"What does that mean?" I asked. "They brought their husbands over?"

"There's an apartment building in Le Havre full of them! Some of the rear-echelon women keep lapdogs. Why not a few husbands, too? So, you see to the conceiving part and once you've done that, switch to light duty when you're twenty weeks pregnant. Then it's nursing leave for a year at half-pay when the little one is born."

I tried to imagine such a state of affairs for an R&E unit in the field.

"It was bad," Punnett said. "When Alice was in First Division, they had women enough to cover for her. Her husband, dear old Jim, found them a love nest in Paris and every third day she would flit off for her 'reasonable accommodations.' But then she got dumped into Fifth Division."

"And Lt. Drale said no?"

"Lt. Drale said we're required by law. We did what we could to let her keep it up. She'd been trying for a year, which could happen to any of us. But then 'reasonable accommodations' became sneaking out an hour or two before her shift was supposed to finish and coming back a couple hours late, blaming it on bad weather. And then, on her doctor's advice, she wasn't supposed to be filling bags or doing overnight board duty."

"Due to pregnancy?" I asked.

"Due to maybe the strain of mild physical labor and sleeplessness were preventing her from conceiving. But there was talk. Not actually trying, or Jim was too well-coiffed in the pictures she showed us and it was a sham marriage, or she was drawing a prophylactic sigil every month and was going to keep taking full pay for half-work as long as we'd let her."

"That's bad."

"Bad for me. I was the new girl, so it was 'Louise, go wake Alice.' And she was a heavy sleeper."

That was a special kind of sin in R&E.

" 'Oh, just give me five more minutes, Louise,' or 'Oh Louise, couldn't you take this one, just this once, and I'll pay you back.' If I get my gold bars, she's the reason."

"So, what does Alice have to do with us camping out in the rain?" I asked.

"A few months back, we did a humanitarian evac. There was a church hit on a Sunday and a lot of French civilians trapped in the rubble. Most of them were dead, but we did what we could to help. The townspeople gave us a case of red wine to thank us. And Lt. Drale agreed that on a certain off day the ban on liquor would be lifted for six hours. After a couple bottles, Millen said a lot of things. Including that maybe a year's worth of unsuccessful 'reasonable accommodations' might be due to a lack of anatomical knowledge by the two parties involved. And in front of the whole wing, she said, 'You take me along next Tuesday and I'll show dear old Jim which hole he's supposed to stick it in.' "

"Lovely image," I said.

"Then Alice got pregnant the next month and everyone was asking

Millen if she'd gone along to help. Somebody reminds Millen of it at least twice a week. Just usually not the wing's second-most junior flier. Anyway, tonight while you were gathering gear, Millen told me, 'Don't get him pregnant—I can't afford to lose another one.' And I said, 'Okay, but which of his holes do I stick it in?' Carmen was trying so hard not to laugh that she started sneezing and fell out of her chair. And so, we're camping."

My shoulders sagged. Millen might live down a line like that, but *I* wouldn't.

"I can trust you, right?" Punnett asked. "Not to do anything? If I knock off for a couple hours?"

"Of course," I said. If there were so much as a whisper of impropriety, it would be a race between my superior officers to see who could slit my throat first.

"You want me to keep watch?" I asked.

"No. Somebody could climb right over us and we'd never see them coming."

Punnett fell asleep almost before the last words were out of her mouth, her head pillowed on her powder bag. Despite the rain, Punnett's snoring, and the muddy ground, I drifted off, too.

I dreamed I was on endless board duty, weeks at a time. Urgent messages flashed by, one after another, too fast to read. My hands were like cast iron. I couldn't draw so much as a letter. Another hundred wounded at Point A. A thousand at Point B. Point C with ten thousand. I had no fliers left to send. I had no harness or I would have tried to run every one myself. If only I could—

I sat up with a start. A couple hours had passed. I wasn't sure what had woken me. Footsteps? Beside me, Punnett snored on. Maybe just the sound of the rain dripping down the canvas tarp.

No, there it was again. The tall grass being trampled, the squelch of boots in the mud.

"Punnett!" I whispered. She didn't move.

My first thought was the German army had seen our lights and was creeping toward us. But they were hundreds of miles away and on the retreat—they had better things to do than hunt down a couple noncombatants. Perhaps the ambulance men, as unlikely as that seemed.

I heard whispers, confused and annoyed. Not overly worried about being heard, though I couldn't make out what they were saying.

Locals, I decided. Shepherds or goatherds. I'd grown up among that sort. They had fantastic intuition about trespassers. They also got lonely way out in the country, so if you were a lost traveler or, say, a philosopher on a mission of mercy, you were more likely to get a hot meal and a dry blanket than a lecture about respecting property lines. Best to take an open, direct course of action.

I shook Punnett by the shoulder. She mumbled in her sleep. Fair enough. I could show some initiative. I ran a hand through my hair and straightened my poncho. First impressions counted for a lot. I crawled out from beneath the fly and called, "*Bonsoir?*"

There was an agitated whisper.

"Sill voose plate," I called, recalling the booklet of French phrases I'd been given in flight training for self-study. "Knee pass a-vahr pear."

The whispering stopped. I felt mighty pleased with myself—reading and practicing alone by lantern light all those evenings.

"Don't move!" cried an accented female voice in English.

So the shepherd's wife, then.

"Gee swees oon fill-oh-soaf-ah," I announced. "Gee swees oon American. Gee swee oon-ah ah-mee-ah."

I heard the unmistakable click of a semiautomatic pistol's safety being switched off. I racked my brain for "don't shoot," but it hadn't been on our list of polite vocabulary.

"Shit!" I said.

A dazzling blue light exploded. I covered my face and dove to the ground, but it was only a flare being lit. When my eyes recovered, I could make out a pair of women wearing skysuits—corpswomen. One held a gun aimed at my head.

"What in the hell are you?" she asked in a Texas twang.

"Sig-3 Canderelli, Fifth Division," I said.

The women looked at each other. The gun came down.

"Whatcha doing out here?" the Texan asked.

"Looking for a bunch of ambulances," I said.

The two of them shook their heads. "Figures Evac Comm would double-dispatch on a turtle hunt like this," the Texan said.

"You're looking for them, too?" I asked.

"We thought you were them. And then we thought you were a trap. What were you shouting when you came out?"

"French," I said superiorly.

"Surely not," said the other woman, who was holding the flare.

"Of course it was!" I objected. "*Je parle français. Je m'appelle Robert.*" Or as I pronounced it, as a Montanan by way of clueless: *Gee parley Frank-ace. Gee maple Robert.*

"What is he saying?" asked the woman with the flare.

"Damned if I know," said the Texan.

"I was introducing myself in French," I said.

The woman with the flare looked appalled. "I grew up in Montreal," she said. "I've heard all sorts of people speak French, but never anything like *that.*"

I was about to object that my training instructors had complimented me on my pronunciation, but Punnett chose that moment to come stumbling out of the shelter. Again, there was nearly gunplay.

"Jesus," Punnett said once introductions had been made. "What unit are you with?"

"First Division, Third Wing," replied the Texan. She looked down her nose at my partner. "I know Fifth Division runs to the eccentric, but this beats all. Y'all planning to stay the night?"

"Unless the ambulances find us first," said Punnett.

"Well that's sweet! Just you and your beau. Was Gen. Blandings the matchmaker? I hear there's nothing she won't meddle in."

Punnett smiled, baring her teeth. "This big lump? It's his second day. He's not allowed to do anything by himself. And I'm sure Gen. Blandings *did* pick him out for our wing. Because some folks just couldn't hack it in an intellectual outfit like yours."

The Texan scowled. "What's that supposed to mean?"

Punnett folded her hands prettily. "Have to be smart enough to keep track of the calls you're actually running and the ones you're pretending to run."

The pair took to the air angrily, heading back toward the First Division's encampment in Amiens.

"I don't think they like us," I said to Punnett as we hunkered back down in our tent.

"No," Punnett agreed. "It's because of Blandings."

"Why?"

"First Division got hammered in '16. They lost a hundred fliers at the Somme, killed, wounded, or captured. Afterward, some of their wings developed a sense of entitlement. They didn't want to risk putting women up, so their commanders faked run numbers. Kept the wings at home and claimed four hundred evacuated, stuff like that."

"Who evacuated the wounded, then?"

"The army board technicians were in on it: They sent fake calls. Run enough of those and you can claim exhaustion when a real call comes and make another division take it for you."

"Nobody blew the whistle?"

"Old Granny Rhodes was the two-star general in charge of R&E back then—she knew something was wrong. She sent her best staff officer to investigate under cover of filling an empty roster spot for a colonel. That was Tommie Blandings. Blandings was her harmless, bubbly self and everybody talked in front of her, right up to the point where she recommended court-martialing every corpswoman ranking Sig-1 or higher in six wings."

"Jesus!" I said. "I never heard about that." We would have gossiped endlessly in training over dozens of commanders being thrown out of the Corps.

"Rhodes retired most of them instead. She didn't want word getting out—she was worried it would make her look bad. But Gen. Fallmarch, who's got three stars and wants a fourth one for running the Corps, found out and fired Rhodes too. So now instead of Gran, who at least knew how to run a wing in the field, we have Gen. Niejenhuis as our two-star—and the Flying Dutchwoman hasn't flown anything but a desk for twenty years. Plus it didn't fix anything. First Division is still rotten as hell."

I shuddered to think of Essie in the middle of that. "I've got a friend in the First," I said. "They bumped her up to Sig-2 right before we came over."

"Well good for her," said Punnett. "Maybe she'll turn them around."

Punnett put her head on her bag and prepared to resume sleeping.

"They probably say the same thing about us," she said.

"What do you mean?"

"Right before Rhodes got the hatchet, she promoted Blandings to brigadier general and created Fifth Division for her. Really, it's just a division on paper, but it means Blandings doesn't answer to anyone except Niejenhuis and Fallmarch."

Punnett yawned.

"Then when Blandings was picking out women, she took a lot of good officers who'd been passed over for promotion eight or nine times, mostly because they were brown. Andrada's one—she should have her own wing by now. And Bernice Macmurdo, if there was any justice in the world, would have Niejenhuis's job, but a Negro's never going to be a general except as a transporter or a smokecarver. So they call us the blackest wing in the Corps and a bunch of backstabbers and spies besides."

"And a man," I said.

"Yeah, you fit right in. It's not any better for Blandings with the bosses. Gen. Niejenhuis doesn't trust her—she thinks Blandings and Rhodes are plotting something, even though Rhodes is retired. So, reinforcements have been scarce. We get shorted on supplies. If the wing falls apart and Blandings loses her command, not many people would be sorry."

"You don't like her?"

"She's dangerous, Robert. Women disappear in the middle of the night to run missions for her. Sometimes they don't come back. We've lost four fliers like that since I've been here. They go off in the dark and the next morning Blandings gives a speech about how some girl had an accident and she was very brave."

"What do they do?" I asked. "In the middle of the night?"

"Spying. Attacking the Germans. Trying to overthrow the Corps. I don't know! But stay away from her. Women who do special missions for Blandings always end up dead."

7

If you ain't broke a bone yet, it's still your first day.

Attributed to Mary Grinning Fox, ca. 1871

WE WERE UP WITH THE DAWN, SEARCHING BY AIR. NO AMBULANCES, not even so much as a road. Off by a mile or ten. After two hours, we landed and I glanced at my wrist board.

RECALL DIV 5. ALL HANDS. PRIORITY ZED. Drale.

Something big was afoot. I drew sigils to look back through my messages and discovered we'd received the recall order three times already.

"Oops," I said.

"Great big oops," Punnett corrected. "The infantry must have attacked this morning. God, I hope it wasn't the big one!"

I packed our gear and made ready to fly home.

"How fast are you?" Punnett asked. "If I carry all that and you sprint?"

"Head down and no cargo, three hundred fifty miles an hour," I said. "Why, what are you?"

"Less. A lot less. I can't believe I'm going to say this, but just go. Better to have one of us than none of us. And I'll hear about getting beat by a boy."

I streaked back for the camp at best speed, leaving Punnett well behind. If this was it—if the army had attacked at Saint-Mihiel—we would need every available flier. I set down on the landing field and jogged to the farmhouse. Carmen was at the message board with Lt. Drale.

"Where the *hell* have you been?" Drale asked.

"Ma'am," I said, "we had orders to search for three—"

Carmen was chuckling. "Oh, little brother. The ambulance drivers were on the board this morning to complain that nobody came to wipe their noses. Then they realized they read their map wrong and they were three miles outside Reims. They walked home."

"Are you serious?" I said. If there had been something handy to murder, I would have.

"I can't believe you stayed out there all night!" Carmen said. "You should have snuck back."

"Punnett said we weren't allowed."

"Just the two of you sitting out there," Carmen snickered, "a romantic night in the mud."

Carmen laughed so hard that even Lt. Drale cracked a smile.

"Sneak back next time," Drale agreed. "We didn't bring you here to be one of the good ones. Miss Delgado, get him briefed and back up, please."

"With pleasure," Carmen said. She pointed to one of the numerous maps on the table. "Our troops made a probing attack this morning. It's not the big one, but big enough. One to two thousand casualties. We have a bunch of squads from First Division assisting in our sector and they're making a mess of it. One landing field is jammed worse than the next—we've got women circling twenty minutes, waiting for an opening. Gen. Blandings went forward to direct traffic."

"Where do you want me?" I asked.

"We just got a request for an ad hoc evacuation point, but we haven't flown anyone over yet to see how many men are there. Go check it out and evacuate it. If you have more than a dozen wounded, message and I'll send additional women to support you. When you're done, go up to Point A to help."

Carmen gave me the grid coordinates and I began plotting a course.

"The field hospital is overwhelmed," she added. "Anyone not in stasis who'll live until tomorrow goes all the way back to the town of Bar-le-Duc—the French brought up a hospital train to move the minor cases to Reims."

Lt. Drale unlocked the supply cabinet and removed two ampoules of silver chloride from a padded box. "This is going to have to last you all day," she said. "Use your discretion. Hurry up."

I scribbled down my course and launched. I could barely keep my hands from shaking and spraying me across the sky as I sprinted to the northeast. My rain-soaked skysuit and a sleepless night and a snappish lieutenant—none of that mattered. *This* was the pinnacle of flight, the greatest selfless good, the end toward which all those countless hours of training had pointed me. As if the war were in perfect concert with my feelings, a few shells burst nearby as I began my descent. The explosions weren't near enough for any risk of shrapnel, but I could feel the rip and thump of the blasts reverberate through my chest.

I saw the ad hoc landing field marked with a bedsheet on which a circle had been drawn in red paint and HERE! written in the middle. A quick circuit of the area revealed every obstacle I'd ever been warned about: barbed wire, impact craters, ditches, observation towers, aerial cables for an electric telegraph, a cavalry unit retreating with sabers still drawn. I found a clear path, landed on the sheet, then lowered myself into the trench.

"Medical evacuation!" I cried as I dropped into the ankle-deep mud.

I found four men sitting on campstools smoking cigarettes. Perhaps they were guarding the more seriously wounded. They stared at me.

"Christ, that's the ugliest woman I've ever seen," said one.

"Medical evacuation?" I said again. I flipped up my goggles, wondering if they had fogged up and I was missing the more urgent cases.

As it turned out, the tally was a lacerated knee, a sprained ankle, knocked in the head by a shelf full of bean cans, and a bad racking cough that had been going on for months. None needed air evacuation, but one of them knew how to message and had gotten hold of the glyph for Evac Comm. Still, it was *my* aid point. And they *were* wounded, however lightly.

"Who wants up?" I asked.

The men continued staring.

"I'm not going with you," said Knocked in the Head. "Tell them to send some girls. Pretty ones."

Well, I was going to evacuate them whether they liked it or not.

Knocked in the Head continued complaining even while I pulled open his shirt and drew a stasis sigil on his chest. For behaving better than the others, though likely only because he hadn't been able to draw enough air to speak, I stasied the Cougher as well. I wrestled them into harnesses, dragged them upright, and clipped in.

"You'd better come back for us!" called Mr. Laceration. "It's a long walk to the field hospital."

I held my tongue and made for the hospital. Stretchers and wounded were laid out so thickly on the grass that there was no place to land. An incoming flier laden with a pair of unstasied wounded cut under me and tried to squeeze into a narrow open spot, only to lose control of her sigils and fall the last ten feet. I could hear all three of them screaming.

"Lord," I murmured. But there was no place to get safely down and try to help her. I finally spotted the only open space left—the cemetery adjacent to the old church. I set down between two crumbling gravestones and the same orderly I'd nearly punched the previous day strode up.

"Two minor," I announced.

"What the hell are you bringing us minor cases for?" the orderly shrieked. "We've got no room. Take them to the hospital train!"

"No, they told me anyone in stasis—"

"What's wrong with him?" the orderly asked, pointing to the man on my chest.

"Umm," I said. "Hit in the head with a can of beans."

The orderly walked away without another word. I muttered a curse and launched.

I had to stop in two different villages to ask for directions before I found Bar-le-Duc, where hundreds of lightly wounded Frenchmen were standing on the railway platform, waiting to be loaded onto the train. I fought my way in among the sea of periwinkle jackets and rounded tin helmets to make a landing. It was fifteen minutes before the French physician in charge could be produced.

"No one with philosophy!" the doctor told me.

"It's just stasis!" I pleaded. "They'll come out of it in a couple hours. They're barely even hurt."

"With philosophy, must go to American hospital."

"I was just there. They told me—"

"No philosophy!"

I strangled a groan and flew back to the field hospital. A different orderly met me between the lines of ancient graves.

"Two minor!" I said.

"Just stack 'em with the rest," he said, pointing to a line of men in stasis that snaked across the ground. "Good job, buddy."

I unharnessed the pair of soldiers and dragged them beside the others. God knew what they would think when they woke up next to a memorial in the shape of an angel with its face worn featureless by decades of rain and one wing lying in pieces on the ground. A demon come to drag them off to hell perhaps. No less than they deserved.

I returned to the ad hoc point, only to discover that the two men who'd demanded that I come back for them had vanished. I cursed and called hordes of faceless angels down on them, then went forward to Point A, which had just cleared the last of its casualties and directed me to Point B; at Point B, I was told that Fifth Division had gone off duty.

"The motor ambulances will evacuate the rest," the chief stretcher-bearer told me.

I just about wanted to be evacuated myself, to an insane asylum. Two thousand wounded and no better employment for me than one fool's errand after another!

I flew back to camp and found the division at breakfast. The only empty seat was next to Millen.

"Never found those trucks?" she asked. I shook my head. "That's ambulance drivers for you."

I had the feeling that was as close as I was going to get to an apology from her.

"Ethel Gelbstein in third squadron took a hard landing and turned an ankle," Millen continued with her mouth full. "Bad sprain probably. She'll be out a couple months. Fucking Fern Cunningham panicked and scrambled our rescue team over it, which put three fliers out of commission instead of one. Did that ad hoc keep you busy?"

"I got the runaround," I said, staring at my bowl of porridge. "Two evacs."

Millen set down her spoon. "Two?" she said. The color drained from her face. "*Two?* We had men dying on the ground for lack of fliers in the first hour! We were tying quadruple stringers to get them out. Gen. Blandings flew fifteen casualties herself. What in the hell were you doing?"

I tried to explain, but Millen wasn't listening.

"You sit there, mooning over the evac count, but you can't even pull yourself together for a Priority Zero recall. If you've got trouble following directions, go back to Maine and haul cargo with those worthless excuses in Logistics."

"I'm sorry," I said. "I'll do—"

"You'll do better or you'll go home!"

8

General Weekes, you have been asked many times to come to the aid of your country, sometimes openly, sometimes in secret, always at great personal cost. I fear I must ask again for your assistance in the matter of the conflict brewing in the Pacific, where our allies are so hard-pressed, but Congress does not permit me to intervene by usual channels. Secretary Hardin once warned me you are a hard man to buy, so my opening offer is no less than this: complete and unconditional amnesty for you and all your fellow philosophers now living in exile.

Personal message from President Franklin D. Roosevelt to
Brig. Gen. Robert A. Canderelli Weekes, May 1, 1941

THE GOOD THING ABOUT FLYING FOR R&E IN THE SUMMER OF '18 was that you never had to wait more than a few hours for a chance at redemption. The ambulances took so long to reach the wounded at Point B that many of the low-priority cases deteriorated and needed air evacuation. We flew another two hundred casualties in the afternoon, ten of which were mine. Millen was too busy to remember she was mad at me. Second squadron was off for the evening and then the entire division came off duty at midnight. I slept deader than I ever had in my life.

Punnett kicked my tent flaps open on the way to assembly the next morning; but for that, I might have slept through the rest of the week. I felt as if someone had taken sandpaper to my brain. I stood, asleep on my feet, as Lt. Drale talked for an interminable length of time followed by Gen. Blandings.

"I'll be serving tea in my quarters from 17:00 to 17:45 if anyone has matters to discuss," Blandings concluded. "Prior to that, I'll be drawing korus for one of our local farmers, Madame Lefevre, whose cheeses have been received by this wing with appreciation on several occasions. Sigilwoman Canderelli, whom I hear is a proficient agricultural sigilrist, will accompany me."

The meeting broke up with most of the women dragging themselves back to bed. I hadn't even recognized my own name before Punnett came over to sympathize.

"Bad luck getting Blandings duty your third day in the war," Punnett said to me.

"I don't even know what that is," I said.

"She does glyphs for one of the farmers and you help. You end up working like an indentured koruist in the sun, with her talking at you the whole while."

"There's nothing wrong with drawing korus," I said. "I spent lots of time doing that kind of work as a kid."

"Yeah, so did I," Punnett said. "That's why I'm sorry for you. She doesn't usually leave until ten. You can get a couple more hours."

I slept. I ate porridge in the mess tent. Sig-2 Andrada intercepted me before I left. She looked worried, rather than homicidal.

"Be careful with Blandings," she warned. "Punnett warned you about her?"

"Yeah," I said.

"Don't say more than you have to. Just 'yes, ma'am,' 'no ma'am.' If she asks you to volunteer for something, say no. If she's putting pressure on you—if she scares you—go to Bernice Macmurdo. Bernice is one of us. She'll put an end to it."

"If Blandings pressures me to do what?" I asked.

"Mutiny."

• • •

The day was warm and pleasant as I followed Gen. Blandings west over pastureland and farms. I wasn't sure what to make of her. Mostly, I was inclined to like her. She'd taken a chance in giving me a position in R&E and I doubted many of her fellow generals could have approved. Yet Punnett had always acted with my best interests in mind, so I took her warning to heart. And what would it take to scare Andrada—an even bigger knife?

After a few minutes, Blandings waved to me for a landing, indicating the cow pasture below. She snapped into a sharp flare and settle. I was happy to do the same. On the ground, Blandings unpinned her plait and undid her braid, shaking out her hair. She'd gone mostly gray, though she couldn't have been more than forty. Her face was wrinkled and tanned from hours flying in the sun; she had the usual hoverer's pale rings around her eyes where her goggles covered the skin. Overall, the effect was of a pleasant country witch out of some fairy tale.

A sturdy Frenchwoman came down the hill, calling out and waving to us. She kissed Blandings on both cheeks and curtsied. She and Blandings conversed for a few minutes. The woman gestured to an apple orchard half a mile up the road—that part was clear enough—but the two of them seemed hung up on some point, despite Blandings's confident French.

"*Soldat? Ou philosophe?*" the woman asked, pointing at me.

"Not for the last time in your life, one imagines," Blandings said to me. "She worries if you're a real philosopher. Will your trees do as well as mine?"

"Tell her my first paid job was drawing korus," I said. And then, wondering if generals did much in the way of agricultural sigilry, I asked, "You ever do fruit trees before, ma'am?"

"No," Blandings said. "I hadn't done any korus at all before I came over."

"It's late in the year for it," I said. "You can end up shocking the trees. Every tenth one ends up dead. It would help if she knows how old the trees are. If she had to choose: larger apples or harvest them sooner? And what will she use them for—to eat, or for cider or brandy?"

They discussed. "She doesn't know how old," Blandings translated. "Maybe twenty years. Sooner. And for eating."

Blandings and I walked up the path toward the trees. She handed me a miniature copy of *Canul's Annual Koru Advisor*, six years out of date, not that I suspected anything had changed for apple trees—they were a valuable crop and their sigils had been among the first ones perfected. I sketched out the shape that our koru glyphs ought to take with a pencil.

"I suppose if I draw korus on half of them, mine will all end up dead?" Blandings asked, as we approached the first row.

"Trees are bad to learn on," I said, trying not to sound like I was accusing a one-star general of being an incompetent philosopher.

Blandings gave me a three-by-three-inch square of glass and an atomizer filled with distilled water. The rhythm came back to me without conscious thought: three sprays to coat the glass, then aim through it at the plant in question and draw the glyph in the beads of water.

We walked up the row and I drew korus on the first dozen trees.

"You're quiet today," Blandings said, her voice high and burbling. "You've been warned off me, I presume?"

"No, ma'am," I said.

"Oh, of course you have! Andrada's never trusted me. And I didn't take for my wing many women who follow instructions blindly, even if it's a general giving them. Besides, Belle Addams told me you would need convincing."

"You know Ms. Addams?" I asked, intrigued. She'd been an assistant dean back at Radcliffe and one of my staunchest advocates.

"Belle Addams and I served together in the Philippines in '99," Blandings said. "Manila was a small town for philosophers back then, much less for those of us developing a conscience at an inconvenient moment. Belle brought you to my attention last October, after you led that evacuation of the wounded protestors in Boston. She told me you were one for R&E."

I'd never even realized.

"I always thought she was looking for an excuse to throw me out," I said.

"She might have wanted to expel you, too, but she and I were trying to find a way to get you into the Corps, almost from the moment you expressed an interest."

I let a smile slip. Mean old Ms. Addams.

"I'd been looking for an outstanding male flier for months," Blandings said. "I need one to win the war."

That sounded too good to be true.

"How do you plan to do that?" I asked.

"Too complicated a question," Blandings answered, waving it away. "Let's start with something simpler: Have you thought about how the war will end if we stand obediently by and let Gen. Fallmarch dictate strategy for the Corps? Have you *really* thought about it?"

We turned and began making our way up the next row.

"Well, we've got ten thousand soldiers coming off the ships every day," I said. "We have numbers on our side. As soon as the American army starts attacking, the Germans won't be able to hold on. They'll pull back."

"And then?" Blandings asked. "When they're desperate?"

"I don't know. Surrender?"

"That's disappointingly conventional thinking, Mr. Canderelli. What weapon hasn't the German army used yet?"

I frowned at that. The Great War had seen the Germans use every manner of new weapon—machine guns, aeroplanes, flamethrowers. And then I understood what she meant.

"Philosophers," I said. "The Korps des Philosophs hasn't fought yet. They can't, though. Germany signed the Rouen Conventions. It's illegal for them to use philosophy in warfare, same as for us."

"The same way it was illegal for the British to evacuate Gallipoli by transporter," Blandings said. "And yet it happened when they got desperate. Though I suppose the man courting Danielle Hardin is unlikely to forget that."

"Yes, ma'am," I said. Danielle might be a hero for saving a quarter of a million soldiers, but she'd violated international law to do it.

"Likewise," Blandings continued, "when the situation gets bad enough, the Germans will use their rauchbauers—their smokecarvers. Doesn't that worry you?"

"No, ma'am," I said. "The Corps has the finest smokecarvers in the world. They've never lost a battle."

Blandings pursed her lips at that. "Never lost a battle. Bravo. That's the line they taught you to parrot in training. But we have two problems. First, the Germans will have the initiative. They'll decide where to attack, when, and with what kind of smoke. We can't defend everywhere. Second, we'll be badly outnumbered."

"How do you figure?" I asked. "We've got two thousand smokecarvers sitting in Le Havre. The peace agreement at the end of the Franco-Prussian War limited the Germans to a thousand women in uniform. They've stood by it. The Société in Geneva checks them out once a year to make sure they don't have extra."

"The Germans rotate the women in their Korps des Philosophs every twelve months. They only have a thousand women in uniform at any given moment, but after two decades they have *twenty* thousand with military training, all of whom can be called up at a moment's notice. They even have plans to house their children with relatives or in boarding schools for a week or two. Twenty thousand. Did you ever win a fight outnumbered ten to one?"

"No," I said. "But Mrs. Cadwallader won outnumbered fifty to one at the Battle of Paris during the Intervention. We can do it again."

"The German Korps is better trained than it used to be and Gen. Fallmarch, alas, is no Cadwallader. Add to that the fact that every German girl learns basic smokecarving in primary school—if they want a million women weaving weapons-grade smoke back in the Fatherland and shipping it forward, then they can do it—and we're set up for a terrible defeat. So, I'll ask you again: How do you counter all that with just two thousand Corps smokecarvers?"

I thought back on some of the impossible situations I'd faced over the past year: a philosophical fight in which I wasn't strong enough to strike my opponent or ward off her blows; a flying race in which I'd competed against women a hundred miles per hour faster than me; an attack by a group of heavily armed men against me and two friends trapped inside a tiny apartment.

"Cheat," I said.

"Very nice," said Blandings. "A few of us in the upper ranks of the Corps decided that if we didn't like trying to win outnumbered ten to one, we ought to try to change those odds."

"What, are you going to put another hundred thousand women in uniform?" I asked.

"Exactly!" Blandings said, beaming. "Not in uniform—they'll be volunteers—but we've been laying the groundwork almost since the day war broke out. We've done it quietly, recruiting women we trust among the transporters and fliers unions. County philosophers, municipal fliers, industrial sigilrists. We've asked them: If your country needed you desperately for a few days, could you assemble and transport overseas to fight? When the time comes, could you persuade your colleagues and bring them, too? It will be a volunteer relief force of civilians. Senator Cadwallader-Fulton will command them."

The senator was Lucretia Cadwallader's daughter—as good as royalty where sigilrists were concerned. If old Josie asked for women to relieve France, no red-blooded American philosopher could say no. Which meant Danielle was surely involved as well.

"If we can match them woman for woman, that'll be an easy win," I said.

"Not if they take us by surprise," Blandings countered. "Gen. Fallmarch guards her intelligence on the rauchbauers jealously. Gen. Pershing is no better. He sees the Corps as a rival. He's heard the whispers that the army hasn't won a war in five decades without its lady consultants, and this time he wants it to be different. He hopes to win single-handedly. So my friends and I have had to gather our own intelligence. Dangerous, difficult work."

I thought of Punnett's description of women gone missing in the middle of the night.

"All my sources suggest the Germans will attack conventionally—twenty thousand women and a pillar of poisoned smoke. The sort of tactic Lucretia Cadwallader might have used during the Civil War or that the Korps itself tried at the end of the Franco-Prussian War."

"Roll right over the trenches and suffocate the men in them?" I asked.

"Precisely. Put a big enough scare into the British and French and seize enough territory that Germany can negotiate a favorable peace. But the real potential for disaster lies less in their attack than in our response to it. If we're losing—if the American army is overwhelmed and the German Korps is driving toward Paris—then Gen. Fallmarch will be tempted to take drastic measures."

"What does that mean?"

"The destruction of nations," Blandings said.

We turned and had already come upon the last row of trees.

"I don't think I understand," I said.

"That was my job, before the war," Blandings said, "devising new ways to cheat. I ran something called the Experimental Wing in Nevada. You've heard of it, perhaps?"

"Once or twice," I said. "An instructor in flight training threatened to send me there."

"We could have put you to good use! In Nevada we asked how the Corps would fight on the day the Rouen Conventions collapsed. How does a flier best attack an aeroplane? How should she drop a bomb—from high altitude or low? One large bomb or many small ones? What if we resorted to total war? How do you best destroy a nation if your army lies in ruins?"

"How?"

"We had smokecarvers who developed a strain of influenza with a vapor booster that infected nearly everyone who inhaled it and caused encephalitis—an infection of the brain. Not invariably fatal, but in more cases than not. They asked me: Should we drop it in a bomb or spray it? How do you best hit a city without infecting the flier carrying it? I thought it was a fascinating question at first. Then after a few years I began to find it horrifying."

"Why would we ever develop something like that?" I asked.

"Because the Germans already had a similar strain of plague that they could unleash. They wouldn't dare hit us if we could hit back. Peace through strength."

I could see the trouble with that line of thinking. "Until we get desperate and hit them and then they hit us back."

"They would have to cross the Atlantic to do it," Blandings said. "Possibly they have fliers talented enough to try it, but I've never heard of a German hoverer that good."

Indeed, even among American philosophers only a handful had been able to fly from New York to London.

"No, the trouble is *we're* likely to use it," she said. "We can hit every city in Germany within a few hours and they would be lucky to hit even one in America. But the Germans could still strike Paris, London, Rome. To Gen. Fallmarch, that would be a small price to pay. If it's not American lives, she won't much mind. Just as long as she's the instrument of American victory."

I remembered sitting in the dean's office at Radcliffe a few weeks before, where Ms. Addams had brought up concerns about what attacks like this would mean for philosophy generally.

"It would be a gift to the Trenchers," I said. "It's everyone's worst fears about sigilry come to pass. The backlash would be terrible."

Blandings raised an eyebrow at that. "That's a politician's answer. I'm more worried about the short term. The simulations we ran in Nevada suggested that for a limited strike and reprisal, ten million lives lost would be a conservative estimate. I'd like to avoid that."

I thought of a big chalkboard in the sky for evacs and "ten million" written next to my name.

"That's a plenty good reason," I said.

"So, we'll do our utmost to prevent it," Blandings said. "We'll make sure the Corps is ready to meet the German attack. We'll have our civilian volunteers ready to reinforce. But if they fail and I get word that Gen. Fallmarch is planning to bomb Berlin with plague, I have a fail-safe. A means of winning the war bloodlessly. Radcliffe has been at the center of developing it. It's experimental, it's not finished yet, and it may never come to fruition. But if the situation becomes desperate, we'll use it. And it requires an expert male hoverer."

"To do what?" I asked. "Why do you need a man?"

She chuckled. "Mr. Canderelli, I hope you'll forgive me if I don't tell you *all* the details. You're serving in a frontline unit that routinely lands within two hundred yards of the Germans. And Gen. Fallmarch may still decide she wants to court-martial me and my friends, in which being able to plead ignorance will save you a great deal of trouble."

Blandings lit a cigarillo. I could smell mint and tea leaves mixed in with the tobacco. She drew a sigil in the smoke cloud so that it circulated back through the paper.

"When I joined Rescue and Evacuation, I swore an oath to protect life," she said. "But after four years of hauling the wounded, it seems to me that the higher good is seeing that soldiers need not be evacuated in the first place, much less tens of millions of civilians. If my superior officer feels differently because she's a three-star general who wants a fourth star, then I believe she's unfit for command. But there's a word for that sort of thinking, you know."

Andrada had called it by its right name.

"Mutiny," I said.

"Or treason. I don't need to tell you how they punish those crimes during wartime. It's not a light thing that we'll undertake. It'll be the end of my career and that of any sigilwoman who follows me. It will require you to forsake the Corps and abandon your comrades. It's a great deal to ask of anyone."

I was so puffed up with all the talk of conspiracies and secret plans for victory, with the idea that Blandings had picked me specially to help and ten million lives at stake, that I hardly gave it a second thought. Besides, if Ms. Addams and my mentors at Radcliffe were working to make it happen then it must be the right thing to do. I never stopped to ask what the price might be, for me or for American sigilry.

"When do we start?" I asked.

"Soon," she said.

PART 2

THE MUTINEERS

Like everyone else, I had a carefully worked out formula for taking risks. In principle, we would all take any risk, even the certainty of death, to save life or to maintain an important position. To take life we would run, say, a one-in-five risk, particularly if there was some wider object. . . . Perhaps a one-in-twenty risk to get a wounded German to safety. . . . When exhausted and wanting to get quickly from one point in the trenches to another . . . we would take a one-in-two-hundred risk; when dead tired, a one-in-fifty risk.

Robert Graves, *Good-Bye to All That*, 1929

9

The fliers came and went and kicked up dust each time. A busy day. One body or two and each time the dust flew up. We watched and drank wine from the canteen.

"Would you like me better?" Catherine asked. "If I were one of those philosophical girls?"

"No," I said. "It twists them up. It makes them cold-hearted or easy."

Ernest Hemingway, *In Another Country and Besides*, 1929

I WAS STILL BUZZING WITH EXCITEMENT THE NEXT DAY AS PUNNETT and I shuttled wounded to the hospital for three hours straight, the day after as I scrubbed the stove in the mess tent, all through the off day that followed. But weeks passed without another word from Blandings. July and August melted away. We stood our two days on, one day off. The Americans continued to reinforce and prepare for their offensive at Saint-Mihiel, while the French made one attack after another to the north. When the French ambulances were overwhelmed, we took their wounded. I made two hundred evacuations, then three hundred.

It's the ordinary stuff of which a hundred memoirs of R&E have been filled, though my experience was a little different. When the women were in a good mood, they called me "little brother." Otherwise, I was "our young lady without a bosom," "Mr. Danielle Hardin," or, inevitably, "the new girl." Punnett was the only one who called me Robert, and I would have fought the whole German army for her.

At the start of every shift, I was assigned to do the heavy lifting when we filled powder bags. I got stuck with overnight board duty more often than any other three women put together (usually without the benefit of Dar staying up late to chat). Whenever the farmhouse floor needed mopping or it was time to dig a new latrine or the Logistics fliers had dropped off five hundred pounds of flour and it had to be hauled to the mess tent, it was "Someone fetch the new girl!"

I put my head down and kept working.

Someone pulled the pegs from "the new girl's" tent one night during a rainstorm and it collapsed on top of me; I needed three days to dry out all my gear—just put my head down and work through it. A couple of women from third squadron refused to run calls with "the new girl" out of concern he might force himself on one of them ("Well of course he didn't try anything with Punnett—can you imagine a man desperate enough to violate *her*?" one of them quipped)—put your head down and fly through it. Rumors swirled that I really *was* a woman ("I saw him squatting to piss in a field—he has no man parts!")—fly through it and through a hundred other insults and pranks and cruelties, as if tending to the wounded and the dying each day wasn't cruel enough.

But they let me fly.

When I worked with Andrada, she never again threatened me. Sometimes she suggested how I might rig a casualty more quickly or navigate more accurately, but those were signs of respect coming from her. And Millen always found me extra grabs when she commanded from the field. She understood what I wanted above all else.

"What do I care what you've got under your knickers if you make twenty runs in a day?" Millen said to me after a busy one. I was doing stretches to loosen up my aching back and she was watching my crotch with more interest than I would have liked. "I'll put up a draft horse or an orangutan if he's willing to fly that many."

I was willing to call it a compliment if she was.

• • •

Lt. Drale softened too. One slow, sultry day she tapped me to staff the ready rescue team with her. It was famously easy duty: no evacs, no bag filling, no cleaning. Just sit in the farmhouse waiting to respond in case one of our own fliers went down.

Fifth Division only took two calls the whole morning and by noon Drale and I were struggling to keep our eyes open. She'd set a couple of the tabletop boards to receive under private glyphs and was content to ignore me while I raised Danielle on my wrist board. I spent the next two hours flirting and drifting off to sleep during the minute or two it took Dar to write back.

In the late afternoon, I heard the Lieutenant curse and I woke with a snort. She was scowling at one of the boards.

"Terribly sorry, ma'am," I said.

"Not you," she said. "I need to pop out on a Blandings-related matter. In the extraordinarily unlikely event that one of our ladies needs assistance while I'm gone, ring one bell for Macmurdo and she'll run the call with you. Should that happen, please remind her she's angry at me and not at you."

The ready rescue team was *never* supposed to leave camp, except to rescue our own. I was surprised to hear Lt. Drale suggest it.

"Yes, ma'am," I said.

"One other thing: We may have a visitor before I get back. Show her what hospitality you can. Treat her like a commander."

With that, Drale jogged out the door and launched.

Well, that was Fifth Division for you. I yawned and went to sit on the grass in front of the farmhouse, which was as far afield as ready rescuers were supposed to go. I took a camp chair and set the board for Evac Comm in my lap.

I closed my eyes and put my face up in the sun. A minute later I blinked awake and looked at my wrist board.

An island off the coast, Dar had written. *There are a thousand of them; you'd never know which one unless you'd been there. Have you ever been on a sailboat?*

N, I replied. *Also nvr on island.*

Hah! So you'll have to let me sail. Pines all around the outside of the island, but there's a clearing in the middle. Full of daisies in the spring. Spread a picnic blanket. Devour lunch. Devour you.

Oof.

Told you so. What's yours?

Danielle, who I'd come to admire because she was brave and smart and always concerned over some threat to empirical philosophy at large. We'd spent hundreds of hours talking about history and politics and sigils. Now we couldn't go ten messages without suggesting a way for one of us to ravish the other.

(It's the purest, simplest pleasure I have, thinking about how I'll love you, Dar had written once. *If I have to spend one more minute talking about budget items—even to you—I'm going to scream.)*

I yawned and looked at my board again.

Tell me one! Robert?

Opposite, I wrote. *Wintertime.*

I rubbed my eyes. *3ft of snw on th ground. Cold, but not 20-below. Spend all day buildng snow hut.*

You know how to build an igloo?

Y, a littl one. Line floor w/ wool blankets. Save rabbit skin blanket to pull over top of us. Softest fur you ever—

I caught sight of an incoming flier. She was hovering in a bizarre posture, three-quarters upright, making good headway in spite of it. Not one of ours. She transitioned beautifully into a straight drop landing. Any hoverer good enough to do that ought to be streamlined, flying head-down, not bulling upright through the air. Not unless she had cargo or a passenger that I couldn't see.

Stndby, I wrote to Dar. *Maybe trbl.*

The flier came to a dead hover three inches above the landing field. She unsheathed something long and wooden from a scabbard on her left side.

Rifle?

I sprang to my feet, knocking the Evac Comm board out of my lap and spilling sand on the ground.

The woman's face was covered by a balaclava instead of a standard crash helmet. Not normal. I ran toward the landing field and pulled my belt knife.

The woman settled to the ground, partially taking her weight on the crutch she'd just secured under her arm. She freed a second crutch from her right side and pulled off her mask.

"Ahoy the Fifth!" she called, using the formal Corps protocol for a visiting hoverer, though she was out of uniform.

"Ahoy the flier!" I answered from behind her, slowing to a trot.

She turned and looked at me in a panic—a man running at her with a knife. Then she threw her head back and laughed.

"Fucking hell, but you scared me!" the stranger said. "You have to be Robert Weekes, right?"

I startled at that. "Yes."

"Up Radcliffe, sister! I didn't get a single letter from Jake this past year without some mad story about you."

And then I understood, too, though we'd never met before. She was the best friend of one of my best friends from school.

"Are you Ruby?" I asked.

"I go by my given name these days," she said, making her way toward me on her crutches. She extended a hand and clasped mine. "Edith Rubinski."

"Well, Edith, I'm flying under my father's last name. Robert Canderelli."

"A pleasure, Sigilwoman Canderelli. We should chat after I've seen your local brigadier."

"Gen. Blandings is out today," I said.

"Your lieutenant, then?"

"Also gone for the moment. I'm happy to pass a message along."

"Robert, I say this with all the goodwill in the world and having been a brandy-new Sig-3 not so long ago myself—"

"You need the boss?"

"Yes. I'll wait. And please don't tell me they have you running a squadron all by yourself on your third day in the war."

"Fifth week—and I'm on for ready rescue. Can I offer you a chair, at least? Or something to eat? Fresh powder bag?"

"Chair, yes. Lentil soup, no. Never would be too soon. And I'm perfectly capable of filling my own bag."

"I don't doubt it," I said. "It's gotta be a pain and a half, though."

She lowered herself into my camp chair and laid her crutches on the ground. "It is. Since you're being a gentleman, twenty-eighty mix, twelve-pounder."

I stepped away to replenish her bag. She wasn't at all what I'd expected. Back at school, the girls had whispered over her: Ruby, Radcliffe's finest flier in a generation, who'd signed up for the Corps the day America had declared war and had become one of R&E's best young Sig-1s. Then in August of '17, she'd been called out for a night evac, during which one of the board monkeys back in Le Havre had transposed two numbers in the coordinates for her impromptu landing field. Ruby had set her women down in front of a German bunker instead of an evacuation site. They'd been plastered with machine-gun fire, all of them hit. Despite four bullet wounds, Ruby had grabbed a pair of injured wingmates and managed to get back in the air. She'd just crossed into friendly territory when her powder bag failed—soaked through with blood. She'd tried an emergency landing in a British trench, only to be shot by a panicky sentry and go down in no-man's-land instead. She'd laid there for hours, tangled up with the bodies of her comrades as they bled to death. She'd nearly died herself before the British troops rescued her in the predawn light.

Ruby had suffered shattered legs, a broken back, broken ribs, a broken nose, and broken bones in her face. It was a miracle that she'd survived, much less to be able to walk in any form. (To say nothing of flying.) At Radcliffe, Jake hadn't been able to speak more than a few words about her without getting teary.

It was the sort of nightmare that could happen to any of us in R&E on any mission. I figured that if I'd gone through all that, I would have been bitter or shaken or empty. But there was a lightness to Edith, a vein of joy that ran through her.

I carried the powder bag back to the farmhouse.

"You did say twenty-eighty mix, right?" I asked as I handed it over.

She grimaced. "Yeah. It burns me up to say it, but what would I do with a higher-powered mix? My legs droop too much to manage anything more than a three-quarters stance."

"Did that happen when you . . . ?"

I stopped myself. If it had been me, an accident like that would have been the last thing I ever wanted to talk about.

"Yes, it happened when I *crashed*," Edith said.

I tried not to flinch at the word. Fliers had a morbid fear of calling it by its right name. We might say someone *went down* or *dug a hole* or *bought the farm* or *experienced an unexpected encounter with the ground*. But never *crashed*.

"You gonna tell me I'm brave?" Edith asked. "People love to tell me I'm brave for flying after breaking my back. You have that look."

"No," I said, though I *had* been on the verge of saying something a lot like it. "I was going to ask if you invented that landing you did today. That was brilliant."

"Thank you! I did invent it. Maybe some of the other women who bought a piece of it land the same way—God knows there are enough of us. I ought to give it a cute name. The halt and hobble."

Were you allowed to joke about something like that?

"The touch and crutch," I suggested.

Edith howled at that, a yipping, barking laugh like a coyote's. "Oh you're naughty! No wonder Jake liked you."

She sighed, closing her eyes and holding her face up in the sun, as I'd been doing before she landed. She had a beaky nose that had healed crooked, her front teeth were chipped, and she had the worst case of helmet head I'd ever seen, a short flier's bob with frizzy black hair sticking out in every direction. Dark circles under her eyes like she hadn't had a full night's sleep in a couple years. But with the light streaming down on her she looked—well, am I allowed to use the phrase that every soldier ever evacuated uses and say, *like an angel*? Like the working older sister of one of the heavenly host, then.

"Have you heard much from Jake?" Edith asked me.

"She tried to send me liquor while I was in training," I said. "They confiscated the bottle, but gave me the letter. She's back home in Baltimore working for her dad. There were a lot of words in her note, but they didn't say much."

"Yes, that's a Jake letter exactly," Edith said. "She's the assistant distribution manager for Mid-Atlantic Logistics for Harnemon's Philosophical Supplies."

"That's a mouthful," I said. "I never imagined her as a businesswoman."

"You knew her mostly in the aerodrome?"

"Yeah," I said.

"She was a different woman away from the other fliers. None of the clowning. Good student. Serious woman. Put her with a couple of hoverers, though . . ."

"Hell-raiser in chief."

"*Exactement*," Edith said. "I miss her. She was the prettiest flier I ever did see. Almost pretty enough to make me jealous."

It was faint praise of the sort that only one R&E flier could say to another. A pretty flier was fast, graceful, and had an intuitive sense of her body in the air. A pretty flier did not read books about rigging or practice landing under fire or understand how to position the body to minimize instability while carrying two unstasied wounded men who were screaming and bucking. A pretty flier did not learn how to fly all over again while carrying a pair of crutches strapped to her sides.

"I'm jealous of Jake like I'm jealous of a hummingbird," I said. "Weighs a tenth of an ounce and doesn't take passengers."

Edith grinned. "She never warned me you were a poet. Just a damned good ugly flier."

I smiled too. "Nobody here's willing to admit the 'good' part."

Her smile vanished. "Are they not letting you take evacs?"

"Three hundred seven," I said, glancing toward the chalkboard in the farmhouse. Not that I needed to look.

"Oh, good for you!" she said. "I thought maybe it was a stunt, maybe they'd stick you with the board all day. But 307. Good for you, Sigilwoman."

Her eyes were full and I could guess what she wanted to be doing more than anything.

Lt. Drale passed overhead and landed. We met her in the farmhouse.

"Miss Rubinski," Drale said. "A pleasure, as always."

"Dispatches for you, ma'am," said Edith. She removed a set of sealed folders from her satchel. "I'll save you the trouble of reading them: Fourth Division didn't find anything."

"I didn't expect so," Drale replied. "But Second Division seems to have. About half an hour ago."

"Really!" Edith said.

"Found what?" I asked.

They shared a look.

"He's in on it, right?" Edith asked. "You don't just *happen* to have a Radcliffe man in your division because you're trying to strike a blow for equality of the sexes."

Drale chuckled darkly. "Yes, he's one of us. Mr. Canderelli, we're trusting to your complete silence on this matter. We've had word that a few days ago the German rauchbauers began moving prefabricated heavy smoke forward. A lot if it—millions of cubic yards in barrels. Poison, too. The good stuff that they'll use in their offensive."

"The German Korps was talking about launching their attack straight at Saint-Mihiel and trying to wipe out the entire American army," Edith said. "But they seem to have abruptly changed their mind. They're moving their philosophical materiel back, but we don't know exactly where along the front lines they have it stored."

"Until now," Drale said. "Maybe."

"How sure are you?" Edith asked.

"Fifty-fifty," said Drale. "Second Division spotted a huge convoy of wagons loading barrels in the village of Étain. Unfortunately, the Germans saw our fliers and brought in aeroplanes for cover before we got a good look. We're flying a woman with a Trestor device over it to see if it's radiating philosophical energy. If so, then it's the smoke. And we'll organize a team to grab a barrel or two."

I couldn't even count how many ways that violated international law. Smokecarved weapons were outlawed by the Rouen Conventions; R&E fliers were forbidden from performing reconnaissance on enemy troops; and having corpswomen launch an attack on the Germans to capture smoke was perhaps most illegal of all. We were noncombatant philosophers permitted to be on the front lines only for purposes of rendering humanitarian aid. We were to carry no weapon larger than a knife.

Though I had to admit, the idea of R&E going on the offensive was exciting.

Drale drummed her fingers on the table and watched the message boards for word from the woman with the Trestor device. "The waiting kills me sometimes," she complained. "I need to get myself a nice girl back home, like little brother here. Have her send me smutty messages all day to break the tension."

"They weren't—" I began.

"Is it still Danielle Hardin?" Edith asked.

"Jesus," I muttered, "how does everybody—"

"Don't tease him about it!" Drale said. "Nineteen years old and besotted? That's exhausting work. I've done it myself. Besides, I'd rather it's someone back home and not a girl in the division."

"I knew Danielle," Edith said. "I liked her. Sitting next to her was like having a hurricane in the chair beside you—you were just glad it was on your side."

"That's one way of putting it," I said.

"You're bringing her over to Paris for a couple days when you go on leave, right?" Edith asked.

My love life was at the top of the list of things I didn't want Fifth Division talking about. I could just imagine the talk: *He's Hardin's lapdog. Sit boy! Roll over!*

"I don't know," I said.

"Addie, you should give him a liberty pass when they rest your division," Edith said to Drale. "Your break is coming up, right?"

"If Pershing delays his offensive until mid-September, then, yes, in a couple of weeks," said Drale. "We'll have three days off. Really, I'm not opposed to sending Sigilwoman Canderelli to Paris. We'll have documents we'll want to get to Senator Cadwallader-Fulton and Ms. Hardin could deliver them. It's just that I worry he'll come home pregnant."

I blushed and stammered.

"And he's shy!" Edith sniggered. "That's adorable. Now, lieutenants aren't allowed to give you this kind of advice," Edith said, "but when you get to Paris, the first thing you do is—"

"Got it!" Drale said, pointing at her message board. "The scouts from Second Division got a huge energy spike on those barrels with their Trestor device. They claim they had twelve aeroplanes chasing them and a thousand men on the ground shooting."

"It always feels like a thousand," Edith said. "You're going to make a grab at them tonight?"

"If I can assemble a team in time."

Then Drale looked at me with a thoughtful expression. "Mr. Canderelli, how much do you weigh in boots and skysuit?"

"One ninety," I said.

"You know how to shoot?" Drale asked.

"Yes, ma'am," I said.

"What kind of weapons?"

"Rifle," I said. "Shotgun. Pistol."

"Machine gun?"

"Umm, no."

"Well, nobody's perfect," Edith said.

"Do you care to take the fight to the enemy, Mr. Canderelli?" Drale asked.

I grinned. "Yes, ma'am."

"Then you're off duty. Go sleep until it gets dark."

10

BLANDINGS: Perhaps in the eyes of God, the value of one life is equal to another. But as soldiers, you and I abided by a different arithmetic. May I ask, Captain, in your estimation, how many German civilians was one American serviceman's life worth?

CAPT. DAVIS: It's hard to put a number on it. One of mine was worth more than one of theirs.

BLANDINGS: Would you have risked one of yours to save ten thousand of theirs? Because I was facing the same ratio.

Transcript of the Court-Martial of
Tomasina Blandings, March 15, 1919

AFTER SUNSET, I CROWDED AROUND THE FARMHOUSE TABLE WITH Blandings, Drale, Kiyo, Carmen Delgado, and Eira Eirasdottir, the phlegmatic, unflappable daughter of an Icelandic fisherwoman. Kiyo was loading bullets into a circular ammunition pan for a Lewis machine gun. It was a big, thirty-pound weapon that I couldn't imagine trying to fire while flying.

Kiyo laughed and cracked her knuckles. "This is glorious! I've waited all war to shoot back. They can't even do anything about it. Complain that we attacked them whil e they were moving an illegal weapon?"

"Can you actually hit anything with that?" I asked her.

"Listen to the new girl!" Carmen clucked. "Such a pessimist."

"Eira carries me and I carry the gun," Kiyo said. "I'll have both hands free to shoot."

"Warn her before you open fire," Gen. Blandings reminded Kiyo. "The flash is going to be blinding in the dark."

"Good thing Eira flies better blind than Kiyo does with both eyes open," Carmen quipped. "Miss Takahashi is R&E's finest smokecarver and its worst hoverer."

Kiyo stuck her tongue out at her.

"Ladies, let's get organized and get launched, please," said Lt. Drale.

Blandings unrolled a map on the table and we leaned over it.

"According to our friends in Second Division," Blandings began, "at least two hundred wagons loaded with barrels left the village of Étain late this afternoon. They were traveling on the main road toward the city of Metz, where the Germans have their railroad terminus. They'll reach Metz by morning and then they'll be able to ship their smoke anywhere on the Western Front. We may not get another chance to capture a barrel if we don't do it tonight."

Blandings marked the position of the two towns, thirty miles apart.

"Reportedly, the convoy is well guarded, but the wagons will be spread out over a mile or two," Blandings continued. "Lt. Drale will use the Trestor device to identify a barrel with the German poison in it, which is our primary goal tonight. Robert will carry the Lieutenant so that she can operate the device. Eira will carry Kiyo with the Lewis gun to provide fire support. Carmen will dash in to make the grab. How long will you need on the ground, do you think?"

Carmen laid a sling made from a thick band of reinforced cotton webbing on the table.

"Thirty seconds, tops," she said. "I loop this around one of the barrels, cinch it down, and we're gone."

"My biggest concern is that they have aircraft escorting the column," Gen. Blandings said. "We should send one more woman with sticky bombs to attack them, if it becomes necessary. I could ask Millen to—"

"Absolutely not," Drale said. "Millen almost got me killed the last time I took her on a raid. We'll go just the five of us. Have Carmen take some grenades and give a couple to Robert. We'll handle it ourselves."

Blandings unlocked a chest full of strange-looking gadgets. The ends were metal spheres the size of a softball, connected to a two-foot-long piece of metal tubing. There was a half-dollar-sized ring on the sphere and a second ring on the end of the pipe.

"We developed these during my time in Nevada," Blandings said. "It's one pound of high explosive covered in birdlime, with a metal shell over top. When you see your target, pull the front ring to detach the shell . . ."

She yanked the ring on the ball and the cover fell away in two pieces.

"Then when you want to start the fuse, pull the ring on the handle and slap it against the aeroplane. The adhesive will keep it in place. Ten seconds. A pound of nitroglycerine is devastating when you're flying a rickety balsa-wood-and-cloth contraption full of gasoline."

"Got it," I said.

"The glue is *really* sticky," warned Carmen. "It sticks to hands, shirts, hair . . ."

"I understand how glue works," I replied.

Blandings gave me two of the long-handled bombs and I strapped them to my harness.

"Do you have moral objections to carrying a sidearm?" Drale asked me, opening a second chest with several pistols inside.

A flicker of doubt passed through my gut, brief but painful as a cramp. The last time I'd carried a gun I'd killed a man. No question it had been justified, but I'd hated the way it made me feel. That was not what I'd come to France to do. And yet I couldn't say no. Not in front of my wingmates.

"No objections when I'm carrying bombs," I said, taking a large, beautiful Colt automatic.

"He killed Maxwell Gannet with a .22 caliber," Carmen snickered. "God knows what'll happen if you give him a .45."

(Every philosophical tabloid had carried lurid accounts of my gunfight at

Radcliffe the previous spring. They'd invented lots of interesting details, but all of them had reported correctly on the minuscule gun I'd been carrying.)

"I'll make a larger hole," I said.

We needed only twenty minutes to reach Étain, on the German side of the lines. I carried Lt. Drale on my chest and she carried the Trestor device, a metal box the size of a suitcase that could detect philosophical energy. Strapped to my back, I had eight giant lead-acid batteries on a special reinforced harness to power the machine.

Drale ordered me to circle the village while she scanned. The Trestor device picked up only a quiver or two of philosophical energy—probably a German soldier sending a message home on an illicit message board.

"They didn't leave anything behind," Drale said. "Let's head up the road toward Metz and see if we can catch them."

Twelve miles on, we came across three wagons that had been unhitched from their horses and were covered with tarps. A handful of soldiers were guarding them, some of them sleeping under the wagons, others sitting around a fire. They'd unhitched the wagons from their horses. We fell into a loose huddle in the air to confer.

"That can't be it, can it?" Carmen whispered.

"It should be a huge convoy with hundreds of wagons," Drale said.

"Those ones broke down, maybe?" I suggested. "Or got stuck?"

Drale lit a fresh safety flare for light and aimed the Trestor device toward them. The needle on the machine's gauge bounced merrily.

"They've got something, all right," she said.

"I wouldn't bite," Kiyo said. "It's probably just a few barrels of the condensed smoke that they'll use as a carrier for the poison. If I spent forty years developing a philosophical poison, I wouldn't leave it in the care of these distinguished gentlemen."

Two of the soldiers below had begun singing a drinking song. The rest were laughing.

We flew farther up the road. After a few miles more, we heard aeroplane engines and then spotted three of them ahead of us, circling low above the ground, lit up by electric lanterns. Beyond, we could see a large convoy: hundreds of wagons and motor trucks guarded by at least a thousand infantry—the women from Second Division hadn't been exaggerating. A few platoons of women in plain gray dresses marched beside them. Rauchbauers.

"Now *that's* how I'd move it," Kiyo said.

Drale adjusted the Trestor device. The needle swung all the way to the top of the scale and stuck there: smokecarved material, huge amounts.

"We can't attack that many," said Carmen. "Even with all of Blandings's friends, we wouldn't have enough women. And they've got their own smokecarvers. They're not going to break and run over a couple of Lewis guns and some grenades."

"Tell Blandings to bomb it," Eira suggested. "She's got all those artillery rounds stashed in camp. Send somebody up to drop them. It'll bring the whole convoy to a stop. Kill a lot of them on the ground."

"No!" Carmen said. "That'll bust open a bunch of barrels filled with plague and it'll spread all over the countryside. That would be a disaster."

"What about the first group of wagons?" I asked. "The broken-down ones. Those would be easy to hit."

"It's just heavy smoke," said Drale. "It's useless."

"No, Robert's right," said Kiyo. "It's a lot better than nothing. When the Germans attack, they're going to need millions of cubic yards of plain heavy smoke to act as a carrier for their poison. Our smokecarvers can attack the plain stuff, too, but they'll need to know the structure so they use the right kind of dispersant. If we can get ahold of it, the ladies at Radcliffe will want samples—I'm a hundred percent sure."

"That sounds worth the risk, then," Drale said. "I saw about six men guarding those wagons?"

"Yeah, I counted six," Carmen said. "Listen, I flew air assault for Blandings in Nevada—we practiced this sort of thing. I'll fly down the middle of the road and drop flares to light it up, then Kiyo shoots the hell out of them.

I'll set down on one of the wagons and grab a barrel. Kiyo and Eira will cover me from the air. Thirty seconds for me to nab a barrel and get back up. We can do it just the five of us. Bernice is going to throw a fit if half the division sneaks out in the middle of the night to help."

"I like it," said Drale. "I'll check with Gen. Blandings to get the—"

The whine of one of the aeroplane engines changed in pitch as it went to full throttle and came around toward us. We looked toward Drale's safety flare, which was still lit.

"Shit!" she said and threw it away.

The plane continued climbing and opened fire.

"Scatter!" shouted Drale.

Burdened with the extra weight of the batteries, plus Drale and the Trestor device, weapons, and extra ammunition, I was much less maneuverable than usual. I drew sigils to drop away and duck under the plane.

"No!" Drale snapped. "Up! You can always outclimb him."

I reversed and pushed straight up to one thousand feet before leveling out. I saw several more bursts of gunfire, now well below us, as the aeroplane turned to chase the safety flare, which was fluttering to the ground.

"Jesus," said Drale. "I never thought the day would come when an aeroplane could sneak up on me. We're a lot faster than him, so as long as everyone—oh, Christ!"

We heard the distinctive chatter of the Lewis machine gun. Short bursts of eight or ten rounds.

"Is that Kiyo?" I asked.

"She's never going to hit him in the air with that!" Drale said. "Not in the dark, not unless Eira has them right on top of him. We need to get everyone out of here before someone gets hit by mistake."

Another longer burst and another. Then one more volley, a flash, and flames. The aeroplane engine howled and a trail of fire streaked across the sky. A moment later we heard a boom and saw a plume of burning gasoline splash across the ground.

Drale shook her head.

"Hell," she said. "We've done target practice a couple times. Kiyo was good, but I never imagined she could hit one."

Below us, the German convoy was springing into action. They threw out their own hot-burning magnesium flares for light. An artillery piece we hadn't even noticed fired a star shell for illumination, which burst beneath us. I added another couple thousand feet of altitude.

The German philosophers lit smudge pots that put out plumes of dense black smoke. They wove and funneled it to form a bubble over the trucks. More star shells burst beneath us.

"Can they see us?" I asked.

"No," Drale said. "Those illumination rounds are designed to light up the ground, not the sky. They're as good as blind looking for us."

The silhouettes of the other two planes passed below us. A moment later, an explosion rocked one of them, blowing the tail off. The aeroplane spun toward the earth and slammed into the ground. No fire this time.

"Carmen?" I asked.

"Probably. I don't want our people messing around any longer—someone's going to get hurt. Let's get those first wagons before the Germans have the chance to bring up reinforcements."

"Okay," I said.

I lit a pair of blue safety flares and attached them to my ankles to signal *Form up*. It would give away our position, but the aeroplane was only half as fast as we were—if it even dared to follow. I took us back along the road toward the three broken-down wagons. Eira and Carmen lit up, too, and pulled in close to us. We coasted to a stop a half-mile before the soldiers' cookfire.

"Did you shoot the bastard?" Carmen asked Kiyo, laughing darkly.

"Eira got me right next to him," Kiyo said. "*Right* next to. The last burst went into the cockpit. I think . . . shit, I hit him in the face."

"So, you and I can go to confession together," said Carmen. "The sticky bomb was perfect. I've got more. I could go back and get the last one. It's a biplane, a big one."

"We're not going to win the war by taking down planes," Drale said. "Let's grab a barrel and get out."

We drifted farther down the road until we had a clear view of the wagons. The guards were roasting sausages over their fire.

"Could they make it any easier?" laughed Carmen.

"They're drunk?" I suggested. "Or they don't understand what they're guarding?"

"Let's do it and be gone before they reinforce," Drale said. "Go!"

Carmen kicked forward, speeding toward the wagons. She lit a handful of flares and scattered them as she passed over the soldiers. Then she snap-turned and climbed away.

The Germans fled. Kiyo and Eira flew a pass, firing the Lewis gun after them. I couldn't see anyone else coming up or down the road. We'd taken them by surprise.

Carmen set down and ran up to the last wagon in line. She pulled back the tarpaulin covering the bed. It was empty.

"Nothing!" she shouted up at us.

She jogged up to the middle wagon, but that one was empty too.

"Oh, come on!" muttered Drale.

Carmen made her way to the first wagon in line and pulled back the cover. It was full of metal barrels.

"Got it!" she shouted.

She secured her sling around one and tried to launch but the barrel didn't budge. She set right back down.

"Too heavy!" she shouted. "Not smoke."

She knocked on the barrel and it thunked dully, instead of echoing. The next one thunked too. The three after that rang hollowly. Smoke or empty?

"Hey, Lieutenant," Carmen called. "Point your machine at one of these and tell me if I'm taking a good one!"

"Put us down," Drale said to me.

I swung around to the end of the convoy and touched down hard, under the weight of Drale and two hundred pounds' worth of batteries. I was pleased as hell not to have ended up flat on my ass. The landing had been more dangerous than getting shot at.

"Nicely flown, Robert," Drale said and unhooked from my harness.

Carmen knocked on the final barrel in the front wagon and got another low thunk. Then there was a flash of light and a deafening roar.

11

I have learned there are at least twenty-one different flavors of panic. Many of them are useful.

Comfort Tyndale, *Reflections on the Franco-Prussian Intervention*, 1888

I CAME TO ON MY BACK. LT. DRALE WAS LYING ON TOP OF ME, STUNNED. My ears were ringing.

Kiyo stood over us, shouting something. Eira ran up behind her, pointing upward, also shouting.

They pulled Drale off me and dragged her under the last wagon in line.

I blinked and tried to get up. I couldn't. Something was wrong with me.

Kiyo came back and put her face right in front of mine. I could see her lips moving: *Some. Smoke. Five. Minutes.*

"What?" I shouted back.

Drale was lying on her side in the fetal position, beneath the wagon, palms pressed against her ears.

Smoke, Kiyo shouted. She thrust the Lewis gun at Eira, who was pointing to the sky. Eira extended a hand like a wing and mimed a dive.

"What?" I shouted. I touched my left ear. My fingers came away streaked with blood.

Eira pointed at the sky, her Lewis gun, and the sticky bombs on my harness. She pounded her fist into her chest: *The third aeroplane is coming. Me with the gun, you with the bombs. Kill it.*

I tried to stand up, but still couldn't get off the ground. I felt like I weighed four hundred pounds.

Eira pulled out her belt knife and sawed through the pockets on the back of my harness, pulling out the oversized batteries and heaving them away. She hauled me to my feet.

"I think my hearing's coming back!" I said. I couldn't tell whether I was yelling or not.

"Can. You. Fly?" Eira shouted. "Bomb. The. Plane."

"Let's get out of here," I countered.

"Kiyo's. Getting. Samples."

Kiyo *was* the best smokecarver in the division—she might be able to collect a trace amount of the German smoke still hanging in the air.

"Is Carmen gone?" I asked.

Eira nodded.

"Get up," she yelled. "Tag him!"

My hands worked. I could see, though the flares on the ground were blinding. My regulator was functioning. My powder bag was intact.

I drew sigils and launched.

From the air, I saw a crater where the front wagon had been and understood what had happened. The Germans must have faked a breakdown and loaded the wagon with barrels packed with explosives—maybe run a wire off to the side of the road where one of the soldiers had been waiting with a plunger box to set it off. Leave a couple barrels with common heavy smoke to lure us down. We'd flown right into their trap.

Kiyo was standing in the crater, taking smoke from a canister on her harness, drawing sigils on it, folding and refolding her material into a netlike structure. Trying to capture wisps of the German heavy smoke. The middle wagon in the row had been overturned. Eira was standing next to it, working to secure the heavy Lewis gun with a strap so that she could fire one-handed and get into the air.

I climbed higher, but couldn't see the German aeroplane. Below me, Kiyo finished her smoke construct and sprinted out of the crater to take cover under the last wagon with Drale. Eira took a knee and braced the Lewis gun against her shoulder, aiming.

I finally spotted the aeroplane as it lowered its nose to open fire, spraying bullets toward the wagons. Eira returned fire, then did a three-step running launch and flew clear.

I couldn't tell if Kiyo or Drale had been hit, but I wasn't about to let the aeroplane come around for a second pass. I matched course with the big biplane and caught up to it, sidling in from behind. Just slap the sticky bomb against the tail. Easy, provided I didn't slam into the aeroplane myself.

I yanked one of the grenades off my harness and pulled the ring on its head. The metal shell popped free, exposing the glue-covered sphere of high explosives. I drew it across my body, getting ready to slap it against the plane, but it brushed against the crotch of my skysuit, sticking to the fabric.

"No!" I said and tugged at it. It was stuck fast.

"Come on!" I yelled, frantically trying to work it free.

It wouldn't come off.

Stupidest way to die ever! *The Corps regrets to inform you that your paramour . . .*

Then I remembered the ring on the handle. I hadn't started the fuse. It wouldn't go off.

"Christ," I whispered.

The plane had come around into position for a second attack. Below me, Eira was parked in the air over the road with the machine gun. She opened up on the aeroplane, firing wildly without a way to support the weapon.

The plane shot back, then lost its nerve and veered away without attacking the wagons.

I saw a red safety flare ignite—Eira signaling *Bad*. Wounded? Or out of ammunition? She climbed rapidly, heading west, back in the general direction of camp. That left just me in the air.

I had to take the plane down before it could make another pass at Kiyo and Drale.

I put on speed to follow the aeroplane back around as it lined up for its next strafing run. I slid in behind it and matched speeds. I took a grenade and this time used my teeth to pull the ring and eject the cover, then the ring on the handle to arm it. I reached toward the plane's tail.

One, two, three . . .

The plane hit a patch of rough air and bounced down a few feet.

Four, five, six . . .

Still out of reach.

Seven, eight . . .

"Fuck!" I said and lobbed the grenade at the plane's fuselage. It stuck just behind the cockpit. I dove and the bomb exploded, ripping the aeroplane in half and spraying a shower of burning gasoline into the air. The front half of the plane cartwheeled through the air and smashed into the ground, erupting in flames. The tail landed with a thud.

I let out the breath I'd been involuntarily holding. I was shaking.

I circled back to the wagons and landed.

"Up the Fifth!" I shouted.

Kiyo popped out from under the last wagon. "Robert!" And then she got a look at me. "Jesus, Robert, you've got a bomb stuck to your pants!"

"I know! It's not armed."

Kiyo drew her sheath knife and grabbed the waist of my skysuit.

"Careful!" I said.

The handle was sticking out two feet in front of me, like a bad joke: *Is that a grenade or are you just happy to see me?*

Kiyo gave a half laugh, half sob and took hold of it, cutting away the crotch of my skysuit to free it.

"Do you wear anything underneath?" she asked.

"Shorts," I said.

"Well, thank God for that. Don't get any ideas."

She finished cutting and pulled the bomb away, still stuck to a swatch of fabric. She pulled the ring on the handle and flung it into the bushes. We took cover behind the wagon.

"What did you do that for?" I asked.

"We don't want to leave it lying around. If the Germans find it, then they've got physical evidence we were here."

The bomb exploded in the bushes. We heard a couple of shouts. The German soldiers who'd been guarding the convoy hadn't fled far.

"Let's get out of here," I said to Kiyo.

She pulled her smoke net out of the crater and stuffed it into its canister with traces of the German heavy smoke adhered to it—we hoped.

I dragged Lt. Drale out from under the wagon.

"Did we get it?" she groaned.

"Sort of," Kiyo said.

"Was Carmen hurt?"

Kiyo glanced at me.

"I'll tell you later," Kiyo said. We hauled Drale to her feet and buckled her into the front of my harness.

"Ready?" I asked Kiyo.

"Where's Eira?" she asked.

"She lit up and ran for home," I said. "Out of ammunition. Or wounded."

"She was my ride!" Kiyo said. "We didn't rig me with a bag."

"I was hauling those batteries. I don't have a double-passenger harness."

"You're sure as fuck not leaving me!"

Rifle fire broke out from the bushes. I drew my pistol and shot back into the darkness. Make them keep their heads down at least.

"Piggyback," said Kiyo.

The soldiers opened fire again, more sustained this time.

Kiyo grabbed me from behind, both arms around my neck, and wrapped her legs around my waist. Precarious as hell. I launched and sputtered along the road, trying to fly belly-down so Kiyo wouldn't slide off.

"Concentrate on flying," Kiyo shouted. "I can hold on all night." The way her knees were digging into my sides, I didn't doubt it.

"I don't know where we're going!" I yelled. "Lieutenant, do you know the compass headings home?"

"She's dead, isn't she?" Drale mumbled, only half-conscious.

I set us down and looked at Drale's map.

"Étain isn't even on it," Kiyo said, her voice trembling for the first time. "We're never going to—"

"Don't say that," I said. I measured with my fingers. "I'm going to call camp forty miles to our south-southwest. We'll message ahead, ask Blandings to launch a couple fliers all lit up with flares and then light the hell out of the landing zone. Okay?"

"Okay," said Kiyo. She cut the straps from my holster so that she could tie her harness to mine.

"You care if I go forward-facing?" she asked.

"However you want," I said.

We launched again with Kiyo more soundly attached to my harness, though she kept her arms around me in a bear hug. To ensure stability, maybe—though I could hear her crying and I didn't mind having someone hold me. I managed a couple of messages to Blandings and tried to keep us on a steady course.

After twenty minutes, we spotted a flier in the distance lit up like a Christmas tree—a dozen green and red safety flares attached to arms and legs. Punnett.

I fired Drale's revolver into the air and Punnett found us.

"Not terrible," she called. "You only missed Commercy by two miles." And then she saw the state of us. "What happened? Where's everyone else?"

12

> Radcliffe College is a hotbed of anarchism, Sapphism, and freethinking that threatens every aspect of our efforts in France. Constraining its agents should be a top priority.
>
> Gen. Gillian Fallmarch, transcribed message to
> Gen. John J. Pershing, May 8, 1918

KIYO AND I SAT WITH GEN. BLANDINGS, GOING OVER EVERY DETAIL of the ambush and our counterattack. Blandings kept up a veneer of cold professionalism throughout. Only at the end of our interview did her facade fall away, leaving the general looking weary and heartsick.

"You both performed bravely tonight," she said. "What happened to Carmen was awful. And it was awful that you saw it. The responsibility for that lies with me, not you."

Blandings composed herself.

"Kiyo, as soon as you're able, I'd like you to begin analyzing the smoke you collected. The rauchbauers may have decided that Étain is the wrong place from which to launch their offensive, but they're repositioning somewhere. The sooner we know how to efficiently destroy their heavy smoke, the better."

"I'll do what I can," Kiyo said, "but I don't have a real chemistry lab here. We need to get a sample back to Radcliffe."

"That will be complicated," Blandings said. "The Corps has been searching sigilwomen crossing back to America on the transatlantic transporter chain. We'll have to consider how best to hide the smoke. In the meantime, we should see to Mr. Canderelli's ear. Kiyo, do you think you could—"

"That's beyond what I can fix. He needs Bernice. Even if he gets a lecture."

Bernice Macmurdo carried her leather smokecarver's bag into the mess tent and rummaged through it in the lantern light. It brought back every bad memory of the doctor and dentist, especially as she pulled out her instruments: tweezers, forceps, a finely honed paring knife, crochet hooks in four sizes, a long, curved needle, and an assortment of glass vials and ampoules filled with smoke that swirled and writhed under its own power.

"It's better if you don't look," Macmurdo suggested, as I grew progressively paler eyeing her tools.

"I'd rather know what I'm up against," I said.

Punnett brought in a basin of hot water.

"We had word from Eira," Punnett told us. "She got hit in the shoulder and the leg. She got lost, but she spotted Reims and set down in the town square. The night watchmen tried to arrest her before he figured out what she was."

"Well, thank God for small blessings," Macmurdo said. "Louise, dear, would you wait outside? Shoo everybody else away."

Macmurdo took a large metal syringe from her bag and drew up warm water into it. She spread a towel over my shoulders. I flinched as she touched my ear.

"I'm just washing it out," she explained. "I won't do anything to surprise you."

She sprayed the water into the outer part of my ear, loosening dirt and dried blood, which she wiped away with the towel. She worked deliberately and the steadiness of her hands against my face calmed me. Not her first day in the war.

"How bad is it?"

"Looks like a piece of shrapnel slashed it open from the top all the way down to the canal. Just about ripped half your ear off." She picked up a big pair of needle-nosed pliers. "Hold real still."

She inserted the pliers into my ear and caught hold of something. She pulled. I gritted my teeth and tried not to fidget.

"Any chance of doing a stasis?" I asked, panting. "Numb it up?"

"If I put a stasis on your ear, I can't sew it up. The sigil protects against the needle."

She pulled again and I yelped. Fresh blood trickled out of my ear. Macmurdo dropped a jagged, half-inch metal fragment on the table.

"You want to keep that as a lucky charm?" she asked. "Because if it had gone an inch deeper, it would have hit your brain. *That* I can't sew back together."

She pinched the gashed part of my ear between two pieces of gauze to slow the bleeding. A wave of nausea hit me. The pain was only part of it. The cumulative weight of everything over the last few hours—aeroplanes shooting at us, a grenade stuck to my skysuit, the barrels in the wagon exploding. The dark. I put a hand over my eyes. I didn't realize how badly my body was shaking before I tried to move.

"Sweetie?" Macmurdo said. "Are you still with me?"

"I'm going to be sick," I said.

Macmurdo cracked open a tube of smoke and held it under my nose.

"Take a snort," she said.

I inhaled. The vapor didn't have a smell but it did something to me—like all the muscles in my face twitched at once and caught fire. When the sensation passed, the nausea had dulled.

"Better?" she asked.

I nodded.

"If you're kind enough to forgo puking on me," Macmurdo said, "I'll tack your ear back together. It's not going to look pretty."

"I'm already not pretty."

"It might be better to send you to the Corps hospital up in Le Havre. Have a surgeon do it. You could get yourself a couple days of rest in the bargain, too."

"I'd rather . . . I don't want to leave after . . ."

"After what happened. You want to stand with the women who stood next to you."

Macmurdo began combining smoke from two of the vials. She used a pair of miniature crochet hooks to draw her sigils and pull wisps of the smoke together. A fabric-like strip began to take shape. Half the threads were red and half were yellow.

"You know, I have twenty-five years in R&E," Macmurdo said as she worked. "And there's only one thing I know for certain: Stand with the women next to you. All the rest—saving the wounded, winning the war—all that's impossible if we don't protect one another. You did that tonight for your sisters. You brought the Lieutenant and Kiyo back to us. I hope someone thanked you."

"You're not supposed to get a thank-you for doing your job," I said.

"Attacking the German army *isn't* your job," Macmurdo replied with elaborate mildness. She let that hang in the air a minute until the threat behind it had taken on shape and form as sure as the smoke between her fingers.

"As for Carmen," Macmurdo continued. "I don't know what to say except that it's a shame. She was a promising young woman."

"I barely knew her," I said.

"Long as you've been here, you barely know anyone. Not Carmen, not me, not Gen. Blandings."

Macmurdo had finished crocheting her square. With the tip of the paring knife, she drew a sigil in the middle of it and the latticework of red and yellow threads merged, turning orange. Macmurdo pressed it to my ear, folding it over to reattach the two pieces of cartilage that had been flayed apart. The smoke was frigid against my skin as it hardened to a consistency like clay.

"Tomasina Blandings is a good talker," Macmurdo said. "She always has been. What's the line right now? She has a secret plan to win the war and needs your help to do it? It's all for the greater good?"

"Something like that," I said.

"Maybe it's true. I hope it is. But I'll tell you one thing: Tommie Blandings won't end the war by playing spy with five girls and a machine gun, but she sure as hell can *provoke* the German army into attacking. You blow up a few biplanes and that's enough to make the Rouen Conventions fall."

Macmurdo picked up a shirt button with a pair of tweezers and swished it in a cup of rubbing alcohol. Then she pressed it into the smoke dressing over the flat part of my ear and held it there a moment. I grimaced.

"How'd you know about the aeroplanes?" I asked.

"You weren't back in camp three minutes and everyone was talking. I don't want to hear what you did. The less I know the better. But if I know, you can bet the Germans do too. How many of them saw you?"

If the ones guarding the convoy had spotted us—and it was hard to imagine they hadn't—then a thousand, at least.

"Blandings will get the Corps pulled into the fighting," Macmurdo said. "That's her real goal: Remind the good people back home how badly they need the Corps when it all goes to hell. She's done it before. She's responsible for the Spanish-American War. Your mother was one of the corpswomen in Cuba in '97—you ought to understand it better than most. Did your mom ever explain to you what she was doing over there?"

Ma had talked very little about her mission in Cuba, which had taken place a few weeks before the official declaration of the Spanish-American War. I knew what everybody else knew.

"They went to scout landing fields," I said. "It was a humanitarian mission. There was a rebellion—the Cubans rising up against the Spaniards. It had been going on for years. Everyone knew America might get involved. R&E was maybe going to evacuate casualties, Spanish and Cuban both. But then the Spaniards attacked them."

"They were set up," Macmurdo said. "The Spanish knew they were coming. Those corpswomen were *supposed* to be attacked. That was the whole point."

"What?" I asked.

"Gen. Yeates led the Corps at that time. She was a fine battlefield commander, but she had no sense of politics. There was talk in Congress of disbanding the Corps—why spend money to have a lot of women in uniform when we weren't even allowed to use them? So, Yeates needed a war. Moreover, she wanted a war in which philosophers on a mission of mercy had been attacked and thus the Corps was allowed to fight back under the terms of the Rouen Conventions. Yeates wasn't creative enough to engineer something like that, but she had lots of bright, ambitious staff officers. One of them was a captain by the name of Blandings. She persuaded Yeates to send over that scouting party, then leaked their location to the Spaniards—said they were spying. The Spanish army killed a bunch of nice, unarmed American ladies on Cuban soil. The newspapers went wild with it—murderous Spaniards. And so Blandings started a war for Yeates. The Corps got to bombard Havana until it surrendered and nobody called philosophical warfare 'irrelevant' again. Blandings got herself promoted to major. She just had to trade a couple dozen sigilwomen and a few hundred thousand civilian dead in the Pacific. I've never asked Tommie if she thinks she got a good bargain."

I considered that a minute. I'd never heard the Spanish-American War explained that way before, but it had the ring of truth to it. As bitterly as my mother had commented on her service with the Corps elsewhere, she'd said almost nothing about her brief mission in Cuba.

Macmurdo checked the smoke patch on my ear. Finding it to be sufficiently solidified, she took up her needle and thread.

"I'm going to sew the button in place," she said. "It'll splint your ear in the right shape."

"Umm," I said, "how do you sew it?" I couldn't imagine any answer I would want to hear.

"Through-and-through the ear."

I closed my eyes and tried to steady my breathing.

"Is it too late for me to say I want to go to Le Havre?"

I felt the needle pierce through the cartilage of my ear and I cried out.

"It's going to be four stitches," Macmurdo said. "Then four more for another button on the other side."

"Just do it."

She made stitch number two and I ground my teeth to avoid whimpering. Macmurdo pressed a piece of gauze to staunch the fresh bleeding from the hole she'd just made.

"That's Blandings's story to tell," Macmurdo said. "Maybe your mother's story to tell. What I *ought* to tell you is my own family's story. It's an older one. About what happens when you mix philosophy and war. There are few enough left who've seen it."

"Tell it then," I said, swallowing down a mouthful of saliva. Anything for a distraction.

"I had kin in Atlanta, back during the Civil War," Macmurdo said. "My grandmother was a slave until Mrs. Cadwallader's army took the city and burned it to the ground. Then she was free. She was part of the mob that followed the Corps on its march to the sea. Some of them thought Cadwallader was a goddess or the Devil or Jesus Christ come back to earth in the guise of a woman."

Macmurdo made another stitch and the pain in my ear was so intense that I saw flashes of light, even with my eyes shut.

"Granny followed the Corps all the way to Petersburg, Virginia. She witnessed the battle there—or the slaughter, whatever you like to call it. For months afterward, she told every person she met, 'Don't plow or plant this year, because we're living in the end times. I've seen the plague from Revelation, I've seen how the world will end.' "

She took the second button up in her tweezers and sterilized it in the alcohol, then sewed it to the back of my ear, which was numb with pain.

"The 'end times,' " Macmurdo spat. "That was a piddling little massacre of forty thousand souls with old-fashioned heavy smoke and a few drums of chlorine gas. Cadwallader whipped it up in twelve hours. If you want to know what the Apocalypse will look like, it's whatever plague the Germans have spent the last forty years working on. It's whatever Gen. Fallmarch has stockpiled in Le Havre. We ain't going to stop it with a couple dozen women, but we may well bring it about."

Macmurdo packed gauze around my ear and wrapped the dressing in place with a roller bandage.

"I pray Blandings is what you think she is," Macmurdo said. "But if she's not—"

Macmurdo taped down the end of the bandage. "You're a smart kid, Robert. Smart enough to understand that you don't meddle where you could cause the end of the world."

Blandings designated me temporarily out of action. I slept through the remains of the night and the whole next day.

Macmurdo's warnings had done their work: Half my dreams were about inadvertently triggering the Apocalypse. Sitting in the farmhouse, plotting the next raid, when all around us flames boiled up out of the earth, intelligent fire that crept up the walls and moved to block the exits, sending plumes of smoke bouncing and laughing toward us. The whole world in flames.

My fault. Our fault. A thousand Germans had seen our handiwork. We'd left behind the batteries and Lt. Drale's Trestor device. If the German army wanted to say that the Corps had violated the Rouen Conventions and that they were justified in launching an attack that would wipe out a million American soldiers and most of France, then they weren't wrong. I was being naive. I was being used in ways I barely understood.

The other half of my dreams were of Carmen silhouetted against the flash of the barrels as they exploded.

I didn't want to think about it. I didn't want to talk about it. But I didn't want to be alone.

I shuffled into the mess tent at the same time as the rest of Second Squadron. They looked awful—Punnett had red eyes and a puffy face.

Andrada, who normally made up for being five foot one with her perfectly erect posture, was slouched over her oatmeal.

There was no Kiyo—she was sequestered away in the farmhouse, working to purify and analyze her samples. No Eira, whom I hadn't known well. She'd liked to sneak up behind people right before they sat down and covertly slide their chair back a couple inches so that they missed the seat and fell on the floor. (She'd gotten me twice.) No Carmen, who'd always gone out of her way to crack up Andrada by yelling dirty jokes across the mess hall in Spanish, which Andrada would have to translate for Punnett. And then, often, translate a second time. (As Punnett's most famous line had gone: "Yeah, okay, but what's the English word for sodomy?")

The only one who looked untouched was Millen. She had the same grim calm, the unchanging sour competence. Sitting alone as ever.

"Robert A," she called and pointed to the seat next to her. She looked me over, not with friendly concern, but more like a farmer who'd loaned her wheelbarrow to the neighbors, only to have it returned damaged.

"Can you fly?" Millen asked.

"Yeah," I said.

"Then we have to have you tomorrow. The squadron's down two women and the Lieutenant's hurt. If you and Kiyo decide you need a couple days off, then second squadron will collapse. If we break, Fifth Division falls apart. Then we all get recalled and split up as replacements to the other divisions. Blandings will have nobody left to spy with. So, tomorrow morning at six: Canderelli, first-up—yes or no?"

"Yes."

"Good. Thank you."

I must have looked stunned to hear her say those last two words.

Millen tried to laugh but she looked more like a cornered animal baring its teeth. "Am I so mean to you as that? You know, I was the sweetest, politest, most demure girl in the world when I came over in '14."

I cleared my throat. "Ma'am, I'm not sure I believe it."

"Well, never demure, then."

Millen stirred a handful of raisins into her oatmeal. "A night like last night will knock the sweetness right off you. I've had a few of them—it's not something I'd have wished on you. All the stories I heard before you came over, I figured you must be the hardest, steeliest-eyed man in the world. Then you turned out to be a sweet young kid."

Much as I wanted to dispute that, I knew there was a time you were permitted to disagree with your Sig-1 and a time when you were obliged to listen.

"I don't know how you keep the sweet on you, Robert A. Punnett cries. Maybe that's the way—washes the evil humors out of the body. I never could. I just close my eyes and fly. I can't promise that'll keep you sweet, but it'll keep you alive if it doesn't kill you. Fly enough evacs and everything else gets buried."

I made thirteen runs the following morning.

Punnett got choked up every time she saw my bandages. Andrada scowled any time I spoke to her, as if I'd been the one who'd killed Carmen. So, Millen and I paired up. We flew and flew.

I came to crave the constant, shocking hammer blows of seeing the wounded, dying, dead: Men hit while scouting enemy fortifications, men with self-inflicted gunshot wounds, men crushed by trenches that collapsed in the rain. For them, you could allow flickers of the feelings you didn't dare have for yourself—regret, horror, rage, terror, the sickly acid splash of recognition that all life ends. For them, we might let slip for a moment the cloaks of cool, numb aloofness we wore to protect ourselves. For them, we might mourn a moment in our profane way—"That poor son of a bitch," "Yeah, poor stupid bastard"—and our faces might do something other than sneer or smirk for a fraction of a second as we said the words.

We backed up the French ambulances at Amiens, where the infantry had broken through at a cost of thirty-eight thousand wounded. Enough stasied bodies to keep us flying for months.

"Enough work to keep you sane," Millen said.

Or some semblance thereof.

13

The sentry in Le Havre is standing guard on a dark night. She hears footsteps approaching. “Halt! Who goes there?” calls she. “Fourth Logistics Wing!” comes the answer. “Pass, the Fourth.” Then footsteps again. “Halt! Who goes there?” asks the sentry. “Medical stasis platoon!” “Pass, the stases.” Then more footsteps. “Halt! Who goes there?” “Mind your own damn business!” “Pass, General Blandings.”

General Jill’s Joke Book, 1917

A FEW DAYS LATER, BLANDINGS INVITED ME TO ATTEND KIYO’S report on the German smoke she’d collected during our raid.

“Nine-tenths of it was residue from the explosives—picric acid and TNT,” Kiyo explained to Blandings, Drale, and me. “But the Germans did have a couple barrels of heavy smoke down in that wagon, enough to set off the Trestor device. I’ve purified a few grams. It’s funny stuff. It’s light.”

“Light heavy smoke?” Lt. Drale asked. She’d recovered enough from her concussion to carry on a sensible conversation, but still had piercing headaches whenever she went out in the sunlight. We expected it would be another week or two before she was fit enough to fly.

“If you don’t mind an oxymoron, yes,” said Kiyo. “Light heavy smoke has a lot of advantages. It’ll flow forward faster and they can mix it with poisons more easily. They just can’t use it to suffocate the enemy directly.”

Blandings nodded. “So, you think they’ll attack over a long distance with a large smoke cloud that has a toxic agent mixed in along the leading edge?"

"That's why I would build it that way," Kiyo said. "But the smoke is knit in the German style. It's closer to what Bernice does than what I do—not that I'm suggesting we show it to her. My best guess is that they have a lot of women sitting at home back in Germany with knitting needles who churn out a yard or two every night. Their better-trained ones baste the sections together and condense it to store it. The true army rauchbauers will mix in the poison when the time comes."

"Can you offer any recommendations on how best to attack it?" Blandings asked. "A dispersant or dissolving agent? Something we could stockpile?"

"I have no idea," said Kiyo. "You'll need a real professional and a real lab."

Blandings and Drale conferred with a glance.

"Radcliffe College it is, then," said Blandings. "Lieutenant, you're confident that your plan for smuggling the samples home will work?"

"Reasonably," said Lt. Drale. "Let's send Edith with him. That'll make it look more credible."

Drale stood. "Mr. Canderelli, rise and put your hand over your heart. As the executive officer of the Fifth Division of R&E, I hereby assign you to detached duty. In order that you may carry out your mission with greater probability of success, as well as in recognition of outstanding service to the division, you are granted temporary promotion to the rank of Sigilwoman First Class for the duration of your special detail."

Drale gave me a hand salute, as did Blandings and Kiyo.

"Congratulations, *ma'am*," Kiyo said with a snicker.

"Sig-1 Canderelli," Drale continued, "you will proceed to Le Havre at best speed. We'll have Miss Rubinski meet you there and the two of you will take the transporter chain to Boston."

It was the sort of duty we dreamed of—no evacs, the possibility of a decent meal, a full night's sleep—but I could barely muster any feeling about it, other than I didn't want to be away from my wingmates. Time to think. Time to reflect. Too much of that and you'd crack.

"Lucky, lucky, lucky!" said Kiyo. "You couldn't send me, too? I did all the chemical analysis."

"No," said Drale. "After that fracas you started in Le Havre the last time you were on leave, I believe the gendarmerie still has orders to arrest you. We can't risk that."

"We'll find something else for you," Blandings assured her. "Robert, I would like to stress that this is a covert mission. You're not to tell your old college friends that you're coming home. Should a picture of you end up on Page Two of the *Tattler*—'General's Cup Medalist Has Wild Night Out on Town'—the only question I'll ask upon your return is whether you'd prefer I send Sigilwoman Andrada or Sigilwoman Millen to kill you in your sleep. Am I clear?"

"Very," I said.

"Godspeed, then. Give Dean Addams my best."

An hour after sunset, I flew out of camp carrying only a light satchel and a twenty-pound powder bag. I headed northwest, passing over the city of Reims, before finding Rouen and turning for Le Havre.

I messaged Danielle while I flew. It was against the spirit of "covert," but we might be able to spend the night together and neither of us was likely to notify the *Boston Globe*. She replied that she was in California with Sen. Cadwallader-Fulton, lending support to a political ally who was running for reelection. Danielle, in her old role as Hero of the Hellespont, was one of the featured speakers at a rally the following afternoon.

Can you wait in Boston a few days? Danielle asked. *We'll be back day after tomorrow. I could see you.*

I thnk 1 day only, I answered.

Why didn't you tell me sooner? I would have stayed behind. This is so disappointing.

Srry. Jst found out.

I almost added a line or two describing the raid that had earned me the time stateside, but Danielle would only have worried over it. I swallowed my disappointment and flew on.

The main Corps installation in Le Havre housed our two thousand smokecarvers, plus clerical staff and messagists, dozens of warehouses packed with supplies, and the final destination sigils for the transatlantic transporter chain. In the warehouse district near the harbor, the Corps had established a permanent landing field for its Logistics hoverers. It was exquisitely maintained; rumor had it a woman went over the grass with manicure scissors once a week. They also had the brightest electric arc lamps in all of Europe for illumination. I couldn't help but feel all that was wasted on a base hundreds of miles to the rear of the fighting. I touched down and the night watchwoman emerged from a guardhouse.

"Ahoy the flier!" she called out.

"Fifth Division!" I answered.

Prior to my departure, Lt. Drale had given me two additional bars of rank for my collar and coaching on how to best converse with the comfortable women who never ventured outside the Corps compound. The fewer questions they asked the better. If they discovered I was smuggling a German weapon of war home for analysis that would be the end of my career, Blandings's conspiracy, and Fifth Division itself.

"Gen. Blandings's compliments, Miss," I said to the watchwoman, who was a mere Sig-3. "I need a guide to the transporter arena."

"Holy hell!" she said. "Are you—"

"I'm a corpswoman with five hundred souls evacuated," I snapped, trying to load my words with the same casual viciousness that Millen would have used, had her authority just been questioned by a woman two ranks beneath her. (And a Sig-3 using a cuss word without prior written approval—tsk, tsk.) "Any rear-echelon messagist who doesn't like it can come down to Commercy and join a working division. Are you volunteering?"

"No sir," she spluttered. "Or ma'am?"

"A superior officer is called ma'am," I said, hitting a note of real menace.

"Yes, ma'am. I'm so sorry. Happy to guide, ma'am!"

She led me toward the transporter arena at a trot.

I felt bad for scaring the girl, but I'd succeeded in avoiding the questions she ought to have asked: What kind of mission brought me in during the middle of the night? Why no advance landing notification? And might I provide my name and destination so that she could log it properly?

We rounded the corner and I saw the rickety old stadium with its wooden bleachers lit up by more arc lamps. It was the same arena I'd come across on the day I'd deployed to France. Outside the main entrance stood a woman in a blue dress and starched white apron, white cap, and red cape. The effect was something like the Virgin Mary meets the Angel of Mercy, especially with the harsh electric lights lending the white cloth an unearthly glow. I had to blink a moment to recognize it as a nurse's uniform. She was standing on crutches.

I dismissed my guide and went up to her.

"Ahoy the Fifth," Edith murmured to me.

"Miss Rubinski," I said. "You look . . ."

I hadn't seen a pretty young lady in a dress instead of a skysuit in months. I could understand how wounded soldiers were forever falling in love with their nurses.

"Oh, quit gawking!" Edith said. "The outfit's one size too small—it's uncomfortable as hell. We keep one around for missions like this."

"It's beautiful," I said.

"Aww. I'll tell Danielle Hardin that you go soft for a girl in a cape. Maybe she'll play dress-up for you someday."

Danielle probably would have if I'd asked, though she would have made the most incongruous nurse on the entire Western Front. I rather liked the thought.

"Keep doing the addled look you're doing right now," Edith said. "That's perfect. Lt. Drale says our cover story tonight is that you were wounded and we're rushing you back to the States for an operation. You had a head injury and lost your hearing."

I took off my helmet. I'd replaced the dressings on my ear before launching, but with the helmet rubbing against it during the flight, I'd bled through the fresh gauze.

"Shit," said Edith. "This is going to be easy to sell. Are you—"

"I'm fine," I said.

"So, just pretend you're hard of hearing. I'll do the talking. They usually transport the wounded home on the morning run, but occasionally the hospital sends a man up with a nurse at night. It should be easy."

Edith sounded like she was trying to convince herself. If we were caught, it would be bad for her, too, civilian or not.

"Drale packaged up the smoke for me special," I said. "They're not going to look at it too close."

We entered the arena and found a sleepy-looking guard in the main corridor.

"Evening," she said.

"This is Sig-1 Canderelli of R&E," Edith explained. "Head injury. Lost his hearing. They want to try surgery on him in Boston in the morning. I'm supposed to get him back tonight. Can we tag along on the midnight service?"

"Yeah, sure," the guard yawned. "They've got men in R&E now, huh?"

"Anyone who can do the work," Edith replied.

"Well, good! It's about time the men started pulling their weight."

Edith handed over the pass that General Blandings had written for us and the guard initialed it. "You're the only ones going back tonight. Just army coffins and empty cargo barrels. Departure time is 00:05."

The guard leaned in close. "You didn't hear it from me, but this transporter team has balked their last two transits. One of them shaved the outer two rows of benches off the stadium last time. Find yourselves a spot real near the center. Try not to spook them. There's a reason we've got them doing the graveyard run instead of taking passengers."

"Terrific," Edith said drily.

The guard turned to me. "Ma'am?" she said, raising her voice. "Excuse me, but I need to search your belongings." She pointed to my satchel. I opened it and passed it to her. She gave the contents a cursory glance—just my harness, a spare skysuit, and my shaving kit.

She started to hand it back, but then held up her hand. On the ground next to her was a Trestor device. She flipped the switch and the machine hummed to life. Edith and I looked at each other in horror: the smoke samples would set it off.

"New procedure," the guard explained. "All personal baggage gets scanned. General Jill's orders."

The guard ran the detector head over Edith's workbag and got no activity. Then she scanned my satchel and the device's needle flickered.

"Are you kidding me?" the guard complained. "Stupid machine."

She scanned my satchel a second time and again got a positive result. She groaned and went through it more thoroughly, this time finding a gelatin capsule in my shaving kit. It was the length of my pinkie and filled with swirling smoke that oscillated from red to purple to blue. The guardswoman pulled out a syringe-shaped applicator as well.

The guard held them in her palm and frowned at them. "Medicated smoke?" she asked Edith. "Is it a pill?"

Edith tapped me on the shoulder and pointed at them.

"Rectal suppository," I shouted. "Reusable."

"Oh, God!" the guard said. She dropped it back in my bag and looked around for something to wipe her hands on. Edith offered her a handkerchief.

"Sorry, ma'am!" the guard shouted at me. "Hope they fix you. Safe trip!"

Edith and I walked out onto the field in the middle of the stadium. A platoon of Logistics fliers was hovering empty powder barrels into a stack so that they could be taken home and refilled. We tried to stand out of the way. Just us, a few thousand barrels, ten transporters, and a hundred coffins.

"God, I thought she saw right through us," Edith whispered to me.

"I'm glad your lieutenant has a scatological sense of humor. How would you make a reusable suppository?"

I hadn't even realized how tense I was until I chuckled at that. "Drale said nobody would think too hard about it."

We sat on crates and watched the transporters, who had huddled in the middle of the field. Each of them had her little black book open to the page with the destination glyph she would be responsible for. Some of them were air-drawing their lines.

"They do one sigil and then get a month off," I said. "How do they make this look so hard?"

"God knows," Edith said. "Do you? Transport?"

"No."

"I thought you might, since you're in love with a transporter and all."

"No. I talked about learning a couple times, but Danielle discouraged me—it's a lot of strain on the body while you're building up resistance. You end up exhausted even if you're only going a hundred yards. Lord knows I had enough to do last year. Do you?"

"No, but I've thought about it, too," Edith said. "It would be useful now. Crosstown hops. My dorm room to the library. Better than crutches or a wheelchair."

I grimaced in sympathy. "You had one semester left to finish at Radcliffe?"

"Yes. I think about going back sometimes and it just . . . it'll be so different."

"Danielle always said so, too. She was only in the service a few months, but most of her friends had graduated when she came home."

"And she came back famous," Edith said. "That must have been hard. You know, I admired her when we were at school together. She was always talking about the big picture, how to unify philosophers from different disciplines. I like the idea of the two of you together. I always figured she'd settle for some rich New Englander who could get her into a country club with a good golf course. I'm glad she found someone more interesting."

I had to rate that as among the two or three kindest things anyone had said to me in months.

We heard the guardswoman ringing a hand bell; she called out to the transporters that she'd walked the perimeter and found it free of obstructions. "Ten out of ten destinations are reporting clear!" she continued. "Draw rapid sequence when ready."

Edith's face tightened. "God, I don't want to think about going back to school," she said. "I'm dreading the way those little society girls will look at me. It's one thing to talk to you—you've been through it. But the first young lady who sat out the war who tells me how *sorry* she feels for me, I'm going to hit her."

She let out a ragged breath. "Thinking about Radcliffe reminds me of what I can't do, instead of what I can. It makes me sad. And sad is fine, but I have things to do right now. I'll have plenty of time to be sad later. So, I try not to think about it."

I was caught off guard by how quickly my emotions went from still to boiling. That someone else felt the same way I did. It made me—

The arc lamps vanished as we jumped to the unilluminated field in London. I gasped, reaching out reflexively to grab Edith's arm. The dark.

"Sorry!" I said. "Sorry."

The only light in the stadium was from the oil lanterns that the transporters had positioned around themselves. I could barely see Edith's face.

"It's okay," she said. "You're okay."

My heart was banging like I'd just sprinted up a hill.

"It happens to everybody on transports, right?" Edith said. "Fliers especially. We're used to being in control. Now we have to trust someone else not to cut us in half."

I tried to pry my fingers off the sleeve of her dress. "It's not that. It's . . ."

She put a hand on my shoulder. The position of the moon changed above us—London to Manchester.

"I heard you had a bad night last week," she said.

"I . . ."

I thought of Millen, burying the bad days with more work, more flying. The model R&E corpswoman: hard, cold, invincible.

"Tell me," Edith said.

We jumped to Scotland.

"I sort of saw a woman get blown up right in front of me."

"And?"

We flipped back to the Faroe Islands.

"And I screwed up an attack on an aeroplane. One of the women on the raid got hit—she was trying to distract him and if I'd gotten him on the first try, she would have been okay. I came real close to killing myself with a grenade."

We jumped back to Iceland.

"And—and I'm going to start bawling if you make me say any more."

"Okay," said Edith. "It's okay."

We made the hop to eastern Greenland, then across to western Greenland. The long jump to Canada would be next. I could hear the transporters talking nervously among themselves.

"And every time I think I've seen all the ways you can mangle the human body or dismember somebody," I said through my tears, "I get to see a new one. And if you talk about it, you're soft. You're the oversensitive little sister. Just shut up and keep flying."

Edith looked at me with sad, warm eyes. "Oh, pal. You're not the only one. Every woman in R&E feels that way."

"They can afford to. Me, I've got to be perfect twenty-five hours a day. Every insult, every indignity—swallow it. Show it and they'll rip me apart and send home the pieces. I feel like I'm losing my mind. And who the *fuck* can I admit that to?"

The transporter in charge of the long jump drew her glyph. One of the women yelped, but neither I nor the stadium had been cut in half. The sun popped back above the horizon—five hours earlier compared to Le Havre.

"Me," Edith said. "You don't scare me."

"I've got no right complaining to you."

"You've got every right. Your war's different than mine was. And I never had to dig my own hole to piss in."

"Yeah," I said and wiped my eyes. "Edith, was there—when you had your bad night, afterward, was there anything you did that helped?"

"No. I didn't do anything. I couldn't. They drugged me in the hospital, all the broken bones, lots of surgeries. Morphine and smokecarved opium for the pain. I had wild dreams. Sometimes I was back there in no-man's-land. I would wake up from the nightmare, only I was still on the cold ground out beyond the trenches, full of holes, tangled between the bodies of my women. A dream inside a dream. And I would wake up and wake up and wake up and be back there every time. When they weaned me off that medicine, I was scared to sleep."

"God," I said.

"After I got my discharge, I didn't know what to do. I didn't want to go home. I went into the wards at the Corps hospital and counseled some of the wounded women, fliers mostly, listened to their stories, tried to lift their spirits. That was good. Then Blandings found me. She gave me interesting work. Useful work. I had the chance to believe in something bigger than myself again."

We jumped to New Brunswick.

"You believe all that?" I asked. "That Blandings is what she says? That it's worth it?"

"It will be," Edith said. "In the meantime, you just got to keep standing with the woman next to you."

She couldn't have voiced an idea closer to my heart.

"Yeah," I said, sniffling. "If I quit, my partner would get stuck with all the shit jobs that I have. My Sig-2 would have to make all the same threats over again to the new girl and she hates repeating herself. My Sig-1 would have to redo the duty roster. And my lieutenant would have to fill out a bunch of forms."

And the next boy who wanted to join R&E—well, if I cracked, then there might never be another. But that was the one I held secret in my heart.

"For God's sake, don't do that to your Sig-1," Edith said. "I feel for her. I used to hate rewriting the duty roster, nasty old commander that I was."

I gave a flicker of a smile. "You couldn't have been a mean Sig-1. Were you?"

"The girls called me Ru-bitch-ski. Seven of them tried to transfer out of my squadron on the same day. It's true!"

I smiled at that.

We jumped to the Corps chain's terminus in Maine.

"Come on," said Edith, and we made our way out into the evening sun.

A wagon hauling coffins gave us a lift to the civilian arena, just in time to catch the last scheduled service of the day to Boston.

"These quick trips back are bizarre," Edith warned me, as we made our way through the bustle of the Boston arena. "It's like looking at the world through grandma's eyeglasses. Everything's warped."

And indeed, I was remembering my first trip through Boston's main transporter station a year before, fresh from Montana, overwhelmed by the noise and chaos.

"Robert!" someone shouted. "Rob!"

He was running toward us, waving. I hadn't realized how much I missed him until I saw him.

14

We are embarking upon a military endeavor, to be sure, but more importantly on an experiment to see if sigils may be created through rational methods. I urge all of you to consider what this could mean, not only for the conclusion of the present conflict but also for the future of humankind.

K. F. Unger, Memo to the Radcliffe Working Group, June 22, 1918

FREDDY UNGER CAUGHT ME UP IN AN EMBRACE. HAD I BEEN A smaller man, he would have lifted me off the ground and danced around in a circle with me.

My old roommate. He was a little plumper, a little paler. Still with his tangle of poorly combed brown hair, his glasses full of smudges, and an outrageous yellow-and-orange bow tie like an exploded marigold. And still with streaks of ink on his face and hands that couldn't be washed away, the result of a serendipitous philosophical breakthrough (or disfiguring accident, depending on your perspective) that he'd made the prior spring.

"Hey there, Freddy," I said as he released me.

"I only heard you were coming home a few hours ago!" he said. "Ms. Addams suggested that I might retrieve you." He thumped me on the back. "Gosh, Robert, it's good to see you!"

People were turning to stare.

"Thanks, buddy," I said to him. "We're trying to keep this quiet, though."

"Oh, no one's going to recognize you with that disguise!" Unger said, pointing to my bandages.

How could I possibly explain it to him? Freddy had been my best friend during my time at Radcliffe. He was the epitome of an inept male philosopher; except for the glyph for temporary permanent ink that he'd accidentally discovered, he'd never gotten a sigil to work. I wanted to protect him like I would have a child—from the reality of R&E, from the war itself. Or maybe it was simple arrogance: I didn't want his pity.

"It's not a disguise," said Edith.

Unger frowned at her in confusion. "Well, I happen to think it's quite an effective . . . oh, dear! Robert, were you injured?"

"Minor," I said, wishing I'd kept my helmet on to hide the bandages.

"Freddy," I said, trying to change the subject. "This is Edith Rubinski. She's a Cliffe, too. Class of '17 originally, before she signed up with R&E. She's the one in disguise."

"So pleased to meet you, Miss Rubinski," Freddy said. "Welcome home to you both! Robert, may I carry your valise for you?"

Much as I didn't want to play the part of an invalid, I allowed him to take my satchel. In fewer than ten steps, Unger managed to snag the strap on a railing and get tangled up with a man walking a Pomeranian.

"That's the boy genius who's inventing the secret plan to win the war?" Edith whispered to me.

"He is?" I asked.

Before I'd left for training, Freddy had mentioned that one of his professors had recruited him to do research for the war effort, but I had a hard time imaging how that would work. Freddy was a fine ideas man, but you'd need to surround him with a bunch of practical philosophers to get anything done. Those kinds of women tended not to take instruction well from nineteen-year-old boys who needed help to retrieve their own messages.

Freddy led us out into the street in front of the station, where I spotted one of Radcliffe's automobiles, an anonymous, overpowered Packard. I recognized the driver a second before she saw us: Ms. Addams herself, the Special Assistant Dean of Empirical Philosophy, who was in charge of the care and feeding of Radcliffe's sigilrists, as well as mitigating death threats and the occasional assassination attempt. She was a severe, stately woman of about forty-five, Harlem-raised, a retired Corps smokecarver who'd fought in the Philippines.

"Dean Addams!" Freddy called.

Addams turned toward us, wearing a rare sardonic grin. "Well if it isn't Big Sister Trouble and Little Bro—"

She caught sight of us and the words died in her mouth. Her first time seeing Edith since she'd suffered her injuries and her first time seeing me since I'd gone over.

"—Little Brother Trouble," Addams finished in a whisper. She looked at us and clenched her jaw.

"I'm old news," Edith said. "Cry over him. He's the one who just ruined his career modeling hats."

"Well, if the hat covers my ear . . ." I suggested.

Addams gave a wan smile at that. "Welcome home," she said.

I helped Edith into the back seat and sat beside her. Freddy climbed in front. He was still bouncing with excitement.

"You'll barely recognize the campus!" he told me. "We've been building left and right. Labs, refineries, a Trestor device the size of a train car. Dr. Brock has masterminded most of it and Dr. Yu, plus a lot of scientists from Harvard and MIT. People from all sorts of different disciplines. It's been fascinating."

"What are you working on?" I asked.

"Goodness!" Freddy said. "Where to start . . . Well, in 1916, Professor Yu came up with some very interesting theories concerning exponential enlargement of—"

"Freddy!" Addams snapped. "No specifics."

"Robert's going to be involved," Freddy objected. "It only seems fair he know about it."

"I'm sure I wouldn't understand anyway," I said.

"You *would* understand," Addams said. "That's the trouble, especially for a man who was close enough to spit on the German army last week."

"In broad strokes, then," Freddy suggested.

"Very broad," Addams allowed.

"We're making a few tweaks to the transport sigil," Freddy said. "Still a work in progress, but we've come a long way."

As we drove onto campus, I was struck by how *unchanged* it looked—the gray hulk of Cadwallader Memorial Library, the bell tower on top of Moss Hall ringing out seven o'clock, the women's philosophical dorm, empty except for a handful of summer students, who were playing a raucous game of croquet on the neatly mown quad. How familiar it all was, how untouched by the war. I wanted to resent them for it. Instead, it struck me as lovely. Uncorrrupted.

Addams parked the car in the alley behind Garden Hall. Across the street, an abandoned stable had been razed and four Nissen huts erected in its place, their half-cylinder, corrugated steel roofs incongruous among the crumbling brick buildings, like a crop of metallic mushrooms that had sprung up overnight. The one on the end had a huge chimney belching black smoke that bulled straight into the wind instead of blowing with it.

"The last one's my lab," Freddy said with a grin. "Though I should perhaps check on that experiment we're running. The output looks rather high. If you'll excuse me . . ."

He leaped out of the car and jogged toward the building.

"Same as ever," I murmured to Addams.

"His lab has burned down twice," Addams complained to me. "We've spent almost a million dollars on equipment for him and Jenny Yu. Though even Dr. Yu doesn't understand some of what Freddy's trying to do. I think there's only one person who does."

Addams and I walked into the office of Radcliffe's Dean of Empirical Philosophy. The lights were off and the curtains drawn. It took me a moment to spot Dean Murchison, sitting cross-legged on the floor, barefoot and with his pants rolled up to the knees. He was petting the wall, murmuring to it in soothing tones.

"Him?" I asked.

"The dean may very well be the finest sigilrist in the world," Addams said.

Murchison stroked his fingertips over one particular brick, as if searching for a ticklish spot.

"I've never seen him do anything more than take apart his furniture and play with ink," I said. And occasionally predict the future with a frightening degree of accuracy.

"He doesn't think like you and me," Addams replied. "Nor does he have a great deal of raw philosophical power—less than you, probably. But he knows where every grain of powder lands when he draws a sigil. It allows him to shape glyphs with a precision that no one else on earth can match. He's the secret weapon."

Murchison gave a quiet, cooing laugh as if the brick had told him a joke.

"It's just that he's also insane?" I asked.

"No!" Addams objected. "He's very well-adjusted for a cartogramancer! They're all like him. Imagine having a sixth sense, an intuitive grasp of distance and position—of where one thing lies in relation to another—so powerful that it drowns out everything else. The idea that there's a piece of sandstone measuring 3.7 inches by 4.2 inches that's buried 14.4 feet beneath your left foot is so compelling that you don't notice a person shouting a question at you from six inches away."

"That's what the world's like for him?"

She shrugged. "It's what I tell myself to keep from murdering him."

The dean was sticking out his tongue to taste the brick that he'd taken a special interest in.

"Lennox," Addams said. "Lennox! Robert's here. Talk to him."

She reached out to shake the dean by the shoulder.

"No!" screamed Murchison, pulling away as Addams's hand made contact with him. "No! No!"

"Sorry!" Addams said. "Sorry. Lennox, relax. Be still."

Murchison needed several minutes to calm down, during which he fixed Addams with a look of betrayal, as if she'd thrown hot oil on him. I'd always heard that a cartogramancer couldn't touch a woman or he'd lose his mind, but I'd never seen it happen.

"Freddy has a lot of theories on *that*, too," Addams says. "He thinks there's some kind of harmonic resonance when a cartogramancer touches a woman that intensifies his natural philosophical ability—the rocks shout louder if I lay a finger on him."

"What does Murchison say about it?" I asked.

"He doesn't. Not to me. Why don't you try chatting with him? A man, even a philosophical one, is safer for him. He's always liked you."

He was scrabbling over the floorboards, trying to catch hold of a piece of wood as if he would pry it up with his fingernails.

"Sir?" I said.

He blew on the crack between two of the boards and plucked out a speck of dirt, which he held next to his ear. I could only think of one sure way to catch his attention. I placed the smoke capsule on his desk.

Murchison leaped up and rushed over to prod at it.

"Wonderful!" Murchison exclaimed. "Oh, wonderful, wonderful."

"Good to see you again, too, sir," I said, amused. "Nobody else has called that stuff 'wonderful'—it's just ordinary heavy smoke."

"Not the smoke," Murchison said, looking up at me for the first time, wearing an expression of confused delight. "That you use both your hands."

"What?" I asked. "Well yeah, I've been working on flying left-handed sometimes. You've talked about that before. Is that important?"

Murchison frowned. "What year is it?"

"Nineteen eighteen," Addams and I said together.

"Oh," Murchison said disappointedly. "We haven't done it yet, then?"

Addams and I shared a look.

"I'm not sure what that means," Addams confessed. "He's been even stranger than usual lately."

"Sir?" I said. "We were hoping you could analyze the smoke. So that we know how to counter the German attack when it comes. Its structure. How best to break it up."

Murchison picked up the capsule between his fingers, considering it this way and that.

"Trivial," he said.

"It's not going to seem trivial when the rauchbauers are rolling a hundred million cubic yards of it toward the American lines," Addams retorted.

"Inessential," Murchison answered and popped the capsule in his mouth, swallowing it.

"Lennox!" Addams shouted. "We were going to study that."

"Don't need to see it," Murchison said. "Internal contact is quite efficacious where structural analysis is concerned."

He took an eyedropper filled with sparkling gray ink from a desk drawer and squeezed a few drops into his palm. They beaded up instead of sticking. He cast them onto a sheet of paper and they skittered and slid across it, like droplets of water on a hot skillet. He trailed a finger through them dreamily, then drew a blazingly fast series of sigils on the paper. The ink coalesced and danced across the paper in a flickering parade of lines and pictures that looked like fragments of mesh.

"A puzzle," Murchison mused, "with nine-tenths of the pieces missing and the rest made by a hundred different hands. And mixed in with it, motes of ash that speak Japanese."

"It talks to you?" I asked. "The smoke?"

He gave an annoyed snort. "Not talk. Its essence. Its truest self. It doesn't speak. It's folded in the Japanese style—the bits added by your smokecarver as she analyzed it. But easy to filter out. What's left isn't complicated. What do you need to know?"

"Everything," Addams answered.

"The smoke is knit with a standard repeating unit of thirty-four throws and knots," Murchison said, altering the ink on the paper to diagram the steps. "There's considerable uniformity in the needles used to knit it . . . stainless steel, with an unusually high proportion of chromium. Standard issue to thousands of women, I would assume. Ash composition is 77.4 percent woodsmoke, sixteen percent coal smoke, with most of the remainder a mix of incompletely combusted fuel oil and kerosene. A preponderance of northern German trees for the wood, primarily three species of pine including . . ."

"Thank you," Addams said. "You could make us a fresh sample?"

"Of course."

He took a candle from another drawer and lit it, holding his hand cupped over the flame, collecting the smoke in his palm, making it adhere to itself with a series of sigils he drew with a pocket knife.

"He should stay," Murchison said to the candle.

"I should stay and watch?" I asked.

"No. Stay," Murchison repeated.

"We'll keep Robert for the night, yes," Addams said.

"No, no, no!" Murchison said. "Why is it so hard? He has it in him, however weakly. Here. Keep him here. He will be difficult to replace. Don't let him leave."

Addams gave the new smoke sample to Edith, who flew it to our allies at the University of Detroit for further analysis and safekeeping—it was one thing for your pet cartogramancer to scribble out the structure of the German material after eating it, but quite another for a team of professional philosophers to confirm it.

Freddy returned from his lab, pleased that it was in no danger of burning down, merely a philosophical reaction running more energetically than anticipated.

"Shall we go out for dinner?" Freddy asked me. "There's a new smoke-carver bistro on the other side of the square, where that German restaurant used to be. It's just the sort of thing I know you adore! They have this dish where they whip foamed butter together with marrow and foie gras to make little . . ."

After weeks of oatmeal and beans, the thought of rich foods made me retch. I closed my eyes until the bout of nausea passed.

"Are you all right?" Freddy asked.

"Something simple," I suggested.

We got sandwiches wrapped in wax paper from a deli and took them across the bridge to Radcliffe's aerodrome. The building was closed for the summer, the landing field overgrown and full of dandelions. We sat on the bank of the Charles River and ate, watching the moon rise, reflected in the water. Freddy blathered about the properties of the transition metals and methods for separating naturally occurring isotopes. Even as I knew he was telling me too much, it was comforting to hear him ramble on in the old way.

Perhaps a hundred yards away, I'd nearly drowned; an eighth of a mile up the field I'd taken a hard landing that would have killed me but for the experimental skysuit I'd been wearing; just past that, I'd punched out an old man and run my first mass casualty evacuation.

It was home.

" . . . so density *does* matter more than oxidation state—quite a lot more, in fact—where energetics are concerned," Unger concluded.

"Uh-huh," I said.

"I'm boring you, aren't I?"

"Not at all," I replied.

Freddy sighed. "You've been so quiet that I can't help but think . . . well, is it asinine for me to ask what it's like? Is it terrible over there?"

"Not always."

I took a last bite of my sandwich and barely tasted it. I thought of the burned man with his eyelids charred shut; of Carmen knocking on the last barrel; of watching the aeroplane tumble out of the sky after I'd stuck the bomb to it, flames trailing behind.

"A part of you hopes for busy days," I said. "Casualties badly enough injured so that they wouldn't survive without air evacuation, but not so severe that they can't be helped. It's what we trained for. It's why we're there. But when you stop to think about it, it's ghoulish. You're praying someone gets hurt."

I wiped mustard off the corner of my mouth.

"Part of you hopes for quiet days so that you can rest. But you can never quite relax. You go to bed at noon under a blazing sun and even when you're asleep, you're always listening for the bell and counting down: ten women left before I'm up; now six, four, two . . ."

I wadded up the piece of wax paper.

"You want both things and neither thing," I said. "It grinds against you."

We stood. Freddy skipped a stone across the water.

"How's Danielle?" he asked.

"I don't know," I said. "Busy. We might get a few days together in Paris in September, if we're lucky."

"You don't sound as if you're looking forward to it."

"Sure I am. But it won't be what it used to be. Afterward . . . after everything is done . . . I don't know. I'm not who I used to be."

"It would take more than a war to change you," Unger said.

We walked back to the apartment that we'd shared and in which Freddy still lived. My old room was empty, except for the same single bed, which Unger had made up for me.

I lay down and for the first time since I'd left for France, I couldn't make myself fall asleep. I thought of Danielle, of how her hair used to catch on my stubble and get in my eyes as we were pressed together in my narrow bed, her snoring quietly, me with one arm under her going all pins and needles, the other across her chest, drawing her closer.

Then, unbidden, I saw Punnett's face, stout and unimpressed, one corner of her mouth turned down in an expression of exasperated resolve ("Yes, ma'am, right away, ma'am, you're going to get us killed, ma'am"). Kiyo raising an eyebrow as she played a card, Millen's scowl. Carmen's curious look in the last moment as she reached out to knock on the barrel, as if she'd figured it out but couldn't quite believe it.

They shuffled and reshuffled through my head all night long. Hours later, after sunrise, Addams called for me. We went back to her office.

"I've been considering what Dean Murchison suggested," she said. "I agree with him. We should keep you here."

"What do you mean?" I asked.

"At Radcliffe for the duration. Until the last day of the war. Murchison is irreplaceable, but you're nearly as important. Blandings wanted to take the measure of you and you've more than proven yourself. It's reckless for us to have you in a frontline division. We'll pull you back to Radcliffe. Student, convalescent, groundskeeper—I don't care what we call you. I want to keep you out of the line of fire until we need you."

I frowned at that, even as my chest ached at the thought. Decent meals, a hot bath whenever I wanted, the old oak trees in the quad that dropped their acorns from such heights that the Radcliffe girls ran about holding their books over their heads like shields on windy fall days. Danielle on the weekend—or any day I chose to visit her in Washington.

"I'm a commissioned officer," I said.

"Honorable discharge," Addams offered. "Medical. I can make it happen by this afternoon."

"I . . ."

I thought of Millen, furious, as she went over the flight rotation, scratching my name out with a fountain pen. Kiyo's archly disappointed eye roll—*you can't count on a man*. Punnett hunching her shoulders and waiting weeks for whatever castoff flier got partnered with her next.

"I'm on duty tonight," I said. "My squadron's expecting me."

"They can find someone else. I can't."

I buttoned up the neck of my skysuit.

"No, ma'am," I said. "I'll fly with my people till it's time to do whatever you need me for."

Addams gave a half-smile. "Still a little fight in you, Robert. I'm glad to see it, however inconvenient you're determined to make this for me."

She stretched and regarded me more closely.

"I worry over all the children I send off to war. I worry about them over there and I worry about them when they come home. Some come back wild. Some come back quiet. I was the second kind, you know."

"Were you?"

"I was. So let me know you're going to be all right. Scream or yell or tell me a dirty joke."

"I don't know any jokes," I said.

"Oh, come on! There was always some line going around in Manila, something awful you would never tell in front of a polite Radcliffe girl. There must be one in France right now."

"I don't know."

"I'll tell you ours. So, Gen. Yeates goes to a gala in San Francisco. All the society men and women are out and Yeates is standing in the middle of them, stiff as a post in her dress uniform with all her medals. One of the ladies tells her she ought to relax and enjoy herself. Yeates barks, 'Yes ma'am.' The well-bred lady stands with her and whispers, 'I don't mean to be cheeky, General, but I wonder, when did you last have a man?' Yeates nods matter-of-factly and sings out, 'Nineteen hundred!' 'Well, no wonder!' says the lady. 'It would make anyone cross to be celibate that long.' Yeates looks surprised. She checks her wrist chronometer and says, 'Is that a long time for a civilian, ma'am? Because it's only 21:10 now.' "

I smiled.

"No," I said. "I never heard that one."

And then I realized that we *did* have that sort of thing, incessantly, in the mess hall. You couldn't shut Carmen or Kiyo up when they got started with one of those.

"Yeah," I said. "Our good one is that Gen. Fallmarch gets her morning briefing from a colonel, who finishes with, 'And I'm afraid there's a little bad news from overnight. The Germans shelled the international brigade and killed two Brazilian women.' Fallmarch puts her head in her hands and starts wailing. The colonel's surprised. She says, 'General, we lose sigilwomen all the time and I've never seen you this upset.' Fallmarch looks up at her and says—"

" 'Yes, but how many's a brazillion?' " Addams said. "It never changes. What you're seeing, what I saw—it's different every time, but it never changes. So, hang on with the tips of your fingers and your claws and your toes. You hang on and come back to us, Robert. If it's too much, send word and I'll have you home before your Sig-2 has time to threaten your life. We need you on the last day."

"If I'm so important, then why don't you tell me what you're planning?"

"We're going to capture Berlin."

15

> "The first time you see one land hot," crows Sgt. Shouter, "mercy! If she comes out of the sun, to your dazzled eyes she'll appear an angel. She'll make a falcon look clumsy."
>
> Brian F. Mayweather, *The Last Barrage*, 1927

I WAS BACK IN CAMP BY SUNDOWN. NO ONE REMARKED ON MY absence. They'd had a quiet off day, replenishing stores and cleaning. I, on the other hand, went around that night feeling like I had a bomb in my chest—a way out, any day I chose. Like holding a winning lottery ticket that any number of my comrades would kill for. I wanted to tell someone, anyone, in the worst way. One more smart remark from Millen and I was out. Go to Cambridge for the duration, clean sheets, rich food, one mission to fly. Just let her try it! Stick me with board duty, latrine duty, extra flights in a downpour—gone so fast it would blow the polish right off my boots. Not that I ever would, but knowing that I *could* made all the difference.

Kiyo, Punnett, and Andrada were playing cards in the mess tent, as always.

"Little brother, I do believe you're smiling," Kiyo said. "Louise, have you ever seen him smile?"

"Never," Punnett said. "I've seen him laugh, but I've never seen him smile."

"Secret," I said.

"He got laid," Kiyo said.

"I certainly hope so," Andrada said, eyeing her knife. "Better there than here. Safer for him."

"Oh, don't!" Punnett said. "Don't say that. He's got the Hero of the Hellespont waiting for him."

"I didn't say it *wasn't* her," Kiyo demurred. "Maybe she flew up to see him."

"She can't fly," said Punnett. "Can she fly?"

"Middling well," I said and grinned as they dealt me in on the next hand.

Such a relief to be back, to be understood. How many comforts would you trade to be with people who stood next to you when it all went to hell? All the hot baths and warm beds, or near enough. So, I flew on and smiled from time to time.

We had moderate casualties all week. Then came the awful day on which the Canadians won a glorious victory at the Second Battle of the Somme. I flew a hundred of them. They seemed to take it as a badge of honor that they not be put in stasis, much to our inconvenience.

"We tell that one about Field Marshal Haig!" said one of them, who would certainly lose his right arm above the elbow, as I lifted from the landing field with him on my chest and an unconscious critical on my back. "A brazillion men!"

"Could you move your hand, Corporal?" I asked him. "You're bleeding on my powder bag."

"Terribly sorry, ma'am," the man replied.

A few days later, the whole division was buzzing over something the German rauchbauers had done. No one could quite agree on what.

"They dropped a barrel during their retreat," Punnett said to me in the morning while we were scrubbing the mess tent. "They wiped out a village in Belgium by accident. Some kind of germ that eats the skin right off you."

"They did it on purpose," Andrada muttered that afternoon while we were doing regulator inventory. "A little old lady yelled *Vive la France* in Metz and they destroyed the whole neighborhood. It was a plague that makes your throat swell shut and it's spreading. Half of France is going to be dead by the end of summer."

"No," Kiyo said that night, while she was relieving me on board duty. "It was a test. You never know exactly how your smoke will move until you try it. So, they set it loose somewhere isolated. And it's not a plague—the philosophers at Radcliffe say the structure of the heavy smoke is wrong for carrying germs. It was chemical."

"Where'd they do it?" I asked. "The test?"

"Blandings doesn't know," Kiyo answered. "She's got her women in Second Division scouring the whole route the convoy took. They haven't found anything."

In the days that followed, Blandings sent half our wing on reconnaissance missions, too, with flimsier and flimsier pretexts. She and Bernice Macmurdo had sharp words over it.

"Too obvious!" we heard Macmurdo shout in the farmhouse. "If they haven't used it yet, you're going to convince them to!"

Meanwhile, I couldn't help but notice I was the only one of the conspirators whom Blandings hadn't sent to investigate three or four different towns.

"Belle Addams says I ought to be more careful with you," Blandings told me, when I complained about being held back. "I think she regrets letting me have you."

"I didn't come this far to sit out the war," I said. "Besides, you're letting me take evacs. That's more dangerous than a flyover to check on a village."

Blandings compromised by putting me up to receive dispatches from a courier, with an aerial handoff to be done out of sight of the wing. There was a time when that sort of mission would have excited me, but by now it felt routine. I made my way northeast until I was quite near the front and circled, waiting, ten thousand feet above a bombed-out church.

It was languid, mindless flying. I hovered half-asleep, sinking into carnal thoughts about Danielle. Just a few days more before I saw her. What article of clothing would she strip off me first? Which one of hers would I remove last? It hardly mattered. What does a starving man eat first at a feast? I thought of the taste of the drops of sweat that collected between her breasts. The tickle of a strand of her hair caught on my tongue when we were kissing so madly that we couldn't be bothered to break apart for a second to pull it away. The . . .

The drone of two aeroplanes passing beneath me brought me out of my reverie. I yawned. Biplanes, single-seaters, German markings. At least a mile below. Harmless. They shouldn't even be able to see me at that range.

But one of them was making a stuttering, whining noise and throwing out clouds of black smoke. The second plane had dropped back and well below the first, waggling one wing up, then the other, trying to see where his comrade had been hit.

The Germans might have shot at me only a couple weeks before, but this was a different situation. I crept closer until I was a hundred feet above the damaged aircraft, crawling along at seventy-five miles an hour to match speeds.

The engine on the wounded plane sputtered and died. It glided along for a moment, shuddering and threatening to roll out of control. Bad situation. The pilot stood up in his cockpit and peered at one of his wings, then glanced at the ground. He wore a leather helmet and goggles just like mine.

I happened to admire the hell out of aeroplane pilots. There was a period early in the war when their average life expectancy was something like eleven days—even worse than R&E. They flew fragile cloth-and-wood machines, the design for which some mad engineer had dreamed up the month before. I, on the other hand, had the advantage of sigils and equipment that had been perfected over decades.

Below me, the pilot put one foot on the edge of the cockpit. The plane rolled slightly beneath him.

"Oh, God, don't do it!" I whispered.

Better than dying in a fiery crash? Better to—

He jumped.

I had no hope of reaching him in time. But then I heard the thump and snap of fabric and saw a huge silk parachute spread out above him. Magnificent! Parachutes of that design had only come into use in the past few years. It looked as if it would slow him enough to survive the fall, but I decided I ought to follow to make sure he didn't need help at the end.

I was moving to shadow him when a gust of wind hit us crosswise. One of the main straps on the parachute snapped, turning half of it inside out. The man fell faster and began to tumble. The second aeroplane tried to veer away, but plowed right into the parachute, which caught on the wing. In an instant, the chute's lines were hopelessly tangled with the aeroplane's control wires. The second aeroplane pitched violently.

"Hell!" I whispered.

The second pilot managed to hold level, but this wouldn't end well. Either the first man would fall to his death or the second aeroplane would lose control and plummet right out of the sky.

Secret weapon, more careful, sit the war out in Cambridge—it was all so much horseshit. You didn't let a man die in front of you if you could stop it.

I dove toward the plane.

It would be a bad idea to surprise the pilot of a half-ton contraption—he might hit me if he tried to maneuver. I needed him to keep his craft steady. I moved alongside the cockpit. The pilot was watching the man stuck on his wing and didn't see me. I pounded on the side of his plane with my fist. He whipped his head around and went so wide-eyed that I could see the whites of his eyes through his tinted goggles.

"Amerikaner!" I shouted. *"Ich hilfe!"*

He looked back at the man then at me, as if he couldn't decide which of us were more improbable.

"Wälkure?" he yelled. *Are you a Valkyrie?*

The Germans did very little in the way of hovering, so R&E was a novelty to them. They'd given us the name of the angels that carried dying soldiers off to the warriors' paradise: Valkyries.

"Ja," I screamed. I motioned with the palm of my hand parallel to the ground. *"Flach, bitte. Geh flach!"*

Even if my German was muddled, I thought I'd found the international tone of voice for *Do* not *hit me with your fucking aeroplane, sir!*

I dropped down and back, then reapproached from the rear. I could see the trapped man flopping along, belly toward the sky, holding on with both hands to the remaining strap on his parachute harness. The plane bucked and for a moment I thought the parachute would come free. But it was stuck fast.

Below us there was an explosion as the damaged aircraft finished its long plunge to the earth.

"Shit," I whispered. There was not going to be a good way to do this. I needed to keep one hand on my regulator so that I could draw sigils to maintain my speed.

I came up fast and threw my left arm around him, pulling him to me in a clinch.

"Hallo!" I shouted over the slipstream. *"Amerikaner. Freundlich!"*

He screamed like I was a demon come to drag him off to hell. He tried to push me away, letting go of the parachute strap in the process. I hung on to him and we rolled, spinning on the strap. I lost sight of the ground. The aeroplane wobbled and lurched.

"No!" I shouted. "Hang on to me. Grab my rigging."

Which was a little beyond my two semesters of German.

I seized one of his hands and pressed it against my harness.

"Hand hier!" I shouted.

He kicked me in the shin and I lost my grip on him, falling away and whipping into a full somersault before I regained control.

"You stupid son of a bitch!" I screamed. "I'm trying to help you!"

I added power to come back toward him, intending to catch him in a bear hug, but the aeroplane bobbed. I slammed into the man hard enough to rattle my teeth. Before I had time to drift away, I scissored my legs around his waist and pressed my body against him, like I was riding him. I pulled my belt knife left-handed and pointed it at him.

"*Du. Halt mich!* Hold on to me!"

I put the knife between my teeth. The man was whimpering and pleading. I grabbed his hand again and pressed it to my harness. He held on and grabbed me with his other hand too.

"*Bitte, bitte,*" he wept. "*Bitte, Gott.*"

Please, God.

Well, sometimes God sends a male philosopher.

With my knife in my left hand and my regulator in my right, I tried sawing through his strap to free him, but the heavy cotton webbing turned and slid under my knife. The man clung to me and begged me to stop.

"Goddamn it!" I screamed.

The plane lurched again and I was slow to correct my sigils. We climbed a few feet, yanking on the parachute. I was tiring. I needed to get him clear or give up.

"Stupid, stupid, stupid," I whispered and shut off my regulator so I could use both hands.

Keeping my legs scissored around him, I grabbed the strap with one hand and sawed furiously with the other. We began to sink as the hover sigil's residual power faded. Eight seconds, nine. The parachute strap was bearing our weight, now. It twisted, spinning us. Then, with a pop, it broke.

We were tumbling tits over toes at four thousand feet. I lost the knife. The German clutched my harness. I kept my legs clenched around him.

I fumbled for my reg, drawing for an aerial relaunch. It failed.

"No," I tried to say, but I couldn't hear the word above the rushing air.

We whirled and tumbled. The German was holding my harness and screaming something—a prayer, maybe.

I drew again and failed, then again. Falling upside down and backward now. The blood was rushing to my head. My vision went blurry red.

I drew and the sigil finally took, its thrust kicking me back upright. The pilot lost his grip and slid farther down on my harness, until my legs were wrapped under his armpits instead of around his waist.

"Hold on!" I shouted. "Hold on!"

I drew a flurry of sigils, trying to stabilize us. Then I started on the fastest descent I dared, straight for the ground. No possibility of landing with dignity. I pulled up hard two feet above the earth and tried to get the German's feet on the ground. I set him down too hard, he fell over, and I toppled over him, smashing into the earth.

I lay there a moment on my back, stunned. In the cloudless blue sky above us, the parachute was fluttering down. The second aeroplane came toward us, dipping a wing. The pilot I'd rescued climbed to his feet and waved. He helped me sit up.

He pulled off his goggles and helmet. I climbed to my feet and did the same.

He couldn't have been more than twenty. He stared at me, then rubbed his eyes and burst out laughing. He howled and slapped his thigh.

"*Du bist ein Mann*," he said.

I didn't know whether he'd been expecting a woman or a devil.

"*Ich bin Philosoph*," I said. "*Amerikaner.*"

He unbuttoned his greatcoat and unbuckled a holster underneath. He took out a pistol.

"*Gebe auf*," he said and chuckled. "Surrender."

The world went silent. I froze my hands. I slid my right foot back a few inches so I could hop-launch if I got the opportunity.

"*Ach, nein, nein, nein*," he said. He reversed the pistol and handed it to me butt first. "Ich *gebe auf.*" And then in heavily accented English, "*I* surrender, *I* surrender."

His name was Johannes. Not a German, but an Austrian from Innsbruck who, after the day's adventure, never cared to pilot an aeroplane again. He also didn't care to be left someplace where he could sneak back to his own lines, as he would be put in the army and sent to the front lines if he refused to fly. So, he wished to surrender. He was delighted to do so to me, as he'd heard prisoners of the Americans were sent to the States, where they were fed extremely well.

I'd never accepted a surrender before. I messaged back to camp for instructions. Millen, who was at the message board, took a long time in getting back to me. At length, she replied that under no circumstances could I bring him home. *Violatn of internatl law*, she explained. *Noncombatants cant take prisnrs.*

"I'm really sorry," I told him. "I wish I could."

"Please," he said. "Prisoner in America. Anything. Tell anything. Where are airfields. Aeroplanes—how fast. I fight! Fight for America. Or translator."

"Smoke?" I asked. "Poison?"

"I don't understand."

I switched to German. "Three weeks earlier from now," I tried. "There was long line of trucks. And horse carts. They drive from Étain to Metz. They carry smoke. Aeroplanes over them, they shoot and fly."

"Yes! Yes. I know about that," he said. "The whole air force talked about it for days. Flying at night is very dangerous for us. We lost four aircraft in crashes while they were trying to land after their patrols. Then three more—well, we don't truly know what happened. We joked the Valkyries got them, but maybe just accidents for those ones, too."

"We also hear," I said, "a few days later. There was, by the rauchbauers. . . umm . . . chemicals that are bad to eat? Chemicals in the air that make you dead?"

"Poison?" Johannes suggested.

"Yes, poison," I said. "In a little city? Poison that makes all the people dead."

"Yes, of course! We've all been talking about it, too. You mean Neuville, don't you?"

"Where?"

"The village of Neuville. My God, it was awful! The rauchbauers set off a container in the middle of village during the night. By the next morning, everyone was dead. They made us fly laps, patrolling to make sure no one tried to get in. Night and day, they had us up. For three days, while they dragged the bodies out of the houses to burn them."

"You were there?" I asked.

"They rotated hundreds of pilots through. No one was allowed to fly near the village for longer than two hours or he might get sick, too."

"Say for me again: Where was this? Many cities are called Neuville."

"I'll show you on a map, if you have one."

"Please, to wait for one minute," I said.

I messaged Millen: *relay to Blandings—he claims hav intel re: Germn poisn.*

We waited ten minutes. At last, Millen replied, *Oh, fuck you! Was Q-U-I-E-T afternoon until this. Bring him straight back.*

I put Johannes in a spare passenger harness and we flew to camp. He was ecstatic. This was flying in the fashion of birds, he kept telling me. Real flying. He wanted me to visit his family in the Alps after the war, teach everyone in his hometown how to hover.

I landed to a large audience. Devereaux and Andrada had us covered with pistols. Millen was in full harness with a Lewis gun strapped in place.

"Nobody move!" Millen shouted.

"Oh, for Christ's sake," I said.

"Put your hands up!" Millen shouted with such force that I raised my hands before I realized she didn't mean me. Johannes was happy to comply.

"You didn't tie him up?" Millen asked me.

"What would I tie him up for?"

Millen searched him and took away a knife and a second gun.

"Farmhouse," Millen said. "Now."

We followed her.

"*Alle Mädchen*?" Johannes asked me as we proceeded inside.

"Yeah, it's all girls except me," I said.

Lt. Drale and Gen. Blandings were waiting for us.

"Sit," Blandings said. The way she was glaring, I was glad she was unarmed. "I send you for paperwork and you come home with a prisoner. If I tell you to fetch a bottle of milk, would you come back with the Crown Prince?"

I provided an account of the rescue. Blandings grew progressively angrier.

"Until we find a backup for you, no unnecessary risks!" she snapped. "I hope to God your German pilot knows how to hover, because I'll be happy to keep him and shoot you."

"No, ma'am," I said drily. "He doesn't hover. He does know where the rauchbauers conducted their test."

Lt. Drale put a map in front of Johannes. He pointed to a spot outside the town of Bavay, near the Belgian border.

"There's not even a village marked there," Blandings objected.

"Very small," Johannes said. "Two hundred persons."

"There's no harm in checking," Lt. Drale said. "We can have a woman from Second Division over top in an hour to look."

"If it's a trap . . . ?" Blandings countered.

"I'll have them send their sprinter," Drale said. "There's nothing that can hit her when she's going five hundred miles an hour."

Drale sent messages and we waited. Sure enough, the report came trickling back: *Small villag at designtd loc . . . No one in streets . . . roadblocks to N and S of town, w Ger sldrs . . . no planes.*

"Today is first day without," Johannes said.

Scorched ground outsid town . . . could be pyre.

"Promising," said Drale. She brought in Kiyo and Sabine Vos, who spoke the best German in the division. Vos was a tall, buxom girl of Dutch background with a figure that the wounded drooled over. (In the right mood, she'd been known to stick out her rump and blow a kiss to the men who catcalled her.) She asked Johannes most of the same questions I had and translated for the group. If we'd had any doubts over his honesty, his expression as he spoke to Vos reassured us—totally smitten.

"What day did they do the experiment on?" Kiyo asked.

Vos translated. "Five days ago. He was there the second day."

"Have him wait outside a minute," Kiyo said. Millen marched him out at gunpoint. "This sounds legitimate. Five days and the poison should have diffused enough so that we can go in safely. If it's heavier than air, there might be traces of it in the deeper parts of town—basements or cellars."

"If we send a team with you, you could collect it?" Blandings asked.

"Five days out?" Kiyo said. "I'm good, but I'm not *that* good. It'll be too dilute. We need a real professional with excellent equipment. Do you have a Corps smokecarver we could borrow from Le Havre?"

"That would be too big a risk," Blandings answered. "The women in Le Havre are watched closely. But I know a civilian stateside whom I trust. I can ask her to come over on the transatlantic line."

"Tell her to hurry," Kiyo said. "Every day we wait, the poison is going to disperse further."

Drale was already on the board, making arrangements.

"That just leaves the question of what to do with our upstanding young gentleman outside," Blandings said.

"He's kind of cute," Vos said. "Can we keep him?"

Blandings rolled her eyes. "That poor little puppy followed you home, Mr. Canderelli, so you take him to the field hospital. They're regular army—they can take him prisoner. Tell him not a word about his visit here. Otherwise we'll have German pilots bailing out over camp every afternoon so they can chat with a Valkyrie before being taken prisoner."

"That could be fun," Vos said. "You'd get good intelligence at least."

"Go!" Blandings barked at me. "And don't do anything heroic on the way home."

16

You can't say civilization don't advance . . . in every war they kill you in a new way.

Will Rogers, December 23, 1929

BY THE NEXT MORNING, EVERYONE IN CAMP—CONSPIRATORS AND Corps loyalists alike—knew that I had won a week of mess tent cleaning duty for rescuing a German pilot and that Gen. Blandings was planning a raid on Neuville.

"This is the problem with R&E," Bernice Macmurdo said to me, as I checked back in following a round of evacuations. "Everybody talks. It's going to be tonight and you're bringing in a specialist from the States, right?"

"Didn't you say the less you knew the better?" I answered. (It had taken Blandings all of four hours to relent and reluctantly include me on the team. Back at Radcliffe, Ms. Addams had several promising leads on other male fliers. I'd proven less irreplaceable than expected.)

"I can't help but hear," Macmurdo said. "Bombing runs for a diversion?"

"Nobody ever said—"

"*Every*body says. You're the last one to know—you bunk by yourself and eat breakfast with Millen. But if *I* know, you can bet Gen. Fallmarch knows. She has her little girls here who listen. And if she knows, then as careless as the officers back in Le Havre are with their message boards, you should assume the Korps des Philosophs knows, too."

"It's worth the risk," I said. "If we get hold of their poison, we could work out an antidote or a neutralizer."

"That'll take weeks of high-order chemistry. If the Germans catch the Corps attacking them again, we won't even have ten minutes. They'll turn their weapon loose on the whole Western Front."

"We'll be careful," I said.

Macmurdo gave a sad laugh at that. "A nineteen-year-old boy is going to be *careful.* Between you and Millen in command, there aren't enough prayers in Christendom for careful."

The strike team held a poorly disguised briefing that afternoon. I saw Fern Cunningham, the Sig-1 for third squadron, writing down the names of everyone who snuck up to the farmhouse. Macmurdo just scowled and shook her head.

Edith, who'd been running reconnaissance flights with Second Division, joined us with their report.

"Neuville is a tiny village," she told us. "About a hundred houses. There's one main road, which runs through the middle of town toward Bavay. The Germans have roadblocks on it, about a quarter mile outside the village on both sides. There are twenty or thirty regular infantry at each—there's no sign of rauchbauers. The town itself looks deserted. We've seen the soldiers patrol along the road from one checkpoint to the other, walking right through the main plaza. They didn't use any kind of gas mask or veil. Second Division landed a woman in the middle of town last night for a few minutes. She was fine."

"There's not enough of the chemical hanging around in the air to hurt us?" Millen asked.

"Shouldn't be," said Kiyo. "The rauchbauers want something that persists for a couple hours, maybe as long as a day or two. If it lasts any longer than that, then you kill your own troops when you try to seize the towns you depopulated. The better question is whether there's enough left to get a good sample."

"Our specialist was optimistic," Blandings said. "She's coming over on the civilian transporter chain later this afternoon. She's a Corps reservist. Highly decorated for her service in the Philippines."

"She should know how to keep out of trouble, then," said Millen.

"We'll get her down into a few of the cellars of the larger houses to collect samples," Kiyo said. "She'll have adsorbent smoke mesh like the stuff I used, except larger and stickier. She's bringing it prefabricated in canisters the size of paint cans. Five or ten of them."

"Crawling around in basements in the dark," Millen sighed. "Lovely. So, Robert A will carry the specialist and Punnett will carry the canisters. Second Division is sending their woman who was on the ground yesterday to act as a guide."

"She thinks the Germans saw her when she dropped flares to light her landing zone," Blandings said. "They came through the town searching not long after she landed. So, I've taken the liberty of organizing a diversion. Ms. Nampeyo?"

Hehewuti Nampeyo was one of our career Sig-2s. She'd served in Blandings's Experimental Wing, where she'd become an expert in aerial bombardment. After suffering shrapnel wounds at the Somme in '16, Nampeyo had been in the hospital for eight months, eventually refusing a medical discharge and persuading the doctors to restore her to active service. She was a woman of few words, but we listened when she spoke.

"I'm going to take eight of the 155-millimeter howitzer rounds that we borrowed from that French ammunition dump," she said. "When you're ready to light up a landing zone, I'll drop half of them on one of the roadblocks. That'll make them put their heads down long enough that they don't see your lights. I'll keep a few rounds in reserve, in case you need me to bomb anything else."

"You're flying two hundred miles carrying live artillery shells?" I asked.

Nampeyo turned to look at me, glaring like I was a child who'd just interrupted the grown-ups. "Hey shithead," she said. "I'm not going to screw the fuses in until we get there. They won't go off by accident. If the thought of flying next to high explosive scares you, then why don't you crawl back under Millen's skirts and let a real corpswoman fly the mission."

I struggled not to snap back at her, but much of the division still had doubts about me, even on ordinary evacs, much less a raid behind enemy lines.

"Ladies," said Blandings with a warning tone. "Mrs. Millen, will you need anything further?"

"Yeah. I want a machine-gun team," Millen said. "Vos and Devereaux would do nicely."

"That's unwise," said Blandings. "If you have a Lewis gun, you'll be tempted to use it. Stealth will be your greatest asset, so small arms and smokecarved weapons only. Assemble at nightfall and we'll get you underway as soon as it's dark."

I had the jitters for the rest of the afternoon, so bad that I turned the wrong way coming out of evac point B carrying casualties. Punnett had to chase me down and reorient me, so that I ended up at the hospital instead of in Switzerland.

"*I'm* the one who should be nervous," she said after we landed. "You blew up a plane last time. I've never done one of these."

I tried to chuckle, but the thought of Carmen knocking on barrels lodged in my throat. That and infiltrating a town that had been wiped out with deadly poison, with the Germans watching for us.

"It's going to be okay, little brother," Punnett said. "Kiyo will bust down a few doors and the smokecarver will get her samples. Nothing to it, right? All you've got to do is give her a ride."

"Sure," I said.

The strike team gathered in the farmhouse at sunset.

"Our smokecarver's delayed," Millen told us, looking up from her message board. "Couple hours, maybe. Problem with the transporter chain."

We passed around a pair of nail scissors. I snipped the threads holding the single brown bar of rank in place on my collar. Off came the American flag patch from my right shoulder, my unit number, and the R&E insignia—an eagle holding an olive branch in one talon and a caduceus in the other. I cut the armband with a red cross on it away from my left sleeve. The spots without patches stood out a darker shade of olive drab against the rest of our skysuits, which were faded from the sun. If any of us were killed or captured, the Germans might suspect who we were, but they wouldn't have proof.

Second Division's guide joined us just as the sun dipped beneath the horizon. It was almost nice to see a familiar face.

"Ooh, a nighttime mission with Mr. Tight Pants!" she tittered. "Ain't we got fun."

"Miss Pitcairn," I answered.

At the General's Cup the previous May, Sig-1 Melissa Pitcairn had planted a kiss on me in front of the entire crowd (including Danielle), soundly beaten me, and then given me an invitation to test for the Corps. I didn't know whether to thank her or spit at her.

"Lord, did he ever give us a show in that racing skysuit!" Pitcairn said. "I'm going to find a glassblower to make ice cream dishes in the shape of his derriere—you could lick the hot fudge right off it. I'd sell a million of them."

I tried not to die of mortification in front of half my squadron.

"You're sure that's the right buttocks?" Millen sneered.

Pitcairn looked me up and down. "It's skinnier, but I'd recognize it anywhere. Besides, you know a lot of other men who make 375 miles an hour?"

"Nope," Millen answered. She glared at Pitcairn and me, then stalked out of the farmhouse to check her equipment yet again. Punnett, Kiyo, and Nampeyo followed.

"Well, shit," Pitcairn said, "I don't know who takes a joke worse, you or your Sig-1."

"Her," I said.

Pitcairn looked at the chalkboard with our numbers recorded on it. "Millen's got eleven thousand evacs? She must have been over here since the first day of the war. Nobody's laughing after four years. Plus, I hear you got hammered on your last raid."

"Pretty bad."

Pitcairn borrowed a board and ran through her messages, stopping to answer one or two. She was a puzzle to me. A townie whom the University of Detroit had admitted on the strength of her flying, only to discover she was better than they'd ever dreamed. Pitcairn had set the world hovering speed record during her junior year at the U of D, a hero to millions of girls—and to me. She was a voluptuous, dark-haired beauty who could have made a fortune endorsing skysuits or vitamin pills. Instead, at the peak of her celebrity, she'd joined the Corps.

She stopped writing and glanced up. "You're looking at me awful hard. Something I can help you with?"

"No, ma'am," I said, swallowing hard. "I was wondering why you joined up, was all."

"Why I joined," she snorted. "Lord, I don't know. Because I was bored—shoot, I'd never been out of the state of Michigan before I was twenty-one. Because I was stupid. Because they asked me."

Really, it wasn't a bad summary of how three-quarters of us had ended up in the service.

"What about you?" she asked. "They must give you an extra helping of hell every night for supper. Why'd you join?"

"Because I'd always wanted to," I said. "And because they wouldn't let me."

She laughed at that, too, a warmer, more genuine sound.

"They're idiots. You impressed the hell out of me in Boston. If you hadn't had fifty girls crowded around you at the finish line, I would have asked to buy you dinner."

The idea made my chest tingle. I hated myself for feeling that way.

"I might have liked that," I admitted.

Pitcairn raised an eyebrow. "Really? And that was before you shot the big bad wolf. Now—well, dang, you can walk into any philosopher bar for the next hundred years and the ladies will trample each other to buy drinks for the man who killed Max Gannet. I missed my chance."

"Nobody's ever offered me a drink," I said.

"You're drinking with the wrong crowd, then. Come past Second Division sometime. The last couple weeks the only thing the girls in my squadron talk about is 'that man.' As in, 'That man from Fifth Division—I hear he took down an aeroplane.' 'That man—I hear he's going to get his thousand.' 'That man—I hear his face ain't as ugly as it looks in those pictures.' "

"What pictures?"

"A bunch of them have big glossy copies of that photograph the *Tattler* published of you."

I flushed red at the idea—*that* picture.

Detroit's leading tabloid had waited until I was in flight training to print it. "Big Plans for the Big Man," the headline had run, followed by a brief story about how the Corps planned to use me in a frontline R&E division. It would have been the kind of forgettable gossip they traded in every day, except that they'd run a picture of me from the General's Cup, which, out of the dozens of photos they'd had to choose from, was the single one in which I looked, well, erect. Probably nothing more than a shadow that had fallen in the wrong spot on my crotch, though as formfitting as the thin, iridescent fabric of my skysuit had been, I couldn't discount the possibility that maybe, for one minute, I might have been slightly engorged.

Pitcairn went on: "I told them, 'I've seen him up close. He *does* tend to the ugly side. But if you turn the lights down, you won't have to see his face and his bottom will still fit just right in your hands.' I walked past one of their tents the other night, I could hear her inside, twiddling the kitty, moaning your name."

I was blushing so hard that I'd run straight through all the shades of red and gone right back to pale. I felt three-quarters paralyzed, like how a mouse freezes when a snake coils back to strike. I kind of liked the feeling. Pitcairn had a low, rough voice. She might be thicker through the middle and the rump than was fashionable, but Lord, if I'd had a glossy of her back in '16 right after she'd set the world record and I was stuck sitting night watches for my mother back in Montana . . .

"Ma'am," I said. "I don't think—"

"There's no ranks tonight. Just two philosophers. Can I tell you a secret?"

"Uhh . . ."

"I've been in the service two years and I haven't gotten laid the whole time. You want me to say it blunter than that? Let's wait for the smokecarver in your tent."

"They'd throw me out."

"Then I'll gag you so no one hears you begging me for more."

"I'm with someone."

"I heard Danielle Hardin dumped you before you shipped out. Besides, you don't think she's got six men a day trying to court her in Washington, rich as her family is? But, hey, if you're still sweet on her, then I'm happy to share."

She was standing right over me, practically straddling my leg. I slid backward and stood, knocking over my chair.

"Think it over, big man. I promise—you'll never go back to a cold eastern girl by the time I'm done with you."

I fled to the mess tent, where Kiyo and Punnett stopped their game of high-low mudge to gawk at me.

"Pay up," Punnett said to Kiyo.

Kiyo checked her wrist chronometer. "Six minutes. If he was quick—"

"Pay up," Punnett said again. "Chivalry's not dead."

Kiyo took a silver dollar out of her workbag and handed it to Punnett.

"You look sick," Punnett said to me.

"Nerves," I croaked. Which wasn't wrong. But, God, why had I allowed Pitcairn to be alone with me? Why had such a large part of me wanted her?

Kiyo dealt me in and switched the game to no-look jiggery. We played a three-game match and started another, all without speaking. I couldn't keep my hands still.

"You moron!" Kiyo finally said. "I would do her and I don't even like women."

"Don't," Punnett said.

"You should go up there and tell her that," I said. "She'd probably enjoy it. God, two million American soldiers in France, and she has to make a pass at *me*."

"She doesn't want a soldier," said Kiyo.

We finished our second match and our third. I got tenser and tenser, until my calves were quivering with the effort of holding still.

"That's contagious, little brother," Kiyo said. "You need to calm down or we're all going to be shooting at shadows tonight. I've got one for you: tup her, marry her, throw her off a bridge . . ."

"Can we not do this while he's upset?" Punnett said.

Kiyo had posed dozens of these scenarios to me on night watches and long standbys, always with different sets of names. I'd learned that the best solution was to answer quickly, rather than trying to evade and let her ratchet up the teasing.

"Tup one, marry one, throw one off a bridge," Kiyo insisted. "The theme is luscious breasts: Vos, Devereaux, Pitcairn."

"Oh, don't!" said Punnett. "It's creepy when it's women in the division."

Easy. Devereaux was a devout Baptist with the shapeliest legs in the Corps and a speech to bring hellfire down on any man who mentioned it.

"Tup Vos, marry Devereaux, throw Pitcairn off the bridge," I said.

"Oh wow," said Punnett, setting her cards down in surprise. "Wow! That's not what I . . ."

"Pitcairn off the bridge?" asked Kiyo. "No! Oh, we're going to keep doing these until you get one right."

"They're all wrong answers," I said.

"But some are wronger than others," Kiyo said.

We played round after round of cards. I lost every one. Kiyo posed a dozen more triads, most of them with Pitcairn. I threw her off the bridge every time, even when the alternatives were the corpses of Civil War generals. Somehow it made me feel better.

"I'm running out of ideas," Kiyo said. "Let's see . . ."

"Give him an easy one," suggested Punnett. "Fifth Division Sig-1s"

"You said no people from the division!" Kiyo objected.

"Sig-1s aren't people," said Punnett.

"That's devious," Kiyo said. "He answers this one wrong, he gets court-martialed."

"Tup Fern, marry Bernice, throw Millen off a bridge," I said.

They erupted in laughter.

"Fern?" Punnett shrieked. "How is he so bad at this?"

"Insufficient bridges," I said.

"I don't know," Kiyo said. "I could imagine Cunningham lying there afterward. First time she unpinned her bun in years, hair spread out over the pillow like a mermaid's. Just had a big, wet orgasm—"

"Yuck!" said Punnett.

"—so intense that she figured out how to navigate because she remembered which one's her head and which one's her ass."

"Would this be after she stopped me four times in the middle to ask directions and fill out an incident report?" I asked.

We guffawed.

"Bernice would make a decent wife," Kiyo decided. "Smokecarvers are good cooks. But Millen off the bridge? As much as she wants a good man? She got married to the first boy who smiled at her and he turned out to be . . . disappointing."

"More interested in men than women," Punnett said, snickering. "Good luck trying to get a divorce in Utah, though."

"She used to go on and on about what kind of man she was going to find over here in France," Kiyo said. "Run off with him and never go home. She's the most boring, conventional romantic in the world. He would be kind and tall and brave and have soft lips."

"You couldn't get her to shut up about it once she got started," Punnett said.

"We ought to thank you, though, because she hasn't made a peep about 'the perfect man' since the day you—"

The mess tent flaps flew open and Millen strode in. The three of us froze with expressions like we'd just been caught by mom while taking nips from the brandy bottle.

"We've got word on the smokecarver," Millen announced. "She's ten minutes out. Go gear up."

We put our deck of cards away and filed out. Millen caught me by the collar as I tried to squeeze past her.

"I don't want you to be even a little confused," she said. "When I play that game, I throw you off the bridge every single fucking time."

"Noted," I said.

I kitted out with a forty-pound powder bag and the same semiautomatic pistol I'd carried on the last raid. Millen took a revolver. Punnett and Kiyo, neither of whom shot well, went unarmed. Nampeyo rigged her artillery rounds and snapped at anyone who tried to help her. Pitcairn blew me a kiss. Millen glared.

Well, this had the potential to be the chippiest mission in the entire war.

A flier from Second Division approached, carrying our smokecarver in from Le Havre. The hoverer struggled to land as the passenger on her back bucked and thrashed. They touched down and nearly toppled sideways as the flier got her feet under her.

"Help!" the smokecarver yelped. "Oh, Mother Mary—"

"Stand still ma'am!" barked the woman from Second Division. "Stop moving!"

She got her passenger detached, then tore her powder bag off and kicked it across the landing field.

"Who's the chauffeur tonight?" the flier shouted as she came over to me. "I'd rather get shot at than fly her again. She's the worst passenger I've ever had. You're going to have to drug her to get her into the field."

"Fantastic," I said.

"Sorry!" I heard the smokecarver say. "I'm so sorry! I'm scared to death of flying. I try to keep calm, but—"

I recognized a western drawl in her voice.

"Is that Dr. Synge?" I called out.

She was a rough-faced Irishwoman of forty-five, the medical smokecarver in Helena, Montana. A Corps veteran who'd settled down for a quiet country life, though she'd remained well connected to Ms. Addams and her co-conspirators. Dr. Synge had been the first person to suggest that a career in the Corps might be more than a fantasy for me.

"Boober Weekes!" Synge cried out. "Oh, my Lord. They told me it was your unit. I'll have to tell you all the news from home."

"*What* did she just call you?" Kiyo asked.

My childhood nickname was not one I was going to allow the division to start using.

Gen. Blandings came out of the farmhouse to see us off.

"Capt. Synge," Blandings said. "We're pleased to have you."

"General," Synge answered. "I'm sorry to be so late. They closed the transporter arenas in Le Havre, both the Corps and civilian ones. They're searching the whole city—sounds like they had an outbreak of disease. Typhus, maybe."

"Then we'll have to make up for lost time now," Blandings said.

We got Synge's canisters of netting secured on Punnett's harness. Synge would carry a few smaller containers of concentrated smoke herself in case she needed to improvise.

"We'll want to collect samples from the deepest possible sites in town," Synge explained.

"I was on the ground there last night," Pitcairn said. "There's an eight-hundred-year-old church and a big town hall right on the main square. It'll be creepy as hell, but they should both have big basements."

"Those would be fine places to start," Synge said. "I'll need a minimum of five samples to cross-eliminate contaminants. Any fewer than that will be useless. More would be better."

"As many as you can get before first light," suggested Blandings. "I need remind no one that this could be the difference between countering the German attack and seeing hundreds of thousands dead in the space of a few hours."

We finished arranging our gear. Millen got airborne and lit a safety flare to mark her position. The rest of the team launched one at a time to follow.

"If you would, Doctor?" I said to Synge, reaching to clip into her harness. She flinched away.

"Oh, come on, now," I said, trying to coax her toward me in the same voice I'd used growing up when our old tomcat got himself stuck in the downspout on the house.

"I'm sorry, Robert," said Synge. "I'm always bad, but I keep thinking of the night I met you. You crashed three times in a row."

I winced to hear her use that word.

"Hey," I said. "Those weren't nothing but sit-down landings where I touched a mite too hard. Besides, I'm a better flier than I used to be. Here's what we'll do: I'll put you in front so you can see where we're going. I'll wrap my off-arm across your chest and you hold on to it with both hands. If you get scared, just squeeze my arm. Don't kick or grab my harness, just squeeze. Squeeze as hard as you want. You won't hurt me."

I got her clipped in and we launched with only a little kicking. Millen headed for Neuville, navigating by compass and stopwatch, while the rest of us followed in a column. We had a quarter moon and starlight to see by, for which I was grateful. I could just make out Punnett ahead of me.

My thoughts kept straying in unsafe directions. Six minutes with Pitcairn had uncorked three months' worth of repression. From the first day of training, the mantra had been "don't look, don't touch, don't even imagine yourself with a corpswoman, or you'll win a dishonorable discharge." Now I couldn't stop picturing Pitcairn unbuttoning her skysuit or Fern Cunningham lying naked on my cot or Bernice—Christ, she was old enough to be my mother—calling "Come to dinner, dear" with her warm, ironic grin. Millen with her head thrown back. Vos licking her lips. The girls in Second Division ogling my picture while they put on their pajamas.

Stop it! Danielle. Only Danielle. Tup her and marry her and if there were days I wanted to throw her off a bridge, too, then I could console myself by knowing that she felt the same way about me.

We were an hour in the air. Dr. Synge squeezed my arm so hard that my left hand went numb. At last, I saw Millen's light change directions as she began sweeping in a wide circle to search for the blacked-out village. We missed Neuville twice and then stumbled upon it during our third orbit. The rest of us drew up around Millen and she doused her light.

"We'll drop to two hundred feet," she said. "Nampeyo will get into position over the northern roadblock and hammer them with half the artillery rounds. While the shells are exploding, I'll drop flares to light a landing field in the main plaza next to the church. I want everybody down fast—simultaneous landing. Once you're on the ground, pick up the flares and hide them in your bags so the Germans don't see the light."

Nampeyo pulled up higher to screw the fuses into her artillery shells. The rest of us sank toward the ground in a loose circle. We waited. Dr. Synge relaxed her death grip on my arm.

"You know, flying isn't so bad at night," she mused. "I can't see the ground."

"I have pretty much the opposite feeling," I said.

At least ten minutes passed, though the moon had set and I didn't have light enough to read my wrist chronometer by. Nampeyo was certainly taking her time.

"How's my mother?" I asked Synge. Ma and I messaged a couple times a week, but she was never the sort to let on if something was wrong.

"Oh, Emmaline's well," she answered. "She's having a tiff with one of her new apprentices. It's the problem with being sixteen years old and deciding you're the smartest person in the room. I can remember those days."

"My sisters never let that happen to me," I said.

Synge chuckled. "I believe it. Do you hear much from them?"

"Angela's still in New York, living the life of a bright young thing. Vivian's in—"

An explosion lit up the night a quarter-mile distant. Then three more in rapid succession. Dr. Synge kicked with both legs, throwing us into a spin.

"Easy!" I shouted, drawing sigils to stabilize. "Easy!"

Just below us, Millen began lighting safety flares and tossing them to illuminate our landing zone. She followed them to the ground and the rest of us followed her.

"I need my arm back to land!" I said to Dr. Synge. "I need both arms to balance. Let go! Close your eyes and give yourself a hug."

She did and then kicked anyway. Three feet above the ground, she peeked and panicked.

"No!" I shouted as she thrashed. "No! Hold still."

She couldn't.

I grabbed Dr. Synge to me with my left arm, wrapped my legs around hers, and tipped us backward and downward so that I struck butt-first and slid on the cobblestones in the square. Skysuits had padded seats for just that kind of maneuver, but I still skinned my ass.

"Damn," I said, grimacing in pain.

"Sorry!" said Synge. "I'm so sorry."

I undid her carabiners to get her loose. Our other fliers were picking up the flares and hiding them to douse the light. Millen kept one out to use as a torch. I got to my feet and limped after her. The church doors were unlocked, so she pushed her way inside.

I hadn't realized how silent the town was until we entered the building and it was quieter still. It was a mass of stone and brick and ancient wood beams, more like a fortress than a house of worship. No stained glass, just slits for windows.

We took our flares back out. There was a rack of votive candles beside the door, all of which had burned out. I played my light over the wall and saw a picture painted right on the plaster: A woman being rent apart by horsemen with spears. Their faces were flat and oval-shaped, amateurish. So old that the artists hadn't even figured out how to draw a human yet. I shuddered.

"Beautiful," I heard Millen murmur.

"Are we doing this or what?" Pitcairn hissed.

"Okay," Millen said, her voice echoing through the empty building. "Robert A, stay here and guard the door. The rest of us stick together and find the deepest cellar or crypt or whatever they've got."

They went down a staircase next to a shrine to an unhappy-looking saint who was holding his own decapitated head.

I stood in the aisle, trying not to get the creeps. My own breathing sounded loud enough to tip off the Germans. I waited ten minutes, then fifteen.

There was a series of four more explosions in the distance, powerful enough that I could feel the vibrations through my feet. Nampeyo. There was no reason for her to have made a second bombing run.

Trubl? I messaged her.

Not yr problem, she replied.

I heard another explosion, duller and more prolonged than the others.

Milln not answrng board, Nampeyo wrote. *Tell her: carry strap came loose. Shells banging into each othr. Dumped. Hit something on grnd. Big fire.*

Ok, I wrote.

Will turn for home, Nampeyo wrote. *Don't let Milln do anthng stupid. She gets stupd when scared.*

I glanced down the aisle—still no sign of Dr. Synge or the others. I checked my .45 and magazines of extra ammunition. Everything was in order. I rubbed my left forearm. I was going to have bruises there, too, in the shape of Dr. Synge's claws.

I waited another ten minutes. It was idiotic to have split our force. What the hell was I supposed to accomplish by guarding the entrance, anyway? If a bunch of Germans decided to rush the building, I wasn't going to be able to hold them off with just—

One of the church doors creaked behind me. I spun and drew my weapon.

"It's me!" Punnett squeaked. "Don't shoot."

"Sorry!" I gasped. "Where is everybody?"

"It's like a maze down there. We went up the wrong stairs and ended up in the main square. Come on!"

Punnett and I went outside. We could see the rest of the team on the other side of the square, illuminated in the light of a safety flare. They were crouched around one of the heavy wooden doors of the town hall. Kiyo had her smokecarving kit out and had just removed a piece of smoke the size of a sheet of paper. She began creasing lines into it.

"We can see your light all the way from the church," I hissed. "Put it out!"

"I can't work if I can't see what I'm doing," Kiyo retorted. She turned back to Dr. Synge. "Now, as I was saying, the advantage of folding your explosive charge is that you concentrate more energy in less space. It's elegance incarnate."

"Just do it!" Millen snapped. "I swear to God, I'm never taking you on another raid. You and your theatrics."

"Teeny, you have no appreciation for high art!" Kiyo complained as she doubled the sheet over yet again and added more sigils. "My grandmother helped build the imperial palace at Akasaka out of vaporized gold leaf. Entirely folded. Thirty rooms and only three hundred grams to do the whole thing. The walls are so thin that you can see through them when the sun hits them at the right angle."

"It's going to be dawn by the time she finishes," Pitcairn complained.

Kiyo held out the finished explosive charge in the palm of her hand: a razor-thin hexagon about two inches long.

"If I'd folded it out of paper, I could blow into one corner to inflate it into a cube. With this one, I flow in philosophical energy with a sigil and it goes bang."

Kiyo slid her piece of smoke between the door and the jamb, then rolled a little extra smoke between her thumb and forefinger to make a wire that she attached. She stretched the filament like taffy out to a length of thirty feet and coiled it around her arm.

Dr. Synge seemed amused by the whole thing. "That's a beautiful technique. I do medical smokecarving back home. We use fine knit wires as expanding stents, but folded tubes would work, too. I never even considered that."

"Well, ma'am, if you'd like to try, I'll have you do the initiation glyph on the end of the wire here. You form it into a simple—"

"No!" insisted Millen. "You are not doing lessons at three thirty in the morning behind enemy lines."

"Large, standard expansion glyph," Kiyo said to Synge, unperturbed. "You finish your last line at the point where you began drawing. It autocycles."

"Ingenious," Synge said.

We took cover around the corner. Under Kiyo's direction, Synge shaped the glyph to set off the charge, using the trailing end of the filament.

Nothing happened.

"Oh for Christ's sake!" Millen complained. "We've already wasted too much time—"

The door exploded inward, sending up a shower of splinters from where the lock had been.

"Bravo, Doctor!" Kiyo said. "Maybe a touch stronger than necessary."

"You're going to have the whole German army coming down on our heads!" Pitcairn whispered.

But Kiyo and Dr. Synge were already scrambling inside to collect their second sample.

"Robert A, you wait outside," Millen said. "We'll meet back here."

I waited, one hand on the grip of my gun. Ten minutes. All I had to do was stay in one place and stay calm. I could see flames rising high into the air at the northern checkpoint. Whatever Nampeyo had hit was burning furiously.

I tried Kiyo's game to keep myself loose.

"Tup Pitcairn," I whispered, "marry Kiyo, throw Millen off . . ."

But that wasn't how I'd meant for it to come out. Safer to contemplate the other three.

"Marry Punnett, throw Nampeyo off the bridge, and . . . tup Synge."

Even worse.

"Tup Danielle, marry Danielle, throw Danielle off a bridge."

Correct. Correct answer.

A moment later, I heard a gasoline engine shudder to life at the southern checkpoint. That was trouble. If they'd decided to help their comrades at the other roadblock fight the fire, they would drive through the center of town to get there. A second engine groaned to life a minute later.

Our team emerged from the town hall not long after.

"Ma'am!" I said to Millen. "I heard engines at the southern checkpoint. Two of them."

Everyone stopped to listen.

"Okay," said Millen. "Houses. We'll do three basements and keep everybody indoors. If the Germans pass through the square, they're not going to stop. They're not after us, they're going to put out the fire. They're probably scared of spending too much time here."

"They're smarter than us, then," said Pitcairn.

We chose an old stone house that looked likely to have a deep basement. Kiyo tried the door: unlocked.

The front room was full of bodies: two old women and three young children. Their faces were mottled gray, their eyes wide open, their teeth bared.

Punnett screamed.

"Everybody back!" snapped Millen. "You might catch it!"

"No," said Synge. She went over and touched the old lady's arm. "The bodies are cold. The smoke is an inhaled poison. You won't pick up any more from them than you will from the air."

"That's a cheerful thought," said Pitcairn.

Millen spread a couple of spare tarpaulins over the bodies while the smokecarvers found the root cellar. Pitcairn went with them. Punnett stood in the corner and trembled.

Millen leaned over and looked at a splash of blood on the floor. She rubbed the toe of her boot in it and it smeared. Still fresh.

"Is somebody hurt?" she asked.

I touched the back of my skysuit. My fingers came away bloody.

Millen tried and failed to stifle a giggle. She rocked on her feet, laughing.

"Teeny!" said Punnett. "People died in here."

"Christ, Robert A!" Millen said. "Did you get your period or did Pitcairn fuck you so hard that you're still bleeding?"

"I did a gluteal landing on those cobblestones," I said. "I ripped up my butt cheek."

Millen cracked up again. "Oh, there's going to be a line out the door to watch you get stitches."

I was laughing, too, mostly because the alternative was crying.

"Robert, don't!" said Punnett.

Marry Millen, tup Pitcairn, and throw Punnett off a . . .

The groan of a laboring engine cut me short. We went to the front window and I pulled back the curtain an inch. A small German truck, overburdened with a dozen soldiers, many of them standing on the running boards, chugged up the road from one of the roadblocks.

"Did they see our lights?" Punnett whispered.

The truck came around the bend in the road in the center of town, but took the corner too fast. It skidded and the front wheel smashed off an old stone well a hundred feet away from us. The truck rolled over on its side.

"Damn it!" whispered Millen.

Several of the Germans had been thrown from the truck and were hurt. The half dozen who were least injured were trying to lift the truck off a pair of men pinned under it. One of them was screaming his head off. He had a jagged piece of the running board sticking out through his belly. What might have been loops of intestine were tangled up with it.

"Oh God!" I said. "We've got to—"

"You're not going out there!" Millen whispered. "You already saved your quota of Germans for the war."

Kiyo popped her head up from the cellar. "What's going on? Are we running?"

"No," Millen said. "Their truck rolled over. They don't know we're here."

Synge and Pitcairn emerged from the basement, too. They took a turn watching from the window.

"This is a problem," Synge said. "I need at least two more samples."

I peeked through the window again. A soldier hauled up a bucket of water from the well and sloshed it over a puddle of gasoline that was leaking from the truck's fuel tank, trying to dilute it or wash it away. The eviscerated man was still screaming.

But the well!

"Dr. Synge," I said. "That well. It's probably a lot deeper than any of the cellars."

"Yes!" said Dr. Synge. "That's the perfect spot to sample."

"There are a bunch of Germans standing right next to it!" Pitcairn objected.

"I'll assemble my net here and snake it out," Synge suggested. "Then pull it back in after it's had a chance to soak."

Synge took a blob of semisolid smoke from one of her canisters, stretched and folded it, drawing dozens of sigils with her fingers. It gradually took on a shape like a stout, legless caterpillar about a foot in length, the interior full of coiled tendrils of smoke that would propel it forward as sure as a windup marching soldier.

Outside, the man who'd been screaming went quiet. Punnett whispered a few words of a prayer.

Synge pulled one of the larger cans from Punnett's harness and squashed the sampling net down into a ball, which she stuck to the front of her smoke contraption like a head.

"Ready," Synge said.

She drew a final sigil on her smoke cloud and it leaped forward, wriggling like a snake, flattening itself to squeeze through the gap under the door, writhing and twisting toward the well with a tendril trailing out behind, which Synge kept hold of, bending it to and fro to steer. Under her command, the cloud crept past the soldiers, then over the stone wall and into the well. Synge tied the end of the filament off to the door handle so she would be able to reel it back in after the netting had soaked up its sample.

"Twenty minutes," said Synge. "We'll get better results if we leave it longer."

"Fine," said Millen. "I want everyone rigged to launch in case we need to make a quick exit. Kiyo, go out the back door and find us another house with a basement for the last sample."

I adjusted the straps on my powder bag, making ready for a hasty launch.

Kiyo reappeared a minute later. "The back door goes out to an alleyway. There's another row of houses right behind us. Looks like a good bet."

"Fine," said Synge.

We went out into the alley, which was so narrow I could reach across it and touch the houses on both sides. The windows in the house across from us were blacked out with curtains, same as the last.

Kiyo took another sheet of explosive smoke, folded it into shape, and slipped it between the door and the frame, just below the lock. She attached her wire and began to shape it, making her glyph a tenth the size of the one Synge had used on the town hall.

"Ladies and gentleman," Kiyo whispered, "this is the smallest, quietest breeching charge on the entire Western Front. The Germans will never hear it."

"Hurry up!" Millen hissed.

"Without further ado," Kiyo pronounced then formed the filament into a sigil.

There was a tiny pop as the charge broke the lock and the door sprang open.

Three elderly men in sweaters and wool caps were eating bread and cheese at a kitchen table by the light of a storm lantern. They looked surprised to see us.

One of them picked up an antique double-barreled shotgun from the table and fired.

17

There's no problem so bad that you can't make it worse.

Mary Grinning Fox, "Instructions for Instructors," 1874

KIYO FELL TO THE GROUND, BLOOD POURING FROM HER CHEST like it was being dumped from a bucket. She didn't manage a word. She didn't lift her head.

One of the men was shouting at the one with the gun; the other had his hands on the barrel, trying to force it down.

"C'est une fille!" cried one.

"Femmes!" shouted the other.

"American!" yelled Pitcairn. *"Américain! Nous sommes américains! Ne tirez pas!"*

Millen was on her knees beside Kiyo, pawing through her workbag. She grabbed a bandage and pressed it to the exit wound on Kiyo's back. It soaked through instantly.

"Stasis!" Millen cried. "Synge! You're a doctor!"

Punnett had her hands over her face. The old man with the gun was crying hysterically.

"I can't," whispered Synge.

"What do you mean you can't?"

"It doesn't work if she's already dead," I said.

The blood was soaking into the knees of Millen's skysuit. The Frenchman with the shotgun was still covering us. He was pointing it at me.

"*Ne tirez pas!*" Pitcairn said. "*Américain.* Don't shoot."

"Tell him there are Germans outside," Synge said. "Tell him we're taking samples."

"That's all the French I know," Pitcairn said.

"*Anglais?*" I asked. The men shook their heads.

Punnett was sobbing. Millen was trying to wipe her hands on the thighs of her skysuit, but her coveralls were so soaked that her hands came away bloodier.

"*Je suis une philosophe,*" I said, repeating the prayer from flight school. "*Je suis une américaine. Je suis une amie.*"

The men looked at one another and gestured for me to continue.

"Of course they believe a fucking *man*," Pitcairn breathed beside me.

"The German smoke," I said. "Smoke, umm, *des Allemandes.*"

"*Fumée,*" Synge suggested.

"*Fumée des Allemandes.* We're going to make medicine. *Medizin?*"

"*Médicament?*" tried Pitcairn.

"*Oui,*" I said. "*Médicament pour fumée des Allemandes.*"

The Frenchmen looked baffled.

Pitcairn tried Cadwallader's line upon the liberation of Paris forty-seven years earlier: "*Vive la France! Vive la Paris! Vive la Gambetta!*"

"*Vive le Corps! Vive Madame Cadwallader! Vive Madame Tyndale!*" the man in the center answered. He lowered his gun.

"We need the, umm, *fumée dans* cellar," I tried. The men shook their heads again.

"*Fumée dans* basement," Pitcairn said, pointing at Dr. Synge. "Can someone take her downstairs?"

"*Aidez-la à la cave,*" Millen said, still kneeling on the ground with her eyes closed. "*Elle est docteur. Elle analysera l'air. Elle fera la médecine.*"

At last the men understood what we wanted to do. One offered his hand to Synge and led her down the hall to the basement stairs. Punnett was sitting on the ground, sobbing, her knees pulled up to her chin. Pitcairn knelt beside her and held her, petting Punnett's hair.

"Shh," Pitcairn said. "Sweetie, you have to be quiet."

"*Nous pouvons cacher sa corps*," one of the men suggested to Millen, pointing to Kiyo.

Millen kept her eyes shut. She shook her head. "*Non. Une couverture, s'il vous plait.* We'll wrap her up. We'll take her body with us."

Their conversation was cut short by the noise of another engine in the town square, accompanied by a great deal of rattling and clanking, as well as the shouts of more soldiers. Millen, Pitcairn, and I crept out the door and into the alley to look between the houses at the plaza. There were another dozen infantrymen accompanied by a seven-foot-tall armored vehicle with tractor treads and a cannon pointing out like a snout.

"A landship?" I asked. I'd only ever seen pictures of them.

"Nobody's called one that since '16," said Pitcairn. "It's a tank. A French one. The Germans must have captured it."

"I thought you scouted the area!" Millen said. "You didn't say anything about a tank."

"Maybe they had it under cover," Pitcairn answered. "It wouldn't be hard to hide it, it's just one of the little two-man models."

"It's fifteen feet long!" I said.

The monstrosity came to a stop in the square between the truck and the well. A soldier came up to it with one of the still-glowing safety flares that we'd dropped to light our landing field. He knocked on the tank's hatch and an officer popped his head out. They examined the flare together. A third man joined them and pointed in our general direction.

"Who the hell missed a flare?" Millen whispered. "They know we're here. We've got to be ready to pull out. Robert A, you keep watch from the first house. If they move toward us, yell. Melissa, get Synge out of that basement. I'll— I'll get Kiyo ready."

I ducked across the alley back into the first house. I picked up the items we'd left behind: two lit safety flares, a couple of Synge's canisters, and Kiyo's workbag. I reached for the tail of smoke still tied off to the doorknob, but my hand went right through it. I wasn't a good enough smokecarver to persuade it to solidify under my hands, much less to reel the net back in. We would have to wait for Synge to collect it.

I looked at the filament, still rippling and writhing as it trailed out under the door—which we'd left ajar with light spilling out from the flares. A little careless.

I pushed the door shut and the latch clicked. One of the German infantrymen, despite the racket of the tank's engine, heard the noise. He walked over to investigate.

"No!" I whispered. I retreated to the back room.

The German opened the door and looked around.

"Hallo?" he called.

He held up a lantern. He went over to the tarps and lifted one, gasping when he found the bodies of the civilians. Then he looked at the fresh drops of blood on the floor. He noticed the smoke still tied off to the door handle and poked at it, then shone his lantern along the trail of smoke that crossed the street toward the well.

In the back room, I unbuckled my holster and took out my pistol.

"Go away," I breathed.

He knelt beside the door, trying to untie the smoke. His hand went right through it, just as mine had. Without the proper sigil, he wouldn't be able to manipulate it, but he must have understood what it was. He unslung his rifle.

"Hallo?" he shouted.

I fired four times, putting three rounds in his chest and one in his neck. He fell backward, scrabbling toward the door, knocking over his lantern. The noise of the gunshots alerted the rest of the Germans. Several men ran up to drag the dying man out of the house. One of them shouted back to the tank commander, who had his head up and out of the hatch. The engine revved and the turret began to move.

I ran out the back door and into the second house.

"They know we're here!" I shouted.

"Were you shooting?" Millen demanded.

"He saw the smoke tied to the door. I—"

From the plaza, the tank fired a shell into the first house. The whole street shook. Dust and bits of rock showered down into the alleyway.

Dr. Synge and the Frenchman came running up from the cellar. Synge was stuffing one of her sample nets back into a canister.

"Let's go," said Millen. "Launch in succession from the alley. Column home."

"The well!" Synge said. "This won't work unless I have five samples. Is there any chance—"

"You're insane," said Millen. "Up, now!"

Pitcairn stepped outside to launch and then dove right back into the house as rifle bullets zinged past the door.

"They're coming up the alley!" she said.

One of the Frenchmen ran to us from the front room of the house, where he'd been keeping watch from the window. *"Ils viennent de l'avant aussi!"* he cried.

"From the other direction, too," Millen said. "We're surrounded."

"Roll smoke!" I said. "Doctor, whatever you've got for a smokescreen, down the alley. Right now!"

Synge took one of the canisters off her harness and shook a semisolid block of smoke into her hand. A ready-made smokescreen—one of the first techniques Cadwallader's corpswomen had developed five decades before. Synge drew sigils and the conglomeration of smoke crackled with static electricity.

Outside, a volley of bullets struck the heavy stone wall of the house. I reached out the door and fired my last four shots blindly back at them before taking cover inside.

"Robert, cut open your flare for me," Synge said.

I pulled a safety flare out of my pocket and plunged my knife into it, piercing the cardboard and glass tip. The knife and my fingers came away blue, as the phosphorescent liquid leaked out. Synge shook the fluid out over her cloud of smoke and drew glyphs to mix the two.

The tank fired again, hitting the second story of the house across the alley.

"If one of those rounds goes through the back wall—" Pitcairn warned.

"Just one minute," said Synge. "Let me add a noisemaker." She swirled a finger through the cloud and drew and drew.

Millen gave me her revolver. I reached out the door and fired it blindly, too. Anything to make the Germans keep their heads down for a few seconds.

"Ready," said Synge. The cloud in her arms was already growing—almost too wide to squeeze out the door. She whispered a word of encouragement to it and applied a final glyph, shooing it through the door with a *go on now* gesture.

The cloud popped into the alley and rolled like a tumbleweed, expanding to thousands of times its original volume within seconds. It whistled as it moved, the pitch rising as the cloud grew, shrieking like a banshee or will-o'-the-wisp or whichever demon ate the flesh of men in the stories of your childhood. It spread down the alley toward the soldiers and spilled into the plaza like a tidal wave. We could hear the soldiers screaming as they broke and ran. The tank fired wildly at the cloud, sailing a round right through it. The shell soared over the roofline and exploded in the distance.

"Fucking hell," whispered Pitcairn.

Punnett was hanging on to Pitcairn's leg, crying.

"Go!" I said to the Frenchmen. "Run. That way. The smoke won't hurt you."

They dashed out the door and into the glowing cloud. Millen attached cargo lines to the shroud she'd fashioned for Kiyo's body and followed.

"I'll light up at a thousand feet," Millen said. "On me!"

She launched. Pitcairn moved to follow, but Punnett was still clutching her.

"Louise, you've got to let go," I said. "Louise!"

All Punnett could do was shake her head. Shock or simply terrified. We didn't have time to calm her down.

"Missy," I said. "Take her as passenger."

"You've got to be goddamn kidding me!" Pitcairn complained.

I pried Punnett's fingers off Pitcairn and clipped her into the back of Pitcairn's harness.

"Go!" I yelled.

Pitcairn dragged Punnett behind her out the door and launched. I opened one of the carabiners on the front of my harness and reached for Synge.

"Time to go," I said.

"Like hell it is," she said.

18

Mrs. Gower looks around the saloon, the walls now redecorated with a spatter of fine pink dots. "What happened to him?" she asks. "Eleven gallons of dynamite in a ten-gallon hat," I say.

Edwin Fitzenhalter, *Fresh Gale on the High Sonora*, 1888

THE TANK FIRED AGAIN AND THE WHOLE CLOUD LIT UP GREEN.

"We either grab that last sample or this whole mission was for nothing," Dr. Synge said.

"Let's do it, then," I answered.

We crawled out the door, trying to keep close to the ground, where the cloud was thinner. The smoke shrank back from Synge as if it were frightened of her. We crossed the alley and found the back door of the first house. Synge caught a handful of the cloud and applied a sigil, clearing it from the house's interior. The first shell from the tank had left a gaping hole in the front wall. The door, with the smoke streamer tied to it, was nowhere to be seen.

"I'll have to pull the net out of the well by hand," Synge said. "But that tank is right next to it. If I had an hour, I could build a thermal charge that would melt it to slag, but the smokescreen's going to be gone in five minutes."

I looked at Kiyo's workbag, still slung over my shoulder.

"What about Kiyo's breaching charges?" I asked.

I gave the bag to Synge, who searched through it. There were another ten whisper-thin sheets of explosive smoke. Synge laid them on top of each other in a stack.

"If I can just remember how she shaped it . . ." Synge murmured.

She folded the sheets, creased them, folded again. Synge worked with frightening speed—faster than Kiyo, even. A professional and not in her first war, either. In less than a minute, she'd produced a bomb the size of an index card, but still thinner than a blade of grass. She took a vial from Kiyo's bag and pulled out a long, thin strand, worked it into a filament, and wrapped a couple hundred feet around her arm. She tacked the end of it to the explosive and handed the tiny charge to me.

"Get as close to the tank as you can. Give me a shout and I'll dissolve the smokescreen so you can see what you're doing. Slide the packet through one of the hatches and run. I'll draw a big glyph like the first one. The shock wave inside an enclosed space will be devastating."

I tried to tell myself that Kiyo would have wanted it that way. Mostly, I thought she would have wanted to live.

"Hurry up before the screen dissipates any further," Synge said.

I crawled through the main square, the cloud glowing around me like a fog bank out of a nightmare. The tank fired again. The smoke held the energy for a moment, glowing a bright ghostly blue-green, before allowing it to seep away. I went on hands and knees across the paving stones, moving toward the sound of the tank's engine. The filament on the explosive charge trailed out behind me. I advanced until I could see treads a few feet in front of me.

"Up the Fifth!" I screamed.

"Up the Corps!" Synge shouted back.

The smokescreen came apart, swirling into the sky and fading like drops of phosphorescent dye that had fallen into the ocean.

I ducked below the tank's cannon and slid the charge into the driver's hatch. The thin square of smoke leaped out of my hand, as if it were pleased to have gotten inside.

I ran.

The tank commander must have realized something was wrong—the disappearance of the cloud or our shouting. Maybe he'd caught a glimpse of me. He made the wrong decision. Instead of bailing out, he began to traverse the turret, looking for a target. But I could run faster than he could turn.

The shock wave hit me in the back a moment before I heard the dull thump of the explosion. A few seconds later, I heard a clang as the driver's hatch, which had been blown fifty feet into the air, hit the ground, followed by a second clatter, as the panel from the commander's door landed. The tank was still upright on its treads, but the armor plates had burst outward along their welded seams. I didn't even want to think what the inside looked like.

Synge was bent double over the well, pulling up her sampling net, jamming it into a canister. She screwed the lid on.

"*Now* let's go," she said.

We found Millen circling above, too frightened and furious to properly chew us out for ignoring orders. She led the rest of the team back to camp, while I swung north to deliver Dr. Synge to the civilian transporter arena in Calais, so she could rush the samples back to the States.

"I'll have the smoke to Radcliffe in a few hours," Synge told me. "We'll do everything we can to make sure it was worth it."

I looked at her hollowly.

I flew home, endeavoring to keep my mind blank. Concentrate on the compass. On my sigils. On body posture. Don't think about what you saw. What you did.

Punnett was sitting in the mess tent, staring at the deck of cards. Pitcairn had an arm around her shoulders. When she saw me, Punnett buried her face in my chest and clung to me, wailing.

"Louise," I said. "Easy. It's okay."

"No it's not!" she sobbed.

"No," I said. "No, it's not."

"I told her I'd wait with her until you got back," Pitcairn said.

"Thank you," I said.

"She cried the whole flight home."

"I'm sorry," I said.

I led Punnett back to her tent, and she lay on the cot.

"You okay to be alone?" I asked.

Punnett sniffled and nodded. I felt numb.

Pitcairn and I walked out to the landing field. Her eyes were wet, too.

"Shit," she said.

"Yup," I said.

She put on her helmet. "Listen, big fella. You were great. I hope that when everything goes to hell, you're the one fighting next to me."

She wrote her personal glyph in my message book.

"In a few weeks, all the church bells in Europe are going to ring and there'll be a celebration like you won't believe. I'll buy you that drink."

"Thanks," I said. "I'll need it."

I was angry and desolated and exhausted. But I wasn't going to be able to sleep. Not yet.

I found Andrada in the tent she'd shared with Kiyo. Kiyo's belongings had already been packed and labeled, her personal effects to be delivered home to California and her Corps-issued gear to be returned to Le Havre.

Andrada was sitting on the edge of her cot, sharpening her big belt knife.

I sat on Kiyo's cot and watched.

"She put her sister on her Form 41," Andrada said. "I didn't even know she had a sister. Six months bunking together and we never talked about her family."

Andrada pointed her blade at me and looked down the edge with one eye closed, checking for dings.

"Tell me it was worth it," she said.

I couldn't even imagine what "worth it" would mean.

"I don't know," I said. "We got what we needed."

"She got shot in the back while taking a bow?"

"Something like that," I said. "From what Millen understood, a couple Frenchmen came back to the town. One of them had gold coins hidden in his attic. They wanted to make sure no one stole them. It was an accident."

Andrada breathed on the knife, blowing away a fleck of metal. "That's more than Blandings told us. She said Kiyo was a brave soldier. Gave up her life so that others could live. That's a load of shit. Kiyo played with that machine gun a few times and then the general sent her to die. So that we can spare some German lives at the end of the war?"

"And some American ones," I said.

"What a beautiful sentiment! The Germans kill four million soldiers and we're asking how we can make the end easier for them."

Andrada drew the knife against the hair on her forearm to test its sharpness. Finding it too dull, she flipped her whetstone over to the finer side and continued scraping her blade over it.

"Or maybe Kiyo *was* a soldier," Andrada reflected bitterly. "Maybe she thought of herself that way. Back home, everybody did, even the girls. Maybe it was like that for Kiyo, too."

I'd rarely heard Andrada talk about home.

"Tell it to me?" I asked.

"I'm supposed to tell you a sad story and it'll make me feel better my best friend is dead?" Andrada asked.

"Yeah."

"You're a fool if you think that."

Andrada added a drop of water to her stone.

"Back home was Mindanao," Andrada said, "the big island in the south of the Philippines. When I was a girl, the Spaniards were the enemy. We'd been fighting them for four centuries. Every year or two, they'd send out an army, which would take two steps into the mountains and get lost. They'd burn down some empty villages, kill a few old men. A month later, their armor would be rusted, their weapons lost, half of them dead from disease. They would declare victory and go back to hiding in the fort. Then when I was twelve years old, the Americans came. Their battleships blew up the

Spanish fleet in an hour. We fought alongside their soldiers and after ten days, the Spanish army was finished too. We danced in the streets. But a funny thing happened. The Spaniards said, 'We'll surrender, but only to the Americans, not to the brown people.' Then the Americans decided they ought to stay for good. Teach us how to take care of ourselves, protect us from the Russians and Japanese."

The knife still not to her liking, Andrada flipped the whetstone back to the coarse side and began sharpening it again from the beginning.

"So, we fought the Americans. That war didn't last long on most of the islands, not after the Corps gassed Manila. But my people had more experience at fighting. Eventually, the Americans rounded up all the civilians on Mindanao, put them in *reconcentrados*—in camps. To protect us, they said, from bandits, from the bad men in the countryside. The Americans burned our fields so the bandits wouldn't have anything to eat. But there was nothing to eat in the camps, either. They were ringed with marines who shot anyone who tried to leave. We were very well protected. Except from starvation and dysentery and cholera. We died and died and died."

"God," I said.

"I lived in one of those camps for months. My mother and I. Then she died. I got sick. I should have died, too. But the purple angels visited us."

R&E. They'd worn navy-blue skysuits, made with cheap dye that had bleached purple in the hot Pacific sun.

"One of them took me—I don't know why. She flew me back to their base in Manila. They fed me. They gave me medicine. They found a family in the States from the same island who'd known some of my mother's cousins. They decided that was close enough. One of the fliers who could speak Spanish took me across on the island transporter chain. *Pop-pop-pop* and we were in San Francisco. I told the big woman who was holding my hand, 'Thank you. God is great. May he protect you.' She said, 'Sweetie, God is a she. If you want to thank me, learn to fly and join up. Help some other little girl.' "

"You have eight thousand evacs," I said. "You more than did it."

"None of them a little girl. But, yes, I came to save lives. Not to play politics or shoot down planes or blow up tanks or decide to bomb this village or that one."

She ran a cloth over her blade to polish it.

"Maybe I'm being unfair. Maybe if there had been a Blandings in Manila, she would have plotted to save *my* people. Maybe we all would have sat down and had tea. Or, maybe Kiyo was worth a million Germans."

"You're going to have a mutiny in the middle of your mutiny," I said to Lt. Drale as I took over board duty that night, sitting gingerly on the sutures that Bernice had used to close the gash on my butt.

"Alta's taking it hard?" Drale asked.

I nodded.

"She'll pull through," Drale said. "She always does. I'm less worried about a mutiny than I am about Saint-Mihiel. The offensive is going to go off before we get any replacements."

Including commanders, we were down to twenty-five women.

"It's really happening this time?" I asked.

"Pershing is borrowing a thousand warplanes and a thousand tanks from the French. It'll take a week or two to get them all in place. Then they'll attack. Nobody's going to be surprised. It should go off right after you get back from your leave. So, enjoy Danielle. Enjoy Paris. Fatten up."

I hadn't written to Dar about the raids. Really, I hadn't written her much at all over the last few weeks. The less I thought about any of it, the better.

"We used to have a tourist's guide to the city," Drale said. "I forget who had it last. Millen, maybe."

Millen and I ran six evacuations together at dawn because we didn't know how else to mourn. We didn't even have to speak to each other until after the last one, when I inquired about the book.

"Yeah, I've got it," Millen said. "I'll beat you to death with it, unless you'd prefer I use Alta's knife. Disobeying orders. Blowing up tanks. You and that madwoman."

"I was trying to do the right thing," I said.

Millen dug the guidebook out of her tent. "I was going to visit gay Paree the last time I had a couple days' leave, but it just seemed too pathetic. Paris all by yourself. I don't know what you'll even need it for—the two of you will just lie in bed and fuck the whole time."

I didn't dignify that with an answer. I turned to leave.

"I never say the right thing, do I?" Millen said. "I screwed up that raid. Kiyo died because of me."

"No," I said. "It was sheer dumb luck we picked the wrong house."

"I ran like a scared little girl. We should have stayed to cover you. I should have been the one to think of the smokescreen. Instead I let the most junior boy in the division give orders."

"Did you just admit I'm not a woman, ma'am?"

Millen laughed a single *ha*. "Are you trying to make me feel better?"

"Yeah, I am. If we lose you, who else could be Sig-1 to me? Cunningham?"

"She'd have a breakdown worrying over you."

"Bernice?"

"Even worse. Besides, you married her—she can't command her husband in the field. There's a regulation against it. No, if you want to make me feel better, lend me a book to read. You're a college man, you must have something."

"I've got Tintinalli, *Hovering Emergencies and Recov—*"

"No, a *book. Frankenstein* or *Wuthering Heights* or *Adam Bede* or something."

"I don't much like reading made-up stories," I said.

"Then bring me back something to read from Paris."

"French or English?"

"Whatever's more promising."

That started the endless string of requests from my wingmates over the next week.

"Bring me back some chocolates," Punnett said. "Five francs would be enough, right?"

"Knitting needles," said Bernice, as I lay on my cot and she changed the dressing on my buttock. "If you go to the Louvre, there's a shop next door that sells them. They aren't meant for smokecarving, but they're the slickest instruments I've ever used. I'll write down the model number. Bring me back a set."

"I messaged ahead to a cobbler's," Andrada told me when I sat beside her in the mess hall. (She'd been taking her meals alone, but didn't turn me away.) "They've done boots for me before, they still have my measurements."

"Nail polish," Cora Devereaux said. "Bright red."

"Brassieres," Sabine Vos said, handing over her most prized undergarment to me. "I bought this in a shop in the second arrondissement and it's the only thing in my life that's ever fit me right. You show them this and tell them I want half a dozen each just like it in white and tan. And one black one with as much lace trim and ribbons as they can put on."

"You going to model for me?" I asked.

"Sure. Right after I pluck out your eyes."

I was in touch with Danielle every day. Le Havre had reopened to transporter traffic, having weathered whatever scare they'd had. She was planning to come across the Atlantic on the Corps chain; they made the crossing faster than their civilian counterparts. She would book a hop to Paris once she was in Le Havre. It would be the easiest thing in the world. She'd reserved a room at a hotel in the Latin Quarter for us.

The day before my leave, we had a busy morning, then some sort of fleeting catastrophe for which the entire division was launched without a destination, only to be immediately recalled. By six in the evening, all was quiet.

In Le Havre, finally, Dar messaged. *See you soon!*

The wing had no further use for me. They had their scheduled three days off beginning at midnight and were practically pushing me onto the landing field.

"Get going, then!" Andrada said.

"Comb your hair at least," Punnett clucked.

"Repeat this," Nampeyo said—the first spontaneous words she'd ever spoken to me. "*Je voudrais le vin de Bourgogne, s'il vous plait.* That's all you need to say at a restaurant."

"But not escargot," warned Fern Cunningham. "That's snails."

"A dozen roses," Millen reminded me. "Red."

"Check your board every hour, even in the middle of the night," Drale warned. "If Saint-Mihiel blows up early, we'll need you back."

Once the rest of them had left, Blandings pressed a satchel full of documents into my hands. "For the senator's eyes only. See that Miss Hardin delivers them."

And then with the goodwill of my wingmates, I was away on a date or shopping expedition or covert courier mission.

I headed west, flying at best speed. It would be only an hour. I glanced occasionally at my compass, but Paris was going to be hard to miss. Find the hotel first. Punnett was right—comb my hair. A proper bath. A shave with very hot water. Roses. Danielle.

Halfway there, I caught sight of my message board—it was crowded with notes. I drew sigils to reset it and ran back through from the top.

In Dar's neat script:

Corps is canceling scheduled transporter service to Paris. Not sure when next one will be.

Outgoing civilian line is down too. I might have to hop back to London then cross to Calais.

Actually, all transports in every direction are canceled. I've never heard of anything like this.

I may have to take the train. It's 4 hours. You could meet me here and we'd ride together?

Soldiers at train station. All trains canceled. Robert, will you answer please?

And then, from the division:

Divert to Le Havre. Message for further orders. Drale.

I replied to the Lieutenant first: *Situatn?*

Corps plague smoke got loose in Le Hv, she replied. *Quarantine in progress. Land at Corps field. Find Hardin. Take shelter.*

19

That's the wrong way to tickle Mary,
That's the wrong way to kiss.
Don't you know that over here, lad,
They like it best like this.
Hoo-ray pour les français,
Farewell Angleterre.
We didn't know how to tickle Mary,
But we learnt how over there!

British song of the Great War, to the tune of "It's a Long Way to Tipperary"

I SET DOWN IN THE MIDDLE OF A WHEAT FIELD TO PLOT A NEW course. If I missed Le Havre, I'd hit the English Channel, so there was no risk of overflying the city too badly.

On my way, I wrote Danielle. *Y ok?*

I'm fine, she answered. *The whole city is in a panic, though.*

Plague got loose?

Maybe. Some people sick by the Corps warehouses is what I heard. The gendarmerie are telling everyone to stay indoors. Do you want me to find us a place? The corpswomen at the arena know a room we could rent for a few hours.

Y. Will be aprox 1hr. Send drct or addr.

What?

Directions or address. Srry.

Love you. Fly safe.

Love you, I replied.

It was a phrase the two of us used far too rarely. We managed our carnal messages here and there—they never failed to lift me up after a bad day of evacs. But thinking of something deeper poured steel into my bones.

I was beginning to lose the daylight when I reached the sea, with Le Havre a few miles off to my right. I turned and found the Corps landing field near the docks, beautifully lit up under its banks of electric lights.

"Fifth Division!" I called as I touched down.

A woman came out of the guardhouse.

"What the hell!" she said. "Are you lost?"

"Sig-3 Canderelli, Fifth Division of R&E. On leave."

"Shit, you can't be here. The field is closed."

"You're all lit up."

"They're not letting us land anyone. We're supposed to be closed."

"I'm on leave," I said. "I was supposed to meet someone here."

"Oh my God, *you're* the corpswoman. And you brought your wife or girlfriend over?" the woman asked with a note of sympathy.

"Yeah. She came in by transporter right before they locked the city down. How worried should we be?"

The guardswoman shrugged. "We had a panic just like this a few days ago. Poison gas. Nothing came of it."

I pulled up a fresh set of messages from my wrist board with the address of the place Dar had found. The woman read it along with me.

"That's only three blocks away," she said. "But there are soldiers at the entrance here—they're not allowing anyone in or out. They've got squads in the streets, too. You could make a short hop?"

She drew me a rough map and pointed me in the right direction.

"Thanks," I said.

"You should see some of the husbands who get smuggled in. The last time I brought mine over, it took three different—"

There was shouting at the front gate.

"Well, hurry up!" she said.

I launched and counted street corners, found a park with a statue of a man on horseback, turned left, and settled to the ground halfway up an unlit side street. I checked the number on the house. It was an anonymous three-story private residence with red lanterns hanging on either side of the door. I'd expected an inn or a pension. I messaged Dar, but she didn't reply. I decided it was better to get off the street if there were patrols out. I knocked.

A woman answered the door wearing a feather boa and an elaborate corset with more frills and lace than all my sisters had ever owned while I was growing up—and very little else. She had a constellation of jeweled hairpins to keep her tresses in an elaborate updo.

"*Bonsoir*," she said, apparently unconcerned by her state of undress.

"Umm, *bonsoir*," I answered. "*Anglais*?"

"You're supposed to call ahead!" she said, her English precise and teasing. "American soldier?"

"Philosopher," I said. "I'm looking for someone."

"You should know better than to come unannounced. Who is it you want?"

"Danielle. Mademoiselle Hardin?"

The woman looked flummoxed. Perhaps Danielle was traveling under an alias?

"We don't have any woman by that name. But I think you'll like it here. Can I take your bag? We'll look at some pictures. You tell me what you like in a girl."

I realized what I'd walked into and blushed crimson.

"No, no, no. I was supposed to meet my . . . a friend here. The Corps sent her. You rent a room sometimes? A pension? An apartment?" I showed her the address on my message board.

"Oh, you're for upstairs. *Merde*. Jeanette!"

An older woman, in a plain black dress, came out carrying a broom.

She threw a key at me and made an *around back, use the exterior staircase* gesture.

"Robert," someone said through the still-open front door.

It was a stout, dark-skinned young woman with a sprinkle of gray through the black wavy hair around her ears. I stared at her in confusion. She looked like Danielle, only older and sadder.

Three months. It might as well have been thirty years.

"It's around back!" Danielle said, annoyed. "I specifically said don't go through the front door."

"Dar, you did *not* tell me that," I said, and showed her my wrist board, bringing up the message with the address—and then one after that, in which she'd warned me it was a brothel, so go around to the back.

"Sorry," I said. "Sorry!"

"Can we *please* go?" Danielle said.

She hustled me outside and around back to a rickety wooden staircase that led to a cramped two-room apartment. It had low, slanted ceilings and a single dormer window. There was a lumpy straw tick mattress on the floor. Thin, gray cotton sheets. A wobbly table and two chairs. A water closet with a sink and toilet.

Danielle glared at the room and I stood stupidly beside her like my joints had rusted in place. Rain began to patter against the roof and it took only a few seconds before water started dripping onto the bathroom floor. I couldn't summon up the strength to look for a bowl or bucket to catch it. I couldn't do anything.

"I have to sit," I said.

"At least hug me first," Danielle said.

She felt the wrong shape in my arms. Her perfume smelled different.

"God, you're thin," Danielle said. "You're not going hungry, are you?"

"No," I said. "It's just sometimes my body's not sure if it's day or night. Or we're busy. Or I forget. Or you come back from a—from something and you can't sit down and just eat soup afterward."

Danielle held me tighter.

"Oh, Robert, I can't even imagine. Tell me?"

How could she ask that? I worked so hard to protect the raw spots and now she asked me to rip them open? It was like living in a half-collapsed house—try to pull one beam out of the tangled pile of rubble and the whole roof falls in on you.

"No," I said. "You don't want to hear what it's like. Nobody would. It's just that I've seen a lot of wounded who must've died quick when they came out of stasis. Two of my wingmates got killed in front of me and I couldn't do anything about it. And . . ."

"I'm sorry, Robert. I'm so sorry."

We sat. My chair creaked beneath me as if it would fall to pieces. We could hear grunting and the squeak of bedsprings in the room below us.

"God, this place is a pit," Danielle said. "I promised I wasn't going to whine in front of you, I wasn't going to complain, not after everything you've been through."

"You hold my hand," I said, "and tell me every single little infuriating thing and I'll say it's not complaining if it's true."

Danielle slid the fingers of her right hand between those on my left.

"Everything," she said. "I don't know where to begin."

"Washington," I said.

"It's awful, except for ten minutes a week when it's wonderful. You mustn't tell anyone this: Josephine had a stroke about two months ago. Not a bad one, but it's made it hard for her to walk and she tires so quickly. By four in the afternoon, she's falling asleep at her desk, forgetting names. She's deputized me to—well, to do too much. Meetings and negotiations. She should be sending someone with more experience and everybody knows it. The old men sit there with their fat, red faces, leering at me like they can't decide whether it'll be more fun to break my spirit or swindle me or make lewd propositions. Not that some of Josephine's senior aides are any better. They're jealous. They heard I was coming over and they started calling it my 'conjugal visit.' Josephine started saying it too—I don't think she knows what it means. I heard it so many times, I felt cheap. I went to a department store to try on lingerie and it made me look like a trussed-up pig. One of the salesladies asked if it was for my wedding night and I just broke down crying. So, there's that."

"What are the ten good minutes?" I asked.

"When I come out of those meetings having gotten what I was supposed to. When Josephine and I are alone for a moment and she starts strategizing—'when you run in '22 . . .' And when you write."

I smiled. A better, less exhausted man might have felt a pang over how infrequently he sent his lover a message.

"The trip over was a fiasco. Then the corpswomen at the arena told me they could get me a room by the hour. I should have understood what they meant, but I walked right into the whorehouse and they thought I wanted a girl. I couldn't stop thinking of how the *Tattler* would write it up in the gossip column if they got word. I finally came upstairs and said to myself, 'If I'm with him, none of the rest matters.' But the mattress was just too much. It's probably got fleas. I don't want to contemplate what might be on the sheets. There may be mice nesting in it—I heard a squeak. Robert, I've never in my life slept on straw and tonight isn't going to be the first time, even for you."

I bristled at the last bit. *Rich little princess.*

"Oh, God, I didn't mean—did you have straw mattresses growing up?"

"For a few years," I said. "You're right. They're uncomfortable as hell. And this room is foul. Could you jump us to Paris?"

"I don't have a destination glyph. Could you fly us?"

"I don't have enough powder to make Paris with a passenger."

"And you look exhausted. How long have you been awake?"

It was the wrong question. Better to ask how many hours out of the last twenty-four. Kiyo had been able to count hours awake out of the last seventy-two and venture an accurate guess for the whole war.

Kiyo.

"Maybe if I lie down, just for an hour," I said. "Then we'll figure out how to get dinner. And a fresh powder bag. We'll fly to Paris. Or Fifth Division camp. My tent is nicer than this."

By the time I'd finished speaking, I'd already shook out the mattress to fluff it, stripped off my harness, and laid the tarp from my rope bag over the sheets. I didn't want to contemplate what was on them, either.

"Of course," Dar said. "It still feels like the middle of the afternoon for me. I have a few messages to . . ."

The smell woke me. Whatever ambrosia was, this was it. I was so tired I couldn't move, not even a fingertip. Couldn't open my eyelids.

"He's awake, isn't he," a woman's voice said. "He just heard every word I said."

"I can never tell with him," Dar said. "I don't think so."

"All I'm saying is that Blandings told me both raids would have failed without him. That's six veteran corpswomen he saved, plus the samples. I wouldn't have believed it if I hadn't met him."

"It's probably true. Edith, the stories he tells about his mother—she fought in the Disturbances. She raised him to fight."

"Does he have a brother? Oh, don't give me that look—to recruit! We don't have another man who can fly nearly well enough."

"Three half sisters. You should recruit *them*. The two oldest were Jayhawks. They fought alongside their mother. The youngest is a secretary. Rob's younger than her by seven years."

"Oh, no! Had my three girls and then when I thought I was too old, along came a boy?"

"It might have been on purpose. She'd just gotten married. I don't think he's ever asked."

Then Danielle let out a shuddering breath. "I'm so scared I'm going to lose him, Edie. He's a different person. The way he looked at me—he didn't even recognize me."

"He was stunned, maybe. It's a terrible shock to come back to civilian life so quickly. I remember visiting the Louvre a few days after I got my discharge. Something about the building put me on edge. I couldn't stop thinking, 'In the event I come under fire, fly for that skylight or that door or take cover behind that pillar.' I had a breakdown in the powder room. I still have days like that. Was it bad for you when you went home?"

"I thought I was losing my mind," Danielle said. "I mean, I *did* lose my mind, after my big night. I was delirious. But when I went home, it happened all over again."

I managed to move the fingers on one hand. I pushed myself up into a sitting position.

"Hey, sleepyhead," said Dar.

Edith had brought a roast chicken and vegetables and a bottle of white wine from a restaurant across the street. Heaven.

"How?" I asked, nearly falling over as I stood.

"The ladies of the night downstairs know where to find just about anything," Edith said. "There's a fresh powder bag for you, too. Gen. Blandings is requesting that you stay overnight to receive documents. The smokecarving accident was contained, but she wants details. I'll bring information tomorrow."

"You know a nicer place we could sleep?" I asked.

Edith laughed. "This is as plush as they come in Le Havre. Eat before you collapse."

I shoved a roast fingerling potato in my mouth. "How long was I asleep?" I asked with my mouth full.

"Four hours," Dar answered. "She brought us forks, darling."

I switched from wolfing my food with my hands to more refined gorging.

"I remember what I used to want most," Edith said. "They have a tub downstairs you can borrow. You'll have to haul the hot water up two flights of—"

"I don't mind," I said.

"I've stayed here before," Edith said. "They're professionals. They're not going to rob you or cause trouble. Listen, I have a few more matters to see to tonight. I'll come past in the morning. Is ten o'clock too early?"

The last delivered with a wink.

"Give them hell, sigilwomen," Edith said and slipped out.

• • •

I wrestled the tin washtub up the stairs and into our apartment.

"You squat in it?" Danielle asked, eyeing it with distaste.

"Indeed, madam," I said. "Until you throw me out. Or, if you want a bath, too, you should go first and have the clean water."

"I'm not going to allow you to bathe in dirty water!" she said. "If you have to make an extra ten trips up and down the stairs, I don't care. That makes me a spoiled brat, doesn't it?"

I grinned. "Not if you wash my back."

One of the women downstairs boiled hot water and I carried it up the stairs by the pailful, mixing it with cold water from our sink.

"You gonna watch?" I asked.

I wore the top three buttons of my skysuit undone, in the style of an off-duty flier. Danielle undid the rest of my buttons down to my waist. I stripped in front of her and felt her eyes burning holes into me. We still had the gaslights all the way up. She'd seen me naked plenty of times, just usually not so well illuminated.

I sank into the little bathtub with a groan of pleasure.

"You've never made a noise that lascivious for me," she said.

"I'll start," I said.

She poured water over my head. Her fingertips played over my shoulders. I sighed.

"May I shampoo your hair?" she asked.

She soaped my hair with a bar from her toiletry kit and combed it out with her fingers. I closed my eyes. The familiar jasmine and lavender scent. Soap, not perfume. I'd forgotten.

"I'm going to smell like you," I said. "It'll keep me awake."

"No, *I'll* keep you awake. Besides, it's better than smelling like you haven't had a bath in months. How does your wing—"

"We have a field shower. You pour water into a bucket on top and pull a cord. It spills down on you. It's marvelous. Every three or four days when I get around to it."

She squeezed my shoulders. I gave a milder version of the same groan as before.

"Your skysuit's a mess. Should I even ask about the stains?"

"You don't want to know. Or, exactly what you think. Cold water doesn't take blood out very well, contrary to the old wives' tales. Especially if it's a couple hours before you get a chance to soak it."

Dar poured more warm water over my head to rinse my hair.

"I don't think I've ever just looked at you," she said. "I like it. And I like seeing you out of uniform. That thing makes you look like a woman."

"My skysuit? I always thought it made women look like men. You can't see anything underneath. Leaves everything to the imagination."

"You're doing a lot of imagining about the women in your wing, are you?"

I was glad I couldn't see her expression.

"Ain't none of them offering to give me a bath," I said.

I stood up. Danielle watched me all the while. She gave me a towel.

"Your turn?" I asked.

"I had one this morning," she said. "A real porcelain tub, with hot water that ran out of a faucet and everything. No, I want to play a game. Spread that towel out on the bed and lie on your belly."

She had a bottle of oil that she'd been warming between her hands.

"I want you to lie there. I'm going to rub you down. Don't reach up or try to kiss me. You tell me where it feels good, where to linger. While I'm working, I'm allowed to ask you any question in the world and you have to answer honestly. I'll go from shoulders to toes. And afterward whatever happens, happens."

"I should give *you* the massage," I murmured as I lay down. "You traveled four thousand miles."

"If I let you do it, I would get a one-minute shoulder rub and then you'd knead my bottom, roll me over to oil my breasts, and we'd end up rutting on the floor like wild dogs."

"That sounds wonderful."

"Yeah, but I wanna play with my food," she growled.

She knelt beside me and rolled up the sleeves of her blouse. She drizzled oil on her hands and rubbed them together.

"It's essence of rose," she said. "For healing. Put your head down. Shut your eyes."

She half sat, half knelt astride me, her skirt all spread out around her, her weight just above my buttocks. I could feel her pubic hair poking through her knickers against the small of my back.

She dug into my shoulders with her thumbs. I groaned.

"There," I said. "Right there. For years."

She worked over my shoulders—all the spots that had to carry weight from my harness. Every muscle I'd ever strained leaning against a stasied passenger.

"More," I mumbled into the towel beneath me.

"I like this," Dar said. "Here—" and she sank her fingers into the meaty part above my shoulder blades—"or here?"—and she pressed beside my spine.

"God," I moaned. "How'd you learn this?"

"My unit had a book we shared while we were sitting in the Dardanelles for three months. Sex magic. How to make a man do your bidding. Massages for amnesia. Lovemaking to see the future. But hush. I'm supposed to be the one asking the questions."

She resettled her weight on me.

"Do you love me?" she asked.

"Yes."

"Do you want me?"

"Eight times tonight," I answered.

She gave me a swat on the bottom, just hard enough to make me tingle.

"I hit the last girl who tried to spank me," I warned her.

"That's just an age-old technique for improving blood flow. Answer the question better."

"I want you, eight times, ten times, ten thousand times. Or once tonight and twice tomorrow."

Danielle resumed massaging my back. "If I dump you, do you have another girl who's going to be sitting on top of you before I even turn around?"

The way she was pressing her hips against me suggested we weren't about to break up.

"Nobody. I couldn't. Not a corpswoman."

"Nobody making eyes at you?"

I'd sworn to be honest. "Missy Pitcairn flew a mission with us. She wants to lick ice cream off my bottom."

Dar gave me another swat and then shifted off me so she could run her tongue up the inside of my leg, taking a wide curve over my buttocks. I moaned. She did my other leg in similar fashion, detouring around my stitches. I ground my teeth in ecstasy.

"If that's your secret perversion," Danielle said, "then I'm happy to find a scoop of vanilla. Give me twenty minutes to talk to those—"

"No," I grunted. "Turn me over and—"

"Not yet," she said. I heard rustling and then she climbed back on top of me. Still in her skirt, but naked beneath. I could feel her heat pressed against me.

"Would you with Missy Pitcairn?"

"She's mean."

"*I'm* mean. And she's gorgeous."

I really was under Danielle's power. "If I were single. Yeah."

She brought her hand down hard on my right flank three times. It smarted beautifully.

"She'd break you in half," Dar said.

She started back from the top of my shoulders once more. "What will you do after peace breaks out?"

"I don't know," I answered. "I try not to think more than a day or two ahead."

"Do it now."

"There are days I think I should move to Washington. Be a house husband. Join the fire brigade if I'm bored."

There was no playful swat.

"I can't even tell you how happy that would make me," she said. "You say it like you never would."

"I liked visiting Radcliffe. I'd finish a degree there, maybe. If Addams could find me a job to cover my tuition."

"Of course she would." Dar was running her knuckles up and down my spine. "I would never begrudge you the time at Radcliffe. But I can't spend three years not knowing. It'll eat me up."

She was back to my buttocks, gentle, running her fingers over my tingling skin.

"It's not fair of me to ask," Danielle said. "You're nineteen. But sooner or later 'I don't know' becomes 'no.' All I want is that you don't string me along. If you mean no, don't take three years to say it."

"Dar, I don't know if I'll survive to next week. I don't know if they'll line up the mutineers at the end of the war and shoot them or throw them in prison. I don't know anything."

She was working on my calves now, the tendons of them between her thumb and forefinger, sliding down toward my ankle.

"They say it'll be over by winter," she said. "May I ask you again then?"

"Yes," I said.

"Then give me something to look forward to."

She flipped me over. I was so hard that I ached. She caught me with her oiled hand and lowered herself onto me.

I made a high-pitched grunting shriek that must have upset the clientele downstairs. Danielle rode me, unbuttoning her blouse, and pulled my hands to her breasts. She bent low over me, her hair cascading over my face. She put her lips to mine and rocked on me. I was going to have no endurance at all.

I reached under her skirt and grabbed her by the hips, sliding her up my body. She left a wet streak across my belly, my chest, my chin. I got her over my mouth, my head up under her skirt, and licked the length of her. She tasted of salt and rose oil, like electricity.

"That's not the game!" she gasped.

"I want a different game," I growled. I licked her again, plunging my tongue into her.

"Don't tease. Do it if you're going to— oh!"

I caught hold of the right spot with my tongue and sucked. She jerked and pressed down against me. I slid a finger in and stroked. She ground harder, her short, curly hairs scraping over my upper lip.

Danielle's climax caught hold of her quickly. She clamped her thighs around my head and yanked my hair with both hands, holding me fast. She bucked and shook and shouted. When she'd had enough, she rolled off me, falling off the mattress entirely. She slipped out of her skirt and kicked it across the room.

"Lord, yes," I said. And she was back on top of me. I grabbed hold of her breasts, caught her nipples a moment between my fingers, then took her by the hair and pulled her lips to mine. She clenched her knees to my sides and that finished me.

It was nothing nobody hasn't done a million times. But to us, it was like we'd washed up on some deserted island paradise, having only half planned it that way.

"Like you threw me down a flight of stairs," Danielle whispered as she lay beside me, her complaints over the straw mattress temporarily forgotten. "Flying and tumbling."

"Sex magic?" I asked.

"Must be. Maybe you changed the spell."

She took her blouse the rest of the way off and lay against me.

"What was it supposed to do?" I asked.

"Make you my slave."

"Don't need magic for that. But you'd get bored with me if I didn't put up a fight."

She kissed my collarbone, the base of my throat, my Adam's apple, my lips.

"No I wouldn't," she whispered. "Come be my slave by day and I'll be yours by night."

20

> Fliers would employ the high-altitude bombing method to drop canisters, with targets to include frontline enemy divisions as well as select civilian populations such as those in Berlin, Hamburg, Munich, and Vienna. Our preferred biologic agent has a ninety-five percent fatality rate and cannot be passed from one person to another. We have sufficient quantity to cause between three and ten million casualties within a week, depending on weather patterns and which population centers are chosen.
>
> Col. Tomasina Blandings, "Briefing #4 on the Conduct of Potential Offensive Operations," November 3, 1914

WE BREAKFASTED AT THE LITTLE CAFÉ ACROSS THE STREET. I WAS ravenous for fresh bread and jam and Danielle. Despite the quarantine, we saw dozens of people out, doing their marketing or walking to work.

We had the rented room and ourselves looking almost respectable by the time Edith arrived. She handed me a sealed folder.

"This is from a woman in the smokecarving who worked with Blandings in Nevada," Edith said. "She doesn't want anyone repeating her name. Regarding the recent incident."

"What did they find?" Danielle asked. "Senator Cadwallader-Fulton needs to know."

Edith looked uncomfortable. "I don't have any problem telling you, Danielle, but Robert doesn't need to hear this. If he were captured . . ."

"Tell him," Danielle said. "Anything you would tell Senator Cadwallader-Fulton, you can tell Robert. I speak with the senator's full authority on that."

Edith blew out a breath. "Okay. Sigilwoman Canderelli, I hope you hold up well under torture, if it comes to that. So, the smokecarvers in Le Havre had an accident the day before you conducted your raid on Neuville. They were taking a vial of plague smoke out of storage, to run tests on it to ensure it had retained its potency. They dropped it."

"Oops," I said.

"That's the understatement of the decade. Seven women were exposed. They initiated a proper quarantine and saved countless lives."

Which would explain why the transporter chains had closed right around the time Dr. Synge arrived.

"They all died, within a day, as they knew they would," Edith continued.

"Jesus," I said. "What kills that fast?"

"Augmented yellow fever," Edith answered. "Twenty years ago, we had thousands of soldiers and corpswomen in Cuba fall sick with the regular strain. While the smokecarvers were working on a cure, they found a way to introduce the virus into the lungs using a vapor carrier. It made the disease much, much deadlier. They thought it would make an ideal weapon, because an infected person can't spread it to another without a mosquito to carry it—there would be no risk of it running wild during the cold months. But it didn't work the way they thought it would. A few days later, all the doctors and nurses who cared for the first group of victims fell ill. They died too."

"Oh, Lord," I said.

"When the second group started dying, the Corps reinstituted the quarantine," Edith continued. "That was yesterday. They isolated everyone who came in contact with the medical staff, but no one else has gotten sick."

Danielle rubbed her chin thoughtfully. "This may actually be a good thing. The danger with biological weapons was always that Gen. Fallmarch might be stupid enough to use them. If this was the 'safe' one and it spread anyway, it may discourage her."

"You have a higher opinion of Fallmarch than I do, then," Edith said. "She doesn't want to start a panic, so she's planning to reopen Le Havre by tonight. It would be smarter to keep the city closed a few more days."

"Could we get out today?" Danielle asked. "A jaunt to Paris."

"I'd advise against it. Fallmarch has a combat air patrol up—the fastest Logistics fliers in the Corps armed with Lewis guns. They shot down a pair of nurses last night who broke out of the hospital and tried to flee the city."

"No!" I said.

Edith nodded. "It would be disappointing to lose the two of you. In the meantime, the police *are* letting people go out of their houses so long as they don't leave the city proper. A romantic tour of Le Havre, perhaps?"

Dar and I went down to the beach, which had been a popular destination in the prewar years. Rows of cabins and saltwater baths lined the shore, now with their doors all chained shut. I rolled up my pants and waded knee-deep into the water, racing the waves back in. Dar watched, amused, from the strand.

"I always forget the sea is novel for you," she called.

"It just keeps going!" I yelled back.

I misjudged a big wave, slipped, and ended up sprawled face-first in the surf.

"Dumb country boy," Dar said. "From way out on the plains."

We retreated to the apartment and Danielle took me back to bed to warm me up. As we lay there afterward, she studied me intently.

"May I ask something rude?" Danielle said.

I nodded, my whole body soaking in her touch.

"Maybe it's that I haven't seen you in so long. Or that you've been out in the sun all summer and you're wearing your hair longer. But are you a lot darker than the rest of your family?"

I chuckled. Nothing that my half sister Angela hadn't remarked on a hundred times at the swimming hole growing up. "Complexion-wise?" I said. "A good deal, yeah."

"Your dad?" she asked. "He was, too?"

"I've only seen one picture of him and you couldn't tell anything from it," I answered. "He was born in Chile, but that can mean anything. European or Incan. I get the impression he blended in well in Cuba when he deployed there with the Société. If you're asking did he have a drop of African blood or Indian—probably."

"Did you ever have a name for what that makes you?" she asked.

"No," I said. "Always thought of myself as a dumb white country boy until pretty recently. Or deviant male philosopher."

I pulled the duvet over us. The ladies downstairs had loaned it to us. It was improbably thick and had a wonderful weight to it.

"You'd like me better if I said I was colored?" I asked.

"No. But it would give us something else in common."

I could guess what had prompted this. "Folks being mean to you in Washington over your ma?"

"Over how many sixteenths of this and that. They all want a name for me. It's happened my whole life, but now deciding what I am—what words to use—is part of my job. They do it under the guise of being polite. 'Should I call you colored? Do you prefer mixed? Do you call yourself a Negro?' Why the hell do they have to put a name on it?"

"Oh, you're as white as they come," I said. "This great-great-somebody on the Mayflower and that one signing the Declaration of Independence."

"Constitution," she corrected. "And that's three greats on my dad's side."

"And which fork is for the fish and which one for the salad. And Daddy and I played golf last weekend and I need a new two-iron."

She laughed. "Only if I wanted to lose would I hit a two-iron. I've been playing from the men's tees and crushing the old lechers Josephine sends me to mind. Add that to my ten minutes of happy."

"Only question they ought to be asking is whether you prefer Miss or Ms."

"I'm only twenty-two. I'm too young for a Ms."

She ran her hand over the pockmarks on the left side of my face—scars from the shotgun blast she'd hit me with while we were fending off the Trenchers back at Radcliffe. (If the gun had been filled with buckshot instead of fine birdshot, she would have shot away half my head.)

"Washington is so awful some days," Danielle said. "I feel like if we make one mistake, it could set philosophers' rights back fifty years. I come home to my apartment and I just want someone to dump half my troubles on. I want you."

"Love," I said. "It's going to be—"

"It's going to get worse before there's any chance of it getting better. I can't sleep at night for worrying over the end of the war. When we come over—when Josephine's supposed to be in charge of tens of thousands of women in the field, but needs to excuse herself for her three o'clock nap—she's going to lay it on me."

"She couldn't choose a better deputy," I said.

"Yes she could! I'm going to be in so far over my head. Could you come to help? When Blandings calls for her mutiny? Come find me. Don't let Blandings send you on whatever suicide mission she's planning. If you're out there behind German lines with a sack full of grenades, I'll lose my mind. I can't afford to worry over you and Josephine at the same time."

"It won't be a suicide mission," I said.

"Oh no?" Danielle said, pulling away from me. "You didn't tell me you blew up an aeroplane. Or a tank. How many of your friends got killed on those raids?"

"How did you—"

"Edith told me. You didn't even say a word."

There was no possible reply that didn't make me sound like an ass. I gave the simplest one: "I didn't want you to worry."

"You don't think I'm sick every morning, looking over the casualty lists in the newspaper? Especially when I haven't heard from you in a couple of days?"

"I'm sorry, Dar."

"You're not sorry! You're the biggest volunteer in the history of the Corps. I want you to promise me: When everything goes wrong, you'll come and find me. If it's a question of where you can do the greatest good, then come to wherever we set up headquarters and help plot strategy. You'd be invaluable. You've been on the front lines. I'll give you a pile of maps and you tell us how to beat the Germans."

"Okay," I said.

"I need more than *okay*," Danielle said. "I need to know you're on my side. Robert, this isn't about you having one more opportunity to prove yourself, it's about the life and death of millions of people. Because I don't trust Gen. Blandings."

"Why not?"

"Robert, you should hear the things people say about her in Washington! She's a German spy, she's working to overthrow the lawful American government, she's engineering a takeover of the Corps. I don't believe any of that, but I know she's holding out on the senator. She sends plenty of useful information about German smoke and what kind of dispersant to use and how many reinforcements she thinks we'll need. But not a peep about her big fail-safe plan. We're talking about how to bring over twenty thousand women to fight without violating international law and she's plotting something that'll destabilize the whole situation. It's infuriating—it's like trying to juggle flaming knives while someone blindfolds you and claims she's helping. Do *you* know anything about her plan?"

For the first time I wondered if Danielle's visit might be less social than I'd assumed.

"Not much," I said. "Blandings needs a male flier. She'd been looking for one for a long time before she heard about me."

"Why?"

"I have no idea. She hasn't told me."

"And you really let it go at that? No questions, no digging for more information? Just 'Yes, ma'am. Of course, ma'am.' That's not you."

"She's a one-star general, Dar! All I know is that she's planning something, she'd rather not go through with it if she doesn't have to, and she thinks that maybe it could win the war overnight. Bloodlessly. That's it. And Radcliffe's involved."

"Of course Radcliffe's involved!" Dar said, exasperated. "They've splashed out so much money that even the German army has commented on it. Labs, equipment, precious metals. They purchased an entire *ton* of platinum. They've bought so much iridium that the price on the international markets has quadrupled. Do you know anything about all that?"

"They need Murchison and me for something," I said. "Ms. Addams is coordinating it."

"Addams," Danielle scoffed.

The two women had never gotten along, even when Addams's job had been protecting Danielle.

"Freddy's involved," I said.

Danielle cocked her head at that. "Fred Unger? Whatever for?"

"Research of some kind."

"On what?"

"The transport sigil, I think."

"With what goal?"

Danielle had gotten out of bed and was digging through her bag for a pencil and paper.

"Oh, you know Freddy—he needed all of eight seconds before he got completely incomprehensible. Energy and efficiency. It sounded like the same thing they've been trying to do for fifty years. Jump farther with a bigger radius."

Danielle was writing down every word.

"Do you remember anything he said specifically?"

"Something about the oxidation state of metals not mattering. For powder, I think."

"Of course it matters!" Danielle said. "You can only run a transport with powder made from an element in group 3A on the periodic table. Aluminum or boron. Aluminum's easier."

"I never knew that."

"Why should you? You're a flier. What else did he say?"

"That's all I remember. And Addams said they want to capture Berlin."

Danielle set her pencil down and gave a half laugh. "Berlin? That's insane. What army is she planning to do *that* with?"

"I don't know. Yours?"

Danielle really did laugh at that. "God, but you can see the trouble, right? Trying to plan with all that going on in the background. Would you promise me something? Whatever you find out, you'll tell me right away."

"Yeah, of course," I said.

"Robert, if you love me—tell me I'm yours and you're mine. Tell me that when I give you the word, you'll stop whatever you're doing and come. Wherever you are, whatever's happening, you'll come to me. Even if the world is ending. Come be with me. We'll do everything we can. We'll do it together."

I nodded and my mangled ear rubbed against her face.

Having decided that the second round of yellow fever had died out, the Corps reopened the transporter chains the following morning. Back in Washington, a minor crisis had broken out over a spending bill and the senator messaged Dar to ask whether she could possibly come home early.

"She has a whole staff of aides," I complained. "Let one of them handle it. We'll have our last night together."

"She's suspicious of them," Danielle said. "It's worse since the stroke. I don't know why she's latched onto me as much as she has."

"Because you're you," I sighed.

Danielle and I exchanged the documents that Cadwallader-Fulton and Blandings had sent each other. We packed. It was like she'd poured a pail full of sadness down my throat and I could feel it backing up into my mouth and eyes. I tried not to look at her too much.

"You should fly to Paris for the afternoon," Danielle said. "You'd like it."

"We'll go together," I said. "After."

She kissed me and my lips felt dry and clumsy on hers. "Come safe home, Robert," she said.

"Give 'em hell," I replied.

And then I was alone.

I settled our account with the ladies downstairs and wandered the streets for an hour. I bought chocolates for Punnett, a copy of *Les Trois Mousquetaires* for Millen, and the most lurid shade of red nail polish I could find for Devereaux. No hope for the other errands—but as I messaged back to camp, I learned that Blandings had sent Andrada to Paris, so at least the boots had been secured, along with the knitting needles and brassieres.

Know you're just terribly disappointed not to get to play dress-up in my underwear, wrote Vos, who was watching the board. A flicker of a smile played over my face.

No need, I replied, *Danielle lets me wear hers.*

And then a moment later: *Well played! Drale just read that while eating soup and it came out her nose.*

How could I ever leave them, even for Danielle? If it ever came to choosing, should I fight alongside the women I'd been under fire with or the one I loved? Maybe I wouldn't have to decide. Maybe the German army would collapse and sue for peace.

I flew home.

"He goes to the least romantic city in France and comes back a day early," Millen crowed to me in the mess tent, in front of the whole division, which had liberated a bottle of spirits or ten during its days off. "I love it. Did she dump you?"

"Not yet," I yelled back. "Did you finally dump Mr. Millen?"

A howl went up from the women.

"Canderelli," Millen shouted, "you tell your Radcliffe friends to get to work on a sigil for time travel. I'm going to send a divorce attorney back to 1909 and it'll save me a lot of trouble."

"You didn't get married until 1910, ma'am," Devereaux deadpanned.

"So, I'll marry the divorce lawyer and never have to work a day in my life, much less be mother to the worst-behaved squadron in the Corps."

A cheer went up for that, too.

I gave Millen the novel I'd bought her. "It's about a bunch of mutinous soldiers who get caught up in politics," I said. "You wanted something made up, right?"

Millen looked pleased. "I've never read it. Thank you."

I slipped Punnett the chocolates and she had an expression on her stout face like I'd handed her a chest full of gold.

"Oh, gimme one!" Andrada said.

"No!" Punnett said cheerfully. "Nobody gets one. I'm going to save them."

"I order you . . ." Andrada said, only three-quarters joking.

"Chocolate is outside the chain of command, ma'am," Devereaux countered.

"They'll never be better than they are right now," Andrada cajoled. "You don't *save* chocolates, you eat them!"

"If it's so offensive to you that no one gets one . . ." Punnett said.

She took one of the chocolates and shoved it into my mouth. It had a horribly over-sweetened cherry-cream center, but I chewed theatrically and swallowed it.

"You bastard," Andrada said. "I'll get my knife and cut it out of him."

"Run," Devereaux suggested. "Run!"

It was as familiar and comfortable as home. If you'd asked me on what day I went from being a curiosity to "just one of the girls" I couldn't have said. You didn't abandon your sisters. But then again, Danielle and conspiracies and Radcliffe and true love.

I took the documents to the farmhouse and turned them over to Gen. Blandings, who broke the seal and read, her face impassive.

"For a man who was just on leave you look weary," she observed.

"Worries for the future," I said.

"Hmm," Blandings said. "Danielle pumped you for information?"

"Yeah."

"And you told her everything?"

I gave a rueful grin at that. "How'd you know?"

"Because you're nineteen and in love. And because she *is* an extraordinary woman."

"She asked me to go help her and the senator if things fall apart," I said. "She says you're withholding your plan from them."

Blandings folded her hands demurely. "I've learned that senators make very bad co-conspirators where details are concerned. They talk for a living. Even senators' aides with the best of intentions and a reputation for discretion talk too much."

I shifted in my chair. "She said you're planning a suicide mission for me. I want to know what."

"Robert, I say this with all possible goodwill and with deep appreciation for your exemplary service and valor: Not merely no, but *hell* no. Telling you is as good as telling Miss Hardin."

"Then I hope you'll forgive me, ma'am, for saying this, but if the Apocalypse is coming, I'd rather be with her than you."

Blandings looked at me calmly. "If when the time comes you decide your energies would be better spent supporting Danielle, on whom so much will rest, I'll give you my blessing. I'll send you a nice bottle of wine on the day we celebrate our victory. But you remain our best option. It's one of the few things Belle Addams and I agree on fully. You're the one we chose."

I didn't want to hear one more vague compliment from her. "I think you should pick out that bottle of wine, ma'am."

"I will," Blandings said. If she was disappointed, she hid it well. "All I ask is that you think it through. Besides, we'll have to survive the next week first."

Suddenly, I understood what had provoked the dark, drunken atmosphere of the mess tent.

"The Americans are attacking at Saint-Mihiel?" I asked.

"As soon as the rain stops."

21

A creeping bombardment is only as good as the least accurate wristwatch involved.

Brian F. Mayweather, *The Last Barrage*, 1927

WE HAD THREE MORE DAYS OF RAIN. EVACS WERE QUIET. PUNNETT, Andrada, and I played cards for hours. We said very little. The riotous mood gave way to slow, grating dread, like a rasp being drawn across your knuckles at the rate of one inch an hour.

When Pershing attacked with the American Expeditionary Force, we would have no rest for days. The offensive was set to go off in the middle of our sector, which meant we would be the first women in, with the rest of R&E to reinforce per our instructions. If you liked to bet, you'd wager we would lose a flier or three trying to evacuate all the wounded—aid stations positioned too close to the fighting, bad landings, crashes from exhaustion.

The water dripped through the holes in the mess tent's roof like the acid in my stomach.

Lord, but th waitng is alwys hard, Mother wrote. *We used to play stupd games to pass the time. We smokd mint mixd w/ tbaco in litl cigars—who cld make hers last longst. How mny pebbles y cld stack in a column. Asinine stff.*

"Run of three," I said, slapping a card on the table.

"Queen for a mudge," Punnett countered. She picked up one of her chocolates, rolled it gently between her fingers, and set it back in the box. The chocolate had become misshapen from all the handling.

Do the best y can, Ma wrote. *Protect yr wingmates. Always gets messy on a big one.*

Put Mother aside. Put Danielle aside. Put "after" aside. Don't think more than two days ahead. Not more than one day ahead. Not more than half a day.

"It's going to be tomorrow," Punnett predicted.

"You've said that two days in a row," I replied.

"I'm going to be right eventually. Then I get to say 'told you so.'"

I had board duty in the afternoon and got to witness the ninth act of Millen and Drale's days-long shouting match.

"It's not safe for us to go out there with only two squadrons!" Millen insisted. "You're going to put me at a forward aid post with three women and how many hundred wounded? They're going to eat us alive."

"We have two squadrons from Fourth Division and another four squads from Second on immediate alert," Drale replied. "That's seventy-two extra women."

"Then bring them into camp tonight and we'll go out in the morning with sixteen fliers each instead of four."

"That's not how it works. Saint-Mihiel is in our sector. We're first-in."

"First-dead, you mean."

"Teeny! You're going to scare the girls."

Drale glanced at me as she said it.

"So, get Gen. Blandings on the board with Gen. Niejenhuis!" Millen countered. "Niejenhuis is fucking this up and it hasn't even started yet. She's leaving three hundred fliers from First Division uncommitted because they're on the wrong side of a line that she penciled in on a map. Tell Blandings to refuse orders unless Niejenhuis commits First Division. Tell her!"

"Gen. Niejenhuis will mobilize them soon as the numbers start coming in."

"Well, First Division is going to have to dig our graves before they start running casualties and I know how you hate that kind of inefficiency."

"Teeny—"

"You are not sending me out there to die! I will resign. I will resign *right now*!"

"Go cool off," Drale said.

"I will *not*! The infantry is going to get slaughtered and then we're going to get slaughtered trying to get them out shorthanded."

The impressive thing was how long the two of them could go at it without one striking the other or storming away. The rain pattered on the roof and they argued. After three hours, Drale took over the board and shooed me out of the farmhouse. I wandered back to the mess tent, where Punnett had fallen asleep in her chair. Andrada, having gotten bored with sharpening her knife, was playing solitaire.

"Should I be scared that Millen's scared?" I asked.

Andrada shrugged. "She always gets upset before a big one. She was in Third Division in '16 at the Somme, when they put their landing fields too close to the lines and the Germans overran them. Total chaos. Women captured or shot down. That day is the reason R&E doesn't have a Third Division anymore—it's an unlucky number. Millen might be the only survivor still flying."

Another story not to tell Danielle. I should write her and tell her . . . what? That I was waiting and frightened? That we had an incompetent for a two-star general in Niejenhuis and could Danielle's pet senator fix it for us?

Andrada ran out of moves. She gathered her cards and reshuffled.

A noise woke me in the small hours of the night. I rolled over and tried to understand it. It was the sound of the absence of rain. Silence.

It would be today, then, if the weather had cleared. The ground was bad, but not impassable. Pershing had borrowed a thousand tanks and a thousand aircraft. He couldn't afford to wait any longer.

I tried to go back to sleep. After an hour of staring at the tent flaps, I got up and rubbed mineral oil into my harness. I polished my boots. I dug through my duffel and found the chain with my good luck charms on it—a medallion of Mercury and a vial of silver chloride—and tucked it beneath the collar of my skysuit, regulations against necklaces be damned.

"From ghoulies and ghosties and long-leggedy beasties and things that go bump in the night," I whispered, "Mother, deliver us."

I still said it before every overnight watch. Anyone's guess whether it worked during the daylight hours.

I hauled myself up to the farmhouse, where the rest of the insomniacs were trickling in. Millen patted me on the shoulder. Andrada picked a stray blade of grass off my sleeve. Punnett chewed her nails. Lt. Drale had her map out and was measuring distances for the four hundredth time. She motioned me over.

"Robert, you'll be at casualty point F for Frances with Millen, Punnett, and Devereaux," Drale reminded me, though our assignments had been set for days.

Point F was the southernmost of the six new evacuation points that the army had designated for the opening hours of the attack. Since the Americans hoped to push northeast toward Metz, we expected the majority of casualties to pour into Points A and B. F should be the least busy—perhaps no mistake that Drale had assigned Millen to command that one.

At three in the morning, the thunder began, rolling without end: every American artillery piece in the theater firing. One gun for every fifty feet of line along which the infantry would advance. The noise rippled through your body in a way that conspired to give you palpitations or loosen your bowels. It went on that way for an hour.

Then at four, a five-minute pause.

"Not yet," Devereaux said. She was putting a third coat of polish on her nails with tiny, perfect strokes. "They're letting the guns cool down. They'll send the engineers over the top at five thirty to clear obstacles. Then they'll launch the real attack at six once it starts to get light."

The firing resumed. Devereaux's nails dried. We kitted out in our harnesses and waited. Bags enough to resupply our division three times over were filled and stacked in the supply shed.

A second lull in the artillery came at five, followed by a fresh round of all-out firing. I wouldn't have believed there were so many shells in the world.

"Robert?" Punnett said. "Can I tell you something?"

"What?"

"If anything happens, I don't have an Aunt Della. I made her up on my Form 41. I don't want my parents getting my personal effects. They can go to hell."

That frightened me more than all the rest: that Punnett, no good with a gun, but steady as a draft horse, unflappable in the field, always the right word to a soldier or orderly, plodding, phlegmatic, enduring, felt moved to make a confession.

"Why, what'd they do to you?" I asked.

"What'd they *do*," Punnett scoffed. "What a man's question. I had four brothers. Them, they all finished eighth grade or twelfth grade, even if they didn't have half a brain between them. Me, I got to fourth grade and my pa said, 'Louise ain't too bright. Let her keep house.' When I was older, I learned to draw korus. Drew them for our farm. Drew for the neighbors to earn a little money. Saved up for months so I could pay for flying lessons. Pa found my jar full of silver dollars one day, took it. 'No good comes of a girl having money.' I wanted to move into town and get a job. Ma said, 'Not a woman's place.' Wanted to join up. 'Can't spare you.' "

"That's terrible," I said.

"No, it's not! That's better than most women in the world have it. But I couldn't abide that kind of double standard. So, I ran away to join the Corps. Made it to the recruiting office in Chicago and lied through my teeth. 'Sure, I know a few stasis sigils. Expert messagist.' Maybe they felt sorry for me."

"They knew quality when they saw it."

"That's sweet, coming from a boy. I learned to fly in the Corps. Took me three tries to join R&E. And now I'm the worst flier in the division."

"Second worst. Cunningham."

"She flies pretty, at least."

"She flies *dainty*. Not what I'd want being evacuated."

Punnett nodded in agreement. "Sure. Right. Just, if something happens, tell the Lieutenant I don't have an Aunt Della to send my effects to."

"Drale's right over there," I said. "Tell her yourself."

The Lieutenant was checking message boards and quietly cussing out Second Division.

"I'll tell her tomorrow," Punnett said. She considered her chocolates and popped one in her mouth.

"Any good?" I asked.

"It's fine," Punnett said, chewing like it was a piece of gristle. "It's great."

At six, Gen. Blandings joined us, wearing her dress uniform jacket over her skysuit—the working general's solution to having enough medals and ribbons so that everyone at an evac point understood who was in charge. She had her saber strapped to her leg.

"Ring for assembly please," she said.

We took lanterns onto the landing field and lined up by four-woman flight team.

"Good morning," Blandings said. "They're attacking today. It will fall to us to save as many as we can. I could not ask for a finer division. Every one of you has proven yourself a hundred times over. Today will be another trial. We will pass it, too, resoundingly."

Beside me Punnett hooked her thumbs under her shoulder straps to hide her hands' shaking.

"There is a high risk of the Germans shelling the casualty stations or even overrunning them in a counterattack," Blandings continued. "That's how we lost Third Division at the Somme. I do *not* want fliers pre-positioning out there and getting pinned down. Wait in camp until your evacuation point requests you and confirms that they're not under fire. If your assigned station hasn't messaged by seven thirty, we'll deploy you elsewhere. I'll be at Point A to organize the reinforcing squadrons."

Millen yawned and stretched beside me.

"Fly to the utmost," Blandings said. "Protect and help each other. Come safe home."

"Up the Corps!" Bernice roared—the senior Sig-1's foremost duty.

"Up the Fifth!" we bellowed in reply.

The artillery increased in volume. Devereaux retched. Punnett tried not to cry.

"Ready positions," Blandings called out. "Mr. Canderelli to take over the board, please."

Blandings grabbed me by the harness as I jogged to the farmhouse. "Don't let Millen go freelancing," she whispered. "Take your saber."

For all the good a sword would do me. The most they'd done in training was show us how to wear it for a parade. But I retrieved it from my tent all the same.

"In what century were you frocked, Robert A?" Millen asked me as I took my place at the board, scraping against the table with my scabbard. "Your sword's from before the Civil War."

I hadn't even taken it out since the day Dean Murchison had given it to me. It must have been handed down to him, too.

At 6:20, before there was even enough light to land by, Point A was bawling for help.

"Point Alice reporting one hundred plus, moderate to severe," I announced. "Not under fire. They're requesting all available fliers."

"We'll drop flares to illuminate," Gen. Blandings called out. "A-flight on me!" And they were gone.

Before I could message Point A to acknowledge, the next request came in.

"B for Bethany says 'many,' requesting two full wings."

"They're dreaming," said Lt. Drale. "My three ladies, on your feet!"

Charlotte and Diane made their requests a few minutes later. They estimated twenty-five and forty casualties, respectively.

"Not terrible, maybe," I said.

But Blandings and Drale were already sending messages over the Divisional glyph, calling two squads from Second Division to A and another two to B. They directed one extra flight team from Fourth Division to C. None to D. Then Blandings ordered all remaining reinforcements to A.

"Would be nice if they'd left some for the rest of us," said Andrada, who would command Point E for Elizabeth, now without any available backup.

"There's another message from the Lieutenant," I said, showing them the Divisional board. "This is bad."

Casualties vry hvy at A & B. Artillery mistimed barrage, hit our own first-wave infntry. Drale.

"Shit," said Andrada. "That's the army for you."

"Why aren't the southern points calling?" Punnett asked. "That should be like hundreds of men hit in the first minute, right?"

"Maybe the southern evac sites got shelled?" Devereaux suggested. "Killed the board technicians?"

"Or they're shunting casualties north," I suggested.

"It's six miles from Point F to Point D," Punnett said. "It's too far for them to walk."

"We should launch someone and check," Millen said.

"Absolutely not, ma'am," said Andrada. "Blandings told us we stay put until the evac points call us or it's seven thirty."

"What good does that do?" Millen snapped. "You want to leave the wounded out there to die?"

"Millen!" Andrada said.

"Go to hell, you want to shirk like that!" Millen snarled. She walked out of the farmhouse.

"We're at the ready, ma'am!" Andrada shouted after her. "You can't just leave! Teeny!"

We couldn't not have our Sig-1, not on the day of the biggest American offensive in the entire war.

"I'll flip you for command of Point F, Louise," Devereaux said to Punnett.

"Not me," Punnett said.

"Robert?" Devereaux suggested.

"Does that mean you have to chase Millen down instead of me?" I asked. I unsheathed my sword and handed it to her.

"Don't you ever sharpen this?" Devereaux said. "It's blunter than a hammer."

Millen came marching back into the farmhouse with her own saber, a much newer model that had been honed within a hair of its life.

"You want to tell me what I can't do?" Millen shouted at Andrada, pointing the sword at her.

"Teeny, put that away before you hurt yourself," Andrada said. She put her feet up on the table in what seemed to me a remarkable display of cool nerves. Though possibly it wasn't the first time Millen had threatened her with a weapon in hand.

"Oh, God, look!" Punnett said.

On the Divisional board: *Cungham put her team dwn on wrng sid of lines at D. Thyr undr hvy fire. Injrd x3. I will attempt rescu. Send any furthr 5th Div rescue requsts to Bvt-2 Candrli. Drale.*

"Oh no," I said. Brevet Sig-2 Canderelli—field promotion to head the ready rescue team.

"Congratulations, ma'am," Devereaux said, handing my sword back. "*You* reason with her."

The clock showed seven.

E for Elizabeth. 100+ severe. Send all avail.

"Oh for Christ's sake!" Andrada said. "They didn't all just show up. Did their tech think they couldn't message us until after seven?"

"Go," said Millen. "I'll stab you when you get back."

Andrada and her three lifted away. But still nothing for us at F.

"If we're putting you in charge of the ready rescue team," Millen said to me, "we should move you to the northern part of the line. That's where they've got the highest volume, so that's where someone will end up digging a hole with her landing. Let's make sure F is clear and get you north."

"Ma'am, Gen. Blandings said I'm supposed to hit you with my saber if you try to freelance," I said.

Millen sneered at me. "Hit me with your saber? Sweetie, I went through training in '14, when it lasted six months and we did an hour a day of fencing. Try it."

"No swordplay," said Devereaux.

"Fine," said Millen. "But either something's really wrong at F or they've closed it and didn't bother to tell us. Waiting a half hour won't change that. We have to know. Let's go."

I shared a look with Punnett and Devereaux—balancing a direct order from Blandings with the gnawing feeling that Millen was probably right.

We launched as a group. Millen led us southeast, a hard, short flight, keeping us low at one hundred feet. The fighting was east of us, though as close as a couple hundred yards in spots. Shells from the big guns arced over our heads.

Half a mile short of Point F we saw a huge collection of men on the downslope of a shallow ridge. We huddled in the air.

"Tell me that's their reserves getting ready to charge over the hill," I said.

But we could see the bandages, blood-soaked, hear them screaming out in pain, the roar of their voices rising in intensity as they caught sight of us. They were pointing toward us, reaching up, calling out prayers or curses.

"Maybe the stretcher-bearers dumped the first round and ran?" Millen said. "There's no landing field. There's no board tech or medical officers to keep order. Maybe Point F proper is doing better . . ."

We flew on another thirty seconds and found Point F beautifully marked, with a labeled tarpaulin staked out on the ground and a command tent. Empty. There was no time to figure out what had gone wrong. We looped back to the collection of wounded.

"Okay," Millen said. "There's a thousand of them at least. They're on terrain with a greater than twenty-degree incline—we *cannot* land in the middle of them. We'll set down at the base of the hill and organize triage. Robert A will put a couple dozen in stasis. If things get out of hand, we'll grab a few and fly them out. That might calm down the rest."

Millen wrote to the Divisional glyph: *Point F musterd wrong. 0.5mi NW of intended site. 1K+ wnded, rpt 1000+. No techs or triage. Send multpl wings. Need MPs, ordrlies.*

"Follow me in," Millen said. "Slow landing. Stay close."

We headed toward the base of the ridge. The wounded surged toward us, blocking our approach.

"Break off!" Millen shouted. "Up!"

One of the injured men caught Devereaux by the foot, trying to pull her to the ground. His entire left cheek was shot away—you could see into his mouth, see the teeth. Devereaux thrashed and landed a kick to his face. He let go.

Near riot at new F, Millen wrote. *Send rnfrcmnts armed.*

"Okay," Millen said. "Last try. We'll back off two hundred yards and land again. If they swarm us, we'll launch and wait until Blandings sends us another fifty women."

This time, we had enough room to touch down before the injured men came hobbling toward us.

"Robert A, hold them back," Millen ordered. "I'll stasis. We'll load Cora, then Louise, then me. Everybody—if you get in trouble, launch."

I approached the wounded at a steady walk.

"Stop where you are!" I shouted. "We'll get everybody out. Everyone flies today."

They didn't stop. A couple dozen came toward me, with another hundred following more tentatively. Not the worst wounded, but rather the ones able to get to us.

"Stop!" I shouted. "Stay back. You got a buddy worse off than you, help him up front."

Nobody listened. The first one, deathly pale, arm in a sling, and face slick with sweat, tried to push past me. I caught him by the front of his uniform.

"Stop," I said to him. "We need room to work."

I pulled him to the ground so Millen could draw a stasis on him.

"Don't you touch him!" another man shouted. His left ankle was turned almost backward, his entire pants leg hanging in shreds. He was leaning on a rat-faced man who was clutching a bandage to the side of his neck.

Millen got the first man stasied. A half dozen men were already past us, converging on Punnett and Devereaux.

"No!" I shouted. "Everybody back!"

I drew my saber and scored a line in the earth with it.

"Stay behind the line!" I shouted.

Millen separated the man with the shattered ankle from the rat-faced one and stasied them, too.

"What do they get to go for?" a man objected, pushing his way up. "I got a friend who's worse off—"

"Then bring him up. We'll take him."

"You bring 'em!" someone else shouted. "We been here two hours! Where *you* been?"

I looked back at Devereaux, whom Punnett had loaded with a pair of stasied men, fore and aft. Three other wounded had a hold of her. Millen was pointing her saber at one.

"Get off her!" I shouted at the wounded. "Get back!"

I ran to Devereaux and grabbed one of the men, but he wouldn't let go.

"Get off them!" shouted a man from the crowd. He came staggering forward, a giant, six inches taller than me, yanking the soldiers off Devereaux, batting them about the head with a fist the size of a sledgehammer. His other arm dangled uselessly at his side.

"They can't fly if you're grabbing on!" he roared.

Millen got another one harnessed and that made two casualties for Punnett as well.

"We're getting everyone out!" I shouted. "Line up. We'll put you under one at a time. Form up!"

The idea seemed to be taking hold among the front rank, but then shells began to fall on the peak of the hill. The walking wounded stampeded toward us, carrying or dragging the more severe cases.

I held my saber in front of me to push them back. They went over and around and through me. The giant man shouldered in beside me. One or two others joined him, but we were overwhelmed.

"Go!" Millen shouted to Devereaux and Punnett. "Get to the hospital. Go!"

The pair launched. The sight of them leaving threw the rest of the casualties into a panic:

"Don't leave us!"

"Come back!"

"You bitches! Leaving us to die."

"Help!" Millen screamed. "Get off! Get back!"

She was ten feet away but I couldn't see her through the crowd.

"Millen!" I shouted. "Teeny!"

I flailed at them with my blunt weapon. A man coughing up blood reached for me and I swung at him, feeling the bones in his wrist shatter under my saber's blow; I shoved a gut shot man to the ground; I smashed my pommel into a man's face, breaking his nose. At last I saw Millen—tall, skinny, alone—striking out at one man after another with the flat of her sword. Her eye had already bruised black. She stumbled toward me.

"Up!" she said, spitting out blood and a tooth.

We launched together and nearly hit Punnett, who was circling above us. She'd stayed; Devereaux had continued on to the field hospital.

"You were supposed to go!" Millen shouted at her.

"I wasn't going to let them just—"

Someone fired a shot at us. Two or three others joined in.

"You bastards!" Punnett shouted.

"Get clear! Go!" Millen shouted.

Another shot, then a thump and an "oof," as if Punnett had had the wind knocked out of her. She didn't call out. She pulled the release strap and dropped her forward passenger, pulled again to release the rear. The stasied bodies tumbled to the ground. She sagged in behind them. The mob was over her in a second.

"Louise!" I screamed.

I pulled the release on my rope bag, which fell twenty feet to the ground and hit hard enough to make the wounded nearby take a step back. I followed it to the ground and drew my saber.

22

Quis salvet ipsas salvatores?

Motto of R&E ready rescue fliers, 1898–1918

THE SMELL OF BLOOD ALL AROUND. MEN REACHING FOR ME. Punnett screaming my name.

I thrashed my way toward her. I hit a man in the back with my saber, then slashed a wounded man and a dying man. I saw Punnett and lost her. I hammered a man in the side of the head and he fell, moaning, and at last I was close enough to reach her.

"Get up!" I shouted.

"I can't," Punnett cried. "The bullet got me in the hip. I can't."

"Somebody help me!" I said, raising my sword. "Somebody fucking help me!"

The wounded were falling back into a loose ring around us. They looked frightened. I couldn't see of what.

"I gotta get you out of here," I said. "Help me get you up."

"It's my left side," Punnett said. "I'm going to scream. Just do it."

I pulled her to her feet. She screamed. I lifted her over my shoulders into a fireman's carry. I could feel the broken bones grinding together in her leg every time I moved.

"Stay back!" I snarled at the wounded, brandishing my saber.

Millen landed hard next to me, sword drawn. "Get back!" she screamed.

"Stop it!" Punnett sobbed. "God, oh, God. Stasis. Please."

"I don't have any hands," I grunted. We had to, though. I couldn't fly her like this.

Millen shoved one of Punnett's sleeves up to expose bare skin on her forearm. Millen took a tube of silver chloride from her workbag. Punnett heard her crack it open.

"Him," Punnett said. "Have him do it. Under long enough for a real hospital. They won't work on me here. Soldiers before women. Him."

"She's right," Millen said. "We've got to get her up to Le Havre."

I dropped my saber and Millen put the tube in my hand.

"Give 'em hell, Louise," I said. I reached for her arm and drew, the largest figure I could manage. Punnett went rigid over my shoulders.

Millen waved her sword, but the walking wounded were closing in around us again. I would never get Punnett rigged.

"I will run through the next man who touches him!" Millen shouted. "Move back!"

She slid in beside me. A man swung at me with the butt of a rifle and Millen parried it and struck back, raking him down the face from forehead to chin, puncturing his eyeball. She hacked another across the thigh, nearly lopping his leg off—blood sprayed from the wound. A man pointed a revolver at her and she stabbed him in the chest, then lost her sword when it stuck between his ribs as he fell to the ground, gasping and clawing at it.

"I'm sorry, Robert," Millen muttered. "Fuck, I'm sorry."

Five or six men were grabbing me. I lost Punnett off my shoulders as I fell to the ground. A boot stepped on my hand. Somebody kicked me in the head. Millen was shouting.

Black smoke popped all around us.

Mortar rounds, I thought. But we would already be dead.

Smoke billowed out.

"First squadron!" I heard someone roar from above in the thundering, carefully enunciated cadence of a female officer giving a particular order for the first time. "Blades out! Charge the ground. Charge!"

Twelve women in a tight wedge formation, sabers bristling in front of them, flew right over our heads, advancing at a walking pace. Men ducked or dove out of their way.

"Second squadron, drop!"

Canisters exploded around us, throwing out a thin, sickly pink vapor. I got a whiff of it and started choking. Water streamed from my eyes. I couldn't breathe.

"Dress the line!"

I pulled the neck of my skysuit over my mouth. Didn't help. I couldn't see. I heard a man making high-pitched, gasping wheezes every time he took a breath. Then I realized it was me.

Somebody had me by the harness, dragging me to open ground.

"Shit, she's a big one," the woman pulling me grunted.

I crawled and then staggered to my feet.

"Oh, shit!" the woman said. She had a swath of smoke across her face like a veil to ward off the effects of the tear gas. "How many of you?"

I was gagging too badly to answer. I held up three fingers. She kept a hand on my back to guide me. "Lt. Stewart!" she called.

"Where's the bottle of neutralizer?" the woman with the drill sergeant's voice asked. "Give it here!"

She splashed liquid into my face and rubbed it over my eyes and mouth. The burning sensation dulled. My breathing sounded less horrific. I could see women pulling Millen and Punnett clear, too.

I wiped my eyes and saw Essie Stewart standing next to me with the bottle.

"Essie," I said.

She had her lips pressed together and her jaw clenched. Her eyes were full.

"We couldn't—" I said. "We couldn't—"

Essie pulled my head next to hers. "Robert."

"They ran right over us," I blubbered. "There were only four of us."

"Stop it," she said. "Stop it!"

"They went right over her, they just—"

"Robert, would you *please* shut up? If you start crying, I'm going to lose it."

And Essie was away again, giving orders to clear the lachrymatory agent and establish a marked landing field. At least a hundred women were circling overhead.

Gen. Blandings was beside me now. "They're volunteers from First Division," she explained. "They came early."

"Punnett got shot," I growled. "I was hitting dying men to get to her."

"Put your fists down," Blandings said. "You look like a berserker about to murder the whole company."

I unclenched my hands.

"Ma'am, Punnett was begging for a Corps hospital," I said. "Not stacked up with the men at the field surgery. I dropped her. I lost—"

"We have her," Blandings replied. "I'll see that she gets to Le Havre."

My eyes started watering again, maybe from the tear gas. Blandings frowned.

"Mr. Canderelli, are you certain you're up to leading ready rescue?"

"Yes, ma'am."

She handed me a canteen and I drank. It had a bitter metallic taste that burned my throat—the tear gas antidote, still smeared on my lips.

"Then go back to camp," she said. "Wire cutters, gloves, and the heavy rescue bag. Go forward to Point D to assist. They're . . . trying to recover Lt. Drale's body."

"No," I said. "No!"

"You don't have the luxury. Comport yourself like a Sig-2. You *cannot* cry in front of the women you're commanding."

I wiped my eyes. "Yes, ma'am. Which— who for a partner?"

Blandings looked about. We had none of our own women left.

"Lt. Stewart!" Blandings called. "Give me a woman for detached duty in ready rescue, please. Sig-2 Canderelli needs a partner."

"Griesbach!" Essie called. "With Fifth Division for double-R!"

The girl who'd dragged me free jogged over. She looked about seventeen years old, wide-eyed. "With him?" she asked. "You're the one who blew up the tank?"

"No tanks today," I said. "Can you read a compass, Miss?"

"Yes, ma'—uh, ma'am? Are you a ma'am?"

"I am. Chart us a course to Fifth Division encampment and then Point D for Diane. I've still got tear gas in my eyes, so I'm following you."

"Very good, ma'am."

With my partner navigating, we flew back to camp, picked up equipment, and continued on to Point D. There was a tarp to mark the landing area; orderly rows of wounded, military policemen helping stretcher-bearers unload a few new cases. Only a couple dozen men remained to be evacuated. We entered the small group of circling fliers and set down when our turn came.

"Ready rescue for the Point D commander!" I sang out to the woman coordinating landings. She ran to fetch Sig-1 Pitcairn, who'd assumed command of D.

"What a hell of a day," Pitcairn said to me.

"Yup," I said, swallowing hard. "What's the situation out there, ma'am?"

"Your girl Cunningham thought she saw the landing zone a quarter mile farther east and put her team down right in the middle of the fighting. They ducked into a trench and got mortared. Your lieutenant came to bail them out with three women from my division and they got hit, too. All the wounded are out except Cunningham, who's refusing to go until someone gets your lieutenant's body."

"It's buried under rubble or what?" I asked.

"Hung up on barbed wire."

"God," I said.

I was trembling. Drale, who'd trusted me before anyone else had. Who'd been under fire with me. Who'd made sure I got my leave. I took a step toward the trenches and my whole body seized up. Pitcairn put a hand on my shoulder. It was like she was pushing heat and strength into me.

Keep breathing, Punnett had told me on our first evac . . . Punnett.

"Take a minute, big fella," Pitcairn said, her arm around me. Her skysuit was damp with sweat on a forty-degree morning.

"Yeah."

"Drale landed here before she went up to the trench. Told me she was promoting you. She said, 'If I need help, I want a six-foot-tall man with a giant pair of wire cutters jumping into the shell crater next to me.'" Pitcairn lowered her voice and leaned closer. "If it's any consolation, Robert, I agree."

"Thanks, Missy," I said.

My borrowed Sig-3 was looking on, scandalized—I couldn't decide whether by my informality with a superior officer or touching between the sexes or the fact that her new boss needed a hug. I drew myself up to my full height and hooked my thumbs under my harness, as Punnett had done.

"Guide for the rescue team, please!" I bellowed.

One of the MPs led us through the former no-man's-land, across the cratered ground, over old trenches that had been bridged with rickety boards, through holes in the endless rolls of barbed wire that had been cut and marked with yellow flags. In the third trench in, we found Fern Cunningham and a blood-spattered rescue flier from Fourth Division.

Fern was staring at her hands, prim and cool and baffled.

"I was sure I was right," Fern said to me. "I saw the landing field. I swear I did."

"We ought to evacuate you, ma'am," I said.

"Drale came for me. She was right up on the edge. Then there was an explosion and she was gone. I tried to pull her off the wire. I couldn't. I gouged my thumb."

There was a long, ragged cut over the finger pad on Fern's thumb.

"You've got to get that stitched up," I said.

"How long do you think?" she asked. "How long will I be out?"

"A few weeks," I suggested.

"It'll be over by then?"

"Yeah," I said. "Yeah, it will." Over for Cunningham one way or another. She allowed the woman from Fourth Division to stasis her.

"Thanks," the Fourth Division woman told me. "You're gonna want to look ten yards forward from this trench and to the left."

What was left of Lt. Drale was tangled in the barbed wire. Half the back of her head was sheared off, both legs gone below the shins, her arms ripped away. She didn't look real. Didn't look human. Meat and bone, hair and cloth.

"Do you want me to help?" Sig-3 Griesbach asked.

I shook my head.

I took the tarpaulin out of my supply bag and draped it over Drale's body. Twelve cuts with the long-handled wire cutters and her remains came free. There was no pretty way to do it. I lowered her to the ground, blood and innards sloshing on the tarp as I moved her. I folded it around her, then secured it with straps. I flew the body a couple hundred yards back to the D landing field and set down.

"You have a graves registry person in among all them?" I asked Pitcairn, indicating the dozen soldiers rendering aid to the wounded. A number of covered bodies were set off to one side, men who hadn't survived long enough to be evacuated.

"We'll find one," Pitcairn said. "Make sure her name's on somewhere."

There were tags in the rescue bag. I wrote *Drale, Adelgundis. Lt, USSC* on one and tied it to the tarp.

"They screaming for me anywhere else?" I asked Pitcairn.

She shook her head. "They're shifting my women down to F. I need to get them ready to move. Godspeed, Robert."

• • •

I returned to camp and set the message boards in the farmhouse to receive on the Divisional and Evac Comm glyphs.

"This is it for your whole division?" Griesbach asked. "One cottage and some tents?"

"There were only twenty-five of us this morning," I said. Now . . . nineteen?

"Gosh, I knew you all were short, but we have three hundred women in Div One. You're covering the same amount of front as we are."

"You'll have to take it up with Gen. Niejenhuis," I said.

I opened the file cabinet where we kept the Form 41s. I broke the seal on Punnett's. Notification to Aunt Della, only in the event of her death. Personal effects to be used by wingmates if able or sold. No special friend, but a request: *I never would have been able to join, except a woman in Springfield slipped me $10 for a ticket on the transporter chain. If I have enough in back pay, give $10 to every woman in my squadron, tell them give it to a lost girl someday.*

Well, if Punnett pulled through, she could hand out the banknotes herself. All it meant for me was no one to notify that she'd been wounded. I initialed the envelope and put it away.

I took out Drale's next. She'd updated it two days before: Notification to her mother in New Jersey, letter only, no message. Special notification to a Jelena Simic, possibly of Princeton, NJ, letter only. *My first love. Might have moved. Don't have a newer address. If you find her, would you write that I still think of her every day? I wish I'd been kinder and wiser, but doesn't everyone look back at herself at twenty and say that? Tell her I found what I was looking for. I hope she did, too. Drale.*

"Step outside, please, Sigilwoman," I said to my assistant, struggling to keep my voice even. "Close the door."

A quarter of an hour later, after I'd composed myself, I messaged Danielle. *I love y. Today has bn awful. Dnt even knw how to describ. If I'm evr hurt—who shld tell y? How?*

I was asking three months too late, but at least I was asking.

Another rescue request came across the Divisional board: *RA, DIV 5 RR. Mech fail. Inj x1, leg. And x1 needs new reg. From B to hosp, down abt 10min flt. Marked. B Macmurd*

Run of the mill mechanical failure, thank God. I tried to put on a dispassionate face as I called Griesbach back in.

"Sounds like everybody's going to walk away from this one," I told her.

"We've just got to find two women in the middle of the whole war, is all," she replied.

It took us two hours, sweeping back and forth between Point B and Reims to spot them. Our women were sitting on the grass in the middle of pastureland, miles back from the fighting, their stasied wounded laid out next to them. It was the French countryside as you might see it on a postcard. The air smelled of clover instead of cordite. Pearl Hanover from our first squad was with Macmurdo, who looked ashen and sweaty.

"My reg jammed," Pearl told me, "so I set down fast. I rolled over, but I'm okay. Bernice saw me hit and landed to help."

"Put my foot in a rabbit hole," Macmurdo said through gritted teeth. "Snapped my ankle."

Pearl was only lightly bruised. We gave her a working regulator and helped her reload her passengers. Griesbach took Macmurdo's casualties and the two launched for the secondary hospital in Reims.

Macmurdo had her eyes squeezed shut. "Is that little girl from First Division gone?"

"Yup," I said.

Macmurdo slapped the ground with her open palm. "Shit, it hurts!" she cried.

The lower part of her shin was bent at a sickening angle. A war-ender. Maybe a career-ender.

"Four years over here and I end up like this," Bernice raged. "Pathetic. Today of all days. We're running out of commanders."

"We'll do okay," I said. "Millen will run one squadron. Blandings will give Nampeyo the other one and bump Andrada up to lieutenant."

"Going to have a bunch of kids commanding kids," Macmurdo complained. "We may as well give *you* a squad."

In the opening days of the war, nothing would have pleased me better. At that moment, though, nothing would have pleased me more than peace breaking out before Blandings had the opportunity.

"I'm not joking," Macmurdo said.

I gave her a smile. "You hit your head, ma'am. But, yeah, I'd take a squad someday."

I cracked an ampoule of silver chloride. "You want me to notify your Form 41? Is it Mr. Macmurdo?"

"Divorced," Macmurdo said. "I haven't seen him in years. Just my sister, Millie. I wrote a hundred glyphs on that paper, but if you try to contact all my relations, you'll spend the rest of the war answering questions."

"Philosophical family?"

"Very. Robert, please not the field hospital?"

"Of course not," I said. "I'll take you to the Corps infirmary in Le Havre."

"Thank you."

I wet a strip of indicator paper with my tongue and stuck it on her neck. I could afford to take an extra two minutes and do this the right way for a Sig-1. She'd been more than decent to me. Even if her capital-P Politics went against mine, she was the epitome of the loyal opposition.

"You be careful," Macmurdo told me. "Blandings is going to rely on you now. And for good reason. You changed a lot of minds about a man. Changed mine."

"Thanks," I said. "Sometimes I forget that I'm not . . ."

I didn't want to finish the thought.

"One of the girls," she said. "I know you do."

She laid back and undid the top buttons on her skysuit.

"When the end comes," she said, "do what you think is right. But promise me one thing—you won't break and run. End the war if you can, but stand with the women next to you. Promise me you won't abandon a flight of scared, green, teenaged Sig-3s in the back country because you get all puffed up over some secret mission."

"Never, ma'am," I said.

"I know you won't. Come safe home, Robert."

I carried Macmurdo to the hospital in Le Havre, then sprinted back to camp and steeled myself for the next one. It never came.

At two in the afternoon, Gen. Niejenhuis relieved Fifth Division from duty, with First Division assigned to clean up the remaining wounded. The American forces had broken through and advanced several miles, before bogging down on the muddy roads short of Metz. No more than eleven thousand casualties. Gen. Pershing was calling it a brilliant success.

Our fliers returned to camp in various degrees of shock and exhaustion. Each of them checked in with me in the farmhouse as they arrived and I moved the marker next to their name to off duty. The state of the chalkboard came as a shock to some of them: seven names erased (six women wounded and out of action, one dead). A Sig-2 couldn't afford to cry in front of the women she commanded, even when they broke down in front of you.

I stole a look at my private message glyph.

What's going on? Danielle had written. *I wake up this morning and you're saying, 'What do you want to happen if I die'? I don't want to think about it! I don't want you to think about it. I want you to come home.*

Of cours, I replied.

Why would you write something like that?

How could I explain?

What happened?

Men left to die on a hill; Drale, cut to pieces by an artillery shell; Bernice Macmurdo, lamed; Essie Stewart, who ought to be giving tea parties, hit with a lieutenant's commission. And Punnett.

Robert?

Millen, who'd continued taking evacs after we were rescued, was the last one to stumble into the farmhouse. She just stood there, stunned. I wanted to be with my burnout of a Sig-1 more than I wanted to hear another word from Danielle.

"C'mon, ma'am," I said, and led her outside.

Millen made it as far as the supply shed, where she sank to the ground, pulling her knees to her chest, leaning against the wall of the building. She closed her eyes and lifted her face into the sun. I recognized the expression: *it could have been me; it was nearly me; it wasn't me.*

She would have cut down the whole German army and then the whole American army to save one of us. She was a son of a bitch; she was my Sig-1. I loved her like a mother and a sister and a schoolboy crush. If she told me to gather supplies so that we could storm the gates of hell and get Drale out, I would have asked her only whether you needed a twelve-pound or forty-pound powder bag to reach the underworld.

Millen's right eye was swollen shut and she had a streak of crusted blood on her upper lip. Straggles of sweat-soaked brown hair hung to her shoulders. I could have called her beautiful and meant it. I eased myself to the ground beside her.

"You're a male," Millen said to me, without opening her eyes. "Explain to me why a man with both hands blown off kept trying to grope my breasts."

"I dunno," I said. And then, because between the two of us I had the more prominent bosom: "Did he find them?"

We laughed together and it was heartless and grim and ecstatic. She reached over and took my hand.

"Shit," Millen said. "Oh, God, Robert. Poor Louise."

"You told her," I said. "You told her to fly for the hospital. If she'd gone ahead instead of circling—"

"You can play the 'if' game all day. But losing her hurts like a punch to the nose."

"You look like you took a couple of those, too."

She opened her good eye and looked at me like she was seeing me for the first time. "I'm glad to have you as a Sig-2, Robert A. I'm only sorry I don't have anyone left for you to command. Just Devereaux. And it's only going to get worse. Pershing will keep attacking every day until the war's over. Not as bad as this morning, but they'll ring up a thousand wounded a day without even trying."

"We can't survive that," I said.

"Neither can the Germans. That's all the army cares about—they don't give a damn whether they destroy R&E, too."

23

DETROIT DEFENDER: The hoverer powering your third-stage booster was a man. Did that worry you?

PILAR DESOTO: Oh, no. He was Sig-2 to me in the war. I was least worried about him out of all of them.

D. Priscilla Conway, "Round and Round and Round She Goes! Desoto Orbits Earth Three Times for Brock-Sudeste Aero," *Detroit Defender Sunday Magazine*, January 28, 1932

DURING OUR EIGHT HOURS FLYING AT THE BATTLE OF SAINT-MIHIEL, Fifth Division suffered the highest one-day casualty rate of any R&E unit during the entire war: seventy-six percent. By midafternoon, the litany of sprains, strains, and landing-induced concussions had left us with only six women who were fit to fly. (The soldier who'd stepped on my hand had cracked a bone in my left pinkie, which put me briefly out of action as well.)

Gen. Fallmarch, the three-star general who had overall command of the Corps, pulled our entire division from active status. We assumed it was the end: She would break us up and use us as replacements elsewhere. But Fallmarch had other ideas. She'd long worried over Gen. Niejenhuis, the ambitious two-star general in charge of R&E. Niejenhuis had spent the past four years maneuvering behind the scenes to take over Fallmarch's job. Niejenhuis's argument hadn't been a bad one: *R&E is the only department that's had women dying on the front lines, so oughtn't an R&E woman have command of the Corps?*

But Gen. Fallmarch seized upon the distribution of fliers at the Battle of Saint-Mihiel as evidence of Gen. Niejenhuis's incompetence. That wounded soldiers should have been allowed to bake in the sun for hours while First Division had two hundred women still aground—disgraceful! And poor Gen. Blandings and her Fifth Division, trying to pull out over a thousand wounded at one of the evac points with just four women. So short on fliers that they'd resorted to using a man.

So, at Gen. Fallmarch's insistence, Gen. Niejenhuis was fired. Fifth Division was delighted! We'd wanted Niejenhuis gone for years. But then came the bad news: rather than promote a one-star general to replace the Flying Dutchwoman, Fallmarch had decided that she would oversee R&E herself.

"Now that's capital-P Politics!" clucked Lt. Andrada (and never was there a better-deserved promotion), as she and I sat in the farmhouse a week later going over duty rosters, preparing to get our women back in the field. "Gillian Fallmarch gets to take credit for R&E's successes *and* she removes her biggest rival."

"General Jill was a Logistics flier," I grumbled. "How does she think she's going to lead R&E when the Corps can't even deliver the mail on time?"

"Careful, little brother. She has girls listening. You would never hear *me* call her a useless careerist who would sacrifice her women to earn a fourth star. Oh, never!"

But we had Gen. Fallmarch to thank for dividing the work equitably. First Division, with nearly three hundred women, would now run the bulk of the evacuations, rather than organizing the front by sectors and dumping the brunt of the flying on the smaller divisions.

With my own promotion to Sig-2 confirmed by the higher-ups ("A man as a flight commander!" Fallmarch had allegedly remarked while signing my paperwork. "How awful that Niejenhuis should have allowed such a state of affairs!"), when the rebuilt Fifth Division went back on duty, I led the first-in flight team for evacuations each morning.

It kept me plenty busy.

Gen. Pershing, having failed to capture Metz, swung his army north to join the grinding offensive through the Argonne Forest. He preferred direct, manly frontal assaults against the German defenses, the better to show off the superb marksmanship and fighting spirit of the American infantry. To be sure, our men shot well and fought bravely, but they were gunned down at an appalling rate, just as Millen had predicted.

I made as many as ten runs a day, loading two casualties on each. By late October, when I looked up at the chalkboard, my number stood at 1,030. I couldn't even remember the evacuation on which I'd made my thousandth.

"Gilded bars, all the same," Lt. Andrada said, giving me new insignia of rank to wear on my collar. The same as my old brown bars, but with a single thread of gold around the edge.

"Isn't there supposed to be a ceremony, ma'am?" one of my new Sig-3s asked me.

That had been another of Fallmarch's changes—reinforcements distributed throughout all the divisions, instead of preferentially to First Division. We now had eight freshly trained Sig-3s, green as new-sprouted sweet peas, to round us out to two full squadrons. There was talk of adding another twelve. I couldn't imagine anything more exhausting. The new women were so . . . enthusiastic. I was responsible for two of them: Misses Franklin and Desoto. It was like they competed to see who could be more earnest.

Millen chuckled over it.

"You got a speech, Robert A?" she asked. "Gilded Sig-2. Very important day."

"I'm pleased to accept this award for showing up to work for three months," I intoned.

"Oh, but you'll wear those the rest of your career, ma'am!" Miss Franklin objected.

Which would only be another couple weeks, God willing.

We ran mornings and evenings. My new girls had a hundred evacs each before I could even remember which was which. Sig-3 Desoto was a Detroiter of Mexican descent, blazing fast, fair landings, spoke good French. Franklin was the other one.

I strove to imitate the best qualities of the women I'd served under. I took my Sig-3s forward for evacuations prior to officially going on duty to take the measure of them (with properly filled out Form 41s); I cautioned them against indiscriminate heroism; I lectured them on the importance of standing by your sisters when things went wrong—Franklin had a little pad on which she took notes. They never once asked me why they had a man in command. For them, my presence was just one of the many peculiarities of serving in R&E, like bean soup and field showers. I loved them for it. But I would have traded both of them and my gold bars to have Punnett back.

"They're like puppies," I complained to Edith, who often dropped by on courier runs. (And, I couldn't help but notice, frequently without documents on days when she knew I was off duty.) "How did you ever manage when you were commanding twelve of them?"

"I made my Sig-2s take care of the children," Edith said with a laugh.

My new girls were not card players—worries over gambling—and Andrada was too busy with her new responsibilities as lieutenant, so the only time I got to play a hand or two of jiggery was when Edith visited.

"They worry me," I confided to her. "The girls. If anything happens."

Edith nodded. "I worried over it, too. The only ones I ever lost—well, that was the night I bought my piece of it. I still think about it, though, what I would have done differently. Three lives. The only satisfactory answer I've ever come up with is that I should have refused the mission."

"Your commanders would have allowed that?"

"Only if I'd resigned. I suppose then they would have given the mission to a different team and it would be four other women shot full of holes."

It took me several visits to notice how good a card player Edith was. She chose her cards slowly, laid them on the table at a glacial pace. Quite the opposite of the other card sharks I'd known.

"Rob," Edith said. "May I ask: Where's Punnett going to be buried?"

I looked down at my hands. The surgeons in Le Havre had spent four hours working on her when she'd come to. The bullet had shattered her pelvis and cut open two arteries and her bowel. Too much damage. But, as she'd once said, clean sheets and a warm bed, morphine and someone to say a prayer over her. We'd given her that much, at least.

"In Le Havre," I said.

Rather than try to explain Punnett's Form 41, I'd simply impersonated "Aunt Della" by message and told the graves registry that it had been Punnett's desire to be laid to rest with her sister corpswomen.

"There's a cemetery near the hospital," I said. "A few dozen other sigilwomen are buried there. Seemed right."

"It *is* right," Edith said.

"They don't do interment ceremonies, but we'll go up in a couple weeks and lay a wreath on her grave."

I closed my eyes and let out my breath and wished I'd said goodbye. I wished I'd told her what it had meant to have someone call me by my given name.

"She knew," Edith said.

"Yeah," I said.

I played a card without looking at it. Edith picked it up and put it back in my hand. She was watching me, her light brown eyes impassive—something beyond sympathy. She'd lived it. No need for a wince or a sigh.

"How do we go back home after this?" I asked.

"I don't know," she said. "Maybe we'll do like the old soldiers do. Get drunk together and tell war stories."

"I'm not very good at drinking," I said.

"You're not very good at cards, either."

Edith ran her finger down each of her cards. I could tell she already knew which one she wanted to play. Delaying for the sake of delay.

"You're worried about being with Danielle?" she asked.

I nodded. "She doesn't understand and I don't know how I could ever explain. She complains about the nastiness in Washington and I don't doubt it, but the Capitol's not likely to get shelled, is it? And then I feel rotten for saying it. She wants me to duck the mutiny. Go sit in the headquarters with her."

"That's a sane thing for her to want," said Edith. "That's a kind thing. You understand that, right?"

"I don't want the kind thing! I want to be with my people."

"Oh, I know that one. God, do I know it." She had an expression of perfect fellow feeling—not sadness or regret, but a look as if we had both been caught in the same raging torrent and there was no way to swim out of it, only to endure.

"Danielle's only part of it," I said. "After this—sit in a classroom for three years? Walk with her on my arm in the botanical gardens? I'll be looking for breaks in the trees for an egress route."

A sincere chuckle from Edith over that, nothing mocking or minimizing in it.

I set down my cards and looked at her: the thin, battered face; a flier's carefully manicured nails; the long, tanned curve of her neck. To be understood so well by someone who was so brave . . . if I hadn't been in love with Danielle . . . if we hadn't been in the midst of plotting a conspiracy that would probably end up with me lined up against a wall and shot . . . if the proscription against fraternization between two corpswomen weren't absolute . . . If, if, if.

I was staring too hard. Edith set her cards down, too, and licked her lips.

"I wish I didn't like the way you're looking at me," she said.

"Edie, the only times I've felt like myself since I came over have been when I'm with you. When you're sitting out there in the sun and the light catches your face, I've never seen anyone more . . ."

She shook her head.

"Rob," she said. "Don't. Danielle might be the philosopher I respect most in the world. If . . ."

If.

Edith slid her hand across the table, stopping a quarter inch before the tip of her finger could brush mine. Her face was pale and drawn.

"When I'm lying awake at night," she spat out, "and I want to feel like shit, I imagine what it would have been like if you'd come to Radcliffe one year earlier. Because I would *not* have waited months for Danielle Hardin to make a move on you. I would have asked you out so fast . . ."

We sat there, motionless, one of us feeling sicker than the other, neither one sure who was supposed to speak next. I drew a breath.

But Sigilwoman Franklin burst into the mess tent. If she'd had a tail, she would have been wagging it and barking in excitement.

"Begging your pardon, ma'ams, but they're calling for assembly!" she squeaked and dashed off.

Edith popped up to her feet on her crutches. She was wearing a relieved smirk.

"Very puppyish," she said. "You're the most incongruous ma'am I've ever met, by the way."

"Thank you," I said.

I could see worry leaking through her façade.

"Robert, if we need to pretend we didn't just say any of those things . . ."

"We've gotta talk somewhere there aren't any Sig-3s," I said.

"Tonight, maybe?" Edith suggested. "At the command post in Belgium."

"Oh!" I said. "Is the mutiny right now?"

"The first phases, yes," Edith said. "Good luck. And I wish—I wish I'd known you before all this, but I'm so glad I know you now."

She pivoted and left the mess tent quickly, before either of us had time to decide whether that conversation ought to end with a handshake or a hug or one of us leaning in, eyes closed . . .

No!

I had Danielle. What more could I want? I took a deep breath and strove to push it out of my mind, to bury Edith in the same part of me where I kept Pitcairn's propositions and my mental picture of the girls from Second Division in their nightgowns, slipping under the covers with their glossy pinups of me. Bury it with work until you had time to take all the pieces out and consider them. Punnett and Drale, Kiyo and Carmen, keep them safely hidden, too. It was an awful lot to keep submerged and if it bubbled up sometimes, well, all it meant was that I was human.

I joined the rest of my flight group. The new women were positively bouncing with glee. Gen. Blandings had her dress jacket over her skysuit. Getting ready to travel.

"Good afternoon," Blandings announced to the assembled division. "I'm sure it has escaped no one that the nights are growing quite cold. Snow may be only a few weeks off."

You could taste the disappointment wafting off the green fliers. The veterans, though, knew the tone of voice. We straightened and stretched and waited for the blow to come.

"This camp is not intended for overwintering," Blandings continued. "We will need to move to more substantial quarters, probably in Bar-le-Duc. I'm flying to the city for several days to find suitable accommodations. Lt. Andrada will be in command during my absence. During that time, I would like you to begin preparing to break camp, including packing high-value equipment."

Andrada began barking out orders concerning which regulators were to be disassembled and crated.

"Oh," Blandings interjected, "I'll also need a brief word in the farmhouse with Aielli, Millen, Vos, Wojciechowski, Nampeyo, Dunphrey, Mondragon, Devereaux, and Canderelli."

It was a little obvious to name all the "bad girls" together, but everyone knew which of us belonged to Blandings. We trouped up to the farmhouse and I closed the door behind us.

"It's happening," Blandings said. "The entire Korps des Philosophs and their reservists have been moved to Metz. They have twenty-five thousand women. They're running trains continuously from Germany—all tank cars, which will be carrying their prefabricated smoke. Not more than a day or two before they make their play."

We'd been expecting it, but we did a poor job of hiding our naked fear: at the coming attack, the mutiny, what came after.

"All indications are that they'll smash through our lines west of Metz and head straight for Paris," Blandings continued. "That will throw the French into a panic, however unlikely the rauchbauers are to actually reach the capital. When the Germans attack, I expect that Gen. Fallmarch will recall you to Le Havre to help position our smokecarvers and their supplies. Teeny, when that happens, I want you to contact Gen. Fallmarch's staff and ask if they can confirm the reports that I crashed and was killed while launching from Bar-le-Duc. Then misplace your board."

"Your friends in the other divisions will be making similar inquiries at the same time?" Millen asked.

"Exactly. Fallmarch will believe I'm dead because she wants it to be true. Once you're in Le Havre, help for as long as you're able. Gen. Witt is the two-star in command of the smokecarvers and I've found her to be a wise and courageous leader. If she's allowed to formulate the strategy, it will be a series of delaying attacks until the Germans run out of supplies and smoke. Not a glorious victory, but an effective one. The Germans will sue for peace. No need for conspiracy or mutiny or rewriting the rules of warfare. Help Witt in any way you can."

That was a more generous assessment of Gen. Witt than one usually heard. In the Philippines, she'd been reluctant to attack, even with huge advantages in numbers—heresy in a department that prided itself on winning outnumbered ten (or fifty or a hundred) to one.

"I fear, though," said Blandings, "that Gen. Witt's plan will not withstand Gen. Fallmarch's desire to make the history books. Fallmarch will likely force Witt to commit to a pitched battle. If we lose there, Fallmarch will escalate. That's when the order to bomb the German cities with plague will come and when we put our plan into action. That's when I'll need you. I'll send word over the Divisional glyph."

"Where are we supposed to go when you call for us?" Devereaux asked.

"Ostend," Blandings said.

There was a moment of confused silence.

"Where?" I asked.

"In Belgium, right on the North Sea," Blandings said. "When the time comes, I'll need outstanding fliers who I trust. That's you lot."

"What about afterward?" Millen asked. "Are they going to shoot us or hang us?"

"I've spoken with Senator Cadwallader-Fulton," Blandings said. "The Corps has always been all volunteer. We've seen the consequence of that in R&E—a woman is permitted to resign at any moment. The senator thinks, provided we win, that we will be allowed to resign en masse, backdated, and be free of charges of mutiny or cowardice before the enemy. I can't imagine any scenario, however, in which you'll be allowed to continue serving after the end of hostilities."

"If they give you Gen. Fallmarch's job," Millen suggested.

"Teeny, don't make threats," Blandings said, and our meeting broke up in nervous laughter.

"A moment, Mr. Canderelli, if you'd be so kind," Blandings added. She'd caught some of the same fidgety energy as the younger fliers—she was unbuttoning and rebuttoning the strap on her scabbard.

"It would be best if you came with us to Ostend now," she said. "Sleep a day or two. Eat a few square meals. Be ready to fly the moment we need you—*if* we need you."

I looked at my feet and tried to come up with an answer. It was the smart thing to do. If Blandings was right, it could mean the difference between ending the war and allowing it to drag on. And yet something in me raged against it.

"Danielle will be in Ostend as well, with the senator," Blandings cajoled. "You can meet her when she comes over. Pick her a bouquet of wildflowers. I'll give her whatever assurances I can."

It wasn't Danielle who gave me pause, though. When I thought of leaving, it was Millen's face that scowled at me. And Andrada. Devereaux, Desoto, and Franklin, to whom I was big sister.

"I'd rather stay with the division," I said. "Stand with the women next to me. I should at least make sure the new girls get to Le Havre. I mean, Miss Franklin spent six hours looking for a can of striped paint yesterday after Millen told her we needed it to touch up the landing field."

"Oh, Mother Mary," Blandings sighed. "That was an ancient joke when I was a new Sig-3. But Robert: When I call for the mutiny, you'll come? Yes?"

"Sure," I said.

"I'll see you in a day or two, then. Come safe home."

Blandings launched and met Edith, who was circling at one hundred feet. They proceeded north-northwest toward Ostend.

"Cold weather," complained Sig-3 Franklin, as I rejoined the rest of the division. "A whole meeting for cold weather! Won't take me hardly any time to pack. I barely got a chance to *un*pack."

Sig-3 Desoto waited for Franklin to walk out of earshot. "Can I come?" she asked me.

"It's by invitation only," I said.

"So invite me."

"Ask Millen."

Desoto spat over her shoulder. "At least tell me where she's going?"

"Bar-le-Duc," I said.

"She's flying the wrong way."

"Le Havre."

"You lie badly, ma'am."

"Go pack."

By that afternoon our civilian allies had descended on Belgium as well. They'd made a chartered crossing on the civilian transatlantic chain, arriving in Calais. After being interviewed by a French customs officer, who was bribed handsomely to misplace their paperwork, they made one further jump to Ostend. So, before the German attack had even begun, we had the most crucial piece of the plan in place: Ms. Addams with a thousand handpicked volunteer smokecarvers, plus Senator Cadwallader-Fulton's staff, hundreds of tons of supplies, and Dean Murchison.

Ostend is devastated, Dar wrote. *The British only retook it a few weeks ago. Everything is shelled to rubble. We'll have to mostly shelter in tents. Could you come now? I need your help.*

We're still flyng casualties, I answered. *Will cm soon.*

Tonight? If you're going to desert anyway, just slip away tonight. You'll do more good here, I promise. So much to do.

I mulled that over the rest of the day. Maybe it was simple egotism to think I would make any difference by staying with my division. They could cover for me. I could even resign in front of Andrada, do it right. I tried to think of what I'd say. Maybe nothing more than "Today." She and I understood each other. But was it better to say something to Millen and Devereaux and a few of the other women who'd quietly encouraged me or simply vanish? A kind word to Desoto and Franklin or abandon them to the tender mercies of whichever woman was promoted to replace me?

Stand with the woman next to you.

But did that mean Blandings or Danielle or my division? All the answers seemed wrong ones.

I couldn't say, Ma wrote, when I laid it out to her. *I nevr much trustd commandrs until I becam one. Funny how it changs y. You'll know what to do wh the times right.*

Thanks, I wrote. *You comin ovr for the big thing?*

We'd never talked about it openly.

Im packed and rdy, she wrote. *Too busy to come w 1st wave. Still crops to bring in. Late forest fire season, terribl big one. Lot of philosphrs fightng it, so we're short as is. Would b nice if y win without us.*

I had a brief pang of homesickness for Montana, a state that never much loved its sigilrists until a hundred thousand acres were burning and the harvest had to be hauled into town. But Mother would come if it went to hell—she wouldn't hesitate or waffle.

I stood and blew out my breath. This was indecisive and unmanly and unworthy. Do it now. Go join Danielle.

I found Andrada at work in the farmhouse, finishing the next day's duty rosters. I came to attention in front of her.

"Ma'am," I said. "Sigilwoman Second Class Robert A. Canderelli is presenting himself to the divisional executive officer to formally tender . . ."

"Oh Jesus, in his purple bloomers, you're not doing this!" Andrada said. "Not today. You desert with everybody else—you don't get to go early! Miss Franklin got lost walking back from the latrine to her tent last night. *I'm* not going to be responsible for her. You get her tucked in in Le Havre before you go. You're big sister."

"Yes, ma'am."

Tommrw, I wrote Danielle. *I promis.*

And then, for the first time in the entire Great War, something happened on schedule. Shortly before dawn I heard three low bells ring out followed by three high: *all scramble for flight, all scramble.*

24

LT. AMANDA RUNABOUT: I'm terribly sorry, madam, but you have the wrong trench. You're looking for the next ditch to the left.

Groucho Marx, *Big Sister in the Sky*, 1933

THAT WAS AT SIX O'CLOCK ON THE MORNING OF OCTOBER 30, 1918. I need remind no serious student of history that the German attack had begun promptly two hours before when a giant smoke cloud a mile deep and five miles wide boiled across the trenches outside Metz. Men who got a whiff of it died where they stood as the cloud flooded west toward Paris.

The Corps generals back in Le Havre needed an hour of discussion before they agreed this was the big one, then another hour to issue orders on the Pan-Corps Emergency Sigil: *Recall, recall, recall. All divisions R&E: Break camp. Destroy supplies useful to the enemy. Assemble Priority Z, main field, Le Havre. Recall, recall, recall.*

I built a bonfire next to the farmhouse.

"Glyph books?" Sig-3 Desoto asked, carrying an armload of binders outside.

"Burn them," Andrada answered.

"Divisional tables and Forms 41?"

"Burn."

"Maps?"

"Burn."

"No, I'll take those," I said. "I have room. They're perfectly good maps."

"Gift to Sigilwoman Canderelli, then."

"Ma'am?" Sig-3 Franklin asked me. "The sand?"

"What?" I said.

"The sand in the storage shed for mixing in powder bags? Our orders were to render all philosophical materials unusable, but—"

"Dump it on the ground and shovel dirt on it," I said. "If the Germans discover the secrets of good, pure American sand, we did everything we could."

"Yes, ma'am!"

Everyone was on their portable boards. Rumors were flying: the Germans were thinning their cloud and expanding it, twenty miles wide now, in the shape of an arrowhead pointing toward Paris. The center of it was moving down the road at fifteen miles an hour, the flanks somewhat more slowly, an astonishingly high speed for such a huge mass. More rauchbauers were following behind, erecting thick, pillowy buffers of smoke along the edges of the territory they'd just seized. No one knew whether those were poisonous, too, but Pershing was wise enough not to charge a company of infantry through to find out.

"They're headed right toward us," I said to Andrada.

"We've got half an hour before they hit," she said. "Make sure your flight is carrying spare bags, forty-pounders. No telling what the supply situation will be like in Le Havre. And get on the board with Pan-Corps Emergency. Ask where they want us to land. If they try to run everybody through the main field it's going to be a mess."

I spent the next twenty minutes trying to solicit further instructions, but the messagists in Le Havre refused to do anything but repeat: *Recall, recall, recall. All R&E divisions muster in Le Havre. Main field. Best speed. Recall, recall, recall.*

Andrada rang the bell and we lined up with our overseas duffels and powder bags.

"We're launching now!" Andrada announced. "Le Havre will be total chaos. Stay with your squadron after we land. Millen and Canderelli—do it!"

I dumped a can of kerosene out on the floor of the farmhouse, popped a tube of sulfur, and drew an ignite glyph. The house went up in flames. Millen did the same for the supply shed, destroying the corn powder and equipment we couldn't take with us.

"Squad-*ron*!" Sig-1 Nampeyo sang out, using the formal call and cadence for orders that I hadn't heard since training—something to put backbone into the girls. "Launch by twos and circle! Rapid *launch*!"

They went up and away. Millen repeated the order and the rest of us launched, joining the parade, with me at the tail end to make sure we didn't lose anyone.

We were terribly behaved; everybody kept sneaking looks at their boards. One of the better Corps gossip glyphs was providing running updates on the attack:

German front expanding. Now 25mi wide. Recon flyby in progress by Logistics dept.

That was Gen. Fallmarch, all right. She wouldn't entrust a reconnaissance flight to anything less than a mail carrier.

Heavy casualties outside Metz. Est. >10k, rpt 10,000+ dead. French and American.

"Wow," I said. That was the sort of number that might make Fallmarch pull out her vials of augmented yellow fever sooner rather than later.

German aeroplanes engaging our Logistics fliers. Our girls are fleeing.

Sending our most plodding fliers right into the dragon's den and unarmed, too. Perfect.

Smokecarvers are assembling on Le Havre landing field.

Surely not *on* the landing field? That was where we were supposed to set down. Near it?

Logistics to insert smokecarvers and supplies as defensive line to oppose Germans.

It didn't take a mathematician to realize that wasn't going to work. There were only a hundred Logistics fliers to fly two thousand Corps smokecarvers to their positions, plus however many barrels and tanks and crates they needed for their prefabricated smoke. Fallmarch was going to have to delegate part of the work to R&E, much as she might have wanted her friends in Logistics to perform the airlift of the century unassisted.

En rte to Le Hvr, I wrote to Dar from the air. *Is this more ordrly thn it sounds?*

Much, much less, she replied. *Chaos here too. So busy. Come now? Please?*

As soon as I gt my girls on grnd.

First Division arrived in the air over Le Havre one minute before us, all three hundred of them circling over a landing field packed with Logistics fliers who were harnessing up smokecarvers and barrels. We fell into line, orbiting too. The landing officer on the ground was waving double red flags to signal *No landing, no landing.*

Priority is for outgoing launches, she messaged to us. *Incoming fliers should ascend to clear the launch corridor.*

It was the sort of ineptitude that drove Andrada mad—we were no good to them stuck in a holding pattern! Andrada raised a fist and pumped her arm twice to signal *Division: follow me.* We pulled out of the circling throng and set down on the beach. Andrada led us a half mile to the landing field at a jog, as we puffed along under the weight of our duffels and forty-pound spare powder bags.

We presented ourselves to a confused Logistics captain.

"Fifth Division of Rescue and Evacuation, reporting!" Andrada announced.

"Oh, wonderful!" the woman said. "How'd you get down?"

"Beach," Andrada said. "You have miles of unobstructed sand. Send up a Sig-3 with a green flag and have her land the rest of R&E on the beach!"

The Logistics woman looked like this was the first sensible thing she'd heard all day. "Lovely! In the meantime, we'll have you lot start moving smokecarvers, plus their kit. That'll be cargo manifests 139 through 182, though some of the women are refusing to wear their numbers. We're still marking the miles outside Reims, so just position them as best you can."

"Marking the miles?" Andrada asked.

"Yes," the captain said. "With chalk and tarps. They're going to form a twenty-five-mile-long defensive line just west of the city. We want to make sure everyone's in the right spot."

I decided I would make one run out to the line, just to make sure my girls knew what they were doing. Only one run. Besides, it was practically on the way to Belgium.

We found a column of eighteen hundred disgruntled Corps smokecarvers lined up on the streets surrounding the arena. They were dressed in passenger harnesses, half of them carrying barrels of concentrated smoke and the rest equipment crates. Paper numbers were pinned to their chests. I again brought up the rear and approached the women wearing numbers 181 and 182.

"What the hell?" my first smokecarver said, as she got a look at me.

"Fifth Division of R&E," I explained.

"Do you really know how to fly?"

"Sig-2 Canderelli beat Aileen Macadoo in the General's Cup!" Miss Franklin chirped from one position ahead of me.

I ran a cargo line to the first smokecarver's barrel, then one to the other's equipment crate.

"How explosive or fragile is this stuff?" I asked.

"Nothing explosive and everything fragile is already busted," said my second smokecarver, a more seasoned woman. And indeed, as I shifted the crate to check my straps I heard the tinkle of broken glass.

"They sent them over four years ago," the second smokecarver said. "Never opened or inspected."

"Fifth Division!" I heard Andrada shout. "Two minutes!"

I clipped the more experienced smokecarver to my chest before trying to hook into the other woman's harness. She backed away from me.

"I can't!" she said. "I can't."

"You can't what?" I asked.

"Backwards. I can't ride backwards for an hour!"

"Oh, for Christ's sake, Winnie!" said the woman on my chest. "Just close your eyes."

"Fifth Division!" shouted Andrada. "Ready to fly. Sound off by number! One, okay!"

"Two, okay!" Sig-1 Nampeyo shouted from the front of first squadron.

"Three, okay!" yelled Brodsky, her Sig-2.

"You're going to hold up the whole line," the woman on my chest hissed at her partner. "Can't she just ride frontwards?"

"Hurry up, then," I said. I got the nervous woman clipped in place as a front-facing rear passenger just in time for me to shout out, "Twenty-five, okay!"

"Group launch," hollered Andrada. "Column, on me. *De*-tail, go!"

We launched simultaneously and climbed slowly until we were clear of the rooftops. My rear passenger was everything I could have hoped for: a bucker, a leg wrapper, a grabber.

"Let go of my arms!" I shouted. She was digging her fingernails into my biceps for all she was worth. I drew sigils to level out and accelerate.

"You gotta put your legs down!" I hollered, as she tried again to scissor them around me.

"Let me stay!" she begged. "Leave me. I can't do it."

We were already making one hundred miles an hour.

"Can't kick!" I screamed. "Please don't kick!"

"Winnie!" shouted my front passenger. "Reach your arms all the way around. Put your hands on mine."

My front passenger had a tube of silver chloride in her hand and got the rear passenger stasied with a quick glyph to the back of the hand.

"Thank you!" I said.

"Nerves running high today," she replied.

We flew for an hour with the sun in our eyes. Andrada's course was good but not perfect and we were a few miles off from our intended landing zone by the time we reached the neatly staked-out mile markers. We swung north along the line.

"What mile are you supposed to be at?" I asked the woman in front of me.

She checked the back of the paper with her number written on it. "Eleven," she said. "We're gonna have trouble though."

"Why's that?"

"We just passed two seventeens in a row."

When we reached mile eleven, I tried to set down gently, but heard more crunching glass from the cargo crate.

"Not your fault," my front passenger said. "Smoothest ride I could have asked for. May I ask for your message glyph?"

That seemed an odd request. I drew it on her paper tag.

"When it all goes to hell and it's every woman for herself," she said. "If you have the chance? If you're unassigned? Come for me?"

"Jesus," I said. "You think it's going to be that bad?"

"The real reason they pinned the numbers to us is so they can identify our bodies. I'll light flares, I'll put out a tarp, whatever you need for a landing zone. And if you don't get the chance—"

She handed me an envelope. "For my daughter. She's about your age. I wrote it while I was in line. When you check the casualty lists for my name—Victoria Clarke. Clarke with an E."

"Jesus, ma'am—" I said.

"I'm a Sig-3—you're the ma'am."

"Okay," I said, taking the letter. "I'll give it back to you, someday."

"Give them hell!" she said.

I considered continuing on to Belgium, but it felt unconscionable. We were sending smokecarvers into the field to die—this was *not* the time to go playing hooky so I could rub Danielle's shoulders and whisper encouragement. This was real work.

Robert? Danielle wrote. *Where are you? Are you on your way?*

We landed again on the beach. I took a young Sig-1 smokecarver and four large barrels of concentrated smoke for my second trip out to the line.

"Gen. Witt's putting us on the wrong side of Reims," my passenger shouted to me as we flew back out to the line.

"Why's that?" I asked.

"We could have saved the city. We've got plenty of dispersant. We'll shred the toxic part in five minutes, then hit them with ours. They don't have a chance!"

"Glad to hear it," I answered. Anybody's guess if it were true.

I set her and the barrels at mile ten on the line.

"It's a hell of a thing, a man flying for R&E," she said to me as I unhooked the cargo. "You have a glyph?"

I drew it for her. "If we have to retreat, I already told—"

"No, no," she said. "There's going to be a great party afterward. You smoke?"

"Not really," I said.

"Oh, we'll get you high and hard, little brother. We've got vapors for that! And there's always room for a man who's good with his hands."

She grabbed the chinstrap on my helmet, yanked my face to hers, and stuck her tongue in my mouth.

"Give them hell!" she said when she let me go, grinning at me.

I wiped my lips on my sleeve and flew back to Le Havre with the rest of Fifth Division.

We hauled two-hundred-pound barrels of concentrated heavy smoke, three each. Then went back and did it again. We were fed and watered and exchanged our bags for ones inexpertly filled by the message staff, then hauled even more barrels to the line.

We could see our defenses beginning to take shape: two long, thin clouds, separated by a half mile, with auxiliary pools of smoke stationed between them. Primary line, secondary line, offensive maneuver materiel. The Germans responded by slowing their advance, expanding their cloud even wider—some reports had it at fifty miles, enough to slip right around the edges.

Our reconnaissance fliers reported they could hear gasoline engines from within the cloud: Every truck and automobile in the German Empire had been commandeered to carry the rauchbauers pushing the line forward. Behind them, German infantry poured into the corridor that had been cut through the Allied lines, digging in to solidify their gains.

We carried still more barrels as night fell. The arc lamps back at the field in Le Havre were blinding. In between, there was only the blue light of a safety flare on my wrist and on Franklin in front of me, my own fear, and my message board.

Robert, it's so awful here. I'm scared I'm cracking up. Where the hell are you?

It should have been simple to reply.

Why aren't you answering? What happened?

The women next to me.

Please? Robert?

If our smokecarvers could rip apart the German cloud, then the whole conspiracy in Ostend would be unnecessary. No tens of thousands of civilian volunteers thrown into the field. No resignation, no mutiny. Win one battle and go home heroes.

If you're breaking up with me, please just tell me? At least message to tell me you're all right.

Am ok, I wrote at one in the morning. *Want to stay w/ Div 5 as long as pos. Will come. I promis.*

We set back down at Le Havre and my head was throbbing. It was philosophical fatigue—that was more consecutive hours of flying than I'd ever done in my life. I had to rest, if only for a couple of hours.

"Ma'am," I said to Andrada. "I'm not safe for another run."

"And that's the problem with boys," Andrada tutted, though she looked ready to fall over as well. "Some of the new ones must be close to the edge, too."

But the smokecarvers had decided they were done with us. They were preparing to engage and destroy the enemy—they didn't want to worry about hitting friendlies by mistake. No fliers were to go near their lines.

The landing officer led us to the main barracks in Le Havre. I plodded in with the rest of my division, but the watchwoman at the door grabbed me by the harness strap.

"You can't mean to sleep in here," she said to me.

"What?" I said.

"I can't allow a man in the women's barracks."

"Where are the men bunking, then?"

She looked at me like I was crazy.

I turned around and bumped into Millen.

"Sigilwoman Canderelli is one of us," Millen said. "You'll let him in or I'll have you flown forward and placed in the front rank on the line. Pick a mile marker or let us in."

"This is perverse," the guardswoman said. "This is immoral."

"Then I'll be the one to go to hell," Millen snapped. "Move."

The guard stepped aside. Millen and I walked inside.

"You wanna snuggle?" she asked me.

"Sure," I said. "As long as I can put you in front of me and Missy Pitcairn behind."

"Robert A, if we're having a ménage à trois, Pitcairn cuddles *me*. God, little brother, I can't believe you're still here."

"It's— it's easier to stay than to leave. I'll go tomorrow."

"You're an idiot."

I found a cot and collapsed.

The next thing I knew four hours had passed and a woman was shouting for R&E.

"They turned! The Germans turned. They're going to go right around us. You have to move our girls."

25

My darling,

I've gone forward to take command. I never intended to make you a widower, but I don't see how we can prevail. My last thoughts will be of you.

Transcribed personal message from Maj. Gen. Christina Witt
to Hiram Witt, October 31, 1918

THE GERMANS HAD PIVOTED NORTH AND CONDENSED THEIR front to twenty-five miles. They could slip around our line and then wheel to attack us from the rear or bypass our defenses altogether and make for Paris or Le Havre. All available fliers were to move our smokecarvers to a new line, twenty miles northeast of the old one, close enough to force a pitched battle at dawn.

"Get out now," Millen told me. "I'll babysit your kids. If you find Franklin tied up in the corner after peace breaks out, it wasn't me."

"Thanks, Teeny," I said. "Come safe home."

I checked my messages.

What are you doing? Where are you? I need you here.

Why won't you answer? You bastard.

Robert? Please?

And then:

To: Robert Weekes.

Fr: Bertie Synge.

In Calais. Need assistance. Most urgent. Come immediate if able. Reply, pls.

What was wrong with me? Go to Ostend, be with Danielle. How hard was this? I'd more than done my duty. But I owed Synge. I would never stop owing her. She'd been the only person in Montana to believe I might join the Corps. Even I had thought it was impossible. Now it only seemed impossible that I had ever wanted so badly to have—this.

I pulled the maps out of my bag and began lining up a course.

En rte from Le Hvr, I messaged to Synge. *ETA 40min. Where are y in Calais?*

And then to Dar: *One more. Then I promis.*

I sped to Calais and found Dr. Synge outside the civilian transporter arena with an equipment box the size of a steamer trunk.

"I can't believe you came!" Synge said. "I can't get through to Blandings. I couldn't think of anyone else. I need a flier."

"Why aren't you in Ostend?" I asked.

"I'm supposed to be. I was coming over with one of the loads of volunteers. But Gen. Witt put out a plea to reservists to report and reinforce the main lines. I haven't been in active service in fifteen years, but my name is still on the rolls. I was already on the way. I should have continued on to Belgium, but I knew Chrissy Witt in the Philippines. I couldn't refuse. Those are my people outside Reims, Robert. All credit to Blandings for what she's about to do, but it's going to be my people—women who served with me and under me—who will do the dying today."

The way she said it scared me.

"How bad is it going to be?" I asked.

"The latest is that Gen. Fallmarch is removing Witt from command and is taking personal control of the line—it's going to be somewhere between a disaster and a bloodbath. She has no combat experience at all. She's not even a smokecarver. Fallmarch wants to hit the Germans with dispersant like

Cadwallader did back during the Intervention, but their cloud is too big. She would need weeks to destroy it. I think I have another way. I need to see the cloud itself to be sure."

"You want me to fly you *toward* it? There are three Allied armies running in the opposite direction."

"We need to know the structure of the cloud itself. The rauchbauers won't want to be anywhere near the toxic part, so the poison will be carried in a compartmentalized section right at the leading edge, probably only twenty or thirty yards deep. Beyond that, they'll have a buffer of ordinary heavy smoke and then farther back it should be hollow—just a thin veneer over their heads to screen them."

"So just attack the front part, then?" I asked.

"Exactly. The question is how. It's devilishly hard to move a cloud that size. You need a lot of women working together to push it forward, which means the temptation is to subdivide as little as possible."

"What do you mean subdivide?"

"You have to split up that front compartment so that if something goes wrong in one spot it doesn't spread through the whole cloud. You put in cofferdams or dividers to prevent one mistake from disintegrating miles of smoke. But those subdivisions make the cloud more rigid and slow down its forward movement. If the rauchbauers were careful and subdivided every hundred feet, then we'll want to concentrate our forces and overwhelm one section at a time. If they've been reckless and the subcompartments are a mile wide so that they can move faster, we have other options."

"Great. So message one of the generals and tell them to send somebody to check."

"I have. Our smokecarvers are scattered, their equipment is lost or broken, and the women who are in place don't have the expertise. It's me or no one. All I need is for you to hover me over their cloud for five minutes. It could make the difference between our lines holding or breaking."

I glanced at my message board. I didn't even want to imagine what Danielle would say if I described what Dr. Synge was asking me to do.

"Robert, you're Emmaline Weekes's son," Synge pleaded. "I've seen you in action. I don't know any other fliers I would trust to do this. Please."

Even now, two decades later, I have trouble explaining it.

Not that I didn't love Danielle, not that I didn't want to be with her. Not a notion that I had some great role to play, that the actions of one person might tip the balance of the war. Merely that I was doing necessary work. That I was nineteen years old and had found my place in the world.

"Let's go," I said to Synge. "We'll do it quick and eat lunch in Belgium."

Synge secured several vials and canisters of preformed smoke to her harness. I rigged her trunk of equipment, which weighed at least two hundred pounds and would make maneuvering difficult.

We launched and, for a bad passenger, Dr. Synge behaved remarkably well.

"How can the new line possibly hold?" I shouted over the slipstream. "It took us all day to move supplies to the old one. R&E can get our smokecarvers into the new position. But they'll never get them enough smoke!"

"They won't need much," Synge shouted back. "They're going to use electrostatic cord."

"What's that?"

"Electrified smoke. Experimental. Each woman will build a coil a couple hundred yards long. Then splice them together and hook up to a generator on the flank. Flip the switch and the German cloud will stick right to it—static electricity. They've never seen anything like it. They won't be able to get their cloud loose. *If* it works. Nobody's ever tried something this big."

We streaked east. Rather than battle tactics, I was worried about missing the German cloud. I'd heard several different descriptions of where it was, in what direction it was moving, and how quickly. As the minutes slipped past, though, my eyelids got heavy. I yawned and closed my eyes for a moment. It was easy. Just redraw my glyph every eight seconds. I didn't need to think to do it. Millen had it right—just close your eyes and fly and fly and—

"Robert," Dr. Synge said. "Robert!"

I startled awake to a dim glow along the horizon. Dawn. We must have flown longer than I'd thought. But the sun looked like it was rising in the south and the light had a sickly gray-green tinge as it hugged the ground.

"That's it, right there!" Synge said. "They injected a luminescent chemical into it so they could see at night."

I slowed and turned to intercept the cloud. It was too big to understand—a thousand yards deep and stretching into the distance farther than I could see. It was a vast, churning sea, all of it in motion, reverberating, reaching out and re-forming, flooding forward unevenly, a tentacle here, a wave there. Yellow patches rose to the surface only to disappear again; dark red spots boiled up and fell away; thin green stripes rolled over the surface. It was mesmerizing.

"Closer," Synge whispered. "Bring us over the leading edge. Right above."

The cloud looked like death incarnate as it lurched forward. Synge took a lead-lined canister the size of a pickle jar from her harness and unscrewed the top to reveal a glob of pale ocher smoke. Just by glancing at it I could tell it was skittish, high-strung stuff looking for the slightest excuse to go bolting off as far and fast as it could.

"Something our friends at Radcliffe cooked up for me," Synge said. "They've been learning how to separate different isotopes of the elements. It's radioactive fluorine. It'll spread through their cloud, but it won't cross the German cofferdams, and it won't diffuse out of the cloud. We'll see how far it gets and that's the size of their compartment."

She tossed it into the cloud and it vanished in an instant. Then she took a smoke filament from another canister, coiling thirty feet of it around her arm. She attached a weight to one end and a handheld detector to the other.

I positioned us ten feet above the front of the cloud and Synge unwound the line. The filament glowed a harsh green as it touched the German smoke. The detector began clicking and popping wildly.

"Move toward the rear of the cloud," Synge said.

I flew and the filament dragged across the ground behind us, mostly hidden by the German cloud. After a few seconds, Synge's detector abruptly went silent. The filament faded to dull gray.

"That's it!" Synge said. "That's the end of their front compartment. It's only ten yards deep. Everything behind it is nontoxic or hollow."

"Hollow?" I said. "There could be rauchbauers right below us?"

"Not *right* below," said Synge. "They'll be spaced out over the whole line. Let's find out how far the compartment extends."

She reeled in her line and I flew us a quarter mile along the German cloud. She lowered her filament again and her detector again clicked and crackled with the radioactive energy.

"Let's try another half a mile," Synge said.

It clicked less energetically at that distance, but still produced a strong signal. We caught it more faintly one mile beyond that.

"They couldn't possibly have done a single compartment for their whole cloud, could they?" Synge mused. "That's beyond reckless."

"Let's go all the way to the southern flank and find out," I suggested.

We flew down to the very edge of the cloud and lowered the filament once more. The signal was weak, but every few seconds we heard one of the characteristic pops on the detector.

"I can't believe it," Synge whispered. "It's one compartment the whole way. It's *got* to be. That's how they were able to move so fast. But if we can get a fire started, the whole thing will burn."

"It's smoke," I said. "It can't burn."

"Oh, you're very wrong. A portion of it is vaporized fuel oil—it's extremely combustible, as are the rest of the particles. The Germans will have taken special care to pull the oxygen out of that front compartment to reduce the risk of it burning. Though maybe I should double-check the oxygen levels with a clean filament. It'll just take a minute."

Synge took out fresh smoke and set about weaving it into a new line.

While she worked, a tentacle of smoke from the German cloud swept lazily toward us, twisting around Synge's old filament, like a vine growing up a trellis. The filament burst into flames and Synge disintegrated it with a glyph.

"That's a good trick," she said, with a ghost of a laugh. "I guess they noticed us after all. I wonder if . . ."

She looked backward over my shoulder.

"Up!" she cried. "Up!"

A much larger plume had been stealing toward us, silent as a fog bank. Now it whipped through the air. I drew for altitude and we pulled away—agonizingly slowly. The plume stretched after us, grazing my boots, causing the soles to smolder. I added power, straining away from the cloud. The wisp stretched after us, wrapping itself around my foot, before it stretched too far and lost coherence, falling back to earth as motes of ash. I could smell burned leather.

"Way too close," I said.

"Agreed," Synge said. "We need to talk to Gen. Witt. Her command post is at the far northern end of our line. If you'd be so kind?"

We had no time to waste. Less than three miles separated the German cloud from our smokecarvers. If the rauchbauers continued creeping forward at their current speed, they would make contact in ninety minutes. I sped toward our lines.

"Is it gonna be safe to be this close to our smoke?" I asked Synge. "They warned fliers clear of the defenses. They said we would get poisoned if we were too close or yanked right out of the sky."

"That's ridiculous," Synge said. "If Fallmarch were smarter, she'd have fliers mixed in with her smokecarvers. They could ferry women to weak spots, move supplies. Instead, she wants a glorious victory for the smokecarvers alone. She doesn't understand how precarious the situation is."

We found the right flank of our line, which the Logistics fliers had kindly labeled with liquid fire so that the R&E flights could see where to land: MILE 0.0, it read in pretty, looping script. There were only nine women there. They waved to us and I slowed for a moment.

One of them was driving metal stakes into the ground with a sledgehammer. The rest were gathering smoke from a large pot and weaving it. They had two lines of electrostatic cord strung in front of them and two more behind. Theoretically, these would run twenty-five miles, all the way to the left flank. Each one was an inch thick, crackling with yellow-blue flashes of energy.

"Oh my God," Synge breathed. "They should have at least a hundred women on the flank to prevent the Germans from pushing around the end."

"R&E is still running smokecarvers up from the old lines," I answered. "Maybe they're still bringing up more on this end."

But as I checked the gossip glyph on my message board, that seemed not to be the case: fliers were complaining about not being able to find the women they'd been assigned to pick up; of smokecarvers refusing to reposition, asking instead to be taken to Ostend to join the mutiny; of entire platoons of corpswomen deserting and walking away into the night when they heard the new plan.

"I think we're gonna have a problem," I said.

We headed toward the command post. With two thousand Corps smokecarvers and twenty-five miles to cover, standard tactics called for them to be evenly distributed: We should have had eighty women per mile. We had perhaps half that, with stretches of several hundred yards left undefended. Then between Miles 12 and 13 there were no women at all. There was also no electrostatic cord.

"This is a catastrophe," Synge said. "The cord's like wire. It won't conduct if there's a gap. Get us up to the command post right now!"

We saw no further holes over the last few miles. The corpswomen were more numerous there and better spaced. As we approached the left flank at Mile 25, we could see huge plumes of oily black smoke rising from smudge pots the size of cauldrons. They had two hundred women—a much more appropriate number for holding the flank—plus the diesel generator and hundreds of barrels' worth of additional materiel.

We set down beside the command tent.

"Pass the word!" Dr. Synge hollered as we landed. "Capt. Synge for Gen. Witt with intel!"

Synge had a good shouting voice. Several women hurried toward a group of officers standing around message boards on folding camp tables. Gen. Witt detached herself and came over to us.

"Mother Mary, but it really is the good doctor!" Witt called out to Synge. "How are you, Bertie?"

"I'm well, Chrissy," Synge replied. "Day for the ages, isn't it?"

"I think—" Witt said lowering her voice, "I really think it could work. The Germans don't understand what they're walking into. We can hold them, at least."

"Not yet you can't. There's a gap all the way from mile twelve to thirteen."

"Christ," said Witt. "Maj. Hideki!"

A smokecarver in hovering harness jogged over.

"Take the maneuver company to mile thirteen with all the cord you can carry. There's a big hole. Patch and report."

"Yes, ma'am," Hideki said.

"Belay that!" shouted a tall, handsome woman who strode over to join us. It was Gen. Fallmarch herself. She looked every part a Corps commandant, with her salt and pepper hair, aquiline nose, and regal bearing—it was just that none of us trusted her to do the actual commanding part. "Mrs. Witt, you are not splitting up my shock troops to man the line!"

Witt conducted herself far more calmly than I would have managed, had I been a general who'd just been demoted to "Mister" in front of my own women.

"General," Witt replied, "it will improve unit cohesion to give the maneuver company a small task, prior to putting them on the offensive. They'll be back in plenty of time to exploit any breakthrough we make."

Fallmarch liked that idea. "Go quickly, then," she said. She looked at us. "Who are these people?"

"This is Capt. Synge, whom you may remember from Manila. She was our chief scientific officer there. She's a reservist who reported at will."

"Bully for you!" Fallmarch said, reaching out to shake Synge's hand. "Brought your own ride, I see."

"Friend from back home," Synge answered. "Sig-2 Canderelli."

"The male from Fifth Division?" Fallmarch asked. I nodded. "Hard-working unit. Terribly sorry to hear you've lost Blandings."

She sounded almost jolly about it.

"Thank you, ma'am," I said.

"Carry on," Fallmarch said and returned to her message boards.

"'Exploit a breakthrough?'" Synge asked Witt. "Does Fallmarch really understand so little?"

Witt shook her head. "She refused to let me attack them by air yesterday—we ought to have had R&E up, bombing with dispersant to slow their advance. But nothing short of smokecarver defeating smokecarver will satisfy her. What choice did I have? Resign and watch her slaughter my whole department?"

"It might not be as bad as you think," Synge said. "We looked at the German cloud. It's ten feet high on the front end and the toxin goes back less than thirty feet. I suspect the rauchbauers are another hundred yards back, pushing the cloud out in front of them. We did a radiological study and you're not going to believe this: They have an enormous front compartment without any subdivisions. The smoke's very dense."

"We can burn it!" Witt said.

"Exactly," Synge said.

"Fallmarch will like that—it's the sort of brute force attack she understands. I'll send orders for the women to fashion incendiaries and build oxygen rams."

Gen. Witt called out orders for her board women to message to the line before turning back to us.

"I hope you'll stay with us here," Witt said to Synge. "I'll put you in charge of a company. We can always use another experienced senior officer."

"I was thinking mile thirteen," said Synge. "That's where you're most vulnerable."

"Our center couldn't be in better hands, then," said Witt. "Good luck."

"Come safe home, General," said Synge.

"I think . . ." said Witt. "I think for me, maybe not today. I had a premonition that . . . Well, Bertie, just promise, if the middle folds—how old are your daughters?"

"Nine and eleven."

"If the cord doesn't light up, run."

We settled in at Mile 13 just as the two dozen smokecarvers who knew how to fly finished splicing in their lengths of cord. The line was patched, with very little time to spare.

"Ten minutes until they flip the switch," one of them told us, before she launched to head back to the command post. She drew a message sigil for me. "Unofficial gossip glyph for the line."

I took my forty-pound powder bag off and set it on the ground. Dr. Synge opened her cargo box and removed an ordinary-sized smudge pot—a metal sphere the size of a cannonball with a narrow neck on top, designed so that the fuel oil inside would burn sooty, putting out thick, ample smoke. Synge lit it and cupped her hands over it to collect the smoke. She drew sigils to cohere it and worked it into sheets, which she began folding and rolling into a spiral-shaped accordion.

"I'm making an oxygen ram," she explained. "It'll separate the oxygen out of the air and blow it toward the German cloud. If Witt got her way, they should be building them all up and down the line. How much smokecarving did you do at Radcliffe?"

"One semester," I said. "I can do simple structures."

"Make us a couple of big blankets with a tight weave to use as shelters in case something goes wrong."

I collected handfuls of smoke from the smudge pot, too, condensed it with glyphs, drew sigils and twisted and folded and wove, until I had two sheets large enough to huddle under. Synge took the sheets of smoke from me, adding powders and complex sigils to reflect heat, to deaden kinetic energy, to repel smoke, to let oxygen through in one direction and carbon dioxide out in the other. Just in case.

Suddenly, I felt a thrum run through me, as if someone had struck a church bell that was vibrating at too low a pitch to hear. I looked up to see both cords on the front side of the line rising up until they were elevated four feet above the ground, hanging a hand's breadth apart. Tiny threads searched their way from one to the other, creating a web.

Dr. Synge was watching too. "It's conducting! The patches held."

And then the German cloud was upon us, its advance silent and inexorable: ten feet high, moving at a brisk walk, the leading edge swirling and feinting, here puffing out and there withdrawing, now advancing three steps and then retreating two, every moment throwing forward a thousand tendrils that collapsed back in on themselves. Stopping it would be like trying to box with a hurricane or turn back the tide. It was a half mile distant, a quarter mile, a hundred feet.

"Oh, Lord," whispered Synge. "Here we go."

Contact, Mile 0.0, read the gossip glyph.

"Step back," Synge said. She grabbed me by the harness. The electrical thrum was clearly audible now. Our smoke net had fully expanded; the bottom cord was flush with the ground and the top cord had risen twelve feet into the air. The threads between them continued to subdivide and tangle with one another.

"Step way back!" said Synge. "They're going to—"

Bits of grass and dead leaves jumped off the ground and stuck to the web between the cords. All my hair stood on end. The metal buckles on my harness sparked and glowed blue.

Synge threw me to the ground and pulled the shelters over us.

"Cover your ears!"

The German smoke was twenty feet away from us, ten feet. And then without warning it was yanked forward and stuck fast to the netting, cracking like a lightning bolt. I could feel the shock wave wash over us, but the blankets absorbed the worst of it.

Synge got back on her feet, pulling me up with her.

The German cloud bulged forward, trying to fling tendrils of smoke over the net, only to have them pulled down and stick to the threads of the web, too. To our right, the rauchbauers pushed up a column that swirled a hundred feet high, crashing toward our line, only for it to be ripped apart by its attraction to the netting.

Similar reports were coming in from all over the gossip glyph:

Stuck fast at 10.2.

Hello from 8.8—they tried to push over, but shredded apart.

Yikes, light-up tore my necklace right off my neck.

THEY ARE TRYING TO FLANK US AT MILE 0.0—RA RA RA—WE'RE THROWING OUT SPIKES OF EXTRA CORD—SEND HELP TO 0.0.

"The right flank can't hold long," Synge said. "Maybe ten, fifteen minutes before the rauchbauers push their way around."

We heard distant shouts in German. The cloud in front of us coalesced more tightly in places, thinned out in others. They were trying to pull back. Our net bowed a few inches backward, but the strain on the German cloud was too great. Flecks of soot floated away from their smoke, vapor rose. If they pulled any harder they would lose cohesion and risk disintegrating their entire front.

They couldn't advance and couldn't retreat.

Stuck.

"Son of a bitch," Synge said. "We did it!"

26

Four decades ago, my mother led a force of volunteers to save France. Now, Paris again is under siege. Our own Corps lies in ruins. Two million of our countrymen in uniform are at risk, as are all the women and men of Europe. Today, I call upon every able-bodied philosopher to join me in a crusade to liberate the world from German tyranny. Our first volunteers are already pouring into France. Will you not join me? Will you not do your part to ensure peace in our day?

Sen. Josephine Cadwallader-Fulton, Speech at the Washington, DC, transporter field, October 31, 1918

I SWITCHED MY WRIST BOARD OVER TO THE SMOKECARVER command glyph.

Witt here: To all miles—Well done! Hold position. Report leaks. Flow forward oxygen. Prepare incendiaries.

"The Germans made their cloud from a beautiful, old-fashioned weave with lots of particulate and oil droplets," Synge said. "And we're bathing it in pure O_2. It'll go up like a cloud of gasoline."

"God almighty," I said, imagining a twenty-five-mile-wide conflagration. I shifted back a foot.

Synge worked on enlarging her miniature cyclone, aiming it more straight on at the German cloud. It continued spinning, stripping the oxygen out of the air and blowing it through our net.

"Do you know how to make a firebomb?" Synge asked.

I'd grown up the son of a county philosopher with a fully stocked chemistry lab and no adult supervision for hours every day. It hardly bore asking.

"I blew up a dead tree with half a pound of thermite when I was fourteen," I said.

"You're lucky to be alive. That would do nicely."

I sorted through Synge's trunk and found jars of powdered aluminum and ground iron oxide—rust. I weighed out the aluminum on an alchemist's scale, poured it into a canister, and added the right amount of iron.

On my wrist board, the right flank was pleading for action: *FROM 0.0: WE ARE ABOUT TO BE OVERRUN. WE NEED TO DO IT NOW!*

Witt agreed. *All Miles: Ready incendiaries. Attack on my order . . .*

I punched a hole in the canister's lid and stuck in a strip of magnesium to act as a fuse. Synge stood in front of me, holding the smoke blanket out as a shield against heat and shrapnel.

"Do you have a good throwing arm?" she asked.

"Good enough," I said. "It only needs to go ten feet."

"Don't hit our net by mistake. There's no telling what—"

"I'm not going to miss!"

Witt here: Do it.

I lit the strip of magnesium and it glowed blue-white, hissing like a sparkler. I reared back and lobbed it over the net into the German cloud. We heard a soft thunk as it landed.

Nothing happened.

I got on my belly to peer through the bottom of our net. The German smoke was thinner along the ground and I could make out my primitive bomb, the magnesium fuse sputtering and going dim.

"Come on," I pleaded. "Come on!"

In the distance, colossal explosions rose, as smokecarver-built clouds of vaporized alcohol and jellied gasoline lit up the German cloud. Finally, my canister flared up and ignited in a flash of sparks, melting within seconds into a puddle of liquid metal. But the grass around it only smoldered. The German smoke didn't take at all.

"Still not enough oxygen!" Synge complained.

She aimed the stream from her ram right at it. The grass waved in the breeze and flickered. Then the cloud flashed over into a roiling firestorm, swirling down the line, sucking air in, screaming like a panicked horse, blinding me with the wind. I scrambled to my feet and we ran.

The heat scorched the back of my neck. The wind roared past us, feeding the flames, which shrieked and whined as if the German cloud were a living thing being burned alive. We didn't turn back to look until we'd put a hundred yards between ourselves and the inferno. Our fire had spread a quarter mile along the line, a roiling red and black sea as the toxic smoke burned.

Farther in the distance, plumes of fire rose, the product of attacks by our fellow corpswomen, accompanied by columns of smoke to which the early-morning sun leant a golden sheen. Smoke burned to white ash and fell back to the earth like snow.

"It's a poor fire that burns but once?" I said to Synge, remembering the old smokecarver's maxim. It hardly seemed biblical enough.

"Pray it works," Synge said.

A huge sheet of anoxic smoke—firefighting material—rose into the air from the rear of the German cloud and crashed down onto our flames, smothering them before they could spread farther. Similar blankets rose over the other fires in both directions. We might have spooked the rauchbauers, but they appeared to be very much alive.

Synge surveyed the line. "We took out maybe half the volume of their cloud. If there'd been twice as many of us . . . damn."

"So, we do it a second time, right?" I suggested.

"They'll beat out the flames as fast as we can light them."

The remaining toxic smoke was flowing forward to fill the denuded areas along our netting. Synge and I walked back to our old position.

Witt here: Mile 0.0 hold fast. Hideki flying squad is en route to reinforce.

Stand clear of the rear cords. We will polarize them to ship dispersal agent to Mile 0.0 and keep the German cloud off our flank. R&E is en route with additional supplies.

The second pair of electrostatic cords, which had been left dead on the ground behind us in case the first net failed and we needed to throw up another layer of defense, now thrummed to life, electrifying and rising. The cords sent threads creeping back and forth, creating a second twelve-foot-high net. Clouds of dispersant from the command post on the left flank began rolling down toward Mile 0, riding the cords like railroad tracks. The women on the right flank would use it to disintegrate the German cloud trying to slip around the end of our line.

"Is this going to work?" I asked Synge.

"As long as our flanks hold, we've forced a stalemate," she said. "It's just a matter of whether the Germans admit it. If they're smart they'll sue for peace by this afternoon."

"No mutiny?" I asked.

"I don't think so."

I sagged to the ground in relief. It might take a few days for the politicians to work out a peace treaty, but no plague. No army of civilian volunteers trying to fight off the Germans with Danielle in the lead. No raid on Berlin. No choosing between Blandings and Dar.

Then I heard the crack of a rifle shot a couple hundred yards away from us inside the German cloud. More shots broke out all up and down the line. Poorly aimed fire, but enough that Synge and I took cover behind her powder chest.

On the gossip glyph, women all over the line were reporting small-arms fire, too. And then on the command glyph: *Heavy mortar fire at 25.0.*

A moment later, the electric thrum running through our netting dropped in pitch and then ceased.

"They must have hit the generator," said Synge. "The netting should still hold, but it'll be a lot less effective."

A few more shots rang out. One of them struck near us, kicking up a spray of dirt. Synge yelped.

At 25.0: Infantry emerging from German cloud. Est 1K, repeat 1000+.

"Oh, Christ," Synge said.

Infntr in the . . .

Then nothing further over the command glyph. I switched to the gossip glyph.

From Mile 24.4: German smoke is running free past our left flank. Our back line is attracting it.

A minute later, a few scattered streaks of German smoke came rolling fast down the electrostatic cords behind us. No different from what we'd done to ship the dispersant. A whole flood of German smoke followed.

On the right flank at Mile 0, Maj. Hideki was reporting that the rauchbauers had swung the edge of their cloud way out past the opposite end of our line and had attached to our rear net there, too. They were sending huge volumes of smoke back in the other direction.

Synge and I watched the cloud along our rear line thicken, running up nearly the whole twelve-foot height of our netting.

"So, we've got a cloud of toxic smoke in front of us, another forming behind us, and they've cut across both flanks?" I said. "A stalemate is one thing, but we're surrounded."

"Agreed," Synge said. "Get your flying gear."

The German smoke surged against the front net. It stretched but held.

I ran for my powder bag, which I'd left right next to the netting. The canvas was scorched. My regulator was melted to slag.

"Oh, no," I whispered.

I looked at the burn marks on my harness around the buckles. When they'd electrified the netting, anything made of steel had gone hot.

The German smoke cloud threw itself against the front netting again; this time it sagged back a couple feet.

"Robert!" Synge shouted. "Let's go!"

I ran back to her with the remains of my powder bag. She looked as if she were going to be sick.

I tried to think of alternatives.

"R&E is on the way," I suggested. "One of my wingmates could get us out."

I messaged Millen, Andrada, Vos, Devereaux. None of them answered.

The Germans hammered at the front line again and it crumpled even farther.

I tried Miss Franklin.

Yes! she replied. *I am happy to help. Where are you?*

Mile 13, I replied.

Where is that? she asked.

"Oh, for fuck's sake!" I said.

"Is that a serious question?" Synge asked.

Between Mile 12 and Mile 14, I wrote.

Where? Everyone says the numbers are covered up.

RIGHT IN THE GODDAMN MIDDLE! FLY UNTIL YOU SEE THE EDGE OF A FUCKING GIANT CLOUD AND TURN RIGHT!

Okay! We are about 40 minutes away. No one is sure who is in charge. Some people are leaving. I will keep coming, though.

The German cloud slammed into our front line again, pushing it back a few more inches.

"Is it going to hold forty minutes?" I asked Synge.

"Doubtful," she said. "What about transporting out? You transport, don't you?"

"No," I said. "Do you?"

"Never in my life," she said. "But we could use the aluminum in the box to put down a destination glyph, then have someone swap us out to Ostend."

"I used it."

"You *what*?"

"I used the aluminum. To make thermite for the bomb."

"Shit."

The German cloud drew back as far as it could and condensed, heaping up smoke until it looked like a thirty-foot-high black wave poised to break over us.

Synge grabbed a protective smoke blanket.

"Get under!" she shouted, throwing it over me.

The wave surged toward us, smashing into the top cable of our net, which disintegrated. The German smoke poured over the top.

Synge dove to the ground next to me and pulled the blanket over us, drawing sigils on it so that the edges bound to the earth, forming a dome. Then the German cloud rolled over us. We heard a soft patter, like sleet falling on tree leaves.

"Hell," Synge whispered. "Oh, hell."

Our shelter was six feet by six. We had only the chemical flare strapped to my wrist for light; it had been burning for nearly three hours and was already fading. I rolled on my side and looked at Synge in its dim blue light.

"We're going to be okay, right?" I said. "R&E's coming."

"They'll need a smokecarver to cut us out. That cloud could be twenty feet deep over our heads."

Synge took her glasses off and put her hands to her face.

"We're going to be okay!" I insisted.

"They can kill us a hundred ways," Synge said. "Carbon monoxide, fire, chlorine gas, explosives . . ."

Before there was time for panic to set in, the part of me that had beat relentlessly forward from the first day in France, pushing always for the next mission, the next evac, the next task, seized control: take inventory, make plan, effect escape. This was no worse than being trapped in a tent. We had . . . a smokecarver cut off from any useful smoke, a hoverer without a regulator, my belt knife, Synge's glasses, assorted buckles and straps, a dying flare, a message board.

It took me a minute longer than it should have to realize the situation was three steps beyond hopeless.

"What do we do next?" I asked Synge.

"Write your family," she said.

I stared at my wrist board. I didn't even know who first. Or how.

Mother. Surely, Mother first.

Unbidden, the memory of an incident from my childhood came back, a disastrous cave-in that had trapped a dozen miners beneath the earth near Helena. Mother and hundreds of other rescuers, philosophical and common laborers alike, had worked around the clock to dig them out. It had taken nineteen days. Mother had been part of the team that finally forced their way inside and discovered the bodies. The miners had written notes by the stub of a candle as they were dying. Ma had come out distraught after reading them, but she'd never told me what they said. I'd always imagined that the men must have been inspired to the heights of eloquence and profundity by their situation. I was now beginning to suspect otherwise.

Hi Ma, I wrote. *In littl bit trubl.*

Mother didn't answer. I couldn't get through to any of my sisters. I gave my wrist board to Synge, who tried to contact her husband.

"Anything?" I asked.

"No," she said. "He doesn't carry a portable. It's— maybe it's better."

I knew I should write Dar.

I pulled up Fifth Division's communication glyph instead. Ten minutes earlier, Blandings had sent the message to start the mutiny: *Now, please.*

I tried Mother again and Angie. Still nothing. Maybe they were on their way even at that moment to rescue me.

I drew Dar's glyph. I licked my upper lip then wiped my board clean.

"What do you say that doesn't sound stupid?" I asked Synge.

"It's supposed to sound stupid," she said.

I'm trapped under the cloud, I wrote to Danielle. *I'm sorry. I love you.*

I sent it.

I wished I were a praying man. I wished I were a better smokecarver and could tunnel out with my bare hands.

"Blandings," I said. "Blandings will send someone for us."

I was her secret weapon, wasn't I? But as I watched the gossip glyph, dozens of women were reporting attacks in Paris by groups of rauchbauers being transported in and releasing clouds of toxin in hit-and-run attacks: the French parliament building was enveloped, Notre Dame, the Eiffel Tower, the main rail stations, French military headquarters.

"This was all a diversion," Synge said. "A twenty-five-mile-wide diversion. Tie up the Corps so that the best rauchbauers could attack Paris unopposed. The Germans have hardly any transporters, but they put them to good use. They succeeded beyond anything they could have hoped for."

"They're coming for us though, right? Blandings and Senator Cadwallader-Fulton and everybody in Belgium—they'll get us out."

"Paris has to be their priority. If they lose the city, the Germans can force peace on their terms."

"Who's left to come for *us*, then?"

I fired off messages to Blandings, Andrada, Macmurdo, Nampeyo. No one answered.

I needed half an hour for that to sink in. Eventually, we heard the drone of aeroplanes overhead and machine-gun fire.

I glanced at my wrist board.

I can't see any mile markers, Miss Franklin had written, *and we are being shot at. Can you mark your position? I could lower you a rope? Or a ladder if I had one.*

Which was the most sensible thing I'd ever heard out of Franklin.

"I don't have anything to mark with," Synge said. "And we'd have to cut a hole in the shelter to get a rope in."

N, I wrote. *No way to mark.*

Oh drat. The aeroplanes are back. Have to go.

The sky went quiet. We waited an hour. One of the other smokecarvers trapped in a shelter under the cloud wrote over the gossip glyph, trying to find out how many of us were similarly entombed. I answered, as did 148 others.

Then something else came across. My hand spasmed.

This is Ms. Hardin's assistant. Danielle is currently occupied. May I relay a message?

I half cried, half laughed.

Synge reached over and squeezed my shoulder.

Situatn bad, I wrote. *Can she come to board?*

She is in a closed meeting. I will forward your request at the first opportunity.

Yet another hour. No word from Danielle. There was no sound but a pair of thrushes singing to each other without ceasing. My flare faded to nothing. The darkness beneath German smoke was total.

"Were you afraid of the dark?" Synge asked me. "When you were a child?"

"No," I said. "I wasn't afraid of anything as a kid. Not till I got older."

The thrushes sang on, a new verse every minute, rising and falling.

"We're going to die here, aren't we?" I said.

"Unless we get a lot of help," said Synge.

PART 3

THE VOLUNTEERS

Never did so many assemble so quickly with so little hope of reward.

Ms. Danielle Hardin, dedication of the American Philosophers War Memorial, St. Louis, Missouri, October 31, 1920

27

NO WEEKEND EDITION: AT THE WAR 'TIL MONDAY!

Detroit Defender, October 31, 1918

11:00 GREENWICH MEAN TIME

OCTOBER 31, 1918

Cambridge, Massachusetts

Freddy Unger had taken to sleeping on a cot in his laboratory, stealing an occasional hour of rest during the frantic string of experiments and rewriting of equations that had filled the past week. When the word came at last—*today, now*—he had only to roll out of bed and begin preparing the powder.

As he lit the burners on the melting furnace and took out his scale, weighing out five pounds of pure platinum ingots, Freddy couldn't help but sing to himself, the same tune that had been running through his brain without ceasing for days:

". . . the Yanks are coming, the Yanks are coming, the drums rum-tumming everywhere . . ."

What a relief to step away from the books and chalkboards! Didn't every theorist dream of a day like this? How exciting that his work might prove useful; how grand that he was doing his part; how worrisome that the stakes were so high. And then, right below the surface, a different feeling bubbled, ugly and gleeful. See if the generals underestimated sigilry after this! See if the practical philosophers still mocked the tweed-wearing, ink-stained theorists after they changed the world.

Not, Freddy reflected, *that one ought to consider this a sure thing.*

Indeed, the final round of tests had been highly concerning. It would have been prudent to run one more experiment with the latest improved sigil, but they'd nearly exhausted their supply of iridium-191. They had enough left either to make their attempt on Berlin or to do the experiment. That was hardly a choice.

Freddy poured the platinum ingots into a crucible then added the duller silver lumps of iridium. He put on a welding mask and insulated gloves, opened the door to the furnace, and used tongs to set the crucible inside.

"We'll be over, we're coming over . . ."

Really, it was impossible to interpret the news coming out of France. It sounded dire: the Corps crippled after their defeat outside Reims; Paris under attack; tens of thousands of women mobilizing for the relief effort. Or possibly the Germans had been stopped cold and were in the process of signing a peace treaty. It all depended which flavor of rumor you preferred.

He had his work, though. Once the metals had melted, he would cool the resulting alloy, mill it into powder, and take a sack to Belgium on the next transatlantic service. A weapon to change the world, but small enough to fit in a woman's handbag. Equal parts theoretical breakthrough and brute-force philosophy. A sigil so powerful that Germany would have no choice but to surrender by this time tomorrow morning. Everything was ready: Gen. Blandings was in Ostend with her team, the reconnaissance flights over Berlin had been promising, Dean Murchison had been trundled off to Europe and had come out of his transporter-related psychosis. (Poor man—break a cartogramancer's connection to the earth too violently and he lost his mind for a few days. Or lost it more than usual, as the case might be.)

The door to his lab banged open as Professor Brock entered. She had a look of worry instead of her usual expression of phlegmatic competence.

"It's going according to protocol?" she asked.

"Indeed!" Freddy said. "It's melting as we speak. It'll be ready by noon and I'm already packed to go. It's like that line in the song that everyone's singing—*we're*—"

"Karl Friedrich," Professor Brock broke in, "is there *any* chance that your roommate might be missing? Any possibility?"

"Who, Robert?" Freddy laughed. "Oh, that's preposterous! He's in Belgium with everyone else."

"Are you *sure* of that?"

"Of course he is! He knows how essential he is to the operation. He wouldn't jeopardize it."

Brock wiped her forehead. "Because I heard from Jake, who heard it from Edith Rubinski, who heard it from one of Robert's wingmates, who heard it from a friend that he went missing on the line outside Reims."

"Now this is the trouble with rumors!" Freddy said with a click of the tongue. "That's at least two too many 'heard it froms' to be credible."

"I hope you're right," Professor Brock said. "Come find me when you're done."

She wandered back out to her own lab next door.

The very epitome of unnecessary worry! Freddy turned up the burners on the furnace as high as they would go, all the while contemplating which bow tie he would wear on the day that victory was declared. The red, white, and blue star-spangled one seemed unforgivably gauche; the red-and-black one with the Radcliffe seal, too self-promotional. Though the new mint-green one with pink and white stripes might do . . .

Oh, but this was going to be exciting!

After twenty minutes, he pulled open the door of the furnace to peek at the crucible. The platinum had melted into a silvery pool, with the iridium still standing in a stubborn lump in the middle. Everything was proceeding according to plan.

"And we won't come back 'til it's over over there!"

15:00 GMT

Ostend, Belgium

Three thousand civilian hoverers launched at the same instant, each carrying a pair of smokecarvers—the largest assembly of American military philosophers since the Civil War. Like a flock of starlings, they wheeled toward Paris, passing silently overhead, closely spaced enough to blot out the sun. Volunteers, every one.

Tommie Blandings only wished there were twice as many. Addams and her team of smokecarvers were scattered across Paris trying to counter rauchbauer attacks, but badly outnumbered. Their command post in the fourth arrondissement was surrounded; Addams was fighting on bravely but running low on smoke.

Given enough time, the volunteers would tip the balance. The National Transporter Chain back in the States had suspended regular service and was running transatlantic jumps every half hour to bring over more philosophers and supplies. In New York City, sigilrists were lined up for eight blocks around the arena, trying to push their way onto the next jump up to Maine; Denver had a ten-hour wait for east-bound service; Sacramento was turning away women and organizing a second wave of volunteers to come over in two days' time. They could put a hundred thousand women in the field if they chose—though if they saved Paris only to see plague and counter-plague kill millions, that hardly seemed a victory.

"*Quis salvet ipsas salvatores*, Tommie?" asked old Gen. Rhodes, whose gravelly voice sounded like it had been quarried in an age when Latin was still spoken. She was buckling the chinstrap on her helmet. "Who will rescue the rescuers?"

"I will," said Blandings, still watching the mass of women flying west. Like the heavenly host going to wreak divine vengeance—or the rebel angels streaming out of hell.

"You ought to have someone carry you," Blandings suggested.

Gen. Rhodes spat on the ground. "I'm not so frail I can't keep up with my own army. It would please me if you had good news by the time I get to Paris. I have to know: Your plan for Berlin has gone tits up or you're going through with it?"

"I don't have a flier," Blandings said. "We lost Canderelli on the line. The postal hoverer from Iowa who we identified as our backup is refusing—his wife's fighting in Paris and they have four children. He doesn't want to risk them both not coming home."

"You had others."

"The Russian boy at Radcliffe hasn't developed as fast as we'd hoped. There's no chance he can cover the distance. The Japanese fellow does have the range, but he's stuck in Tokyo—the trans-Pacific chain is shut down. We're looking for alternatives."

"Lord," Gen. Rhodes said. "This is the trouble with relying on men! If you can't find one, then we need the senator to hammer out a cease-fire before one side starts flinging plague at the other. There's no way I can mount a credible offensive with an army of schoolgirls, retirees, and Sunday-morning sigilrists. We'll be in a purely defensive posture. You either take Berlin or write me a pretty speech to deliver when they hang me. You've always been a good talker—you talked me into this."

"You'll have Berlin," Blandings answered.

Rhodes sniffed. "Sure I will."

She handed Blandings a sealed envelope with *41* penciled on it. "No bagpipes at my funeral and do *not* let them play 'The Keel Row' over me. I hate that song."

"Don't let it come to that, ma'am," Blandings said.

"Then win."

20:00 GMT

Mile 25

Near Reims, France

Edith Rubinski shielded her eyes. The civilian smokecarvers had put up sheets of incandescent smoke to work by, though the harsh blue light didn't penetrate even an inch into the German cloud. The volunteers were driving tunnels into it, isolating and neutralizing the German smoke a few cubic yards at a time, then hauling it out in baskets and dispersing it into the night air in swirls of black ash.

The German cloud just sat there, inert and gray, like a wall or a gravestone: *Here died the Corps' finest.*

An hour before, her women had found the remains of the American command post and had begun dragging bodies out. The German poison was a paralytic, the smokecarvers said. A breath or two and the diaphragm and muscles of the chest were paralyzed along with the rest—you suffocated, still awake. The corpses had expressions of terror frozen on their faces, their eyes bulging, lips curled. All women. When she'd seen the first one, Edith had broken down in her worst crying jag of the war, bad enough to frighten a few of the smokecarvers, who had otherwise gone about their work with grim, methodical competence. They'd recovered Gen. Fallmarch's body and Gen. Witt's.

The rescue teams farther south along the line had had better success, tunneling out a hundred survivors from improvised shelters. But all of those had been in communication with the rescuers by message board to help direct the efforts. They hadn't found anyone alive by accident.

Teeny Millen landed beside her.

"Nothing?" Edith said.

Millen shook her head.

"Where are we *sure* someone saw him last?" Edith asked.

"We dug the whole southern flank out," Millen answered. "The women there saw Canderelli fly over an hour before the German cloud hit. They're sure it was him. They waved. Multiple survivors saw him at the northern flank fifteen minutes later. Then he messaged me, Andrada, Devereaux, and Vos in the space of a few minutes. Said he was trapped, but no location. Blandings had just called for the mutiny—I didn't see his note till an hour later. Then messages to Danielle and his mother about fifteen minutes later. His mother forwarded hers to Blandings. The last ones sounded dire, like his shelter was failing."

Edith set her jaw. "Tell me again: The last place someone saw him for sure?"

"Right here on the flank," Millen said.

"Last message from him was . . . ?"

"Ten hours ago."

Edith had only a hundred smokecarvers with which to conduct search and rescue for the entire line—the situation in Paris was becoming more tenuous by the hour. They couldn't spare any more. She called one of her team leaders over.

"Our group at mile six is struggling to get their tunnel through," Edith said. "They have at least four known survivors there. Take your women to assist. Rescuing the living takes precedence over recovering the dead. If any of your women find a male corpse in a Corps skysuit at any location, I'm to be notified immediately."

"Yes, ma'am," the smokecarver said and began withdrawing her philosophers.

Millen looked like she was on the verge of bursting into tears. Instead, she yanked off her helmet and hurled it at the German cloud.

"That shithead!" she screamed. "He only had one job! He told me he was going to Belgium. Fuck!"

01:30 GMT

NOVEMBER 1, 1918

Ostend, Belgium

Danielle wiped the back of her neck with her handkerchief. The classroom that they'd commandeered in Ostend's secondary school was unbearably warm. The walls were hung with charts and maps next to crudely drawn wax crayon pictures of the Virgin Mary that a grade-school class must have made before the city was evacuated.

Don't think about him. Hopeless. They would try for his body in a day or two; for now, they were racing to save the last handful of survivors. His body. Don't think about him.

The senior aide, standing at the chalkboard, cleared her throat and cut her eyes toward Danielle.

Sen. Cadwallader-Fulton had fallen asleep in her chair again.

"Ma'am?" Danielle said to the elderly woman next to her.

The senator woke with a snort. "Excuse me," she said. She scrubbed at her eyes. "Composition of the next regiment—" she announced. She stifled a yawn. "This is regiment . . . eighteen."

"Twenty-one," Danielle corrected gently. "We put the chart up to help with this."

Danielle pointed at the wall.

"I can't see it without my glasses," the senator said.

"You're wearing them, ma'am."

The aides shared a look. To Danielle it said, *you're the favorite—you suggest it.*

"Would you like to lie down?" Danielle asked. "We'll finish up. You can go out first thing in the morning, give them a speech as they come off the transporter field."

"Lovely idea," the senator replied. "It's a wonderful problem, to have so many of them. Wake me if there's trouble. In the meanwhile, Danielle will speak for me."

One of the young girls who'd snuck over with them on the first transport helped the senator find her cane and shuffle out of the room.

The other women were looking at Danielle. She couldn't afford to show weakness in front of them. She knew she was speaking more softly than usual, less forcefully, less often. Perhaps they credited her behavior to the same worries they all had: fatigue, Josephine's health, reports of the failing defenses in Paris. But enough. Don't think about him. She couldn't afford to have feelings right now.

"Miss Hardin, if you would?" said the senior aide.

"Regiment Twenty-One will go to Gen. Rhodes on the western defensive perimeter in Paris," Danielle said. "We'll make it a standard thousand-woman regiment. Six companies of a hundred smokecarvers each, three companies of hoverers to move them, and one command company—ten messagists, ten short-haul transporters, eighty Logistics fliers. They'll be due in at 03:00."

The women nodded their agreement.

"We have adequate personnel waiting in Maine to fill that," agreed the woman with the tally of available philosophers.

Then came a lull of a few seconds, which was deadly.

When Robert's shelter failed, it would only have been forty-five seconds before he blacked out from lack of oxygen. A few minutes more before he died. Not painful, everyone kept whispering. Danielle didn't believe it. Was drowning painful? Being smothered? Don't contemplate it.

"Regiment Twenty-Two," said the woman at the board.

"That's a relief division going to Belle Addams in the forward staging area in Paris," Danielle said, her voice wavering as she balled up her handkerchief in her hand under the table and squeezed. "She liked the last one, so let's do a repeat of that. Nine maneuver companies each with fifty smokecarvers, forty fliers, five short-haul transporters, five messagists. One command company as above. Due in at 03:30."

05:00 GMT
Paris, France

Essie Stewart pulled her shawl tighter around her shoulders. She reached for the teakettle, but it was empty. A light patter of rain was falling on the canvas of her command tent, but she could see the flames still rising from the first arrondissement across the river.

"Capt. Stewart?" her junior Sig-3 said. "I have a new one. French military police requesting us Priority Zed. Two hundred civilians wounded ready for evacuation at the park next to Point V for Victoria. They have smoke rolling toward them. They need at least two squads?"

"Do you see anyone left to send?" Essie snapped. Just the two of them in the tent, every remaining R&E flier committed, with a hundred requests for aid left unfilled. "Do they think it's American smoke or German that's moving toward them?"

"They didn't say."

"Ask them."

"I don't know how to say in French if it's—"

"Ask them what color the smoke is: *Fumée rouge ou jaune*?"

"Sorry."

"Don't be sorry—do it!"

Poor girl. Only one week in the war before everything went wrong. Essie resolved for the thousandth time to be kinder to her. But it had been too many hours without sleep. Too many wings that had disappeared to Ostend without giving notice. Now Gen. Pym and her three squadrons, which had gone to pull civilians out of the wreckage of the fourth arrondissement, were missing. The Germans seemed to be everywhere. A group of five or ten rauchbauers could unleash a cloud on a neighborhood and move on, leaving terror in their wake. There didn't even have to be poison in the cloud to inspire a panic.

"They say *orange*?" her Sig-3 said. "Is that the same as orange?"

Then again, there was a reason they'd kept this girl out of the fighting.

"Nobody's tinting their clouds orange," Essie said. "Give me the board."

The French board technician elaborated that the smoke was a shade closer to tangerine than pumpkin. More importantly, the cloud was advancing on their position and had run over the man they'd sent to inquire as to the nationality of the smokecarvers inside.

"Send one message to Gen. Pym," Essie said. "If we haven't gotten word in two minutes, we're going to bomb that cloud ourselves."

"Ma'am, we're not allowed to engage the enemy!" the Sig-3 said. "We're Rescue and Evacuation."

"We are going to rescue the wounded on the ground by keeping them alive long enough to be evacuated. And we're not engaging the enemy, just the cloud."

It would have been more effective to bring in a couple dozen volunteers and have them drop canisters of dispersant, but Essie didn't have glyphs over which to contact them. Pym had forbidden any contact between the remnants of the Corps and Gen. Rhodes's civilians.

"Sigilwoman, would you do something for me before we launch?" Essie asked. "You have the glyph for the Corps casualty list?"

"Yes, ma'am. What name, ma'am?"

She'd meant to check for hours now, ever since hints of it had come across her private glyph, but she couldn't bear to do it, much less while in close quarters with a green Sig-3.

"Weekes," she said.

The woman flipped through papers until she found the right glyph. She drew it on the message board to bring up the Ws.

"I don't see anything under—"

"I'm sorry, not Weekes," Essie said. "Canderelli."

The Sig-3 drew again. "Roberta?" she asked.

Essie's heart fell.

"She was confirmed killed in action yesterday evening at 21:30."

Essie struggled to keep her face a mask.

"Thank you," she choked out. "Let's go."

Not in front of the most junior woman in the division. But the rain would hide it.

28

In the final days, rates of acute stress reaction among frontline sigilrists such as smokecarvers and R&E fliers were nearly seventy percent. No intervention was found to reliably ameliorate symptoms, except for removing women from the stressful environment.

Edith Rubinski, "Neurological Complaints of US Sigilry Corps Veterans: Ten Years of Theory and Practice," *Journal of Philosophical Medicine*, November 1, 1928

THERE WAS NO WAY TO TELL HOW MUCH TIME HAD PASSED. WE had no light. Dr. Synge had half a canteen of water, which we passed back and forth, a mouthful every couple hours.

The temperature dropped overnight. I pulled my arms inside my skysuit and crossed them over my chest. We lay back-to-back, shivering. I could feel frost on the grass crunching every time I moved.

We waited.

I couldn't tell whether my eyes were open or shut. Some hours later, I asked Dr. Synge for the canteen and she didn't answer. She still felt warm.

I heard aircraft occasionally. No bombs. No machine guns.

I'd thought about dying before, but never considered that I might have time to contemplate it. Maybe a half second of recognition before I slammed into the ground or a bullet hit me. Not hours. Not days.

I listened to the sound of my own breathing. I fell into a stupor.

Half-asleep or half-comatose—flickers of dreams. I saw lights and they went dark. I heard voices and they went silent.

"Hardened number nine sheet, please. And the slow match."

"I've filtered the section. It's safe to the touch."

"Left-hander, please."

"Are we sure this is the spot?"

"The probe's indicating structural smoke. Should be a shelter."

"Hullllooooo!"

My eyes fluttered open.

I tried to answer, but my parched throat turned it to a groan.

"Shh. Did you hear that?"

"Hello?"

"Help," I rasped.

"Oh my God, there's a live one!"

"Hang on! One minute!"

The smoke above us peeled back to reveal a blinding sunny sky.

"Two of them!"

"Retract it farther!"

I shaded my eyes. There were at least five fliers carrying smokecarvers. A couple more hoverers in high guard position with Lewis guns. They'd cut through the thinner smoke above us rather than tunneling in on the ground.

"Pass the word for the company commander! Someone get the commander right now!"

"Lift them clear! I don't want to dig everybody out a second time."

Two fliers set down next to us. One wore a rough working skysuit bearing the insignia of the International Union of Dockfliers. She had Dr. Synge clipped into her harness and away before I could even manage a word. The second looked like she was fourteen. Her skysuit didn't fit her and had patches on both knees.

I tried to stand and my legs cramped. I fell back to the ground, crying out in pain.

"Is it a man?" the girl asked one of the women above her.

"Army board tech? He's wearing a harness, though."

The girl shrugged. She hooked into my back and lifted me free, setting me down a few yards from the edge of the smoke cloud. They were working on Synge.

"She's got a pulse on the neck."

"Here, try—"

One of the women held smelling salts under Synge's nose. She pushed weakly at the bottle.

"She's moving!"

"Where's the commander? What do we do with live ones?"

More women landed. Everyone was talking at once.

"Oh my God! Oh, no. Robert!"

I could barely keep my eyes open.

Someone put a canteen to my lips. I choked on my first gulp and spit up all over myself. I wiped my mouth and tried again, draining the full quart. Water mixed with sugar and peppermint extract—a philosopher's restorative draught.

A woman was leaning over me on crutches. "Robert," she said again.

"Edith?" I said.

"Can you stand up?"

They helped me to my feet.

"Robert, who's this with you?" Edith asked.

"Bertie Synge," I said. "Captain in the reserves."

"Okay," said Edith. "Label her a volunteer. Let's get her stasied and up to Calais for evacuation home on the civilian chain. This gentleman belongs to Blandings, so he's for Ostend. I'll take him there myself."

"Miss Rubinski, we have lots of hands—you shouldn't have to haul one."

"I'll take him."

"Stasis, surely," one of the women said.

"No stasis," I said. "Please."

"Okay," Edith said. "I want the rest of the platoon to head back to Belgium and resupply. We'll find you new assignments. Outstanding work, ladies."

The women launched, leaving just me and Edith. I squinted at her in the sunlight.

"Wh-what day is it?" I asked.

"It's November first. It's two in the afternoon. You were under there almost thirty hours."

I shut my eyes and swallowed. "How'd you find me?"

"Young Miss Franklin talked to Desoto, who flew to Ostend and kept pestering people until she found me. We were looking for you in the wrong place. We'd gone to search for other survivors before we realized."

"How many did you get out?"

"You were number one hundred twenty-seven. A lot of the shelters failed. You had a hell of a smokecarver."

"Yeah," I said. "Do you have any more . . ."

Edith gave me a second canteen. I tried to go slow.

"There are a thousand people I should message," I said between gulps. "Danielle. My mother. My sisters."

"Send one to your mom," Edith suggested. "Tell her to tell your sisters."

I did.

I drew Danielle's sigil and then couldn't think what to do next. Edith was practically holding me up.

"You want me to?" she asked.

"Would you?"

Please relay to Ms. Hardin: Robert Canderelli is alive. We dug him out. He's alert and uninjured. Edith is carrying him to Ostend.

"I'll fly myself," I said. "If you've got a spare—"

"Oh, no you're not," Edith said.

"You're going to carry me in front of God and my Sig-1 and ten thousand volunteers?"

She fixed me with a look both withering and gentle that said *that is vanity and stupidity and if you survived all this only to crash because you're too exhausted to fly . . .*

"Let me do a stasis for you," she suggested.

I shook my head. "Being under was like being dead and alive at the same time. No stasis."

"Okay. Clip in, then."

"And I pissed myself yesterday," I said.

"I don't care, Robert. Clip in."

Her skin was smoke-stained, her eyes bloodshot, nose crooked, teeth chipped, and her left eyelid puckered whenever she blinked, but there's no face more beautiful than the one that comes to rescue you.

She took me on her chest, a mark of respect for another hoverer, rather than making me ride on her back. She stowed one crutch in its scabbard, leaned on the other, launched, adjusted, secured the second crutch, and lifted away. As smooth a ride as I'd ever had.

The German cloud stretched into the distance like a river, fifty feet wide, still swirling and shrugging in spots, but no longer trying to advance. Our women had set up camps every quarter mile on each side to watch for leakage until we had philosophers enough to render the poison inert and dismantle the whole cloud.

"Are we winning?" I asked.

"No," Edith shouted over the slipstream. "But we're not losing, exactly. The Germans pulled all their rauchbauers off the line. They're using them as reinforcements in Paris. The city's a mess. One of our volunteer regiments walked into a trap at Notre Dame cathedral. Whole thing blew up, leveled the fourth arrondissement. Ten or twenty thousand civilians dead. Five times that many injured. The Louvre's on fire. Lots of pockets of resistance. Gen. Rhodes and her women are spread too thin trying to defend the entire city. They have the Germans mostly contained. But no telling what'll happen if either side presses their attack."

"Is . . ."

I didn't even know what I'd been about to ask, but I couldn't get out any more words.

Edith wrapped her off arm across my chest, holding me to her. I realized I was shaking.

"Hey," she said. "You're okay. Robert, you made it."

My whole body shuddered harder.

"Shh," she said. "It's all right. You're going to be okay."

29

Unable to contain Wainwright's Legion during the summer campaign of 1862, Lucretia Cadwallader sent Mrs. Tyndale back to Detroit to bring up the newly formed Second Division. The green corpswomen were so overwhelmed with well-wishers that they needed several hours to board the paddle wheelers that were to convey them out of the city. Frustrated by the delay, Tyndale requested that the dockside marching band play a faster tune, so that the women would embark more quickly. The bandmaster replied, "Beggin' your pardon, ma'am, but the only double-time march we know is 'The Keel Row.' " To which Mrs. Tyndale answered, "Then play that until everyone is aboard!" One imagines that after four hours of the shrill fifty-one-second tune, she regretted this order.

Victoria Ferris-Smythe, *Empirical Philosophy: An American History*, 1938

THE CAMPFIRES ON THE BEACH AND IN THE STREETS OF OSTEND were too numerous to count. Women were packed around them, cooking lunch or weaving smoke or warming themselves.

Edith set us down on a landing field beside a roped-off transporter arrival zone. An old stone church serving as Ostend's command post stood above the strand, still mostly intact after four years of fighting and occupation. Beside it flew the American flag on a tall flagpole next to the twenty flags from the other Allied powers, arranged at equal heights in a half circle, as if to serve as a reminder that this was not an invasion, but rather a friendly humanitarian intervention open to women of all nationalities. In the center of the half circle stood the old Corps battle standard, made from a patchwork of gray smoke. A thousand shades rippled across its surface in an ever-moving, ever-mixing combination, as it whipped and snapped in a nonexistent wind, waving wildly among the sea of limp flags. Lucretia Cadwallader had fashioned it herself, using obscure sigilry so that, according to legend, it always pointed toward the greatest threat. On that day it blew first in one direction and then another, as if it couldn't decide in which direction the danger lay.

Beside us on the transporter field, a group of women flashed into existence. Several thousand of them, plus piles of loose barrels and boxes, and ten of the largest wagons that Harnemon's Philosophical Supplies used for their deliveries and piles of loose barrels and boxes.

From beside the church an improvised three-woman band—bagpipes, piccolo, and bass drum—struck up the Corps' unofficial march. The thousands of women encamped on the beach all roared along:

As I came through Sandgate,
Through Sandgate, through Sandgate,
As I came through Sandgate,
I heard a lassie sing:
"O, well may the keel row,
The keel row, the keel row,
O, well may the keel row
That my laddie's in."

I knew the words, but I just stared.

After they'd played it through twice, a woman stepped forward with a speaking trumpet.

"Welcome to Belgium!" she bellowed. "Senator Cadwallader-Fulton, Gen. Rhodes, and thousands of your fellow countrywomen are even now fighting to bring about a speedy end to hostilities. Women such as yourselves will ensure we're victorious."

The volunteers on the beach broke into a huzzah for the new women.

"If you have not done so already," continued the woman with the speaking trumpet, "organize yourselves into platoons of ten by specialty. Elect one lieutenant from your platoon. If you practice multiple specialties, we have greatest need for transporters, followed by smokecarvers and then fliers. Transporter platoons, please step to the far right, smokecarvers center right, fliers to the left. All others, come off the transporter field straight forward."

Then the din of thousands of voices as the women sorted themselves out. The wagons creaked forward, trying to force their way through the crowd.

"Come on," said Edith, starting up toward the church. "You can watch the circus tomorrow."

She led me to the command post. A pair of jittery civilian women with rifles were guarding the doors. They saw us and looked horrified.

"You can't come in here!" one of them told us. "Do you need the hospital? We're using—"

"I'm Miss Rubinski," Edith broke in calmly. "I'm the commander of the search and rescue company. Gen. Blandings is expecting me. Send for her runner, please."

One of the women ducked inside and Sig-3 Desoto popped her head out a moment later.

Desoto saw me and her eyes went wide. She nearly tripped over the threshold. "Ma'am," she said. "Are you okay?"

"Fine," I answered. "You told them where to find me?"

"I did. I would have sent them sooner, but we didn't know where you were. All Miss Franklin remembered was 'Fly until you see a giant cloud and turn right.' We thought that meant the left flank. I finally asked her what you said before that and she said, 'Oh, mile thirteen.' "

I winced at that. No less than I'd deserved for snapping at a Sig-3 who was just trying to help.

"Thanks, Pilar," I said.

Desoto gave me a shallow curtsy. "Miss Rubinski," she said. "Did you want to . . . do we want him to see Gen. Blandings looking like that?"

"Yes," Edith said. "Immediately."

"The general's in the rectory. If you two would follow me, please?"

Desoto took us around to a low stone building attached to the church and into a crowded parlor, where a map was spread out on a coffee table and a number of people were waiting on a set of overstuffed couches with flowered upholstery.

Freddy Unger sprang up to embrace me, a geometry book tumbling out of his lap and hitting the floor with a crack that sounded like a gunshot.

"Robert!" Freddy sobbed. "We'd thought— we thought the worst."

He held on to me longer than I was expecting.

"I can't even say how happy I am," he said.

"Thanks, Fred," I said. "I . . ."

I felt numb. I looked at the other faces in the room and could scarcely recognize them.

"You shit," Millen said. She looked as if she had been crying, too. "You complete *shit*! Do you realize how many people we had looking for you! It could have been over by now if—"

"Teeny," Gen. Blandings said. "Enough."

"I told them you were harder to kill than that," Pitcairn said, holding a dainty porcelain teacup in her big hands.

"Is it time?" Dean Murchison asked. "Where are we?"

Someone settled me in a chair, put a cup of tea in one hand, a thick slice of bread in the other. I stared at the cup, letting the heat from it soak into my hand.

"Are we seriously considering flying him?" Pitcairn asked. "He looks three-quarters dead."

"I'm fine," I mumbled. "You need me?"

"We do," Blandings said. "The situation in Paris is precarious. God knows how much more of the city the rauchbauers can level if Gen. Rhodes tries to overwhelm them. We're content to leave them encircled for now. But

Congress held an emergency joint session last night. They voted to put the remains of the Corps under Gen. Pershing's command."

"That's illegal," I said, not so far gone that I couldn't recognize that as an outrage. "It's in the Corps charter. We're supervised by the Department of the Interior. The Corps is independent from the army."

"That changed as of last night. They called our scheme to bring civilian reinforcements over a coup, an unauthorized invasion, high treason. They also felt masculine leadership was necessary to salvage the remnants of the Corps. So, the reserves in Le Havre—the Logistics fliers, the barrels of plague, the R&E fliers who remained loyal—they're all under Gen. Pershing's command now. He sent an ultimatum to the Germans: If they don't surrender by dawn tomorrow, the Corps will drop plague smoke on Berlin. The Germans replied that if he tries it, they'll destroy Paris."

"So, stalemate again," I said.

"No," said Blandings. "Pershing will do it. He gassed Manila in '99. He'll have no compunction about using like means this time, too. Victory by any means necessary and if Paris burns to the ground, that's on the kaiser's conscience, not his."

"You'll use your backup plan, then?" I asked.

"Yes," Blandings replied. "We're going to take Berlin."

All of them looked so calm and matter-of-fact about it that I couldn't help but give an incredulous laugh.

"With what army?" I asked, remembering Dar's words. "Those women sitting on the beach singing songs?"

"No, they're further reinforcements for Paris," Blandings said. "We don't need an army to take Berlin. We're going to capture the city. Seize it."

"How?"

"We're gonna steal it," Millen said. "Transport it right out of Germany and into a big, empty space back in the States."

This time my laugh sounded jeering and cruel.

"That's impossible," I said. "Berlin is huge. You'd need thousands of transporters."

"About 192,000 using conventional means," Freddy supplied. "We really did consider that method, but it would have required placing 192,000 destination sigils, which we found impractical. No, we're going to do it with one. One transporter, one glyph."

I recalled Freddy's chatter back in Cambridge and realized that this wasn't funny or ridiculous or mad. If it was true, it was world-changing.

"You invented a new sigil?" I asked. "For transporting?"

"We redesigned the old one along more theoretically sound grounds," he answered. "We also changed the powder formulation to increase efficiency, which gives us a very long jump range with minimal weight loss for the transporter. And we altered the parameters for the destination sigil and custom-drew it to match the most salient geomagnetic and topographic features of the city of Berlin. The difficulty is that the glyph is huge—two hundred feet wide—and it will have to be placed with exquisite precision, down to the millimeter."

"Sub-centimeter accuracy will be sufficient," grumbled Dean Murchison.

And at last the plan fell into place for me.

"You need him to draw the glyph," I said. "No one else would be able to place it accurately enough. But he's a cartogramancer—he screams and kicks every time he touches a woman. You need a man to fly him."

"Exactly," said Blandings.

I sagged down on my chair. "I'm not your secret weapon. I'm your secret weapon's *ride*."

"We all have our role to play," Blandings said. "Dean Murchison will draw the destination sigil. You'll carry him. Miss Rubinski, who's practiced flying from Ostend to Berlin several times, will navigate and handle communications. Mrs. Millen will take a Lewis gun to provide cover from the air for you and the dean while he's drawing on the ground. Miss Pitcairn will have grenades to bomb any targets necessary to clear the way, as well as canisters with preformed smokescreens and tear gas. The five of you will leave at midnight and we'll seize the whole city in an instant. All we need is for you to say yes."

They looked at me. My arm jerked and I spilled tea in my lap. I wanted to curl up in a ball and sleep for a hundred years and not hear another word of missions or sigils or battles.

"I've gone on a bunch of simple jobs," I said. "They've all gone wrong."

"There's no alternative, Robert," said Blandings. "You're it."

I could think of an alternative.

"I want to see Danielle," I said.

"I don't think that's wise," Blandings said. "See her in the morning when you come back triumphant. See her when every church bell in Europe is ringing for our victory."

"I want to see Danielle!" I shouted.

"Robert, we need a decision," Blandings said. "If you refuse—"

"Let him see her," Edith said. "I'll take him."

"Oh, Jesus Christ in his Easter bonnet," Millen said, with a mordant laugh. "At least clean him up first."

Edith took me to the rectory's bathroom, where I studied myself in the mirror. I looked like I'd died, been buried, and then dug up again. Residue from the smoke had stuck to my skin, turning it flat gray. My hair was gray, too; the heat from the firestorm had singed it and it crumbled to ash in spots as I ran my fingers through. I'd split my lip and had a ring of dried blood around my mouth. Flash burns and blisters covered the back of my neck and ears. My teeth had turned gray, too.

"You're going to be okay," Edith said, as she handed me a cloth.

I didn't even know what the words meant.

I washed. The blood and smoke came away; I went through three washcloths and a towel before I got my hands and face clean. Edith loaned me her toothbrush, but I couldn't get the gray off my teeth. They looked like they were carved out of flint.

"It must have bonded to the enamel," I said.

Men's clothing was harder to come by, so I was stuck in my soot-covered skysuit.

"Shall we go to Danielle?" Edith asked.

I can hardly say what I felt foremost: longing and exhaustion, dread and resignation. No—only an aching need to see her.

Edith and I walked a few minutes up the street through the devastated city. Most of the buildings had been leveled months before, during the British offensive that had retaken western Belgium. Bricks and rubble littered the streets. One of the few other surviving structures was a primary school, which we headed toward.

Overhead, a stream of fliers heavily laden with passengers and supplies made their way south, toward Reims.

"How many volunteers?" I asked. Something dull, safe, practical.

"Fifty thousand so far," Edith said. "Eventually, we'll need another fifty thousand just to neutralize the German cloud. The real challenge will be supplying our women once they're in the field. Nobody brought smoke or provisions for more than a day or two. If this drags on, we're going to have a hundred thousand women in the field with nothing to eat and no powder to fight with."

I inclined my head toward the school up ahead.

"She's the one organizing all of that?" I asked. "Danielle?"

"Most of it, yes."

I'd been off playing at being a common smokecarver on the line while she was trying to win a war. I was never going to be able to justify it.

Edith exchanged passwords with the sentries at the school and one of them escorted us inside. We went up a flight of stairs to the second floor, detoured around a section where the ceiling had fallen in, and then found Danielle sitting in an office with several other women. She had the dark, sunken eyes that she got when she hadn't been sleeping. Someone had messaged ahead to warn her.

She saw me.

"Ladies, let's break for ten minutes to draw up lists," Danielle said to her compatriots. "If we set aside the majority of tomorrow's first transporter run for food, that still leaves room for eight thousand tons of powder. Work up a list so that they can start loading in Baltimore."

The other women filed out.

Danielle stood. Her shoulders were hunched as if to ward off a blow.

I closed the door behind us. I fought to take a breath and then another.

"They told me you were dead," Danielle said.

I nodded.

"They told me there was no hope. I messaged your mother, who was on the way over. She told me the same thing. When she got here, we cried together in a broom closet for ten minutes. Then she went to lead a regiment in Paris. I went back to work. It almost killed me to do that."

She was so calm.

"Why didn't you come?" Danielle said. "I asked you and asked you. I needed your help."

I thought of the stream of messages she'd sent the morning of the attack. The awesome, unearthly German cloud rolling toward us—so few of us. Dr. Synge, who had believed in me when no one else would, who I'd fought beside in Neuville. The desire to be of use. To not abandon my sisters.

"I stood with the women next to me," I said.

It was no kind of answer, but Danielle understood it. She could hardly do otherwise, holding court in a room wallpapered with sheets of regimental message glyphs, running totals of fresh transporters, tons of corn powder, available fliers, and a thousand other details.

"You'll go back into the field?" she asked. "Berlin? If that's where you think you'll do the most good?"

"Maybe," I said.

"There's no maybe, Robert! Stay with me. Blandings's plan isn't going to work. You can't transport a whole city."

I looked at her in surprise. "How do you know about that?"

"Everybody knows! This is the worst-kept secret in the history of modern warfare. Those scientists back in Cambridge couldn't keep their mouths shut if you stapled them closed. Once you told me where to look, it was easy."

"Dar!" I said, horrified.

"I sent a few women to make inquiries. Then, after the rauchbauers attacked, we did what we had to. Rumors and secret plans are one thing, but they won't persuade Germany to surrender or Pershing to hold back his plague. On the other hand, a specific threat might."

My mouth fell open. "You *told* them?"

"Kaiser Wilhelm and Blackjack Pershing—one's dumber than the next where philosophy's concerned. They both believe it. I've got to admit it's a hell of a bluff."

"It's not a bluff! Radcliffe redesigned the sigil. They came up with new powder. It could work."

"You've heard about their tests? They've had one success out of three and it was with a fraction of the size and distance they'll need. They had catastrophic sigil failure with the last one. They burned down a hundred square miles of forest and it didn't move an inch. Did Blandings admit that to you? Or Freddy?"

I felt as if I was trying to wade across a stream and the ground had just dropped out from under me. I fought to keep my feet.

"You used me," I said.

"I'm trying to protect you! And protect Paris and Germany and fifty thousand American volunteers. At best, Blandings is going to immolate Berlin trying to save it. And she'll throw you away to do it. Robert—stay."

"And do what?"

"Go to Le Havre with me and the senator. We're leaving later this afternoon. Help negotiate a peace between Pershing and the Germans. It would be useful to have a man in the delegation. They'll listen to you in a way they won't listen to me."

"I'm no diplomat. I'm a soldier."

Danielle wiped her hands on her skirt.

"Then stay because you want to be with me. Stay because I need you. I'm not going to beg any longer. I can't do both. I can't do all this and be lover to a dead man. It's a suicide mission, Robert. Stay because you love me."

What could I say except that I'd fought and labored and bled beside

Blandings and Millen and Pitcairn and Edith and that was a kind of love, too?

"I hope you do it," I said. "I hope you make peace. If anyone can, it's you."

I held my hand out in front of me and she shook it numbly. Then I staggered out into the hall, trying not to look back, unwilling to contemplate what I'd just done. I stopped to peer at the sky through the hole in the roof. A cool, clear afternoon, the stream of fliers still visible in the distance. I don't know how long I stood there staring before Edith collected me.

"Rob?" she said. She steered me toward the exit. "Do you need a bottle of whiskey or something?"

"I need my mission."

30

General Blandings,

Pershing himself briefed the hundred best fliers we have left. Plan: raid on Berlin with smokecarved weapon at dawn tomorrow. A handful of women walked out. More stayed. I smiled, nodded, memorized the course. Then slipped away with a few friends. Next messages will contain route, escort and armament, & launch schedule. I've no love for the Germans, but damn me if I'll let Pershing do to Berlin what he did to Manila. I'm on my way to help you however I can.

Regards,
Alta

Transcribed personal message from Lt. Alta Andrada, US Army Philosophical Service, to Ms. Tomasina Blandings, Commander of the Volunteer Special Strike Force, November 1, 1918

I FOUND A COT IN A QUIET CORNER OF THE HALF-BOMBED-OUT warehouse where Blandings's team was assembling its equipment. Pitcairn was checking the fuses on her grenades; Millen was cleaning a Lewis gun; Freddy was reading a mathematics book with a lengthy title in French. I lay down, staring at them, trying to uncoil myself. Freddy sat beside me.

"Fred," I said. "I don't know what's—I didn't yell or cry or—what are you supposed to do?"

"I don't know," Freddy said.

Millen loaded an ammunition pan into the top of her Lewis gun and racked a round home.

"Do *not* test that indoors!" Pitcairn shouted at her.

Millen slung the machine gun over her shoulder and stalked outside.

"You know I like Danielle," Freddy said. "I liked the two of you together. But no one thought it would last this long. When you started going out, Brian Mayweather said to me, 'I give it six weeks.' I told him, 'I give it five.' "

I chuckled bleakly and my throat caught. Danielle.

"Is this going to be worth it?" I asked him. "She said none of your tests worked. That we're going to burn the city down."

"Those tests provided invaluable data," Freddy said.

"What are our chances?"

Freddy glanced around the room and lowered his voice. "Fifty percent probability nothing happens. Forty percent the sigil works and we jump the city according to plan. Thirty percent chance of a massive conflagration."

I frowned. "That adds up to one hundred twenty percent."

"The outcomes aren't mutually exclusive. Even if the transport goes off, it's possible we could draw too much energy and transform the excess to heat. So, do make sure you're well clear of the city when our woman stateside makes the jump."

"A one-in-three chance of burning down the city," I said, shaking my head.

"Robert, if we do nothing, there's a one hundred percent chance all of Berlin will drop dead from plague. It's a fair tradeoff."

I rolled up an empty powder bag to use as a pillow. I tried to recall how to shut my eyes. We were going to be flying all night. I needed to rest.

"Freddy, I don't remember how to sleep," I said.

A moment later, I heard the rattle of the Lewis gun as Millen test-fired it outside the warehouse. My eyes fluttered shut.

Then, darkness. I couldn't move my hands or feet. Couldn't take a breath. I tried to cry out, but the noise died before it reached my lips. Alive and dead at the same time. Back underneath . . . but no, I'd been . . .

At last, I flexed the tip of my right index finger a fraction of an inch and the power of movement came slowly back along the rest of my arm, feet, legs, belly, chest. I gasped, filling my lungs.

"You dying, big man?" Pitcairn asked from the chair beside me. She was playing solitaire by lantern light.

"Where's Freddy?" I asked.

"Last-minute adjustments to his sigil."

"Don't go," I said. "Don't go. Don't leave me."

"Nobody's leaving you. He said watch you. I'm watching."

"Don't go."

She gave me an exaggeratedly prim smile. "You want me to climb in with you? Everybody's out. They'll never know."

I shuddered. "Just don't leave."

"I'm not leaving. After what you've been through, what you need is a few square meals, a bed with real sheets, a pint of rum, and a warm body beside you. You've got me, a package of crackers, and a wobbly cot. Trust me, it would be enough. I can take you so hard, you'll forget her name."

"Tomorrow," I said, my eyes shutting again.

Hours later, a hiss of a laugh.

"There are days I hope it *does* go on forever."

"What?" I said.

"This," Millen said. "The war. So I never have to see him again."

I had the vague sense I'd asked her a question a minute before, still half-asleep.

"Who?" I asked.

"*Him.* Don't pretend the whole division didn't talk about it. He wasn't cruel in any of the usual ways. I just felt horrible when I was with him. Stunted, smothered."

"Why'd you marry him?"

"Because he was interested and I was bored. What the hell else was I going to do in Provo, Utah? I just wish I'd figured out I hated him sooner. It doesn't last. It never lasts, Robert A."

"That's supposed to make me feel better?"

"Nah. You were supposed to leave when the mutiny started. We'd have run the mission by now and you'd be with your girlfriend celebrating. You *should* feel bad about it. You should feel terrible."

"Thanks," I said.

I ran my hand over the blisters on the back of my neck. They'd risen up into a tender, angry strip where I'd had bare skin between my helmet and the collar of my skysuit. A couple of them had burst and were weeping thin, sticky fluid.

"Teeny, what *will* you do after?"

"I didn't bother to make plans," she said. "I never thought I'd live through it. I still don't."

"Come to Radcliffe," I suggested.

"And do what? Drink tea and eat petit fours?"

"Study French. Teach flying. Sit outside in the sun and read."

"How much older would I be than the rest of the freshmen? Eight, nine years?"

"A hundred years," I said.

"It's a pretty idea," Millen allowed. She took a rag and ran it over the barrel of her Lewis gun. "We'll be another hour at least. Sleep."

Lantern light and a hand on my shoulder.

"It's time," Edith said.

I rolled off the cot and onto my feet, a response so automatic that I was reaching to open the flaps of my tent before I realized I was hundreds of miles away.

"Belgium," I said. "We're in Belgium."

"That's right. You're okay. You're okay."

I couldn't even panic right. I felt thick and stupid and barely able to speak.

"Am I cracking up?" I asked.

"Only the right amount," Edith answered.

I gave a ghost of a smile at that. She rested her hand on my arm and a thousand things surged up within me. But most powerful of all was the feeling that if I spoke any of them aloud, I would allow it to master me.

"Yesterday . . ." I managed. "I don't want to talk. I don't have room for it. I want to be empty."

"Okay," Edith said.

"I don't want to love her. Or to want anybody. Or anything. Ever."

"Now you're just being maudlin."

"Yup. And it feels good."

Edith took her hand away.

"I'll tell you something," she said. "The soldier who splits up with his best girl is only the second-saddest story in the war. I'll tell you the sadder one: I knew an R&E flier who got sweet on a man she rescued."

"Yeah, they warned me about that in training, too," I said.

"It really happened," Edith said. Her lower lip was quivering. "To me. I went silly for him the day we met—he was kind and funny and brave. I saw him a few more times. I was too much a coward to tell him. And then when I flew him out . . ."

She stifled a sob. She poked her finger into my chest and looked away. I caught her hand in mine and held it.

"I don't care if it's too soon," she said. "I can't not tell you. Because I'll be damned if we win tonight and Missy Pitcairn gets a flask of Scotch into you tomorrow morning and screws your brains out on the beach and I never said a word."

Edith took a breath and pushed her hair back from her forehead.

"You have to say something," she said. "Otherwise I'm going to spend the whole mission thinking about how I just ruined this."

I swallowed. My face was radiating so much heat it was a wonder the room didn't catch fire.

"I got real sick on Scotch once," I said. "I can't drink it. And Missy ain't the one I got a crush on."

I lifted her hand and put it to my lips, which were so dry and cracked that she might have come away with my blood on her skin. She was grinning at me.

"Lord, Edie, but you've got a smile that could punch through steel," I said.

"It's a good thing for you that I can navigate a little starry-eyed," she said. "God, let's hurry up and win this."

31

Dear ma'am,

They are sending us early, they are sending us with plague right now. Some of us will refuse to drop it when we reach Berlin, but some will do it. Pershing will do all he can to stop you. I hope you succeed. I didn't know who else to write. This is Essie Stewart from Radcliffe.

Transcribed personal message from Capt. S. E. Stewart,
US Army Philosophical Service, to Annabelle Addams,
Commandant Paris Volunteers, 12:03 A.M., November 2, 1918

WE ASSEMBLED ON THE LANDING FIELD AT A QUARTER PAST midnight. Millen had the Lewis gun attached to a brace so that she could fire one-handed from the air. Pitcairn had a supply of small bombs strapped to her harness, plus canisters of tear gas and preformed smokescreens to cover our landing. Edith was unarmed but wore three portable message boards. And Murchison was wandering, barefoot, across the beach singing wordlessly to himself, while Freddy tried to cajole him into a bulletproof vest, with heavy steel plates sewn between layers of canvas. Murchison finally consented and Freddy dressed him, then strapped a modified powder bag to his side that contained the ten pounds of pulverized iridium and platinum that Murchison would use to draw the destination glyph.

"They know we're coming," I murmured to Blandings. "I should have warned you sooner. Danielle told everybody—the Germans too."

"Of course she did," Blandings answered unconcernedly. "Why do you think I sent you on a long weekend with her? Or to Cambridge for that matter? If I'd told Kaiser Wilhelm I intended to transport an entire city halfway across the world, he never would have believed me. But a conspiracy that Senator Cadwallader-Fulton's office had to go to great lengths to uncover—now *that* must be a real threat."

I winced at that. "You used me too."

"My dear, I used you every day when I put you up to fly casualties. I used you with the intent of saving lives. And I'm doing the same tonight. You'll forgive me, I hope."

"I'm still standing here, aren't I?"

Blandings gathered the rest of the team together.

"I'm sorry to say this evening's peace negotiations did not go as hoped. Instead of capitulating, the Kaiser has redoubled his efforts at protecting his capital. I've heard rumblings that the rauchbauers are up to something in Berlin, though we don't know precisely what. More troublingly, Pershing has moved up his timeline for bombing the city with plague smoke. Even as we speak, he's launching his hoverers with a heavy escort."

"Lovely," Millen said. "We're going to get shot at by both sides?"

"With only five of you, it's most likely that no one will ever spot you," Blandings reassured us. "They don't know where in the city you're headed. But you *must* hurry. You have a two-hundred-mile head start on the fliers Pershing is sending from Le Havre, but if they send their fastest fliers ahead, they'll be a good deal faster than Robert hauling a passenger."

"Boys," Pitcairn muttered.

"It'll work," Edith said. "We can still be on the ground twenty minutes ahead of them."

"We've got no margin for error," Millen complained. "We're flying overland at night. If we're even five degrees off course, we'll miss the city entirely."

"It'll be fine," Edith insisted. "I've scouted the route several times. Berlin is huge—it's easy to spot. Our landing zone will be the large square in the city center next to their parliament building, the Reichstag. It's a massive building with columns and a glass and wrought iron cupola next to the river. The destination glyph will go in the middle of the square."

"It's defended?" I asked.

"Lightly," Blandings said. "According to our flyover last night, they had six or eight guards at the main entrance and two bunkers in the square."

"Could we put the sigil someplace else?" I asked. "Slip into a dark alley or a park and draw it there?"

"Absolutely not!" Unger objected. "The destination glyph is designed to work at a central location in the city, so we customized it for that square. It would take us weeks to modify it to work elsewhere."

"If it's only ten, twelve men, that's easy," Pitcairn said. "I drop tear gas on them and ring our landing site with a smokescreen. They're expecting to be bombed with plague. They'll be frightened. They'll run."

"Exactly," Blandings said. "Edith will fly point and have overall operational command. Robert will take control on the ground and direct attacks as needed."

"Am I required to call him ma'am?" Millen asked.

Pitcairn rolled her eyes.

"All of you are to protect Murchison at any cost," Blandings continued. "Once the sigil is in place, launch immediately and come home. We'll have our transporter make the grab once you're clear. Any questions?"

"This is not enough people," Millen said. "Do we have backup? Anyone?"

"I have a small number of armed fliers who are launching right now to shadow Pershing's women," Blandings said. "Andrada's commanding them. They'll follow the bombers. If they get close to the city, Andrada will open fire to buy you extra time."

"We're supposed to be the humanitarians," Pitcairn said. "You're proposing firing on American corpswomen? That's sick."

"Andrada might not mind," I said.

"As a last resort only," Blandings reiterated. "I need not remind you of the stakes. This is our chance to atone for Petersburg and Manila. To save lives instead of taking them. To make certain that philosophy has a place in the world to come."

The faces around me were drawn and anxious.

"Up the Corps!" Blandings shouted, her voice going shrill and breaking.

"Up the Corps," we answered, though with only five voices it was a thin, bleak answer.

"One minute for the believers," Blandings said.

And suddenly everyone was praying at once, aloud, in hushed voices.

"He shall cover thee with his feathers," Blandings intoned, "and under his wings shalt thou trust . . ."

". . . the granitic axis of that chain," Murchison muttered, "does not rise so high as a ridge formed by marine calcareous beds, the organic remains of which shew them to be the equivalents of our lower chalk . . ."

". . . nor height, nor depth, nor any other creature," Pitcairn said, her words sure and steady, "shall be able to separate us . . ."

". . . rescue us from the hand of every foe and ambush," Edith whispered, "from robbers and wild beasts on the trip and from all manner of punishments that assemble to come to earth . . ."

". . . *Dein Wille geschehe*," Unger said shyly, "*wie im Himmel so auf Erde . . .*"

It was at moments like these that I felt my lack of religious upbringing. I had to say something. In a low voice I began: "From ghoulies and ghosties and long-leggedy—"

"Oh, for Christ's sake, Robert A," said Millen, who had gone without any words for protection. "Show some respect. We *are* the things that go bump in the night. The whole world's praying for deliverance from *us*. Form up and launch."

We lit one blue flare each. Edith pushed into the lead, I took up position in the middle, and Pitcairn and Millen flanked me so that if I tired and began to sag back they would spot me immediately.

I carried Murchison on my chest so that I could see if he did anything preposterous. But he was a different sort of bad passenger than I was used to, pathetic rather than panicked.

"Where are we?" he whined, five seconds into our flight.

"Over Ostend!" I called back. "We're like ten feet up."

Then twice a minute for the next hour, like an injured, terrified animal, he kept mewling out, "Where are we?" pausing only to beg me to set him down.

"I'm sorry!" I yelled over the slipstream as we bulled along semi-upright at 210 miles an hour. "I can't."

No answer I gave satisfied him—providing an accurate location, being sympathetic, getting angry. Every thirty seconds, like a poorly conceived cuckoo clock: "Where are we?"

One hour underway, we reached the city of Münster as our first waypoint, right on schedule. It was hundreds of miles behind the German lines and all lit up. Edith rechecked her compass heading and led us onward.

"Where are we?" Murchison wailed.

"East of Münster," I yelled. "It's going to be another hour. Can't you just be quiet?"

"Could you put me down?"

"No!" And then because I was desperate for any kind of reprieve from his whimpering, I asked, "Is this because you can't feel the ground?"

"Can still feel it," he replied. "Can feel it through the air. But it's so quiet. So faint. Put me down?"

"No way."

"You'll understand," he said. "You'll have no choice."

I suppressed a shudder at the way he said it. He'd told me once that he'd see me in Belgium, not France, at the end of the war. He'd made a number of smaller pronouncements, too, the meaning of which had only become clear to me weeks or months later when they'd come true.

"Can you see the future?" I asked him.

"Oh!" he answered, surprised by the question.

"Can you?"

"Not the future," he said. "I can sense both position and velocity. I infer consequences. Some consequences are inevitable."

"Is this going to work tonight?"

"I can't tell you from up here. Not without touching the ground."

He turned his head to look up at me and a sly expression came over his face. "But if you set me down . . ."

"Not till we get there."

And yet I was intrigued. "That's what it's like? The ground talks to you?"

"No," Murchison said. "It sings, but without a voice. It speaks, but silently. You'll understand soon enough. You have it in you, you know, weakly. It's in most men. Rarely in women. The antithesis of philosophy. You'll understand."

We reached the city of Hanover dead-on and made our last course correction. Forty-five minutes to go. Dull, stupid flying—follow the light in front of you. Edith was doing the part that required murderous concentration. All I had to do was plod along behind like a pack mule.

I couldn't help but laugh bitterly at that. This was glory? This was the danger so intense that it ripped Danielle apart to imagine it? For this moment Blandings had overturned decades of tradition to bring a man into the Corps, for this I had borne countless insults and sleepless nights, for this I had risked life and love? To be a pack mule? But so be it. Stay awake. Fly on. Follow.

Some time later, Edith waved her flare and we coasted to a stop. Beneath us, I could make out the glimmer of moonlight on a river, surrounded by a dense forest. But no city.

"Where are we?" Murchison whined.

And for the first time I wondered whether he'd been trying to warn us all along.

"It should be right here," Edith said. Her face was pinched. She looked as if she might vomit. With only a twenty-minute advantage over the bombers, we didn't have time to get lost.

"Did we come up short?" Pitcairn asked. "We were flying slower than we thought?"

"No," Millen shot back. "We were flying 210 miles per hour on the nose. We didn't slow down. We didn't drift. I was checking. We're right on."

"Well, we ain't where we're supposed to be," Pitcairn said.

I looked at the ground, squinted into the distance ahead of me and over both shoulders. No city. No landmarks.

"Where are we?" Murchison moaned.

"It *has* to be here," Edith insisted.

"Backtrack," Pitcairn suggested. "Back to Hanover. We'll recheck our course."

"That would take hours," Millen said. "We can't go back."

"Where are we?" Murchison asked again.

"I swear to God, if he doesn't shut up—" Millen growled.

"No, that's it!" I said. "He's a human map. Sir, if I put you on the ground, can you tell us which way to Berlin? How many miles?"

"Trivial," Murchison murmured.

"Those trees are real dense," Edith said. "The last thing you want to do is get hung up in one."

"I'll be careful," I said. "Lots of flares, slow descent—"

"Lights!" Millen barked. "Three o'clock, half mile above, coming down right on us."

At least a dozen red safety flares shone in the sky above us, streaking toward our position.

"Andrada's team?" Edith asked. "Maybe they came to help?"

"Too many," Millen said.

"Scatter?" Pitcairn suggested.

"Hold!" I said. "Hold fast."

Our group drifted closer together.

"Ahoy the fliers!" Edith shouted at the incoming hoverers. "American philosophers."

"Identify yourselves!" a man shouted back.

I wondered for a moment if it could be another male flier. But as he approached, I saw he wore a regular infantry uniform with a motorcyclist's goggles. He was strapped to the chest of a woman in a Corps-issue skysuit. Passenger. Flanked by two other fliers carrying soldiers on their chests with Vickers machine guns—longer-ranged and faster-firing than Millen's Lewis gun. Another nine or ten hoverers with soldiers in like configuration, each with a machine gun, hung back to cover them. Pershing's people, not ours. Not friendly.

"Who's in command here?" the man shouted, squinting in the red light of his flare. "Who's the man here?"

Even if Edith was nominally in charge, I didn't see any choice but to speak up.

"I am!" I shouted, with the slightest hint of irritation that he hadn't recognized me for a male.

"What unit?" he called back.

There was no possible right answer. But as chaotic as the previous days had been, a bluff might stand a good chance of working.

"Maj. Willard Gunch," I said, borrowing my mother's old rank and my childhood best friend's name. And then, thinking back on how the Corps had styled its fliers during the Franco-Prussian Intervention, added, "First Division of Air Infantry, first platoon."

The man wrinkled his brow. "Air Infantry? We don't have any unit by that name."

"New yesterday afternoon," I said. "Pathfinders for the bombers."

"If you're pathfinders, then where's Berlin?" he asked.

Which was an excellent question.

"I have a specialist who can tell us. My orders are to put him on the ground. Your team should take up a high cover position and provide fire support if my platoon gets into trouble."

"Like hell we are!" the man shouted back. "Bring my board woman forward. Send a message back to headquarters. Find out about this 'Air Infantry' nonsense."

"You'll have to wake up Gen. Pershing then!" Pitcairn called from my left. "We were formed by his personal command. Special task force. Do you have any idea who the fuck I am?"

"That's Melissa Pitcairn, sir," said the woman with the message board who'd come up beside the man. "Fastest woman in the world."

"Second-fastest," I heard one of the other army fliers murmur.

I was pleased Pitcairn didn't shoot her over it.

"Pershing himself is going to throw you out of the army if you obstruct us," Millen yelled. "There isn't time for this. The bombers are nearly here. We're landing. Cover us."

"I'm not taking orders from a woman!" the man leading the army fliers said. "All of you are to land slowly and throw down your weapons."

They outnumbered and outgunned us, but hitting a flier moving at two hundred miles per hour, in the dark, while strapped to the chest of a woman who was herself trying to maneuver was virtually impossible. We were only vulnerable while hanging motionless in the air or on the ground.

"I won't tell you again!" the officer opposite us shouted.

Behind him, one of the army fliers fired off a pair of smoke streamers that glowed with an intense blue-white light. They exploded overhead into panels like giant umbrellas that lit us up brighter than midday. We were perfect targets. But they were, too. And their machine gunners were bunching up behind their commanding officer.

At the same moment, though, something else caught my attention. Below us, their lights didn't reflect off the river. They didn't illuminate the trees. I couldn't quite understand it, but the ground wasn't the ground.

"Land and throw down your weapons!" the man ordered.

We couldn't afford to wait any longer. My team must have sensed what I was going to do a second before I did it; they all started to move at once.

I switched my regulator to my left hand, drew my pistol with my right, and shot the man in the chest twice. The bullets went through and through, hitting the woman carrying him.

Pitcairn rocketed up, Edith dove for the ground, and Millen opened up with the Lewis gun, raking fire across the army fliers. She hit at least two of the machine gunners before they scattered.

I wheeled and dove out of the line of fire. The pair I'd shot, still harnessed together, tumbled past me, out of control, then vanished right out of the air. Not under the trees—we were too high for that. I spiraled back and caught sight of the edge of something, like a tear in the air, a piece of fabric flapping in the wind hiding . . . buildings?

Above me, more machine-gun fire, badly aimed though definitely in my direction. I had to dive or climb or fly flat out. The only thing I couldn't do was hang still and hope for inspiration.

I dove, following the path the bodies had taken. I struck something thin and yielding—like punching through wet crepe paper. Once I was through, I found a city beneath me stretching as far as I could see. I was about two hundred feet above the ground. A great hulking building stood a mile ahead with a glass and wrought iron cupola on top, blazing bright with some kind of philosophical energy, casting an image of trees and a river like a movie projector against a scrim of smoke that had been stretched over the entire city of Berlin. Camouflage on a huge scale.

I flew toward the building—the Reichstag. Our target would be the square in front of it. But, as Blandings had warned, there were sandbagged bunkers at both ends of the square, each with a searchlight and a machine-gun emplacement, with the weapon mounted so that it could be aimed upward.

Berln hid undr sheet of smok, I wrote to the rest of the team. *Can brk thru at 200ft. I need covrng fire to land. Rndzv at capitol.*

A minute passed as I circled the square, trying to stay out of sight. No one wrote back.

I could hear the distant rattle of guns in the air, the chatter of Millen's

Lewis gun against the deeper bark of the American machine guns. Then a whole chorus of Lewis guns above me opening fire at once. I couldn't see what was happening on the other side of the screen.

Beneath me, one of the spotlights swiveled and caught me in the beam. I sped away, but somehow it stayed with me. One of the guns on the ground opened up, then the other.

Easy enough to escape.

I climbed, punching back through the layer of smoke and into the harsh light put out by the illumination rounds that the army fliers had fired off. I squinted against it. I could see bursts of gunfire and tracers high above, a handful of safety flares swooping across the sky—blue and red. Blue should be ours. Red would be the American regular army.

"Robert!" I heard someone call behind me. I spun and saw Andrada carrying a Lewis gun like Millen's.

"I've got six women with me," she shouted. "We're trying to drive them off. Where's the city?"

"Right below us!" I yelled. "Two machine guns on the square. I need Pitcairn to bomb them. Where is she?"

"I don't know! I'll find her. Get back under. You'll get killed if you're not moving."

"They're shooting from the ground, too."

"Then fly where the bullets aren't!"

One of the red flares maneuvered toward us and opened fire. Andrada broke away. I dove back under the cloud, right into the searchlight that had been illuminating me a minute before. The guns on the ground opened up. I dove and spiraled toward the river, spoiling their aim. They couldn't track fast enough to keep up with me at full speed.

"Land," Murchison suggested.

Not a terrible idea. I could find a little street away from the machine guns, wait for Pitcairn to hit them. Then fly to the Reichstag so that Murchison—

An army flier carrying a soldier with a Vickers gun ripped through the smoke layer above me. She spotted my flare and wheeled to give chase. I poured on power and dove even closer to the river, pulling up inches above. Bursts of gunfire whizzed past us. I twisted and did a full loop the loop, trying to shake them. The next burst was so close I could feel the heat of one of the rounds as it went past my ear. I snapped us into a punishing vertical ascent, Murchison's body pressed hard against mine, my vision going dim from the effort. We sliced through the smoke layer and I heeled over, reversing direction and diving right back through. Murchison's head slammed against my chin with the rapid change in direction.

The army hoverer stayed right on me, trying to line up another shot. She was a better flier than me—no doubt. Couldn't outrun her. Couldn't outmaneuver her. So, try something cute and hope she was dumb enough to follow.

I reversed again and spun, backing through the smoke layer butt first. I came to a full stop and leveled my pistol with my left hand. Murchison hung from my harness, swaying. Just put the fear of God into her for a second and slip away while she was dodging. Above me, flares and bullets lit the sky.

The army flier crashed through the smoke curtain a dozen feet away, saw me, and came screaming to a stop so her gunner could aim. I fired off all six rounds left in my pistol. She froze and I thought I'd hit her, but then the soldier on her chest opened up with a long, sweeping burst.

Three crushing pings as bullets slammed into the steel and canvas of Murchison's flak vest. Then a fourth sound, softer, half-puff, half-crunch.

I realized first that powder was spilling out of the side of my bag. Then that I couldn't move my right hand. Then, searing pain in my forearm.

The gunner in front of me took aim again, but a thunderous burst of fire broke out from behind me. His head jerked to the side. The flier carrying him went limp. They slipped back through the smoke layer toward the ground.

I dropped my gun and put my left hand on my regulator, trying to add power before my sigil faded and I fell. I could fly left-handed. I'd spent hours learning. It didn't have to be pretty. Just get down fast. Put Murchison on the ground. Nothing else mattered.

But a bullet had caught my reg at exactly the wrong angle. Shattered. Jammed. A last sputter of powder slipped through it and I was able to turn to see Millen behind me.

"Robert A!" she shouted. "Get on the ground. Land, you dumb shit!"

"Help," I got out before my sigil failed and I began to fall. "Teeny—"

And then we were tumbling, ripping through the layer of camouflage a final time, picking up speed. I drew sigils desperately, but nothing took. No powder was flowing through my reg.

"Down," Murchison mused as the square in front of the Reichstag spun into view. "Good."

"Sorry," I grunted. "I'm sorry."

I drew sigils again. Hopeless. The ground rushed up at us.

Then a fist seized a strap on the back of my harness, hauling upward to brake me.

"Not like this!" Millen shouted.

Her heels dug into Murchison's ribs as she pulled.

"Come on!" she yelled.

We slowed.

"No!" screamed Murchison. "Let go! Let go!"

He thrashed and bucked. Below us one of the machine guns opened up, missing high.

Millen heaved against us. The barrel of her gun, still hot, pressed into my skysuit and I could smell the wool scorching. Another burst from the ground, this one closer. Millen roared with the effort of hanging onto us. Murchison kicked and wailed.

Fifteen feet above ground we'd come nearly to a stop. The machine gun on the far side of the square fired again. Murchison thrashed and Millen lost hold of us.

It was the sort of problem I'd often been asked to solve: How fast does a body in free fall accelerate due to gravity? How long to cover twelve feet?

Not even time for a fully formed thought, only the flicker of an image or two: My mother, the last time I'd seen her, stepping onto the transporter field in Boston months before. Danielle's expression of exhausted, resigned disappointment. Millen's scowl, Pitcairn's leer, Edith's grin as she—

32

"The Americans have ways," Albert says. "They can pluck the trenches from the earth and dump them into the ocean."

"That would be an improvement," replies Haie.

Erich Maria Remarque, *A Disappearance on the Western Front*, 1928

I FELT THE CARABINERS ON MY CHEST UNLOCK AS MURCHISON reached back and undid them with confident, efficient hands.

I tried to decide what hurt worst: head, back, gut. The searing pain in my right arm was so intense that it made my hand feel cold.

We were sprawled on the cobblestones in the square beside the Reichstag. There was one machine-gun emplacement three hundred feet in front of us, silent now, its searchlight sweeping the sky. The second machine-gun emplacement a hundred feet behind us, also quiet.

Murchison, whom I'd landed on, crawled a few inches out from under me.

"Stay put," I rasped. "They're not shooting. They might think we're dead."

"Insufficiently mobile to draw," Murchison said.

"What's that mean?" I asked. "You're hurt?"

"Discontinuities in the hydroxyapatite of my bilateral lower extremities."

I rolled off Murchison and onto my side, getting a look at his legs, both of which were bent at unnatural angles mid-shin. Broken. I couldn't understand how he was lying there, caressing one of the cobblestones instead of howling in pain.

I shifted my own legs. They seemed to be working.

"Where does the sigil go?" I asked Murchison.

"In the middle of the square. Eighty-one feet in front of us."

"I could draw it? You could tell me how? Give me directions?"

"No. Miss your lines by half an inch, miss half the city."

"I could carry you? Drag you?"

"How?"

Not with one good arm and two machine-gun nests. I wrote left-handed to Edith: *On grnd in sq. Inj x2. Need hlp. Need bombs on machn guns.*

OK, she replied. *Will help. Hang on.*

Murchison had worked himself into a sitting position.

"We'll have to do it the other way," he mused.

"Stay down!" I hissed. "Don't move. Help's on the way."

He opened a pouch on his harness and sorted through it, pulling out a pair of fountain pens.

"Get down!" I whispered.

The gun crew in front of us began pointing and shouting. They swiveled the spotlight and caught us in its glare. The machine gun on its mount began to turn toward us as well.

I crawled toward Murchison. "Get down!"

He had his head cocked to one side, considering a pen in each hand.

"The blue ink or the green?" he sighed.

"Get down!" I shouted and threw myself onto him.

The machine-gun in front of us opened fire. But it missed high—much too high—sending the bullets flying over the other machine-gun nest. The soldiers at the bunker behind us were screaming and waving at their comrades, trying to get them to stop. And then I understood the problem: The mounts were designed to point the guns upward, so they could shoot at hoverers and aeroplanes. The men couldn't depress the machine guns far enough to hit a target on the ground.

I looked over my shoulder at the emplacement behind us. The soldiers there were scrambling to get their gun off its mount so they could set it on the sandbags and take aim at us.

"Ridiculous shade of green," Murchison complained. He'd uncapped one of his pens and was doodling a figure on his left palm. The ink danced in waves across his skin, forming into strange curling glyphs that shifted into others, vanishing and reforming across his wrist in time with his pulse.

"Let's go," I said to him. "I'll pull you out of the square. We'll find cover."

"No," he said. "We're right where we're supposed to be."

Behind us, the soldiers had removed the last of the bolts holding their gun in place. It dropped free of the mount and fell to the ground. Two of the soldiers wrestled it up. The rest were grabbing their rifles, kneeling behind the sandbags to take aim.

"I'm sorry," Murchison said.

"For what?" I asked. I grabbed hold of him with my good arm.

"For showing you the world as it is. Close your eyes."

"I'm not going to sit here and just let them—"

A pair of fliers lit by blue flares burst through the smoke layer and broke in opposite directions. One of them looped over the machine-gun emplacement on the far side of the square, coming to a dead hover to plaster the soldiers on the ground with a long burst of fire—Millen with the Lewis gun. I looked back at the nearer bunker. The second flier had paused for a moment overtop. Then a series of explosions rang out on the ground as Pitcairn's grenades found their mark.

Murchison caught hold of my shoulder.

"Close your eyes," he said again. "It's important."

"What are you . . . ?"

But the man could see the future, in his own addled way. Don't argue.

I closed my eyes and knelt beside him. I felt the nib of his pen scratch over my right eyelid.

"Hold still," he murmured, as the fire from Pitcairn's bombs ignited a box of machine-gun bullets that popped and pinged into the air. “Keep them closed!”

He drew a sigil on my left eyelid, too, then breathed on each to help dry the ink.

“What’s it supposed to—”

A cacophony of sensations rose up, as if every cobblestone in the square was babbling at once, trying to introduce itself and remind me of the exact distance between it and me. The distant thrum of bedrock beneath my feet overwhelmed them, then an irritable hiss of layers of sand and sediment in the river. Above this rose the noise of the dying men in the bunker behind us, the iron in their blood singing with a fading note, like a guitar string that had been plucked a minute ago and was still vibrating, though barely audible. Then the muttering of my own bones, the shattered pieces of my forearm calling to each other as if they might coax one another back into position.

I opened my eyes and the world returned to normal, except for the echoes of someone screaming. Me.

“—show you how,” Murchison said. “Steady. Steady.”

“How . . . ?” I said. “That’s what it’s like for you?”

“Every moment,” he said. “It can be so hard to hear a person.”

He pressed the sack filled with powdered platinum and iridium into my good hand.

“It knows what it was created for,” he said. “It knows where it belongs. Listen to it and no other. Close your eyes.”

I closed my eyes and saw without seeing, felt without touching, listened without hearing. The bag sang out with a low tone, like the wind blowing over the mouth of a pipe. The destination sigil should begin eighty-one feet in front of me, the powder six-hundredths of an inch deep, sweeping rightward in an arc for forty-three feet plus six and nine-hundredths inches before . . .

But urgent, insistent shrieks interrupted it—on the far side of the square, the gunpowder in the bullets of the rifles and machine gun hooted like a chorus of monkeys, begging to be put to use. Conglomerations of blood and bone crawled toward them. Men. Soldiers. Not dead, but under cover while

Millen had been shooting at them. Whether she'd retreated or was coming around for a second pass, I didn't know. The air was silent to me.

Then came a clack like two tree branches striking each other—Murchison tapping a single finger on the ground to remind me, *Go on*.

The low, blowing noise of the platinum and iridium powder came back to the fore, pulling me forward. I strode with perfect confidence; every rock and crack beneath my feet made itself known to me. I could feel the whole undrawn destination glyph spread out over the ground, huge, two hundred feet wide, bigger than anything I'd ever drawn, more mural than glyph.

I opened the tip on the powder bag and began to pour out the precious metals. How much, how deep? How does one know how hard to press with a pencil without breaking the lead? How far to bend one's knee when walking up a flight of stairs? One simply knows.

As I drew, the thrum changed pitch, higher, questioning, on edge, coming to better understand its purpose and the inexperience of the man drawing. I strode on, spilling out the powder in a broad arc behind me, stopping a moment here to flick out an extra line, slowing a second there to let the powder mound up higher. It was beginning to take shape. The figure begged me to go slower. Why not take an hour, a day, a lifetime to draw it? To appreciate and position each fleck of metal, to inquire over the subtleties—why two crossing lines here and not three? Stop and chat.

But behind me the snare drum rat-a-tat of Murchison tapping his index finger against the ground. *Go, go, go*.

Then a tickle of steel interjected itself: a rifle coming to rest on the sandbags of the bunker on the far side of the square. The growth plates in the femurs of the man wielding it weren't closed—still growing, nineteen years old at most. The same age as me. I knew the distance between us to the hundredth of an inch, the angle and inclination of his gun barrel, how many grains of powder were in the cartridge. He was aiming badly. Stunned or frightened. He would miss twenty feet to my left and high. Inevitable.

I could barely hear the crack of his rifle through the din of stone, metal, powder, bone.

"Robert!"

The young man was preparing to take a second shot, even worse than the first.

"Robert!"

I couldn't understand where the voice was coming from. Then the impact of feet against the ground beside Murchison—a flier landing. One hundred seventy-one pounds with tackle and powder bag. Pitcairn.

But that wasn't important. Across the square, a second rifle came to rest on a sandbag beside the first, turning, aiming, helping the other soldier line up his shot. Bad for me. One near miss and one bullet that would hit me in the belly before shattering my spine on the way out. Too late to run, to dodge, to scream. The howl of my partly drawn glyph took on a disappointed tone. It would never be finished. Inevitable.

But no. Lead fell around the soldiers like pebbles poured out of a bowl, bullets fragmenting as they struck the ground and ripped through the two soldiers. I couldn't understand where they were coming from. Then a third soldier, running to the machine gun, swiveling it and pointing it upward.

I opened my eyes.

Millen was hovering over the bunker, peppering it with a long burst of fire from her Lewis gun. She came to the end of her magazine and pulled up and away as the gun below opened fire.

"Hurry up!" shouted Pitcairn from beside Murchison. She pulled a philosophically built smoke grenade from her harness and hurled it. It spat out a wave of green-black vapor that swept forward with unearthly speed, washing over me so that I could barely see my feet on the ground.

Trivial.

I shut my eyes and felt the glyph sing out again. Not even one-third finished. I began pouring powder again, gently smoothing the break in the line with my fingers, then drawing onward, faster—faster!—breaking into a trot as the powder spilled out behind me, throwing it this way and that. Close enough. I could hear the sigil whispering, describing a place it had never seen, but wanted terribly to visit: *mountains, snow, deep-rooted grass that survives even the bitterest . . .*

Again, the tap of Murchison's finger: *Go, go, go.*

I drew.

I could feel the reverberation of feet rushing toward the square. Another detachment, two dozen men at least. And a pair of daintier boots, too, a rauchbauer. The high-density smoke in her workbag made a rude, unimpressed noise at the smokescreen that Pitcairn had tossed out for cover. They came toward me. Distance: 861 feet.

A whisper of more smoke rushing past me as Pitcairn tossed a second smoke grenade. The rauchbauer threw out her own smoke, which whipped toward me from the opposite direction, grumbling with a different accent as it began to pull the smokescreen apart.

Two-thirds done.

Less complicated, the destination sigil suggested. *Leave that line out, shorten that curve. Simplify, simplify. I'll still work. We'll still go to the other place.*

A hail of bullets, amusing trajectories, toward me but not near me, as the soldiers paused to fire.

I was running now, flat out, the bag of platinum and iridium powder nearly empty, drawing the jumble of lines that would connect, in the end, to the point where I'd begun.

Bullets showered down among the soldiers, who were firing upward instead of at me. A few seconds later, a flier hit the ground in an awkward, sliding landing a hundred yards in front of the German squad. Scrawny, stork-like, furious: Millen.

Beside Murchison, Pitcairn took a long, leaping step and vanished off the ground. She'd pushed off in a direction that would send her toward Millen, whose blood was streaming out on the cobblestones. No! Christ, I had to—

Finish me! the destination sigil screamed. *Now, now!*

I sprinted the last few steps, flung out a final curve, connecting my last line to my first. The glyph's note changed pitch—a ripple of notes like a puff of breath across panpipes, a chord that had never before been played. I still had an ounce of powder left in the bag, but the sigil didn't care.

Ready, ready.

I opened my eyes and staggered back toward Murchison. Edith was pulling out her crutches and preparing to land beside him.

"Pershing's bombers are three minutes out!" she shouted as she set down. "Andrada won't be able to hold them off. There are too many."

"Ready, ready," I gasped.

"What?" Edith said. "Oh, God, Rob! Your arm."

"The sigil's ready," Murchison supplied. "Tell Blandings to go now. The transporter in America should start drawing immediately!"

Edith scribbled a message on one of her boards.

Then the center of the smokescreen parted, as the German rauchbauer finished driving a tunnel through it with her own cords of smoke. She was on the far side of the square. Behind her were the remaining German soldiers. They were fixing bayonets to the ends of their rifles. About a hundred yards separated us. I blinked my eyes to use my cartogramancer's sense—388 feet.

Suddenly, a figure came crashing through the smokescreen, flying backward at ground level, her off arm laced through her passenger's harness, dragging her. Pitcairn pulling Millen to safety. They flopped to a halt in front of us.

Millen had both hands pressed against her upper thigh. Blood was gushing from between her fingers.

"Shit," Millen laughed. "Oh, shit."

"An artery, maybe," Pitcairn said. "Somebody get her in stasis!"

Pitcairn untangled herself from Millen's harness and dropped to her knees. She pushed her hands against Millen's to put extra pressure on the wound.

"Stasis!" shouted Pitcairn.

I reached for my workbag—which I hadn't brought. No need. Just a ride. I looked desperately at Edith. She had three message boards but no silver chloride.

"Teeny," I said. "Tube?"

Millen was covered with a film of sweat. It was the first time I'd seen her look frightened.

"Fuck all," she whispered. She had another six pans of ammunition strapped to her.

Murchison pulled a tube of silver chloride from his belt and slapped it into my left hand. Pitcairn ripped Millen's skysuit open, the buttons flying into the air.

"You're going to do it *lefty*?" Edith objected.

"Him," Millen mouthed.

I thought of all the botches and near misses and too-short stases I'd ever blundered through. I put them out of my mind. I closed my eyes.

I could hear every bone and blood vessel in Millen's body. The laceration in her femoral vein. The spot the stasis glyph should go, just above the sternum, bright like a strip of burning magnesium.

"Do it, you asshole!" Millen croaked.

I drew and every grain of silver chloride fell into place. Perfect. I let my eyes come open.

"Twenty-three hours eight minutes stasis time," Murchison muttered.

I dry heaved and sank the rest of the way to the ground. Maybe. Maybe if she were on a table in an operating room the second she came out of it. (As if any hospital in France had time for that with tens of thousands of wounded.)

Pitcairn was beside me, tugging at the straps and buckles on Millen's harness, trying to wrench the Lewis gun free.

"What's taking so long?" Pitcairn snapped as she worked. "Why don't they make the jump?"

"Any second," Edith answered. "They have to draw the same glyph on the other end. Giant-sized, like that one."

Across the square from us, the German soldiers were preparing to charge. Pitcairn brought the Lewis gun up to her shoulder. It clicked. Empty.

"Shit," Pitcairn said. "How do you . . . ?"

Edith threw her crutches to the ground and flopped down beside us. She pulled an ammunition pan off Millen's harness, detached the old one from the gun, and locked the fresh one in place. The Germans raised a shout as they leveled their guns and ran forward, shoulder to shoulder, through the final dissipating wisps of the smokescreen.

Edith opened up on them, getting off a long burst. A few of them fell, but the rest kept coming. Edith fired again and the gun jammed. She worked the bolt back and forth, but it wouldn't clear.

"God," Edith said. She let go of the gun and reached over to take my hand.

The philosophical energy in her spread across my skin like scalding water. I cried out. Even with my eyes open, the world around me sang out, calling for me, urging me to let go, let my body fly apart, return to nothingness. Let my blood sink into the earth and intermingle with the molten iron in its core, let the river's current wear my bones away to sand, let the air in my lungs escape into the atmosphere from which it had come. End the separation of body and earth. Return to . . .

"Sorry, sorry," said Murchison. He licked his thumb and pressed it against each of my eyelids, smearing the sigils he'd drawn.

I blinked and Edith's hand felt like a hand. The stones didn't have names. The destination sigil was silent. Only Edith's fingers between mine, rough and dry from years of exposure to the desiccants mixed in with the corn powder, spoke to me in the ordinary fashion. A flier's hand. Perfect.

The Germans were charging full out, their boots echoing as they ran. Sixty yards, fifty.

Not like this. Not with one minute left in the war. Shot or run through.

"Missy, fly clear!" I shouted. She was the only one who could save herself.

Pitcairn drew her belt knife. "Thanks, pal, but no."

Murchison was lying on the cobblestones, spread-eagle. "No one else dies tonight," he said.

He struck the ground with his fists.

"Gebt auf!" Murchison bellowed and the whole world shook with his words—the stones, the bricks and concrete in the buildings, the water in the river, the bedrock deep beneath us, the church bells, the metal in the gun barrels—the entire city vibrating, amplifying his voice.

The men broke their charge, looking this way and that, trying to understand how all of Berlin had just cried out, commanding them to surrender.

"This is part of the special transport sigil?" Pitcairn asked.

"No," I said. "This is Murchison being Murchison."

"Ich befehle die Sonne im Westen aufzusteigen!" Murchison shouted. Every grain of sand within a hundred miles echoed it.

"What'd he say?" Pitcairn asked.

"He'll make the sun rise in the west," I whispered.

The soldiers approached us tentatively, staring as if they'd heard the voice of God.

"Look," Edith said, thrusting her wrist board at me.

Sigil in progress. Clear the edge! Blandings.

"Thirty percent chance of a firestorm," I breathed.

"Don't even say that!" Pitcairn snarled. She turned to me. "Kiss me for luck."

Her breath was hot on my face. Her hands were covered in Millen's blood.

"Or kiss her, I don't care," Pitcairn said. "Kiss *somebody* for luck."

Edith grabbed my face and kissed me. She tasted like peppermint, her mouth hot against mine. I kissed her back.

"Oh, yes," I whispered to Edith when she let me go.

"He's too fucking sweet for words," Pitcairn muttered.

"Ich befehle der Erde sich zu bewegen!" Murchison pronounced. The stones screamed with him. *I command the very Earth to move.*

And with that, the sun appeared in the west, low on the horizon, above distant snow-topped mountains—mountains in every direction. The ground shuddered, as pipes and sewers, basements and foundations suddenly found themselves ripped free of their old surroundings and settled into the new. There was a rush of wind as the warm, damp air that had hung over Berlin rose and the colder mountain air swirled in to replace it. The smell was familiar: snow and ponderosa pines. I knew it without any cartogramancer's sense. Montana.

"Oh, golly," Pitcairn said.

I closed my eyes and pressed my forehead against Edith's neck. I felt her hands on my back.

In the distance, a church bell began to ring. Then, all through the city of Berlin, the bells tolled. A warning, or in thanks for salvation from the bombers, or a simple, inchoate acknowledgment that something impossible had happened. Or Murchison's influence—I wasn't sure. He was curled up in the fetal position, looking blindly ahead, stunned by the trauma of having his connection with the earth severed and then reestablished in an entirely different spot.

The soldiers were gazing into the distance with similar expressions, trying to comprehend what had happened. Some of them kept their weapons pointed at us. Others dropped to their knees to pray. One, bolder than the rest, laughed and walked toward us.

"Where are we?" he asked Pitcairn in English.

"America," she said. "War's over, friend."

"Peace?" the man asked. He was young and quite short, with an absurd waxed mustache. "Don't shoot?"

"*Nicht schiessen*," agreed Pitcairn. "You could kiss me though. We just won."

"Excuse me?" the soldier said.

Pitcairn walked over to him and undid the strap on his steel helmet. She mashed her lips against his and, with one hand behind his head and one around the small of his back, dipped him. A few of his comrades cheered.

I collected Edith's crutches and helped her to her feet.

I couldn't celebrate. I could only catalogue the things that had to be done in the next ten minutes: A hospital for Millen—it would have to be

Denver, which was maybe five hundred miles away and with night falling, too. I didn't even know where precisely we were. We needed a hospital for Murchison, who, for all his calm, had a pair of mangled legs in addition to transport-related psychosis. We needed to get word to Blandings that the transport had been successful. Word to everyone else that we'd survived. As the throbbing in my shattered arm became more insistent, I remembered I needed a hospital, too. The German wounded, as well, if there were any we could help. And the city itself, a million people, now cut off in the mountains, which would need—

Edith reached up and hooked a finger in the collar of my skysuit.

"I want one like that," she said.

She had a bruise coming up over her cheek where the Lewis gun had kicked back and caught her, deep impressions around her eyes from two hours with her goggles cinched down, and a sweaty straggle of hair escaping from under her helmet. She was so perfect I could hardly bear to look at her.

"You have a beautiful smile, Rob," Edith said. She tipped her chin up.

I kissed her. My recollection of that moment is how grateful I was that neither of us toppled over. But I was so lost to the world that it's possible the Germans broke out in a cheer for us too or that a minor earthquake shook the city or the sun stood still in the sky. When we broke free, I could have fought the war a second time.

I put my good arm around Edith's waist. In a minute. Worry about all the rest in one minute. A minute to glory in what we'd just done.

The sun sank toward the mountains, going orange and red, the bells rang, and snow began to fall from a clear sky.

EPILOGUE

How is it you forever have the right goal and the exact wrong means of pursuing it? How many times now? Do you have any idea how hard this is going to make it on those of us who stayed behind? Damn you! And please be safe.

Transcribed personal message from Rep. Danielle Hardin
to Robert Canderelli Weekes, December 26, 1926

I'M TEMPTED TO END THE STORY THERE, WITH BERLIN WRESTED away a moment before the bombers arrived, to say that peace broke out and a grateful world acknowledged those of us who had risked everything in the sky and on the ground as heroes.

But the truth, as it tends to be, is a good deal more complicated.

The American bombers, faced with a topographical impossibility, did indeed turn back, their canisters of plague undropped. The German army, no less shocked to have lost their capital, declared a unilateral ceasefire, though the fighting in Paris and across the Western Front continued sporadically for days.

But it was far from a simple victory.

In drawing my destination glyph, I'd committed the cardinal sin of transporting: uttering the phrase "good enough." As a result of my imperfect sigil, our lines came up short and we took only ninety percent of Berlin, leaving behind a ring of buildings and streets on the outskirts of the city, now surrounding three hundred square miles of the Rocky Mountains, which had been ripped out of Montana and plunked down in the midst of the northern European plains. I've heard descriptions from some of the civilians left behind, of houses rent in two, splitting up families, half in America, half in Germany, of people who woke in the small hours of the morning to find a wall of sheer rock where their bedroom door had formerly been and, once they determined they weren't dreaming, had to climb out a window on knotted bedsheets down to the street. The terror of the avalanche that rocked the neighborhood of Spandau, the disastrous flood that raged through the borough of Köpenick as the river Spree suddenly tried to flow uphill. The usual figure given in history textbooks is 1,341 civilians dead, though how anyone ever arrived at that number I'll never know.

It's impossible to describe the depth of the panic that broke out, not only in the captured city, but in every corner of America. Was this the long-dreaded philosophical uprising? A coup? Had the sigilrists seized control of the army and invaded France? Had they transported Germans into the heart of America to launch guerilla attacks? Who was in control in Washington? Could philosophers do to Kansas City what they'd done to Berlin? Could they do it to the house of any God-fearing man who'd spoken out against empirical philosophy?

Gen. Pershing was furious over the sudden turn of events. For months, he'd expected that the American army would be the instrument of final victory in the Great War, the first conflict in fifty years that America would win without the assistance of its lady consultants. Even plague would have been preferable—sigilrists subordinate to the army, carrying out their orders, terrible as they might be, under the command of serious, fatherly men. But his glorious victory had been snatched away by a gang of upstart women. President Wilson and most of Congress were of similar mind.

Wilson and Pershing fumed all through the following afternoon as Sen. Cadwallader-Fulton, Gen. Rhodes, Gen. Blandings, and Miss Hardin led a collection of dignitaries—American, German, French, and British—on a tour of Berlin in the midst of the Rocky Mountains, then across the transatlantic chain to see the remains of the city in Germany. The men chafed when Blandings announced, bluffing of course, that her women had the ability to seize any city they chose, anywhere in the world. (In reality it would have taken months to refine enough iridium and design a glyph for a new city, but none of the senior military leadership was philosophical enough to suspect it.) They raged all through the next days as a peace treaty was hammered out.

Weeks later, when Congress gave Pershing full control of the Corps—or the Army Philosophical Service as it was renamed—he exacted his revenge. He slashed the peacetime Corps to five hundred women, even while Japan and Russia were putting sigilrists into uniform as quickly as they could. Philosophers, he further decided, would be enlisted women only, not officers, in order to avoid future breakdowns in the chain of command caused by infirmity of female will; they would be led by men. A plethora of career soldiers with no philosophical experience whatsoever were put in charge of the various departments. A major in the artillery with a fear of heights took command of Rescue and Evacuation. By all accounts, it was a dismal time to be a corpswoman, but a few veterans stayed on in the new service, trying to keep alive the Corps' storied traditions and standards. One of them was a young sergeant of R&E named Sarah E. Stewart, who would rise through the ranks in the coming years.

That just left the matter of what to do with the mutineers. Not the volunteers—not the civilians who'd been given a miles-long parade through Paris for crossing the sea to risk their lives to save a foreign country. That was forgivable, if misguided, enthusiasm. But the two hundred or so uniformed corpswomen who had engaged in a conspiracy to bring an entire German city onto American soil without the knowledge of the federal government and who had engaged in open warfare (however briefly) with the US Army. No matter that they'd forced peace, they'd done it against orders.

Pershing tried Blandings in a formal court-martial, charging her with thirty-six counts of treason and high crimes against the United States. But along with having spent years planning her conspiracy, Blandings had plotted for the court battle she'd always assumed would follow. The impassioned speeches and legal pyrotechnics that followed in her monthlong trial are the stuff of history books. One prosecutor after another found himself outmaneuvered and replaced, until Blandings and her lawyers had whittled the charges down to a single count of going absent without leave, to which she pled guilty in return for a backroom promise that none of her co-conspirators would be charged. The sentence was ten years' imprisonment at Fort Leavenworth. (I often visited her there for advice and to deliver philosophical journals detailing the latest advances in hover sigilry.)

The rest of the world could scarcely believe that America would imprison its best general. The French responded by awarding the Croix de Guerre to Blandings, along with two hundred of her key conspirators, a list I've always suspected that Blandings herself provided, since it included all the most deserving names—Carmen, Kiyo, Millen, Pitcairn, Edith, Murchison. And me. The Germans followed suit by giving us the Iron Cross.

Those medals did us no favors at home, where the backlash was swift and severe. We were foreign agitators, anti-Americans, radicals. By Christmas, we had a zoning law that prohibited the practice of sigilry over broad swaths of the country; by spring, limits on how many hoverers could be licensed in each state—I was one of a hundred registered fliers for the entire state of Massachusetts.

The story of American philosophy over the decade that followed is a bitter one to tell, a rearguard action to defend sigilrists' rights even as magnificent new philosophical possibilities came into being. For all our hopes and good intentions, the Battle of Berlin was the event that most powerfully set the backlash in action. Maybe we're to blame. Or maybe all the answers were wrong and we chose the least wrong one. I like to think so.

There are a thousand happier stories I could tell, too, of the months after peace was declared, when the real work began. Of the great Berlin Airlift to supply food and fuel to a city that suddenly found itself cut off from every road and rail connection with winter falling; of the painstaking work by Murchison, Unger, Yu, and Brock to get the city back in place following the Treaty of Versailles, which they managed within a finger's breadth (though this left behind a half-inch-thick wall of rock running between the two parts of the city; it's been left standing in a few places as a memorial to the Great War); of the thousands of refugees who wished to stay in America and deserted the city prior to its repatriation, settling in Helena to form Little Germany, in Bozeman as Neue Berlin, in Billings as Blandingsstadt.

I could tell of Teeny Millen, who Pitcairn flew to Denver General Hospital at maximum speed. She came to the next day on an operating table with a surgeon standing by with a clamp to stop the bleeding and a smokecarver for anesthesia; Millen survived with what her doctors called the worst case of blood-loss anemia they'd ever seen in a person who wasn't dead. ("There is no justice in the world," Millen wrote me while convalescing with Andrada in San Francisco, "that I should have lived while Punnett died.") Millen came to Radcliffe the following year as a twenty-seven-year-old freshman, majoring in French, one of a stream of veterans, wounded in body or spirit, that Radcliffe adopted. The girls elected her president of the Class of 1923.

Of Lennox Murchison, who whispered advice and encouragement to the minerals in his broken legs until they knit together so perfectly that he walked the rest of his days without so much as a limp.

Of Danielle Hardin, who continued to act as confidante, aide, and nurse to Sen. Cadwallader-Fulton even as the old woman's health faded, weakened by her efforts in France. I remember the photo of Danielle pushing her onto the Senate floor in a wheelchair to cast the single vote against an even more heinous version of the Zoning Act in the spring of '19, the senator's voice so weak that Danielle had to shout out the "Nay!" for her. The senator died a few hours later. (*Thank you*, I wrote to Danielle afterward. *Don't give up*. Her reply came instantly: *Never, never, never, never.*)

Of Sigilwoman Second Class Robert Canderelli, who was mistakenly marked down as "Killed in Action" and whose name I did not use again for many years.

And of Robert Weekes, who received the highest decorations from two foreign nations as one of Blandings's two hundred, but no American awards for his service. I could tell you of the surgeries and futile exercises I went through, trying to undo the damage done by the bullet that had struck my right forearm, breaking both bones and severing my median nerve, leaving me without any strength in my thumb and two fingers. (Today, they're curled and withered like claws.) Of learning to be left-handed. Of nightmares and sleeping with the lights on and my heartsickness at an America that seemed determined to prevent me from practicing the only kind of work I'd ever wanted to do.

But that's altogether too dark a note to end on.

As we stood there in the fading Montana light, in the center of Berlin, Pitcairn's German infantryman fashioned a sling and swathe from two handkerchiefs and splinted my arm against my chest. Edie rigged me in front, face-to-face, which is a terrible configuration for both hoverer and passenger on a long flight, unless you're hoping to gaze into each other's eyes, clinch together with your off arms, and try to steal the occasional kiss without losing your line of navigation. Which as we lifted off, the Reichstag and Brandenburg Gate behind us, the mountains and a five-hundred-mile journey to the hospital in Denver ahead of us, a couple of love-mad young fools delighted to have found each other and with no notion of what was to come, was exactly what we did.

Appendix

Adapted from *A Girl's Guide to the Great War*, Chapter 3: Equipment and Weaponry, Victoria Ferris-Smythe, 1940.

RARELY IN HUMAN HISTORY HAS TECHNOLOGY ADVANCED SO quickly or been so poorly understood by military and philosophical commanders as during the Great War. All too frequently, this led to nineteenth-century tactics being used to disastrous effect. However, it also produced some of the most heroic, surprising, and memorable episodes of the conflict. In the pages that follow, you will see several pieces of equipment that altered the course of the conflict. Some of them have been made iconic by the most famous pictures and stories of "the war to end all wars." Others may appear commonplace to the modern eye, but were revolutionary in their time.

Lewis Gun

NO WEAPON IS MORE CLOSELY ASSOCIATED WITH THE BLANDINGS Mutiny than the Lewis automatic rifle, a light machine gun that fliers carried on raids for air-to-air combat and fire support on the ground.

Shortly after Isaac Lewis built his first prototypes in 1911, Tomasina Blandings secured several dozen for testing with the Sigilry Corps' Experimental Wing. When the Corps disbanded Blandings's unit in 1914, she arranged for the guns to be "lost"—that is, shipped to France in secret.

Carried on a rigid arm brace or two-handed by a passenger, the twenty-eight-pound weapon had a range of up to two miles, though its recoil made it difficult to hit a target from beyond point-blank range. Capable of firing six hundred rounds per minute, its ninety-eight-round magazine meant that it could provide only ten seconds of sustained fire before needing to be reloaded—an extremely difficult task for a lone flier while in the air.

SMUDGE POT

WHILE SMOKECARVERS HAVE USED SOURCES AS VARIED AS CAMP-fires, gunpowder, and even dense fog as feedstock for their sigilry, the smudge pot has proven itself time and again as an ideal source: portable, durable, capable of using a variety of fuels, and productive of sooty, dirty, utilitarian smoke good for nearly all applications.

Even the widespread use of preformed smoke carried by rail cars and hoverers didn't replace the need for the simple smudge pot. The steel tanks necessary for carrying large volumes of compressed smoke were heavy and bulky, making them difficult to haul into the field. By contrast, even one gallon of fuel oil could produce a huge amount of smoke, provided that a smokecarver had time to burn and collect it. Additionally, the complex philosophico-electrical sigils used by American smokecarvers required fresh smoke, making smudge pots indispensable tools.

SMOKECARVER'S BOX

SMOKECARVERS HAVE LONG LABORED UNDER THE DIFFICULTY OF using more powders, chemicals, vials, and tools than any other philosophical specialty. Their solutions for carrying equipment have ranged from converted tackle boxes to bespoke steamer trunks with padded velvet linings. During the Great War, the US Sigilry Corps produced two standard-issue smokecarver boxes: a ten-pound box adapted from a traveling apothecary's chest, meant to be carried by a single woman; and a two-hundred-pound crate, intended to supply a small group of women and be carried by wagon or hoverer. The latter was based on an unproven design and often left its array of glass bottles and jars a shattered mess. Nearly all smokecarvers also carried preferred powders and favored tools—custom knitting needles, for example—in a handbag or rucksack.

Renault FT Tank

BY 1915, BOTH THE BRITISH AND FRENCH HAD BEGUN DEVELOPING landships capable of repelling small-arms fire, crossing trenches, and tearing holes in barbed wire. Hoping to keep their new weapon secret during its development, the British called their project a "water carrier" and the team that designed it became the Tank Supply Committee. These early behemoths required a crew of as many as eight and were prone to breakdowns. It wasn't until French automobile builder Louis Renault designed the smaller, nimbler FT that the modern tank, with rotating turret, was born. With a top speed of five miles per hour and a two-man crew, it proved to be a much more practical weapon. The American army, with no tanks of their own, borrowed French FTs for major assaults, including the Battle of Saint-Mihiel. FTs were also prized by the German army on the rare occasion they could be taken intact. The Germans reserved captured tanks for its most important missions, including protecting philosophical experiments and supporting attacks undertaken by the Korps des Philosophs.

FOKKER D.VII BIPLANE

IT IS DIFFICULT TO OVERSTATE HOW PRIMITIVE THE STATE OF mechanical aviation was during the Great War. Aeroplanes were slow, rarely reaching even 120 miles per hour, delicate in their wood-and-canvas construction, and prone to mechanical failures of all sorts. The common adage that a twelve-year-old girl flier with a book of matches could take down the finest biplane of the era, surely inspired by the 1927 motion picture *Prudence Fairchild Saves the Day*, is not a gross exaggeration. That said, aeroplanes proved to be quite a stable platform for machine guns. More formidable fighters like the Fokker D.VII, which mounted a pair of Vickers guns, could fire a combined sixteen rounds every second, making them deadly opponents for a hoverer caught in the wrong position for even a moment.

Blandings Mark III Sticky Bomb

YEARS BEFORE THE FIRST SHOTS OF THE GREAT WAR WERE FIRED, Tomasina Blandings correctly identified the possibility that hoverers might need to attack aeroplanes and set about designing a means for doing so. As philosophical fliers were faster, more maneuverable, and extremely hard to spot, the solution of arming them with a small bomb coated with powerful adhesive was obvious from the start. Building a working prototype, however, proved more difficult. Much of the dangerous work of testing early versions fell to Sigilwoman Carmen Delgado, an explosives expert who became one of Blandings's most trusted co-conspirators. The final design, which incorporated one pound of high-grade smokecarved explosive covered in a layer of birdlime, proved an effective (if frequently awkward) weapon. Of the eighteen confirmed "kills" scored by hoverers against aeroplanes during the war, eleven used sticky bombs (with two others employing direct gunfire, four from aircraft crashing while trying to escape from philosophers, and one by Capt. Sarah E. Stewart throwing a pitchfork through an aeroplane's engine block while defending the Orphanage of the Sacred Heart in Paris, in one of the numerous colorful incidents that defined her career).

Smoke Canister

AN EXPERIENCED CORPS SMOKECARVER NEEDED ONLY A FEW minutes to assemble potent tear gas or a smokescreen capable of covering entire city blocks, but when seconds counted, nothing beat a canister filled with ready-made philosophically crafted smoke. This also put high-powered sigilry in the hands of nonspecialists, who could clear a landing zone or disperse enemy troops with ease. After the war, however, the widespread theft and diversion of military smoke canisters led to their use by various factions during the Zoning Riots and Third Trencher War. Despite strict bans on civilian possession of such weapons, similar effects could be created with jam jars or ceramic jugs, with these improvised devices often called "Detroit moonshine" or a "Radcliffe martini."

Smoke Shelter

FROM THE EARLIEST SKIRMISHES BETWEEN SMOKECARVERS DURING the American Civil War, the need to protect military philosophers against large clouds of poisonous smoke was obvious. During the Battle of Halloween (1862) and the First Battle of Paris (1871), American forces under Mrs. Cadwallader were positioned close together and had large-scale smoke walls and dams ready to deploy if their defenses were breached. In the Battle of Reims, however, with the American lines spread out over twenty-five miles, it was left to individual smokecarvers to fashion emergency shelters in case the American line fell. Faced with limited resources and time as they worked to reinforce the main line, many smokecarvers neglected shelters, planning to retreat on foot if necessary, which proved disastrous after the American lines were encircled. The most effective emergency shelters were generally made out of a single sheet of semi-rigid smoke, shaped into a dome or tent-like structure sealed fast to the ground. Some of these makeshift structures disintegrated within minutes of the German attack, leading to speedy deaths for their occupants, but well-constructed shelters lasted for days, allowing eventual rescue.

M-3 Skysuit and Harness

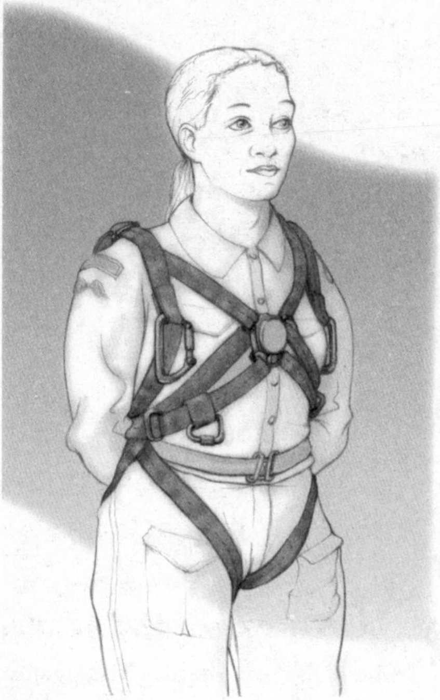

WHEN RESCUE & EVACUATION fliers landed in France in the fall of 1914, their basic equipment was little different from that which their mothers might have used. The skysuit—a one-piece, button-up, long-sleeved coverall with trouser legs—was a utilitarian masterpiece. Meant to protect the body from windburn during high-speed flight as well as the cold of hovering at high altitudes, the suit was made of thick, relatively form-fitting wool, reinforced over the elbows, knees, and seat to protect against hard landings. A heavy leather harness, with straps fitted about the shoulders, chest, and thighs, plus steel carabiners on the chest and back straps for carrying passengers or cargo, was also obligatory. A padded leather crash helmet and shatterproof goggles completed the ensemble. Though perfectly functional, the standard-issue skysuit was famously unflattering on all body types. Veterans who had worn the M-3 viewed the craze for skysuit-inspired eveningwear during the 1920s, with plunging necklines and flowing silk harem pants, with a mix of annoyance and horror.

Powder Bag with Series-1892 Lever Regulator

TO A CONTEMPORARY MECHANICO-PHILOSOPHICAL AVIATOR, THE equipment used by Great War fliers is shockingly crude: a conical waxed-canvas bag for holding up to forty pounds of blended corn and sand powder, a clockwork regulator to ensure that powder ran out at a uniform rate, and a stainless steel tip that screwed into the reg and was held between thumb and forefinger to draw sigils. This setup had two tremendous advantages: the powder flowed by gravity and required no external power source or pressurization, and the lever regulators used by the Corps were extremely durable, containing only eleven parts and requiring no specialized equipment for field stripping and cleaning. (The lever itself could be removed by hand and used as a screwdriver and prying tool to disassemble the rest of the pieces.) The reliability of the classic lever reg is legendary. During the Shanghai Evacuation of 1939, Gen. Stewart ordered several dozen vintage bags and regs taken off the shelf of a museum display and pressed into emergency action; despite having sat unused for twenty years, these proved operational and were flying within minutes.

HISTORICAL NOTES

AS WITH THE FIRST NOVEL IN THIS SERIES, WHEN POSSIBLE I'VE preserved the original timeline of the Spanish-American War, Philippine-American War, Moro Rebellion, and First World War. "Blood Upon the Harness," is an homage to the paratrooper song "Blood Upon the Risers," with some verses nearly unchanged. Mary Fox's adage about making a bad problem worse is borrowed from an astronaut saying popularized by Chris Hadfield. The epigraph involving the sentry is an adaptation of a Great War joke in which the punch line was "Pass, the Canadians!" Likewise, the jokes about "how many is a Brazilian?" (which I first heard with George W. Bush in place of Gen. Fallmarch) and confusion over military time are old ones. The excerpt from Robert Graves's memoir *Good-Bye to All That* is unaltered, as is the line by Will Rogers. Murchison's prayer is from the book *Principles of Geology* by Charles Lyell. The literary works referred to by Erich Maria Remarque and Ernest Hemingway are fictitious, though it pleases me to believe that their experiences in the Great War and the books they wrote afterward would have been different in Robert's world.

ACKNOWLEDGMENTS

THIS NOVEL OWES A PROFOUND DEBT TO THE EMTS AND PARAMEDICS I worked alongside at Eastern Area Prehospital Services from 2006 to 2010—they always suspected I was writing a book about them, but I don't think they ever imagined this. Writing and rewriting would not have been possible without the endless support and interest of my colleagues at the University of Wisconsin Hospital and Clinics, particularly my co-residents. Whenever I wasn't sure how a character would react, I simply asked, "What would a senior resident who hasn't slept in three days do?" My special thanks to Dr. Mary Westergaard for the field promotion that gave me a year of my life back and for never questioning (aloud) whether medicine and fantasy fiction were compatible careers.

I'm deeply grateful for the agenting prowess of Alexandra Machinist and the steady editorial hand of Zack Knoll.

Thank you to my cadre of advance readers who provided feedback and advice, including: Bea, Barry and Nate Carlin, Arianne Cohen, Dom Jonak, Ilan Kolkowitz, Kay Miller, Tom Miller Sr., Max Nichols, Matt O'Connor, and Jan Schowengerdt.

My thanks first and last to Abby, who has believed in this project for a decade now with unflagging faith. And to Owen and Eddie, who get even more excited over airplanes than I do.

About the Author

TOM MILLER grew up in Wauwatosa, Wisconsin. He graduated from Harvard University and went on to earn an MFA in creative writing from the University of Notre Dame and an MD from the University of Pittsburgh. He has worked as a travel guidebook writer, EMT, college English instructor, and emergency room doctor. *The Philosopher's War* is the highly anticipated sequel to his debut novel *The Philosopher's Flight*.